PRAISE FOR THE THRILLERS OF HARLAN COBEN

Missing You

"There is a confidence to Coben's writing that carries the reader along on this literary journey. He knows his subject matter; he knows his characters; he knows his plot. He is supremely confident in all he puts down on paper and this confidence enhances the reader's pleasure. *Missing You* is another winner in Coben's stack of winners. If you are smart, you will grab it up as quickly as possible and start letting the pieces fit." —The Huffington Post

"Harlan Coben, master of the suburban thriller, delivers another outstanding look at the truth behind the facade with *Missing You*. . . . This is a dive-in, lose-sleep and miss-your-bus-stop reading experience."
—The Associated Press Online

"*Missing You* delivers twists aplenty, including—mercifully briefly—a chilling, horrific, and completely deserved revenge scene that makes the recent spate of zombie movies and television episodes pale significantly in comparison." —*The Boston Globe*

"Warning: Under no circumstances do you skip to the ending of this superbly crafted novel. Yes, there is a twist—are several of them, in fact. And you have to work your way through all of them to relish the stinger on the final page. . . . One of Coben's best ever."
—*The Globe and Mail* (Canada)

"Continues to mine the truly terrifying from everyday life. . . . This as the book masterfully explores the costs of our techno-crazed existence in which the emotional costs of these Twitter-age relationships can be shattering and, in this case, dangerous. That's the power of Coben's uncannily prescient ability to guess where the darkness is going to settle next, making the brilliantly staged *Missing You* not to be missed." —*The Providence Journal*

continued . . .

ALSO BY HARLAN COBEN

Play Dead
Miracle Cure
Deal Breaker
Drop Shot
Fade Away
Back Spin
One False Move
The Final Detail
Darkest Fear
Tell No One
Gone for Good
No Second Chance
Just One Look
The Innocent
Promise Me
The Woods
Hold Tight
Long Lost
Caught
Live Wire
Shelter
Stay Close
Seconds Away
Six Years
Missing You
Found
The Stranger
Fool Me Once
Home
Don't Let Go

HARLAN COBEN

MISSING YOU

DUTTON

DUTTON

An imprint of Penguin Random House LLC
penguinrandomhouse.com

Previously published as a Dutton hardcover and a Signet premium mass market.

First Dutton premium mass market printing, 2017

ISBN 9780451414120

Printed in the United States of America
10 9 8 7

To Ray and Maureen Clarke

I

KAT Donovan spun off her father's old stool, readying to leave O'Malley's Pub, when Stacy said, "You're not going to like what I did."

The tone made Kat stop midstride. "What?"

O'Malley's used to be an old-school cop bar. Kat's grandfather had hung out here. So had her father and their fellow NYPD colleagues. Now it had been turned into a yuppie, preppy, master-of-the-universe, poseur ass-hat bar, loaded up with guys who sported crisp white shirts under black suits, two-day stubble, manscaped to the max to look unmanscaped. They smirked a lot, these soft men, their hair moussed to the point of overcoif, and ordered Ketel One instead of Grey Goose because they watched some TV ad telling them that was what real men drink.

Stacy's eyes started darting around the bar. Avoidance. Kat didn't like that.

"What did you do?" Kat asked.

"Whoa," Stacy said.

"What?"

"A Punch-Worthy at five o'clock."

Kat swiveled to the right to take a peek.

"See him?" Stacy asked.

"Oh yeah."

Decor-wise, O'Malley's hadn't really changed much over the years. Sure, the old console TVs had been replaced by a host of flat-screens showing too wide a variety of games—who cared about how the Edmonton Oilers did?—but outside of that, O'Malley had kept the cop feel and that was what had appealed to these poseurs, the faux authenticity, moving in and pushing out what had made the place hum, turning it into some Disney Epcot version of what it had once been.

Kat was the only cop left in here. The others now went home after their shifts, or to AA meetings. Kat still came and tried to sit quietly on her father's old stool with the ghosts, especially tonight, with her father's murder haunting her anew. She just wanted to be here, to feel her father's presence, to—corny as it sounded—gather strength from it.

But the douche bags wouldn't let her be, would they?

This particular Punch-Worthy—shorthand for any guy deserving a fist to the face—had committed a classic punch-worthy sin. He was wearing sunglasses. At eleven o'clock at night. In a bar with poor lighting. Other punch-worthy indictments included wearing a chain on your wallet, do-rags, unbuttoned silk shirts, an overabundance of tattoos (special category for those sporting tribal symbols), dog tags when you didn't serve in the military, and really big white wristwatches.

Sunglasses smirked and lifted his glass toward Kat and Stacy.

"He likes us," Stacy said.

"Stop stalling. What won't I like?"

When Stacy turned back toward her, Kat could see over her shoulder the disappointment on Punch-Worthy's glistening-with-overpriced-lotion face. Kat had seen that look a zillion times before. Men liked Stacy. That was probably something of an understatement. Stacy was frighteningly, knee-knockingly, teeth-and-bone-and-metal-meltingly hot. Men became both weak-legged and stupid around Stacy. Mostly stupid. Really, really stupid.

This was why it was probably a mistake to hang out with someone who looked like Stacy—guys often concluded that they had no shot when a woman looked like that. She seemed unapproachable.

Kat, in comparison, did not.

Sunglasses homed in on Kat and began to make his move. He didn't so much walk toward her as glide on his own slime.

Stacy suppressed a giggle. "This is going to be good."

Hoping to discourage him, Kat gave the guy flat eyes and a disdainful frown. Sunglasses was not deterred. He bebopped over, moving to some sound track that was playing only in his own head.

"Hey, babe," Sunglasses said. "Is your name Wi-Fi?"

Kat waited.

"Because I'm feeling a connection."

Stacy burst out laughing.

Kat just stared at him. He continued.

"I love you small chicks, you know? You're kinda

adorable. A spinner, am I right? You know what would look good on me? You."

"Do these lines ever work?" Kat asked him.

"I'm not done yet." Sunglasses coughed into his fist, took out his iPhone, and held it up to Kat. "Hey, babe, congrats—you've just moved to the top of my to-do list."

Stacy loved it.

Kat said, "What's your name?"

He arched an eyebrow. "Whatever you want it to be, babe."

"How about Ass Waffle?" Kat opened her blazer, showing the weapon on her belt. "I'm going to reach for my gun now, Ass Waffle."

"Damn, woman, are you my new boss?" He pointed to his crotch. "Because you just gave me a raise."

"Go away."

"My love for you is like diarrhea," Sunglasses said. "I just can't hold it in."

Kat stared at him, horrified.

"Too far?" he said.

"Oh man, that's just gross."

"Yeah, but I bet you never heard it before."

He'd win that bet. "Leave. Now."

"Really?"

Stacy was nearly on the floor with laughter.

Sunglasses started to turn away. "Wait. Is this a test? Is Ass Waffle, like, a compliment or something?"

"Go."

He shrugged, turned, spotted Stacy, figured why not? He looked her long body up and down and said, "The word of the day is legs. Let's go back to your place and spread the word."

Stacy was still loving it. "Take me, Ass Waffle. Right here. Right now."

"Really?"

"No."

Ass Waffle looked back at Kat. Kat put her hand on the butt of her gun. He held up his hands and slinked away.

Kat said, "Stacy?"

"Hmm?"

"Why do these guys keep thinking they have a chance with me?"

"Because you look cute and perky."

"I'm not perky."

"No, but you look perky."

"Seriously, do I look like that much of a loser?"

"You look damaged," Stacy said. "I hate to say it. But the damage . . . it comes off you like some kind of pheromone that douche bags can't resist."

They both took a sip of their drinks.

"So what won't I like?" Kat asked.

Stacy looked back toward Ass Waffle. "I feel bad for him now. Maybe I should throw him a quickie."

"Don't start."

"What?" Stacy crossed her show-off long legs and smiled at Ass Waffle. He made a face that reminded Kat of a dog left in a car too long. "Do you think this skirt is too short?"

"Skirt?" Kat said. "I thought it was a belt."

Stacy liked that. She loved the attention. She loved picking up men, because she thought a one-night stand with her was somehow life changing for them. It was also part of her job. Stacy owned a private investigation firm with two other gorgeous women. Their specialty? Catching (really, entrapping) cheating spouses.

"Stacy?"

"Hmm?"

"What won't I like?"

"This."

Still teasing Ass Waffle, Stacy handed Kat a piece of paper. Kat looked at the paper and frowned:

KD8115
HottestSexEvah

"What is this?"

"KD8115 is your user name."

Her initials and badge number.

"HottestSexEvah is your password. Oh, and it's case sensitive."

"And these are for?"

"A website. YouAreJustMyType.com."

"Huh?"

"It's an online dating service."

Kat made a face. "Please tell me you're joking."

"It's upscale."

"That's what they say about strip clubs."

"I bought you a subscription," Stacy said. "It's good for a year."

"You're kidding, right?"

"I don't kid. I do some work for this company. They're good. And let's not fool ourselves. You need someone. You want someone. And you aren't going to find him in here."

Kat sighed, rose, and nodded to the bartender, a guy named Pete who looked like a character actor who always played the Irish bartender—which is what, in fact, he was. Pete nodded back, indicating that he'd put the drinks on Kat's tab.

"Who knows?" Stacy said. "You could end up meeting Mr. Right."

Kat started for the door. "But more likely, Mr. Ass Waffle."

KAT typed in "YouAreJustMyType.com," hit the RE- TURN button, and filled in her new user name and the rather embarrassing password. She frowned when she saw the moniker at the top of the profile that Stacy had chosen for her:

Cute and perky!

"She left off *damaged*," Kat muttered under her breath.

It was past midnight, but Kat wasn't much of a sleeper. She lived in an area far too upscale for her—West 67th Street off Central Park West, in the Atelier. A hundred years ago, this and its neighboring buildings, including the famed Hotel des Artistes, had housed writers, painters, intellectuals—artists. The spacious old-world apartments faced the street, the smaller artist studios in the back. Eventually, the old art studios were converted into one-bedroom apartments. Kat's father, a cop who watched his friends get rich doing nothing but buying real estate, tried to find his way in. A guy whose life Dad had saved sold him the place on the cheap.

Kat had first used it as an undergrad at Columbia University. She had paid for her Ivy League education with an NYPD scholarship. According to the life plan, she was then supposed to go to law school and join a big white-shoe firm in New York City, finally breaking away from the cursed family legacy of police work.

Alas, it hadn't worked out that away.

A glass of red wine sat next to her keyboard. Kat drank too much. She knew that was a cliché—a cop who drank too much—but sometimes the clichés are there for a reason. She functioned fine. She didn't drink on the job. It didn't really affect her life in any noticeable way, but if Kat made calls or even decisions late at night, they tended to be, er, sloppy ones. She had learned over the years to turn off her mobile phone and stay away from e-mail after ten P.M.

Yet here she was, late at night, checking out random dudes on a dating website.

Stacy had uploaded four photographs to Kat's page. Kat's profile picture, a head shot, had been cropped from a bridesmaid group photo taken at a wedding last year. Kat tried to view herself objectively, but that was impossible. She hated the picture. The woman in the photograph looked unsure of herself, her smile weak, almost as though she were waiting to be slapped or something. Every photograph—now that she went through the painful ritual of viewing them—had been cropped from group pictures, and in every one, Kat looked as though she were half wincing.

Okay, enough of her own profile.

On the job, the only men she met were cops. She didn't want a cop. Cops were good men and horrible husbands. She knew that only too well. When Grandma got terminally ill, her grandfather, unable to handle it, ran off until, well, it was too late. Pops never forgave himself for that. That was Kat's theory anyway. He was lonely, and while he had been a hero to many, Pops chickened out when it counted most and he couldn't live with that and his service revolver was sitting right there, right on the same top shelf in the kitchen where he'd always kept it, and so one night, Kat's grandfather reached up and took his piece down from the shelf and sat by himself at the kitchen table and . . .

Ka-boom.

Dad too would go on benders and disappear for days at a time. Mom would be extra cheery when this happened—which made it all the more scary and creepy—either pretending Dad was on an undercover mission or ignoring his disappearance altogether, literally out of sight, out of mind, and then, maybe a week later, Dad would waltz in with a fresh shave and a smile and a dozen roses for Mom, and everyone would act like this was normal.

YouAreJustMyType.com. She, the cute and perky Kat Donovan, was on an Internet dating site. Man oh man, talk about the best-laid plans. She lifted the wineglass, made a toasting gesture toward the computer screen, and took too big a gulp.

The world sadly was no longer conducive to meeting a life partner. Sex, sure. That was easy. That was, in fact, the expectation, the elephant in the date room, and while she loved the pleasures of the flesh as much as the next gal, the truth was, when you went to bed with someone too quickly, rightly or wrongly, the chances of a long-term relationship took a major hit. She didn't put a moral judgment on this. It was just the way it was.

Her computer dinged. A message bubble popped up:

We have matches for you! Click here to see someone who might be perfect for you!

Kat finished the glass of wine. She debated pouring another, but really, enough. She took stock of herself and realized an obvious yet unspoken truth: She wanted someone in her life. Have the courage to admit that to yourself, okay? Much as she strove to be independent, Kat wanted a man, a partner, someone in her bed at night. She didn't pine or force it or even make much of an effort. But she wasn't really built to be alone.

She began to click through the profiles. You've got to be in it to win it, right?

Pathetic.

Some men could be eliminated with a quick glance at their profile photograph. It was key when you thought about it. The profile portrait each man had painstakingly chosen was, in pretty much every way, the first (very controlled) impression. It thus spoke volumes.

So: If you made the conscious choice to wear a fedora, that was an automatic no. If you chose not to wear a shirt, no matter how well built you were, automatic no. If you had a Bluetooth in your ear—gosh, aren't *you* important?—automatic no. If you had a soul patch or sported a vest or winked or made hand gestures or chose a tangerine-hued shirt (personal bias) or balanced your sunglasses on top of your head, automatic no, no, no. If your profile name was ManStallion, SexySmile, Rich-PrettyBoy, LadySatisfier—you get the gist.

Kate clicked open a few where the guy looked . . . approachable, she guessed. There was a sad, depressing sameness to all the write-ups. Every person on the website enjoyed walks on a beach and dining out and exercising and exotic travel and wine tasting and theater and museums and being active and taking chances and grand adventures—yet they were equally content with staying home and watching a movie, coffee and conversation, cooking, reading a book, the simple pleasures. Every guy claimed that the most important quality they looked for in a woman was a sense of humor—right, sure—to the point where Kat wondered whether "sense of humor" was a euphemism for "big boobs." Of course, every man also listed preferred body type as athletic, slender, *and* curvy.

That seemed more accurate, if not downright wishful.

The profiles never reflected reality. Rather than being what you are, they were a wonderful if not futile exercise in what you *think* you are or what you want a potential partner to think you are—or most likely, the profiles (and, man, shrinks would have a field day) simply reflect what you want to be.

The personal statements were all over the place, but if she had to use one word to sum them up, it would probably be *treacle*. The first read, "Every morning, life is a blank canvas waiting to be painted"—click. Some aimed for honesty by telling you repeatedly that they were honest. Some faked sincerity. Some were highfalutin or showboating or insecure or needy. Just like real life, when Kat thought about it. Most were simply trying too hard. The stench of desperation came off the screen in squiggly, bad-cologne waves. The constant soul-mate talk was, at best, off-putting. In real life, Kat thought, none of us can find someone we want to go out with more than once, yet somehow we believe that on YouAre-JustMyType.com, we will instantly find a person we want to wake up next to for the rest of our lives.

Delusional—or does hope spring eternal?

This was the flip side. It was easy to be cynical and poke fun, but when she stepped back, Kat realized something that pierced her straight through the heart: Every profile was a life. Simple, yep, but behind every cliché-ridden, please-like-me profile was a fellow human being with dreams and aspirations and desires. These people hadn't signed up, paid their fee, or filled out this information idly. Think about it: Every one of these lonely people came to this website—signed in and clicked on profiles—hoping it would be different this time, hoping against hope that finally they would meet the one person who, in the end, would be the most important person in their lives.

Wow. Just let that realization roll over you for a moment.

Kat had been lost in this thought, clicking through the profiles at a constantly increasing velocity, the faces of these men—men who had come here in the hopes of finding "the one"—blurring into a fleshy mess from the speed, when she spotted his picture.

For a second, maybe two, her brain didn't quite believe what her eyes had seen. It took another second for the finger to stop clicking the mouse button, another for the profile pictures tumbling by to slow down and come to a halt. Kat sat and took a deep breath.

It couldn't be.

She had been surfing at such a rapid pace, thinking about the men behind the photographs, their lives, their wants, their hopes. Her mind—and this was both Kat's strength and weakness as a cop—had been wandering, not necessarily concentrating on what was directly in front of her yet being able to get a sense of the big picture. In law enforcement, it meant that she was able to see the possibilities, the escape routes, the alternate sce-

narios, the figure lurking behind the obstacles and ob-
fuscations and hindrances and subterfuge.

But that also meant that sometimes Kat missed the
obvious.

She slowly started to click the back arrow.

It couldn't be him.

The image had been no more than a flicker. All this
thinking about a true love, a soul mate, the one she
would want to spend her life with—who could blame her
imagination for getting the better of her? It had been
eighteen years. She had drunk-Googled him a few times,
but there had just been a few old articles he'd written.
Nothing current. That had surprised her, had piqued her
curiosity—Jeff had been a great journalist—but what
more could she do? Kat had been tempted to run a more
thorough investigation on him. It wouldn't take much
effort in her position. But she didn't like to use her law
enforcement connections for personal reasons. She could
have asked Stacy too, but again, what would be the
point?

Jeff was gone.

Chasing or even Googling an ex-lover was beyond pathetic. Okay, Jeff had been more than that. Much more.
Kat absentmindedly touched her left ring finger with her
thumb. Empty. But it hadn't always been. Jeff had proposed, doing everything right. He had gotten permission
from her father. He had done it on bended knee. Nothing cheesy. He didn't hide the ring in a dessert or ask her
on the scoreboard at Madison Square Garden. It had
been classy and romantic and traditional because he
knew that was exactly how she'd wanted it.

Tears started to well in her eyes.

Kat clicked the back arrow through a potpourri of faces and hairstyles, a veritable United Nations of eligible bachelors, and then her finger stopped. For a moment, she just stared, afraid to move, holding her breath.

Then a small cry escaped her lips.

The old heartbreak came back to her in a rush. The deep stab of pain felt fresh, as though Jeff had just walked out that very door, just now, just this very second and not eighteen years earlier. Her hand shook as she moved toward the screen and actually touched his face.

Jeff.

Still so damned handsome. He had aged a bit, graying at the temples, but, man, it worked so well on him. Kat would have guessed that. Jeff would have been one of those guys who got better-looking with age. She caressed his face. A tear leaked from one eye.

Oh man, she thought.

Kat tried to put herself together, tried to take a step back and gain some perspective, but the room was spinning and there was no way she was going to slow it down. Her still-shaking hand came back to the mouse and clicked on the profile picture, enlarging it.

The screen blinked to the next page. There Jeff stood, wearing a flannel shirt and jeans, hands in his pockets, eyes so blue you'd look in vain for a contact lens line. So handsome. So goddamn beautiful. He looked trim and athletic, and now, despite everything, another stirring started from deep within her. For a quick second, Kat risked a peek at her bedroom. She had lived in this co-op when they were together. There had been other men in that bedroom after him, but nothing ever came close to reaching the high of what she had experienced with her fiancé. She knew how that sounded, but when she was with Jeff, he had made every part of her hum and sing. It wasn't technique or size or anything like that that made the difference. It was—unerotic as it sounded—trust. That was what had made the sex so mind-blowing. Kat had felt safe with him. She had felt confident and beautiful and unafraid and free. He would tease her at times, control her, have his way with her, but he never made her feel vulnerable or self-conscious.

Kat had never been able to let go like that with another man.

She swallowed and clicked the full-profile link. His personal statement was short and, Kat thought, perfect: **Let's see what happens.**

No pressure. No grandiose plans. No preconditions or guarantees or wild expectations.

Let's see what happens.

She skimmed toward the Status section. Over the past eighteen years, Kat had wondered countless times how his life had turned out, so the first question was the most obvious one: What had happened in Jeff's life that he was now on a singles' website?

Then again, what had happened to her?

The status read: **Widower.**

Another wow.

She tried to imagine that—Jeff marrying a woman, living with her, loving her, and eventually having her die on him. It wouldn't compute. Not yet. She was blocking. That was okay. Push through it. No reason to dwell.

Widower.

Underneath that, another jolt: **One child.**

They didn't give age or sex and, of course, it didn't

matter. Every revelation, every new fact about the man she had once loved with all her heart made the world teeter anew. He had lived a whole life without her. Why was that such a surprise? What had she expected? Their breakup had been both sudden and inevitable. He might have been the one to walk out the door, but it had been her fault. He was gone, in a snap, just like the entire life she had known and planned.

Now he was back, one of a hundred, maybe two hundred, men whose profiles she had clicked through.

The question was, What would she do about it now?

2

GERARD Remington had been only scant hours away from proposing to Vanessa Moreau when his world went dark.

The proposal, like many things in Gerard Remington's life, had been carefully planned. First step: After extensive research, Gerard had purchased an engagement ring, 2.93 carats, princess cut, VVS1 clarity, F color, platinum band with a halo setting. He had bought it from a renowned jeweler in Manhattan's Diamond District on West 47th Street—not in one of the overpriced larger stores but at a booth in the back near the Sixth Avenue corner.

Step Two: Their flight today would be leaving Boston's Logan Airport on JetBlue flight 267 at 7:30 A.M., touching down in St. Maarten at 11:31 A.M., where he and Vanessa would transfer to a small puddle-jumper to Anguilla, arriving on the island at 12:45 P.M.

Steps Three, Four, etc.: They would relax in a two-level villa at the Viceroy overlooking Meads Bay, take a dip in the infinity pool, make love, shower and dress, and dine at Blanchards. Dinner reservation was for seven P.M. Gerard had called ahead and arranged to have a bottle of Vanessa's favorite wine, a Château Haut-Bailly Grand Cru Classé 2005, a Bordeaux from the Pessac-Léognan appellation, at the ready. After dinner, Gerard and Vanessa would walk the beach barefoot, hand in hand. He had checked the lunar phase calendar and knew that the moon would be nearly full at the time. Two hundred eighteen yards down the beach (he'd had it measured), there was a thatch-roofed hut used during the day to rent snorkels and water skis. At night, no one was there. A local florist would line the front porch with twenty-one (the number of weeks they had known each other) white calla lilies (Vanessa's favorite flower). There would be a string quartet too. On Gerard's cue, the quartet would play "Somewhere Only We Know" by Keane, the song he and Vanessa decided would be forever theirs. Then, because they both liked tradition, Gerard would bend down on one knee. In his mind's eye, Gerard could almost see Vanessa's reaction. She would gasp in surprise. Her eyes would well up with tears. Her hands would come up to her face in astonishment and joy.

"You have entered my world and changed it forever," Gerard would say. "Like the most startling catalyst, you have taken this ordinary hunk of clay and transformed it into something so much more potent, so much happier and brimming with life, than I could have ever imagined. I love you. I love you with my entire being. I love everything about you. Your smile gives my life color and texture. You are the most beautiful and passionate woman in the world. Will you please make me the happiest man in the world and marry me?"

Gerard had still been working on the exact wording—he wanted it to be just right—when his world went dark. But every word was true. He loved Vanessa. He loved her with all his heart. Gerard had never been much of a romantic. Throughout his lifetime, people had had a habit of disappointing him. Science did not. Truth be told, he had always been most content alone, battling microbes and organisms, developing new medicines and counteragents that would win those wars. He had been most content in his laboratory at Benesti Pharmaceuticals, figuring out an equation or formula on the blackboard. He was, as his younger colleagues would say, old-school that way. He liked the blackboard. It helped him think—the smell of chalk, the dust, the way his fingers got dirty, the ease of erasing—because in science, truly, so little should be made permanent.

Yes, it was there, in those lost moments alone, when Gerard felt most content.

Most content. But not happy.

Vanessa had been the first thing in his life to make him happy.

Gerard opened his eyes now and thought about her. Everything was raised to the tenth power with Vanessa. No other woman had ever moved him mentally, emotionally, and yes, of course, physically like Vanessa. No other woman, he knew, ever could.

He had opened his eyes, and yet the dark remained. At first he wondered if he was somehow still in his home, but it was far too cold. He always kept the digital thermostat set at exactly 71.5 degrees. Always. Vanessa often teased him about his precision. During his lifetime, some people had considered Gerard's need for order close to being anal or even OCD. Vanessa, however, understood. She both appreciated it and found it to be a bonus. "It is what makes you a great scientist and a caring man," Vanessa had told him once. She explained to him her theory that people we now consider "on the spectrum" were, in the past, the geniuses in art, science, and literature, but now, with medications and diagnoses, we flatten them out, make them more uniform, dull their senses.

"Genius comes from the unusual," Vanessa had explained to him.

"And I'm unusual?"

"In the very best way, my sweet."

But as his heart swelled from the memory, Gerard couldn't help but notice the strange smell. Something damp and old and musty and like . . .

Like dirt. Like fresh soil.

Panic suddenly seized him. Still in pitch-darkness, Gerard tried to lift his hands to his face. He couldn't. There was something binding his wrists. It felt like a rope or, no, something thinner. Wire maybe. He tried to move his legs. They were bound together. He clenched his stomach muscles and tried to swing both legs into the air, but they hit something. Something wooden. Right above him. Like he was in . . .

His body started bucking in fear.

Where was he? Where was Vanessa?

"Hello?" he shouted. "Hello?"

Gerard tried to sit up, but there was a belt around his chest too. He couldn't move. He waited for his eyes to get used to the dark, but that wasn't happening fast enough.

"Hello? Someone? Please help me!"

He heard a noise now. Right above him. It sounded like scraping or shuffling or . . .

Or footsteps?

Footsteps right above him.

Gerard thought about the dark. He thought about the smell of fresh soil. The answer was suddenly so obvious, yet it made no sense.

I'm underground, he thought. I'm underground.

And then he started to scream.

3

KAT passed out more than slept.

As it did every weekday, her iPod alarm woke her with a favorite random song—this morning's was "Bulletproof Weeks" by Matt Nathanson—at six A.M. It had not escaped her attention that she was sleeping in the very bed where she had slept with Jeff all those years ago. The room still had the dark wood paneling. The previous owner had been a violin player at the New York Philharmonic who'd decided to make the entire six-hundred-square-foot apartment look like the inside of an old boat. It was all dark wood and portholes for windows. She and Jeff had laughed about it, making dumb double entendres about making the boat rock or capsizing or calling for a life raft, whatever.

Love makes the cloying somehow poignant.

"This place," Jeff would say. "It's so not you."

He, of course, had viewed his undergraduate fiancée as brighter and cheerier than her surroundings, but now, eighteen years later, anyone stepping into her abode thought the place fit Kat perfectly. In the same way you hear how spouses start looking like each other as the years piled on, she had started becoming this apartment.

Kat debated staying in bed and catching a few more Zs, but class would be starting in fifteen minutes. Her instructor, Aqua, a diminutive transvestite with a schizophrenic personality disorder, never accepted anything but life-threatening excuses for missing class. Besides, Stacy might be there, and Kat hoped to run this whole Jeff development past her. Kat threw on her yoga pants and tank top, grabbed a water bottle, and started for the door. Her gaze got caught up on the computer sitting on her desk.

Ah, what's the harm in taking a quick look?

The YouAreJustMyType.com home page was still up, though it had signed her out after two hours of inactivity. They splashed an "exciting introductory offer" to "Newcomers" (who else would be eligible for an introductory offer?), a month of unlimited access (whatever that meant) for just $5.74 "discreetly billed" (huh?) to your credit card. Luckily for Kat, Stacy had already bought her a full year. Yippee.

Kat put her name and password back into the fields and hit RETURN. There were messages now from men. She ignored them. She found Jeff's page—she had, of course, bookmarked it.

She clicked the REPLY button. Her fingers rested on the keypad.

What should she say?

Nothing. Not right now anyway. Think it through.

Time was a-wasting. Class was about to begin. Kat shook her head, stood, and headed out the door. As she did every Monday, Wednesday, and Friday, Kat jogged up to 72nd Street and entered Central Park. The mayor of Strawberry Fields, a performance artist who made his living on tourist tipping, was already laying out his flowers on the John Lennon Imagine memorial tiles. He did it nearly every day, but he was rarely out this early. "Hey, Kat," he said, handing her a rose.

She took it. "Morning, Gary."

She hurried past Bethesda's upper terrace. The Lake was still quiet—no boats out yet—but the water spouting off the fountain glistened like a beaded curtain. Kat veered to the path on the left, coming up near the giant statue of Hans Christian Andersen. Tyrell and Billy, the same two homeless men (if they were homeless—for all she knew, they lived in the San Remo and just dressed this way) who sat here every morning, were, as always, playing gin rummy.

"Ass looking good, girl," Tyrell said.

"Yours too," Kat replied.

Tyrell loved that. He stood up, did a little twerking, and slapped Billy five—dropping his cards on the path in the process. Billy scolded him.

"Pick those up!" Billy shouted.

"Just calm down, will ya?" To Kat: "Class this morning?"

"Yep. How many people?"

"Eight."

"Did Stacy walk by yet?"

At just the mention of her name, both men removed their hats and placed them over their hearts in respect. Billy muttered, "Lord have mercy."

Kat frowned.

Tyrell said, "Not yet."

She continued to the right and circled around Conservatory Water. There were model boats racing early this morning. Behind the Kerbs Boathouse, she found Aqua sitting cross-legged. His eyes were closed. Aqua, the product of an African-American father and a Jewish mother, liked to describe his skin as mocha latte with a splash of whipped cream. He was petite and lithe and, right now, sat with a complete stillness so at odds with the manic boy she had befriended many years ago.

"You're late," Aqua said without opening his eyes.

"How do you do that?"

"What? See you with my eyes closed?"

"Yes."

"It is a special yogi master secret," Aqua said, "called peeking. Sit."

She did. A minute later, Stacy joined the group. Aqua didn't give her any admonishment. Aqua used to hold the class on the Great Lawn—that is, until Stacy started showing up and demonstrating her flexibility in public. Suddenly, men found tremendous interest in outdoor yoga. Aqua didn't like that, so he made the morning class female only and now kept it in this hidden spot behind the boathouse. Stacy's "reserved spot" was closest to the wall so that those who wanted to ogle from a distance would have no sight line.

Aqua led them through a series of asanas. Every morning, rain or shine or snow, Aqua taught class in this very spot. He didn't charge a specific fee. You gave him whatever you thought was just. He was a wonderful teacher—instructive, kind, motivating, sincere, funny.

He adjusted your Downward Dog or Warrior Two with the slightest touch, yet it moved everything within you.

Most days, Kat vanished into the poses. Her body worked hard. Her breathing slowed down. Her mind surrendered. In her regular life, Kat drank, smoked the occasional cigar, did not eat right. Her job could be a pure, uncut hit of toxin. But here, with Aqua's soothing voice, all of that was usually flushed away.

Not today.

She tried to let go, tried to be in the moment and all that Zen stuff that sounded like such nonsense unless Aqua said it, but Jeff's face—the one she had known, the one she had just seen—kept haunting her. Aqua saw her distraction. He eyed her warily and took a little more time adjusting her poses. But he said nothing.

At the end of each class, when the students rested in Corpse Pose, Aqua put you fully under his relaxation spell. Every part of you surrendered. You would drift off. He would then ask you to have a blessed, special day. You would lie there a few more moments, taking deep breaths, your fingertips tingling. Slowly, your eyes would flutter open—as Kat's did now—and Aqua would be gone.

Kat slowly came back to life. So did the other students. They rolled up their mats in silence, almost unable to speak. Stacy joined her. They walked for a few minutes past Conservatory Water.

"Do you remember that guy I was sort of seeing?" Stacy asked.

"Patrick?"

"Right, him."

"He seemed really sweet," Kat said.

"Yeah, well, I had to give him his walking papers. Found out he did something pretty bad."

"What?"

"Spinning class," Stacy said.

Kat rolled her eyes.

"Come on, Kat. The guy takes Spinning classes. What's next, Kegels?"

It was funny walking with Stacy. After a while, you no longer noticed the stares and catcalls. You weren't offended or ignoring them. They just ceased to exist. Walking beside Stacy was the closest thing Kat would ever know to camouflage.

"Kat?"

"Yes?"

"You going to tell me what's wrong?"

A big guy with gym muscles, the kind featuring prominent veins, and slicked-back hair stopped in front of Stacy and let his eyes drop to her chest. "Whoa, that's a really big rack."

Stacy stopped too and let her eyes drop to his crotch. "Whoa, that's a really tiny dick."

They started walking again. Okay, so maybe they didn't totally cease to exist. Depending on the approach, Stacy handled the attention in different ways. She hated the showy bravado, the wolf whistlers—the rude ones. The shy guys, the ones who simply admired what they were seeing and enjoyed it, well, Stacy enjoyed them back. Sometimes she would smile or even wave, almost like a celebrity who gave a bit of herself because it was a little thing and made others happy.

"I went on that website last night," Kat said.

That made Stacy smile. "Already?"

"Yep."

"Wow. That didn't take long. Did you hook up with someone?"

"Not exactly."

"So what happened?"

"I saw my old fiancé."

Stacy pulled up, her eyes wide. "Come again?"

"His name is Jeff Raynes."

"Wait. You were engaged?"

"A long time ago."

"But engaged? You? Like a ring and everything?"

"Why does this surprise you so much?"

"I don't know. I mean, how long have we been friends?"

"Ten years."

"Right, and in all that time, you've never been within sniffing distance of love."

Kat gave a half shrug. "I was twenty-two."

"I'm at a loss for words," Stacy said. "You. Engaged."

"Could we move past that part?"

"Right, okay, sorry. And last night you saw his profile on that website?"

"Yes."

"What did you say?"

"Say to who?"

"Whom," Stacy said.

"What?"

"Say *to whom*. Not *to who*. Prepositional phrase."

"I wish I was carrying my gun," Kat said.

"What did you write to, uh, Jeff?"

"I didn't."

"Pardon?"

"I didn't write him."

"Why not?"

"He dumped me."

"A fiancé." Stacy shook her head again. "And you never told me about him before? I feel like I've been had."

"How's that?"

"I don't know. I mean, when it came to love, I always thought you were a cynic, like me."

Kat kept walking. "How do you think I became a cynic?"

"Touché."

They found a table at Le Pain Quotidien inside Central Park near West 69th Street and ordered coffee.

"I'm really sorry," Stacy said.

Kat waved her off.

"I signed you up for that site so you could get laid. Lord knows you need to get laid. I mean, you need to get laid as badly as anyone I know."

"This is some apology," Kat said.

"I didn't mean to conjure up bad memories."

"It's not a big deal."

Stacy looked skeptical. "Do you want to talk about it? Of course you do. And I'm curious as all get-out. Tell me everything."

So Kat told her the whole story about Jeff. She told her about how they'd met at Columbia, how they'd fallen in love, how it felt like forever, how it all felt easy and right, how he proposed, how everything changed when her father was murdered, how she became more withdrawn, how Jeff finally walked out, how she'd been too weak or maybe too proud to go after him.

When she finished, Stacy said, "Wow."

Kat sipped her coffee.

"And now, almost twenty years later, you see your old fiancé on a dating website?"

"Yes."

"Single?"

Kat frowned. "There are very few married people on it."

"Right, of course. So what's his deal? Is he divorced? Has he been sitting at home, still pining like you?"

"I'm not still pining," Kat said. Then: "He's a widower."

"Wow."

"Stop saying that. 'Wow.' What are you, seven years old?"

Stacy ignored the mini outburst. "His name is Jeff, right?"

"Right."

"So when Jeff broke it off, did you love him?"

Kat swallowed. "Yes, of course."

"Do you think he still loved you?"

"Apparently not."

"Stop that. Think about the question. Forget for a second that he dumped you."

"Yeah, that's kinda hard to do. I'm more of an 'actions speak louder than words' girl."

Stacy leaned closer. "There are few people who've seen the flip side of love and marriage more clearly than yours truly. We both know that, right?"

"Yes."

"You learn a lot about relationships when your job, in some ways, is to break them up. But the truth is, almost every relationship has breaking points. Every relationship has fissures and cracks. That doesn't mean it's meaningless or bad or even wrong. We know that everything in our lives is complex and gray. Yet we somehow expect our relationships to never be anything but simple and pure."

"All true," Kat said, "but I don't see what you're driving at."

Stacy leaned closer. "When you and Jeff broke up, did he still love you? Don't give me the 'actions speak louder than words' stuff. Did he still love you?"

And then, without really thinking about it, Kat said, "Yes."

Stacy just sat there, staring at her friend. "Kat?"

"What?"

"You know a hundred ways over I'm not religious," Stacy said, "but this feels a little like—I don't know— fate or kismet or something."

Kat took another sip of her coffee.

"You and Jeff are both single. You're both free. You've both been through the ringer."

"Damaged," Kat said.

Stacy considered that. "No, that's not what I . . . Well, yes, that's part of it, sure. But not so much damaged as . . . realistic." Stacy smiled and looked away. "Oh man."

"What?"

Stacy met her gaze, the smile still there. "This could be the fairy tale. You know?"

Kat said nothing.

"But even better. You and Jeff were good before, right?"

Kat still said nothing.

"Don't you see? This time, you can both go into it with eyes open. It can be the fairy tale—but real. You see the fissures and cracks. You go into it with baggage and experience and honest expectations. An appreciation for what you both messed up a long time ago. Kat, listen to me." Stacy reached her hand across the table and grasped

Kat's. There were tears in her eyes. "This could be really, really good."

Kat still didn't reply. She didn't trust her voice. She wouldn't even let herself think about it. But she knew. She knew exactly what Stacy meant.

"Kat?"

"When I get back to my apartment, I'll send him a message."

4

AS Kat showered, she thought about what exactly to put in her message to Jeff. She ran through a dozen possibilities, each lamer than the one before. She hated this feeling. She hated worrying about what to write to a guy, as if she were in high school and leaving a note in his locker. Ugh. Didn't we ever outgrow that?

The fairy tale, Stacy had said. But real.

She threw on her plainclothes cop uniform—a pair of jeans and a blazer—and slipped on a pair of TOMS. She pulled her hair back in a ponytail. Kat had never had the courage to cut her hair short, but she'd always liked it pulled back, off her face. Jeff had liked it that way too. Most men liked her hair cascading down. Jeff didn't. "I love your face. I love those cheekbones and those eyes. . . ."

She made herself stop.

Time to get to work. She'd worry about what to write later.

The computer monitor seemed to be mocking her as she walked past, daring her to leave. She paused. The screen saver did its little line dance. She checked the time.

Get it over with now, she told herself.

Kat sat down and once again brought up YouAreJust MyType.com. When she signed in, she saw that she had "exciting new matches." She didn't bother. She found Jeff's profile, clicked the picture, read his personal statement yet again:

Let's see what happens.

How long, she wondered, had it taken Jeff to come up with something so simple, so enticing, so relaxed, so noncommittal, so engaging? It was no pressure. An invitation, nothing more. Kat clicked the icon to write him a direct message. The box came up. The cursor blinked impatiently.

Kat typed: Yes, let's see what happens.

Ugh.

She immediately deleted that.

She tried a few others. Guess who; Been a long time; How are you, Jeff?; It's nice to see your face again. Delete, delete, delete. Every utterance was lame to the nth degree. Maybe, she thought, that was the nature of these things. It was hard to be smooth or confident or relaxed when you're on a site trying to meet the love of your life.

A memory brought a wistful smile to her face. Jeff had a thing for cheesy eighties music videos. This was before

YouTube made it easy to watch any and all at a moment's notice. You'd have to find when VH1 was running a special or something like that. Suddenly, she pictured what Jeff would be doing now, probably sitting at his computer and looking up old videos by Tears for Fears or Spandau Ballet or Paul Young or John Waite.

John Waite.

Waite had an early MTV classic, a quasi new-wave pop song that never failed to move her, even now, if she was flipping radio stations or in a bar that played eighties hits. Kat would hear John Waite singing "Missing You," and it would bring her back to that truly cornball video, John walking alone in the streets, repeatedly exclaiming, "I ain't missing you at all," in a voice so pained it made the next line ("I can lie to myself") superfluous and overly explanatory. John Waite would be in a bar, drowning his obvious sorrows, flashing back to happy memories of the woman he will forever love, all the while still chorusing that he wasn't missing her at all. Oh, but we hear the lie. We see the lie in every step, every movement. Then, at the end of the video, lonely John goes home and puts his headphones on, now drowning his sorrow in music rather than drink, and so, in a tragedy reminiscent of something Shakespearean by way of a bad sitcom, he can't hear when—gasp—his love returns to his door and knocks on it. In the end, the great love he was meant to be with forever knocks again, puts her ear against the door, and then walks away, leaving John Waite forever brokenhearted, still insisting that he doesn't miss her, lying eternally to himself.

Ironic in hindsight.

The video became something of a running joke between her and Jeff. When they were apart, even for a short while, he would leave messages saying, "I'm not missing you at all," and she might even comment that he could lie to himself.

Yeah, romance isn't always pretty.

But when Jeff wanted to be more serious, he would sign his notes by the song title, which right now Kat found her fingers almost subconsciously typing into the text box:

MISSING YOU.

She looked at it a moment and debated hitting SEND.

It was overkill. Here he was being wonderfully subtle with the Let's see what happens and she comes on with MISSING YOU. No. She deleted it and tried one more time, quoting the actual line from the chorus:

"I ain't missing you at all."

That felt too flip. Another deletion.

Okay, enough.

Then an idea came to her. Kat opened up another browser window and found a link to the old John Waite video. She hadn't seen it in, what, twenty years maybe? But it still held all the sappy charm. Yes, Kat thought with a nod, perfect. She copied and pasted the link into the text field. A photograph from the video's bar scene popped up. Kat didn't stop to think about it anymore.

She hit the SEND button, stood quickly, and almost ran out the door.

*　　*　　*

KAT lived on 67th Street on the Upper West Side. The 19th Precinct, her workplace, was also on 67th Street, albeit on the east side, not far from Hunter College. She cherished her commute—a walk straight across Central Park. Her squad was housed in an 1880s landmark building in a style someone had told her was called Renaissance Revival. She worked as a detective on the third floor. On television, the detectives usually have some kind of specialty like homicide, but most of those subspecialties or designations were long gone. The year her father was murdered, there were nearly four hundred homicides. This year, so far, there had been twelve. Six-man homicide detective groups and the like had become obsolete.

As soon as she passed the front desk, Keith Inchierca, the sergeant on duty, said, "Captain wants to see you pronto." Keith pointed with his beefy thumb as though she might not know where the captain's office was located. She took the steps two at a time up to the second floor. Despite her personal connection with Captain Stagger, she was rarely called into his office.

She rapped her knuckles lightly on his door.

"Come in."

She opened the door. His office was small and rain-pavement gray. He was bent over his desk, his head lowered. Kat's mouth suddenly went dry. Stagger's head had been lowered that day too, eighteen years ago, when he had knocked on her apartment door. Kat hadn't understood. Not at first. She always thought she would know if that knock came, that there would be a premonition of some sort. She had pictured the scene a hundred times in her head—it would be late at night, pouring rain, a pounding knock. She would open the door, already knowing what was to come. She would meet some cop's eyes, shake her head, see his slow nod, and then fall to the ground screaming, "No!"

But when the knock actually came, when Stagger had come to deliver the news that would cleave her life in two—one person before that moment, another thereafter—the sun had been shining without hesitation or care. She had been heading uptown to the campus library at Columbia to work on a paper about the Marshall Plan. She still remembered that. The damn Marshall Plan. So she opened the door, preparing to head to the C train, and there was Stagger, standing, his head lowered, just like now, and she hadn't had a clue. He didn't meet her eyes. The truth—the weird, shameful truth—was that when she first saw Stagger in the hallway, Kat had thought that maybe he had come for her. She had suspected Stagger had a little crush on her. Young cops, especially those who considered Dad something of a father figure, fell for her. So when Stagger first popped up on her doorstep, that was what she thought: that despite knowing she was engaged to Jeff, Stagger was about to make a subtle move on her. Nothing pushy. Stagger—his first name was Thomas, but no one ever used it—wasn't the type. But something sweet.

When she saw the blood on his shirt, her eyes had narrowed, but the truth still didn't reach her. Then he said three words, three simple words that came together and detonated in her chest, blowing her world apart:

"It's bad, Kat."

Stagger was nearing fifty now, married, four boys. Photographs dotted his desk. There was an old one of Stagger with his late partner, Homicide Detective Henry Donovan, aka Dad. That's how it was. When you die on the job, your picture ends up everywhere. Nice memorial for some. Painful reminder for others. On the wall behind Stagger, there was a framed poster of Stagger's oldest, a high school junior, playing lacrosse. Stagger and his wife had a place in Brooklyn. It was a nice life, she supposed.

"You wanted to see me, Captain?"

Outside of the precinct, she called him Stagger, but when it came to professional matters, she just couldn't do that. When Stagger looked up, she was surprised to see his face ashen. She involuntarily stepped back, almost expecting to hear those three words again, but this time she beat him to it.

"What is it?" she asked.

"Monte Leburne," Stagger said.

The name sucked the air out of the room. After a worthless life of nothing but destruction, Monte Leburne was serving a life sentence for the murder of NYPD homicide detective Henry Donovan.

"What about him?"

"He's dying."

Kat nodded, stalling, trying to regain her footing. "Of?"

"Pancreatic cancer."

"How long has he had it?"

"I don't know."

"Why are you just telling me this now?"

Her voice had more edge than she'd meant. He looked up at her. She gestured her apology.

"I just found out myself," he said.

"I've been trying to visit him."

"Yeah, I know."

"He used to let me. But lately . . ."

"I know that too," Stagger said.

Silence.

"Is he still up at Clinton?" she asked. Clinton was a maximum-security correctional facility in upstate New York near the Canadian border, seemingly the loneliest, coldest place on earth. It was a six-hour drive from New York City. Kat had made that depressing ride too often.

"No. They moved him to Fishkill."

Good. That was much closer. She could make it there in ninety minutes. "How long does he have?"

"Not long."

Stagger started to come around the desk, maybe to offer comfort or a hug, but he pulled up short.

"This is good, Kat. He deserves to die. He deserves worse."

She shook her head. "No."

"Kat . . ."

"I need to speak to him again."

He nodded slowly. "I thought you'd say that."

"And?"

"I made the request. Leburne refuses to see you."

"Too bad," she said. "I'm a cop. He's a convicted murderer about to die with a big secret."

"Kat."

"What?"

"Even if you could get him to talk now—and come on, we know that won't happen—he won't live until trial anyway."

"We can put him on tape. Deathbed confession."

Stagger looked skeptical.

"I have to try."

"He won't see you."

"Can I borrow a car from the pool?"

He closed his eyes, said nothing.

"Please, Stagger?"

So much for only calling him captain.

"Your partner will cover for you?"

"Sure," she lied. "Of course."

"Doesn't feel like I have much of a choice anyway," he said with a sigh of resignation. "Fine, go."

5

GERARD Remington finally saw daylight.

He had no idea how long he had been in the darkness. The sudden burst of light exploded in his eyes like a supernova. His eyes shut. He wanted to shield them too, but his hands were still tied. He tried to blink, his eyes watering with the light.

Someone stood directly above him.

"Don't move," a man's voice said.

Gerard didn't. He heard a snapping noise and realized that the man was cutting the bindings. For a brief moment, hope filled his chest. Perhaps, Gerard thought, this man has come to rescue me.

"Get up," the man said now. He had a hint of an accent, maybe something from the Caribbean or South America. "I have a gun. If you make any moves, we kill you and bury you here. Do you understand?"

Gerard's mouth was so dry, but he still managed to say, "Yes."

The man climbed out of the . . . box? For the first time, Gerard Remington could now see where he had been kept all these . . . hours? It was somewhere in size between a coffin and a small room, maybe four feet deep and wide, and perhaps eight feet long. When he stood up, Gerard saw that he was surrounded by deep woods. The room was buried in the ground. A hidden bunker of some sort. Maybe something to hide in during a storm, or somewhere to store grain. It was hard to say.

"Get out," the man said.

Gerard squinted up. The man—no, he was closer to a teen, really—was big and muscular. His accent now seemed to have a little Portuguese in it, maybe Brazilian, but Gerard was no expert. His hair was short, tight curls. He wore torn jeans and a fitted T-shirt that worked almost like a tourniquet on his bloated biceps.

He also had a gun.

Gerard climbed out of the box and into the woods. In the distance, he saw a dog—a chocolate Lab maybe—run up a path. When the man closed the top of the bunker, the bunker vanished from sight. You could see only two large metal rings, a chain, and a padlock—all on the door.

Gerard's head spun.

"Where am I?"

"You stink," the young man said. "There's a hose behind that tree. Wash yourself off, do your business, and put this on."

The young man handed Gerard a one-piece jumpsuit in camouflage colors.

"I don't understand any of this," Gerard said.

The muscled man with the gun moved right up next to him. He started flexing his pecs and triceps. "Do you want me to kick your ass?"

"No."

"Then do what I say."

Gerard tried to swallow, but again his throat was too parched. He turned toward the hose. Forget washing off. He needed water. Gerard started to run toward the hose, but his knees buckled, almost knocking him down. He had been in that box too long. He managed to stay upright long enough to reach the hose. He turned the faucet. When the water appeared, he drank greedily. The water tasted like, well, old hose, but he didn't care.

Gerard waited for the man to bark at him again, but suddenly the man had patience. That bothered Gerard for some reason. He looked around. Where was he? He turned in a circle, hoping to find a clearing or a street or something. But there was nothing. Just woods.

He listened for any noise. Again nothing.

Where was Vanessa? Was she waiting for him at the airport, confused but safe?

Or had she been grabbed too?

Gerard Remington stepped behind the tree and removed his soiled clothes. The man still watched him. Gerard wondered when he had last been naked in front of another man. Physical education class in high school, he assumed. An odd thing to think about at a time like this—modesty.

Where was Vanessa? Was she okay?

He didn't know, of course. He didn't know anything. He didn't know where he was or who this man was or why he was here. Gerard tried to slow himself down, tried to think rationally about his next move. He would have to cooperate and try as best he could to keep his wits about him. Gerard was smart. He reminded himself of that right now. There, good, that made him feel better.

He was smart. He had a woman he loved and a great job and a wonderful future ahead of him. This brute had a gun, yes, but he was no match for Gerard Remington's intellect.

The man finally spoke. "Hurry."

Gerard hosed himself off. "Do you have a towel?" he asked.

"No."

Still wet, Gerard slipped into the jumpsuit. He was shivering now. The combination of fear, exhaustion, confusion, and deprivation was taking its toll.

"Do you see that path?"

The man with the swollen muscles pointed toward the same opening Gerard had seen the dog run up.

"Yes."

"Follow it until the end. If you step off of it, I will shoot you."

Gerard did not bother to question the order. He started down the narrow path. Running away did not seem to be an option. Even if the man didn't shoot him, where would he go? He could hide in the woods maybe. Hope to outrun him. But he had no idea which direction to head. He had no idea if he would be running toward a road or deeper into the wilderness.

It was, it seemed, a fool's plan.

Plus, if these people wanted to kill him—he assumed that there was more than one since the brute had said "we"—they would have done so by now. So stay smart. Stay observant. Stay alive.

Find Vanessa.

Gerard knew his stride was approximately eighty-one centimeters. He counted the steps. When he reached two hundred steps, which added up to 162 meters, he saw a break in the path. There was a clearing not far away. Twelve steps later, Gerard was out of the thick woods. Up ahead, there was a white farmhouse. Gerard studied it from afar, noticing that the upstairs window shades were dark green. He looked for electrical wires leading toward the house. There were none.

Interesting.

A man stood on the porch of the farmhouse. He leaned casually against a porch post. His sleeves were rolled up, his arms crossed. He wore sunglasses and work boots. His hair was dirty blond and long—shoulder length. When he spotted Gerard, the man beckoned for him to come inside. Then the man slipped through the door and out of sight.

Gerard started toward the farmhouse. Again he noticed the green shades. There was a barn to his right. The dog—yep, it was definitely a chocolate Lab—sat in front of it, patiently watching. Behind the dog, Gerard could see the corner of what looked like a gray buggy for a horse. Hmm. Gerard also spotted a windmill. That made sense. These were clues. He didn't know what they added up to—or maybe he did and that just made the situation even more confusing—but for now, he just let the clues sink in.

He walked up the two porch steps and hesitated by the open door. He took a deep breath and stepped into the front foyer. The living room was to his left. The man with the long hair sat in a big chair. His sunglasses were off now. His eyes were brown and bloodshot. Tattoos covered his forearms. Gerard studied them, trying to form a mental photograph, hoping for a hint as to who the man might be. But the tattoos were simple designs. They told him nothing.

"My name is Titus." There was a lilt in the man's voice. Something silvery and soft and almost fragile. "Please sit down."

Gerard moved into the room. The man named Titus pinned him down with his eyes. Gerard sat. Another man, what one might call a hippie, entered the room. He wore a colorful dashiki, a knit cap, and pink-tinted glasses. He sat at the desk in a corner and opened a MacBook Air. All MacBook Airs look alike, of course, which was why Gerard had put a small piece of black tape on the top of his.

The black tape was there.

Gerard frowned. "What's going on? Where's Vanessa—"

"Shh," Titus said.

The sound sliced through the air like a reaper's scythe.

Titus turned to the hippie with the laptop. The hippie nodded at him and said, "Ready."

Gerard almost asked, "Ready for what?" but the sound of that shush still kept him silent.

Titus turned back to Gerard and smiled. It was the single most frightening sight Gerard Remington had ever seen.

"We have some questions for you, Gerard."

6

FISHKILL Correctional Facility's original name was the Matteawan State Hospitial for the Criminally Insane. That was in the 1890s. It remained, in one capacity or another, a state hospital for the mentally ill until the 1970s, when courts made it harder to arbitrarily commit those deemed insane. Now Fishkill was labeled a medium-security prison, though it had everything from minimum-security work-release prisoners to a maximum-security S Block.

Located in Beacon, New York, nestled somewhat picturesquely between the Hudson River and the Fishkill Ridge, the original brick building still greeted you upon arrival. With the razor wire and the disrepair, the place looked like an Ivy League campus by way of Auschwitz.

Kat used professional courtesy and her gold badge to

get past most of the security. In the NYPD, cops on the street had a silver badge. Detectives had the gold. Her badge number, 8115, had belonged to her father.

An elderly nurse, dressed completely in white with a vintage nurse's cap, stopped her at the hospital wing. Her makeup was garish—deep blue eye shadow, neon red lipstick—and looked as though someone had melted crayons onto her face. She smiled too sweetly, the lipstick on her teeth. "Mr. Leburne has requested no visitors."

Kat flashed the badge again. "I just want to see him"—she spotted a name tag reading SYLVIA STEINER, RN—"Nurse Steiner."

Nurse Steiner grabbed the gold badge, took her time reading it, then looked up to study Kat's face. Kat kept her expression neutral.

"I don't understand. Why are you here?"

"He killed my father."

"I see. And you want to see him suffer?"

There was no judgment in Nurse Steiner's voice. It was as if this would be the most natural thing in the world.

"Uh, no. I'm here to ask him some questions."

Nurse Steiner took one more look at the badge and handed it back. "This way, my dear."

The voice was melodic and angelic and downright creepy. Nurse Steiner led her into a room with four beds. Three were empty. In the fourth, the one in the far right corner, Monte Leburne lay with his eyes closed. In his day, Leburne had been a big, beefy bruiser of a man. If a crime involved a need for physical violence or intimidation, Monte Leburne had been the meathead to call. An ex-heavyweight boxer who'd definitely taken a few too many shots to the head, Leburne had used his fists (and

more) in loan-sharking, extortion, turf wars, union busting, you name it. After a rival family gave him a particularly brutal beating, his Mob bosses—who respected
Leburne's brand of loyalty because it was so akin to
stupidity—had given him a gun and let him work the
physically less demanding task of shooting their enemies.

In short, Monte Leburne had become a midlevel hit
man. He wasn't bright or clever, but really, when you
stopped and thought about it, how smart did you have to
be to shoot a man with a gun?

"He's in and out," Nurse Steiner explained.

Kat moved toward the bed. Nurse Steiner stayed a few
paces behind her. "Could you give us some privacy?" Kat
asked.

The sweet smile. The creepy, melodic voice: "No,
dear, I can't."

Kat looked down at Leburne, and for a moment, she
searched herself for some sign of compassion for the man
who had killed her father. If it was there, it was pretty
well hidden. Most days, her hatred for this man was red-
hot, but some days, she realized that it was like hating a
gun. He was the weapon. Nothing more.

Of course, weapons should be destroyed too, right?

Kat put her hand on Leburne's shoulder and gave him
a gentle shake. Leburne's eyes blinked open.

"Hello, Monte."

It took a moment for his eyes to focus in on Kat's face.
When they did—when he recognized her—his body
went stiff. "You're not supposed to be here, Kat."

Kat reached into her pocket and took out a photograph. "He was my father."

Leburne had seen the photograph plenty of times before. Whenever she visited him, Kat brought it. She

wasn't sure why. Part of her hoped to reach him, but men who execute people are rarely subjected to bouts of regret. Maybe she brought it for herself somehow, to steel her own resolve, to have, in some odd way, her own father as backup.

"Who wanted him dead? It was Cozone, wasn't it?"

Leburne kept the back of his head flat on the pillow. "Why do you keep asking me the same questions?"

"Because you never answer them."

Monte Leburne smiled up at her with peglike teeth. Even at this distance, she could smell the decay on his breath. "And what, are you hoping for a deathbed confession?"

"There's no reason not to tell the truth now, Monte."

"Sure there is."

He meant his family. That was his price, of course. Stay quiet and we will take care of your family. Open your mouth and we will hack them into small pieces.

The ultimate carrot and stick.

This had always been the problem for her. She had nothing to offer him.

You didn't have to be a doctor to realize that Monte Leburne didn't have much time left. Death had already nestled into a cozy spot and started clawing its way to inevitable victory. Monte's entire being was sunken, as though he'd eventually disappear into the bed and then the floor and then, poof, completely vanish. She stared now at his right hand—his gun hand—loaded up with fat, loose veins that looked like old garden hoses. The IV was attached near his wrist.

He gritted his teeth as a fresh wave of pain coursed through. "Go," he managed to say.

"No." Kat could feel her last chance slipping away.

"Please," she said, trying to keep the pleading from her voice. "I need to know."

"Go away."

Kat leaned closer. "Listen, okay? This is just for me. Do you understand? It's been eighteen years. I have to know the truth. That's all. For closure. Why did he order the hit on my father?"

"Get away from me."

"I'll say you talked."

"What?"

Kat nodded, trying to keep her voice firm. "The moment you die, I will arrest his ass. I will say you ratted him out. I will tell him I got a full confession from you."

Monte Leburne smiled again. "Nice try."

"You don't think I'll do it?"

"Don't know what you'll do. I just know no one will believe it." Monte Leburne looked past her toward Nurse Steiner. "And I got a witness, don't I, Sylvia?"

Nurse Steiner nodded. "I'm right here, Monte."

A fresh roll of pain made him wince. "I'm really tired, Sylvia. It's getting pretty bad."

Nurse Steiner quickly moved closer to his bedside. "I'm right here, Monte." She took his hand. What with the garish makeup, her smile looked literally painted on, like something on the face of a scary clown.

"Please make her go, Sylvia."

"She's leaving now." Nurse Steiner started pressing the pump, releasing some kind of narcotic into his veins. "Just relax, Monte, okay?"

"Don't let her stay."

"Shhh, you'll be fine." Nurse Steiner gave Kat the baleful eye. "She's as good as gone."

Kat was about to protest, but Nurse Steiner pressed

buttons on the IV box again, making the point moot anyway. Leburne's eyes started to flutter. A few moments later, he was out cold.

A waste of time.

But then again, what had Kat expected? Even the dying man had scoffed at the idea of a deathbed confession. Cozone knew how to keep his employees quiet. You do your time, your family gets taken care of for life. You talk, everyone dies. There was no incentive to get Leburne to talk. There never had been. There certainly was none now.

Kat was just about to head back toward the car when she heard the sickly-sweet voice behind her. "You handled that very poorly, dear."

Kat turned to see Nurse Steiner standing there, looking like something out of a horror movie with the nurse getup and the paint-can makeup. "Yeah, well, thanks for your help."

"Would you like my help?"

"Pardon?"

"He has very little remorse, you know. I mean, true remorse. A priest stops by, and he says the right words. But he doesn't mean it. He's just trying to bargain his way into Heaven. The Lord isn't so easily fooled." She gave the creepy lipstick-on-teeth smile again. "Monte murdered many people—is that correct?"

"He confessed to killing three. There were more."

"Including your father?"

"Yes."

"And your father was a police officer? Like you?"

"Yes."

Nurse Steiner made a tsk-tsk noise of sympathy. "I'm very sorry."

Kat said nothing.

Nurse Steiner chewed on her lipsticked bottom lip for a moment. "Please follow me."

"What?"

"You need information—am I correct?"

"Yes."

"Please stay out of sight. Let me handle this."

Nurse Steiner spun and started back toward the infirmary. Kat hurried to catch up. "Wait. What are you going to do?"

"Do you know anything about twilight sleep?" Nurse Steiner asked.

"Not really."

"I started my career working for an ob-gyn doing baby deliveries. In the old days, we'd use morphine and scopolamine as anesthesia. It would produce a semi-narcotic state—the expectant mother would stay awake, but she wouldn't really remember anything. Some say it dulled the pain. Perhaps it did, but I don't think so. I think what happened was, the expectant mother forgot the agony she was forced to endure." She tilted her head, like a dog hearing a strange sound. "Does pain happen if you don't remember it?"

Kat thought that question was rhetorical, but Nurse Steiner stopped and waited for an answer. "I don't know."

"Think about it. For any experience, good or bad: If you don't remember it immediately after it happens, does it really count?"

Again she waited for an answer. Again Kat said, "I don't know."

"Neither do I. It's an interesting question, isn't it?"

Where the hell was she going with this? "I guess so," Kat said.

"We all want to live in the moment. I understand that. But if you can't recall that moment, did it ever really happen? I'm not sure. The Germans started twilight sleep. They thought it would make childbirth more bearable for the mothers. But they were wrong. We stopped using it, of course. The child came out drugged. That was the main reason—at least, that's what the medical people claimed." She leaned conspiratorially toward Kat. "But between us, I don't really think that was it."

"Why, then?"

"It wasn't what happened to the babies." Nurse Steiner stopped at the door. "It was the mothers."

"What about them?"

"They had issues with the procedure too. Twilight sleep allowed them to miss the pain, yes, but they never experienced the birth, either. They went into a room, and next thing they remembered, they were holding a baby. Emotionally, they felt disconnected, removed from the birth of their own child. It was disconcerting. You've been carrying a child for nine months. You've started labor and then poof—"

Nurse Steiner snapped her fingers for emphasis.

"You wondered whether it really happened," Kat finished for her.

"Exactly."

"What does this have to do with Monte Leburne?"

Nurse Steiner's smile was coy. "You know."

She didn't. Or maybe she did. "You can put him in twilight sleep?"

"Yes, of course."

"And you think—what?—I can get him to talk and then he'll forget about it?"

"Not really, no. I mean, yes, he won't remember. But morphine isn't all that different from sodium thiopental. You know what that is, don't you?"

Kat did, though it was better known as Sodium Pentothal. In short: truth serum.

"It doesn't work like you see in the movies," Nurse Steiner continued. "But when people are under, well, the mothers tended to babble. Confessing, even. At more than one delivery, with the husbands pacing in the other room, they confided that the baby wasn't his. We didn't ask, of course. They would just say it, and we would pretend that we didn't hear. But over time, I started to realize that you could actually carry on conversations. You could ask and learn a great deal and, of course, she would never remember a thing."

Nurse Steiner met Kat's eye. Kat felt a shiver run down her back. Nurse Steiner broke the contact and pushed open the door.

"I should point out that there is a huge problem with reliability. I've seen it happen many times with morphine. The patient will speak convincingly about something that can't possibly be true. The last man who died in this infirmary? He swore that every time I left him alone, someone would kidnap him and take him to different cat funerals. He wasn't lying. He was convinced it was happening. Do you see?"

"Yes."

"So you understand, then. Shall we continue?"

Kat didn't know. She had grown up in a cop family. She had seen the dangers of bending the rules.

But what choice did she have?

"Detective?"

"Go ahead," Kat said.

The smile widened. "If Monte hears your voice, it will put his defenses up. If you let me handle it, we may get some useful information for you."

"Okay."

"I'm going to need some information about the shooting."

It took about twenty minutes. Nurse Steiner added scopolamine into the mix, checked vitals, made adjustments. She was doing this with all too much a practiced hand, so that, for a moment, Kat wondered whether this was the first time Nurse Steiner had done it for reasons that were not purely medical. Kat couldn't help but wonder about the implications of twilight sleep, the potential for abuse. Nurse Steiner's seemingly cheery justification—if you don't remember it immediately after it happened, did it happen?—sounded too easy.

The woman was off, no doubt about it. Right now, Kat didn't much care.

Kat sat low in the corner, out of sight. Monte Leburne was awake now, his head lolling back on the pillow. He started calling Nurse Steiner Cassie—the name of his sister who died when she was eighteen. He started talking about how he wanted to see her when he died. Kat marveled at how Nurse Steiner seemed to lead him further and further down the path she wanted him to travel.

"Oh, you will see me, Monte," Nurse Steiner said. "I will be waiting on the other side. Except, well, there could be issues with the people you killed."

"Men," he said.

"What?"

"I only killed men. I wouldn't kill no woman. Not

ever. No women, no children, Cassie. I killed men. Bad men."

Nurse Steiner shot a glance toward Kat. "But you killed a police officer."

"Worst of them all."

"What do you mean?"

"Cops. They ain't no better. Don't matter, though."

"I don't understand, Monte. Explain it to me."

"I never killed no cop, Cassie. You know that."

Kat froze. That can't be right.

Nurse Steiner cleared her throat. "But, Monte—"

"Cassie? I'm sorry I never defended you." Monte Leburne started to cry. "I let him hurt you, and I didn't do nothing to help."

"That's okay, Monte."

"No, it's not. I protected everyone else, right? But not you."

"It's over. I'm in a better place now. I want you to be here with me."

"I protect my family now. I learned. Dad was no good."

"I know that. But, Monte, you said you never killed a cop."

"You know that."

"But what about Detective Henry Donovan?"

"Shh."

"What?"

"Shh," he said. "They'll hear. It was easy. I was toast anyway."

"What do you mean?"

"They already had me for killing Lazlow and Greene. Dead to rights. I was going to get life anyway. What's one more, if it provides, you know what I mean?"

A cold hand wrapped itself around Kat's heart and squeezed.

Even Nurse Steiner was having trouble keeping her tone even. "Explain it to me, Monte. Why did you shoot Detective Donovan?"

"Is that what you think? I just took the fall. I was already toast. Don't you see?"

"You didn't shoot him?"

No answer.

"Monte?"

She was starting to lose him.

"Monte, if it wasn't you, who killed him?"

His voice was far away. "Who?"

"Who killed Henry Donovan?"

"How should I know? They visited me. Day after I got arrested. They told me to take the money and the fall."

"Who?"

Monte's eyes closed. "I'm so sleepy."

"Monte, who told you to take the fall?"

"I should have never let Dad get away with it, Cassie. What he did to you. I knew. Mom knew. And we didn't do nothing. I'm sorry."

"Monte?"

"So tired . . ."

"Who told you to take the fall?"

But Monte Leburne was asleep.

7

ON the drive back, Kat kept both hands on the wheel. She focused hard on the road, too hard, but it was the only way to keep her head from spinning. Her world had keeled off its axis. Nurse Steiner had again warned her that Monte Leburne had been disoriented under the medication and that his claims should be viewed with a strong dose of skepticism. Kat nodded as the nurse spoke. She understood all that—about disorientation and unreliability and even imagination—but she'd learned one thing as a cop: Truth has its own funky smell.

Right now, Monte Leburne reeked of truth.

She flipped on the radio and tried to listen to angry talk radio. The hosts always had such easy answers to the world's problems. Kat found their simplicity irritating and thus their shows, in an odd way, wonderfully distracting. Those who had easy answers, be they on the right or the left, were always wrong. The world is complex. It is never one-size-fits-all.

When she arrived back at the 19th Precinct, she headed straight to Captain Stagger's office. He wasn't there. She could ask when he'd be back, but she didn't feel like drawing attention to herself quite yet. She settled on sending him a quick text:

Need to talk.

No immediate reply, but then again, Kat hadn't expected one. She took the stairs up a level. Her current partner, Charles "Chaz" Faircloth, stood in the corner with three other cops. When she approached, Chaz said, "Well, hey there, Kat," stretching it out so that even these benign words carried a sarcastic edge. Then, because Chaz was funny like this, he added: "Look what the *Kat* dragged in."

Sadly, the men with him actually chuckled.

"Good one," she said.

"Thanks. Been working on my timing."

"It's paying off."

Oh man, she was so not in the mood for him right now.

Chaz wore an expensive, chintzy, perfectly tailored suit, the kind that glistens as though wet, a tie Windsored by someone who had too much time on their hands, and Ferragamo shoes that brought to mind that old adage about judging a man by the shine of his shoes. The adage was crap. Guys who always shined their shoes were usually self-involved asswipes who figured superficiality trumped substance.

Chaz had the waxy, pretty-boy good looks and almost

supernatural charisma of, well, a sociopath, which Kat suspected he was. He was a Faircloth, yes, one of *the* Faircloths, a loaded and well-connected family whose members often played at being cops because it looked good when they ran for public office. Still keeping his eye on her, Chaz whispered a little joke to the guys, probably at her expense, and the group dispersed with a laugh.

"You're late," Chaz said to her.

"I was working a case for the captain."

He arched an eyebrow. "Is that what they call it?"

What an ass.

With Chaz, everything was a double entendre that bordered on, if not crossed into, harassment. It wasn't that he hit on women. It was that his entire personality was hitting on women. Some men are like this—they communicate with all females as though they've just met in a singles' bar. He couldn't talk about what he had for breakfast without making it somehow smarmy, as though you'd just had a one-night stand and cooked it up for him.

"So what are we working on?" Kat asked.

"Don't worry. I covered for you."

"Yeah, well, thanks, but do you mind filling me in?"

Chaz gestured toward her desk, flashing emerald-stone cuff links. "The files are all there. Have at it." He checked his oversize and too-shiny Rolex. "Gotta bounce."

He strutted out with his shoulders back, whistling some lame tune about shorties in a club. Kat had already spoken to Stephen Singer, her immediate superior, about getting a new partner. Once Chaz heard about her request, he'd been shocked, not so much because he really liked Kat but because he could not fathom how this woman—or any woman—hadn't fallen under his spell. He reacted by turning up the charm, sure that there was no woman anywhere in the free world he couldn't bend to his whim.

With his back still facing her, Chaz waved a hand up and said, "Later, babe."

Not worth it, she told herself.

There were more important issues at hand. For example: Could Monte Leburne have been telling the truth?

What if they had had it wrong all these years? What if her father's killer was still out there?

It was almost too overwhelming to consider. She needed to unload, to talk to someone who had known all the players and the situations, and the first name to come to mind, the first person who popped in her head, God help her, was Jeff Raynes.

She glanced at the computer on her desk.

First things first. She brought up every file on Monte Leburne and the murder of Detective Henry Donovan. There was a ton of material. Okay, fine. She could read it tonight at home. Of course, she had already read it a hundred times, but had she ever gone into it with the supposition that Monte Leburne was a fall guy? No. Fresh eyes. She would read it with fresh eyes.

Then she started wondering whether Jeff had replied to her YouAreJustMyType.com message yet.

The desks on either side of her were empty. She looked behind her. No one was there. Good. If the guys in here saw her bring up an online-dating site, she would never hear the end of it. She sat at the computer and took another look. The coast was clear. She quickly typed "YouAreJustMyType.com" into the field and hit RETURN.

Site blocked. To access, please ask your direct superior for access code.

Uh-uh, no way. The police department was like a lot of businesses—they were trying to up productivity by not allowing employees to spend time on personal websites or social networks. That was what was happening here.

Earlier she had debated putting the YouAreJustMy Type app on her phone, but that felt way too desperate. It would simply have to wait. Which was fine. Except that it wasn't.

Cases came in through the door. Kat handled them. A taxi driver claimed a socialite was trying to beat a fare. A woman complained that her neighbor was growing pot plants. Minor stuff. She checked her cell phone. No reply from Stagger. She didn't know what to make of that. She sent him another message:

Really need to talk to you.

She was about to pocket her phone when she felt the vibration. Stagger's answer had come in: Assume this has to do with prison visit?

Yes.

The delay was longer this time.

Busy until eight. I could stop by tonight or we can wait till the morning.

There was no delay on Kat's part.

STOP BY TONIGHT.

*   *   *

KAT didn't pretend that she wasn't anxious to see if Jeff had replied.

At the end of her shift, she changed into jogging clothes, ran across the park, hurried past the doorman with a smile and nod, took the stairs two at a time (the elevator could be slow), and unlocked her door in one smooth motion.

The computer was in sleep mode. Kat gave the mouse a shake and waited. The little hourglass popped up and started going round and round. Man, she needed a new computer. She was thirsty from the run and debated getting up for a glass of water, but the hourglass stopped.

She loaded up YouAreJustMyType.com. It had been too many hours since her last visit, so the site had again logged her out. She typed in her user name and password and clicked CONTINUE. The welcome screen came up with six words big, bright, and green:

One response waiting in your in-box!

Her heart pounded. She could actually feel it, the slow, steady thud that she was sure would be visible to the eye. She clicked the green lettering. The in-box came up along with the tiny profile photograph of Jeff.

Now or never.

The subject line was blank. She moved her cursor over it and clicked to open the e-mail. Jeff's message came up:

HA! Cute video! I always loved that one. I know men always say that they love a woman with a sense of humor, but that was really a clever way of reaching out. I'm also really drawn to your photographs. Your face is beautiful,

obviously, but there is something . . . more
there. It's nice to meet you!

That was it. No signature. No name.

Nothing.

Wait. What?

The truth smacked her hard across the face: Jeff didn't remember her.

Was that possible? How could he not remember her? Hold the phone—let's not get ahead of ourselves. She took a deep breath and tried to think it through. Okay, at the very least, Jeff didn't recognize her. How much had she changed? A lot, she supposed. Her hair was darker and shorter now. She had aged. Men are luckier, of course. The gray at Jeff's temples just made him better-looking, damn him. If she was objective, the years perhaps had not been as kind to her. Simple as that. Kat stood up, started pacing, looked in the mirror. You don't see it on yourself, of course. You don't see the changes that the years bring. But now, as she started to search her drawers for old pictures of herself—the bad hair, the chubbier cheeks, the glowing youth—she could almost get it. He had last seen her as a bright-eyed albeit devastated twenty-two-year-old. She was now forty. Big difference. Her profile offered up no real personal information. It didn't list her address or degree at Columbia or anything so that you'd know it was Kat.

So on one level, it made sense that Jeff may not recognize her.

Of course, when she started to think about it a little more, her justification started to, if not fall apart, at least unravel a bit. They'd been in love. They'd been engaged. That song—that video—had been more than "cute" to them, more than something you'd pass off or forget or . . .

Something snagged her gaze and held it.

Kat leaned closer to the computer monitor and saw a beating heart next to Jeff's profile photograph. According to the little grid at the bottom, that meant he was currently online and would accept instant messages from "those who've previously communicated" with him.

She sat down, opened up the instant message box, and typed,

It's Kat.

To send, you had to hit the RETURN button. She didn't waste time or give herself a chance to talk herself out of it. She hit the RETURN button. The message was sent.

The cursor blinked impatiently. Kat sat there and waited for his response. Her right leg started jackhammering up and down. She had never been diagnosed with restless legs syndrome, but she guessed she was on the borderline. Her father used to shake his leg too. A lot. She put her hand on her knee and willed herself to stop. Her eyes never left the screen.

The blinking cursor vanished. A small cloud popped up.

That meant Jeff was typing his reply. A moment later, it popped up on her screen:

No names. At least, not yet.

She frowned. What the hell did that mean? Somewhere in the back of her mind, she remembered reading something during her initial "orientation" to YouAreJustMyType.com, some warning to users not to use their real names until they were certain that the person was someone they'd want to meet in person.

So he wasn't sure?

What was going on here? Her fingers found the keypad and started typing:

Jeff? Is that you? It's Kat.

The cursor blinked exactly twelve times—she counted— and then, the beating red heart disappeared.

Jeff had gone off-line.

8

IF it was Jeff.

That was the other thought that suddenly entered her mind. Maybe the widower in the profile wasn't Jeff. Maybe it was just some guy who looked like her ex-fiancé. The pictures, now that she studied them anew, were grainy. Most of the shots were outdoors, at something of a distance. There was that one in the woods, one on some barren beach with a broken fence, one on what might have been a golf course. In some, he wore a baseball cap. In others, he wore sunglasses too (never indoors, thank goodness). As in Kat's own photographs, the Maybe-Jeff never looked completely comfortable, almost as though he were hiding or caught off guard or avoiding a photographer who had made it a point to include him anyway.

As a cop, she had learned firsthand the power of persuasion, of want, of the unreliability of the eyes when it came to full-on suggestion. She had seen witnesses pick out the person in a lineup that they, the cops, wanted them to pick out. Your brain can fool you with simple inducements.

What can it do with all this want?

Last night, she had been scanning quickly through a website in search of a lifetime partner. Weren't the odds better that she would conjure up the one man who had been closest to that in her life than actually see him again?

The doorman intercom buzzed.

She pressed the button. "Yes, Frank?"

"Your captain is here."

"Send him up."

Kat left her door ajar so Stagger could walk right in without knocking—the last thing she wanted was more memory flashes to that day eighteen years ago. She exited YouAreJustMyType.com and, just to be on the safe side, cleared her browser history.

Stagger's whole being emanated exhaustion. His eyes were red and sunken. His normal five-o'clock shadow had darkened into something closer to midnight. His shoulders stooped like a buzzard too tired to go after its prey.

"You okay?" she asked him.

"Long day."

"Can I get you something to drink?"

He shook his head. "What's up?"

Kat decided to dive right into the deep end. "How sure are you that Monte Leburne killed Henry?"

Whatever he had been expecting her to say—whatever guess he had made as to why she so desperately wanted to speak with him—it wasn't that. "Are you serious?"

"Yes."

"So I guess you got to see him today."

"Yes."

"And what, he suddenly denied that he shot your father?"

"Not exactly."

"Then what?"

Kat had to be careful here. Stagger wasn't just by the book—he was the book, binding, pages, printing press, the whole deal. If he heard about Nurse Steiner and the twilight sleep, he would throw a fit and then some.

"Okay, I want you to listen to me for a second," she began. "Just go in with an open mind, okay?"

"Kat, do I look in the mood for games?"

"No. Definitely not."

"So tell me what's going on."

"I get that, but just bear with me. Let's go back to the start."

"Kat . . ."

She pushed through it. "Here is Monte Leburne, right? The feds nail him as a triggerman for two hits. They try to get him to flip on Cozone. He doesn't. He isn't that type. Too dumb maybe. Or he thinks they'll hurt his family. Whatever, Leburne shuts up."

She waited for him to tell her to get to the point. He didn't.

"Meanwhile, you guys are searching for whoever killed my father. You don't have a lot, just rumors and a few loose threads, and suddenly, voilà, Leburne confesses."

"It wasn't like that," Stagger said.

"Yeah, it was."

"We had leads."

"But nothing solid. So you tell me—why did he suddenly confess?"

Stagger made a face. "You know why. He killed a cop. The heat was ridiculous on Cozone's operation. He had to throw us something."

"Exactly. So Monte Leburne takes the fall. And Cozone gets away with it. How convenient. A guy who is already spending his life in prison gets another life sentence."

"We tried for years to nail Cozone for it. You know that."

"But we never could. Don't you see? We could never tie Cozone and Leburne together on that case. You know why?"

He sighed. "You're not turning into a conspiracy nut on me, are you, Kat?"

"No."

"The reason we couldn't tie them to it is simple: That's the way the world works. It isn't a perfect system."

"Or maybe," Kat said, trying to keep her tone calm, "maybe we couldn't tie it together because Monte Leburne didn't shoot my dad. We were able to independently connect Leburne to the other two murders. But we could never do that with Dad. Why? And what about those fingerprints we were never able to identify? Don't you wonder who else was at the scene?"

Stagger just looked at her. "What happened up at Fishkill?"

Kat knew she had to play this delicately. "He's bad."

"Leburne?"

She nodded. "I don't think he has more than a week or two."

"So you drove up," Stagger said. "And he agreed to see you."

"Sort of."

He gave her the eye. "What does that mean?"

"He was in the infirmary. I talked my way in. No big deal, nothing shady. I flashed my badge, kept it vague."

"Okay, so?"

"So when I got to Leburne's bed, he was in pretty bad shape. They had him drugged up with a hefty dose of painkillers. Morphine, I guess."

Stagger's eyes narrowed. "Okay, so?"

"So he started muttering. I didn't question him or anything. He was too out of it. But he began to sort of hallucinate. He thought the nurse was his dead sister, Cassie. He apologized for letting their father abuse her or something. Started crying and telling her he'd be with her soon. Stuff like that."

Stagger pinned her with his eyes. She wasn't sure if he was buying it, but then again, she wasn't sure how hard she was selling it. "Go on."

"And he said he never killed the cop."

The sunken eyes bulged a bit now. It wasn't exactly the truth, but for the sake of this conversation, Kat figured that it was close enough.

"He said he was innocent," she continued.

Stagger looked incredulous. "Of everything?"

"No, just the opposite. He said that they already had him dead to rights for two murders, so what harm was there to confessing to one more if it provides?"

"If it provides?"

"His words."

Stagger just shook his head. "This is crazy. You know that, right?"

"It's not. It actually makes perfect sense. You're already going to serve a life sentence. What's one more murder conviction?" Kat took a step closer to him. "Let's say you were closing in on the killer. Maybe you were days or even hours from putting it all together. Suddenly, a guy who is already caught and going to serve life confesses. Don't you see?"

"And who would set that up exactly?"

"I don't know. Cozone probably."

"He'd use his own man?"

"A man he knew—and we knew—would never talk? Sure, why not?"

"We have the murder weapon, remember?"

"I do."

"The gun that shot your father. We found it exactly where Monte Leburne said it would be."

"Of course Leburne knew. The real killer told him. Think about it. Since when does a hit man like Leburne save the gun? He gets rid of it. We never got the weapons for the other two murders, right? Suddenly, after he kills a cop, he decides to save it, as what? A souvenir? And again, what about those fingerprints? Did he have an accomplice? Did he go it alone? What?"

Stagger put his hands on her shoulders. "Kat, listen to me."

She knew what was coming. This was part of it. She'd have to ride it out.

"You said Leburne was drugged up, right? On morphine?"

"Yes."

"So he hallucinated. Your word. He muttered some imaginary nonsense. That's all."

"Don't patronize me, Stagger."

"I'm not."

"Yeah, you are. You know I don't buy into nonsense like"—she made quote marks with her fingers—"'closure.'

I think it's crap. Even if we nail everyone involved in his murder, my father is still dead. That will never change. So closure—I don't know—it's almost an insult to his memory. You know what I mean?"

He nodded slowly.

"But this arrest . . . it never worked for me. I always suspected there was something more."

"And now you've made it into that."

"What?"

"Come on, Kat. This is Monte Leburne. You don't think he knew you were there? He's playing with you. He knows that you've had your doubts all along. You wanted to see something that wasn't there. And now he's given that to you."

She opened her mouth to protest, but suddenly, she thought about the Maybe-Jeff on her computer. Want can twist your perception. Was that part of it? Had she so wanted to find a solution—to find "closure"—that she was creating scenarios?

"That's not it," Kat said, but her voice held a little less conviction now.

"Are you sure?"

"You've got to understand. I can't let this go."

He nodded slowly. "I do understand."

"You're patronizing me again."

He forced up a tired smile. "Monte Leburne killed your father. It isn't neat or a perfect fit. It never is. You know that. The questions about the case—all normal and routine and easily explainable—eat you up. But at some point, you have to let it go. It will drive you mad. If you let it get to you like this, you end up depressed and . . ."

His words trailed off.

"Like my grandfather?"

"I didn't say that."

"Didn't have to."

Stagger found her gaze and held it for a long second. "Your father would want you to move on."

She said nothing.

"You know that I'm telling the truth."

"I do," she said.

"But?"

"But I can't do it. My father would know that too."

KAT filled yet another shot glass with Jack Daniel's and started printing out her father's old murder file.

This wasn't the official police one. She had, of course, read that one many times before. This one was of her creation, loaded up with everything in the official file— the detectives who'd closed her dad's case had both been family friends—plus everything, even rumors, she had managed to nail down on her own. The case had been pretty solid, the two keys being that they had a confession from Leburne himself, plus the murder weapon, found hidden in Leburne's home. Most of the loose ends had been tied up nicely, with one notable exception that had always haunted Kat: There were unidentified fingerprints found at the murder scene. The lab guys had found a full, clear print on her father's belt and had run it through the system but got no hits.

Kat had never been fully satisfied with the official explanation, but everyone, including Kat herself, had written that off to her personal connection. Aqua had said it best one day when she ran into him in the park on one of his more lucid days: "You are seeking something in this case that you can never find."

Aqua.

Here was something odd. She could talk to Stacy about her father's murder, but Stacy had never met the man. Stacy didn't know "old Kat," the Before Kat, the one who had dated Jeff and smiled freely and existed before Henry Donovan's murder. But the first name to come to mind—the one person who would understand more than any other what she was going through—was, well, Jeff.

That didn't seem like a good idea, did it?

No. At least, it wouldn't at six in the morning or ten o'clock at night. But right now, at three A.M. with a few belts of Jack coursing through Kat's veins, it seemed like the most brilliant idea in the history of the world. She looked out the window of her apartment. They say New York is the city that doesn't sleep. That was nonsense. When she stayed in other cities, even smaller ones like St. Louis or Indianapolis, people seemed to stay up later, though it seemed more out of desperation than anything else. We aren't New York City, so we will work harder to have a good time. Something like that.

The streets of Manhattan at three A.M.? Still a cemetery.

Kat wobbled toward her computer. It took her three tries to log on to YouAreJustMyType.com because her fingers, like her tongue, were thick from drink. She checked to see if by some chance Jeff was online. He wasn't. Well, that was too bad, wasn't it? She clicked the link to send him a direct message.

Jeff,
Can we talk? Something happened here and I would really like to bounce it off you.

Kat

Part of her brain realized that this was a really bad idea, that this was the online dating equivalent of drunk texting. Drunk texting never worked. Never, ever, never.

She sent the message and managed to half pass out, half fall asleep. When the alarm went off at six A.M., Kat hated her pitiful self even before the hangover rushed in and started shooting pain sparks through her skull.

She checked the messages. Nothing from Jeff. Or Maybe-Jeff. Right, hadn't she realized at some point that maybe it wasn't Jeff, just some guy who looked like him? Didn't matter. Who cares? Where the hell is the Extra Strength Tylenol?

Aqua's yoga class. Uh-uh. No way. Not today. Her head would never take it. Plus, she had gone yesterday. She didn't have to go today.

Except . . .

Wait, hold up a second. She ran back to the computer and brought up Jeff's profile. Other than Stagger, the only person who was really still in her life, who knew her with Jeff and her dad and knew the old her, was, well, Aqua. Aqua and Jeff had grown close via her, even rooming together in that crappy two-bedroom on 178th Street. She hit PRINT, threw on her clothes, made the run over to the east side of the park—arriving, as usual, when everyone was meditating, their eyes closed.

"Late," Aqua said.

"Sorry."

Aqua frowned and opened his eyes in surprise. Kat had never apologized before. He knew something was up.

Two decades ago, Aqua and Kat had been classmates at Columbia. That was where they met freshman year. Aqua was, quite simply, the most brilliant person Kat had ever known. His test scores were off the charts. His brain was revved up, worked too fast, finishing homework assignments in minutes that would take others all night. Aqua consumed knowledge like some consume fast food. He took extra classes, worked two jobs, started running track, but there was nothing that could stop the mania.

Eventually, Aqua's engine overheated. That was the way Kat thought about it. He cracked, though in truth he was just sick. Mentally ill. It was no different, really, from having cancer or lupus or something like that. Aqua had been in and out of institutions since. Doctors had tried everything to cure him, but his mental illness, like those physical ones, was, if not terminal, chronic. Kat didn't know where he lived now exactly. Somewhere in the park, she guessed. Sometimes Kat would bump into him away from the morning class, when his mania was at a more fevered pitch. Sometimes, Aqua would be dressed like a man. Sometimes—okay, most times—Aqua would dress like a woman. Sometimes, Aqua wouldn't even know who Kat was.

At the end of class, when the others closed their eyes for Corpse Pose, Kat sat up and stared at Aqua. He—or she, it got very confusing when someone was a part-time transvestite—stared back, a flash of anger on his face. There were rules in this class. She was breaking one of them.

"I want you to relax your face," Aqua said in that soothing voice. "Relax your eyes. Feel them sink down. Relax your mouth . . ."

His gaze never left hers. Eventually, Aqua acquiesced. He rose from a lotus position in one effortless, silent move. Kat rose too. She followed him through a back pathway heading north.

"So this is where you go after class," Kat said.

"No."

"No?"

"I'm not showing you where I go. What do you want?"

"I need a favor."

Aqua kept walking. "I don't do favors. I teach yoga."

"I know that."

"So why are you bothering me?" His two hands formed fists, like a little kid about to throw a tantrum. "Yoga is the routine. I'm good with routine. You calling me out, wanting to talk like this, it isn't part of the routine. It's not good for me, losing my routine."

"I need your help."

"I help by teaching yoga."

"I know that."

"I'm a good teacher, aren't I?"

"The best."

"So let me do what I do. That's how I help. That's how I stay centered. That's how I contribute to society."

Kat suddenly felt overwhelmed. They'd been friends a long time ago. Good friends. Close friends. They would sit in the library and talk about anything. The hours would fly by—he had been that kind of friend.

She had talked to Aqua about Jeff after their first date. He got it. He saw it right away. Aqua and Jeff had become close too. They became roommates, moving into off-campus housing, though Jeff ended up spending most nights at Kat's. Looking at the bewildered look on Aqua's face right now, she realized yet again how much she had lost. She had lost her dad. Obvious. She had lost her fiancé. Also obvious. But maybe—not so obvious— she had lost something else, something real and deep, when Aqua came apart.

"God, I miss you," she said.

Aqua started picking up his pace. "This doesn't help anything."

"I know. I'm sorry."

"I have to go. I have things to do."

She put her hand on his arm to slow him down. "Will you look at this first?"

He frowned, not slowing down much. She handed him the printouts from Jeff's YouAreJustMyType profile.

"What is this?" Aqua asked.

"You tell me."

He didn't like it. She could see that. This whole break in his routine was agitating him. She didn't mean to do that. She knew there was a danger in upsetting him.

"Aqua? Just take a look, okay?"

He did. He looked at the sheets of paper. She tried to read him. His expression remained perturbed, but she thought she saw something light up in his eyes.

"Aqua?"

There was fear in his voice. "Why are you showing these to me?"

"Does he look like someone you know?"

"No," he said.

She felt her heart crash. Then Aqua started to hurry away.

"It doesn't look like Jeff, Kat. It is Jeff."

9

KAT had just hung up the phone, replaying Monte Leburne's words in her head for the umpteenth time, when
the computer dinged as "YouAreJustMyType Instant
Message!" popped up on her screen.

The instant message request was, she could see from
the tiny profile picture, from Jeff. For a moment, she just
sat there, almost afraid to move or click the READ button
because this contact, this connection seemed so fragile
and tenuous that any sudden act on her part could snap
this thinnest of a frayed thread.

The heart icon next to his profile picture had a question mark on it, awaiting her approval to commence the
conversation. For the past three hours, Kat had been
working on her father's case. The file told her nothing
new and yet held all the old problems. Henry Donovan
had been shot in the chest at close range with a small

Smith & Wesson. This too had always bothered her. Wouldn't you go for the head shot? Wouldn't you come up behind him and put the gun against the back of his head and pull the trigger twice? That had been Monte Leburne's MO. Why change it here? Why fire into the chest?

It didn't mesh.

Neither had something Monte Leburne said to Nurse Steiner when she asked who killed Henry Donovan: "How should I know? They visited me. Day after I got arrested. They told me to take the money and the fall."

Obvious question: Who were "they"?

But perhaps Monte had given her the answer. "They" had visited him in prison. Not only had they visited him, but they had visited him the day after he got arrested.

Hmm.

Kat had grabbed the phone and called an old friend of hers, Chris Harrop, who worked for the Department of Corrections.

"Kat, nice to hear from you. What's up?"

"I need a favor," Kat said.

"What a surprise. I figured you were calling me for sweaty, hot sex."

"My loss, Chris. Can you get me a visitor log for a prisoner?"

"Shouldn't be an issue," Harrop said. "Who's the prisoner and where is he doing time?"

"Monte Leburne. He was up at Clinton."

"For what date?"

"Um, well, it was March twenty-seventh."

"Okay, let me get on it."

"Eighteen years ago."

"Pardon?"

"I need his visitor log. From eighteen years ago."

"You're kidding, right?"

"I'm not."

"Wow."

"Yeah."

"Look, it'll take some time," Harrop said. "The computerization started in 2004. I think the old records are in storage in Albany. How important is this to you?"

"Hot-sweaty-sex important," Kat said.

"On it."

It was when she had hung up the phone that the YouAreJustMyType instant message balloon had popped up. With a shaking hand, she clicked the question mark, said yes, and then, after a small delay, Jeff's words appeared:

Hey, Kat, I got your message. How are you?

Her heart stopped.

Kat read the instant message from Jeff two more times, maybe three. It was hard to know. She saw the beating heart next to his name—he was online, right now, waiting for her response. Her fingertips found the keyboard.

Hey, Jeff . . .

She stopped, trying to think what to add to that before she hit SEND. She decided to go with what was on her mind:

Hey, Jeff. You didn't recognize me, I guess.

Kat waited for his reply—an explanation that would probably be full of some sort of defensive baloney like

"You're even prettier now" or "The new haircut is so flattering," something like that, whatever. Who cares anyway? It didn't make a difference. Why did she even raise it? Stupid.

But his answer surprised her:

No, I recognized you right away.

The heart next to his profile picture kept beating. She wondered about that little icon or avatar or whatever the hell you called it. A beating red heart—the symbol of romance and love, and if Jeff left right now, if he decided to disconnect, the heart stops beating and then fades away. You, the customer and potential partner, don't want that to happen.

Kat wrote: So why didn't you say so?

More blinking heart: You know why.

She frowned, gave it a moment, mulled it over. Then she typed: Actually, I don't. Then thinking even more about it, she added: Why didn't you say anything about the "Missing You" video?

Heart. Blink. Heart. Blink.

It's just that I'm a widower now.

Whoa. How to reply to that one? I saw that. I'm sorry.

She wanted to ask him a million questions—where he lived, what was his child like, when and how his wife had died, did he still think about Kat at all—but instead she sat there, nearly paralyzed, waiting for Jeff's reply.

Him: Being on here is weird for me.

Her: For me too.

Him: It makes me more cautious and protective. Does that make sense?

Part of her wanted to answer: "Yes, of course. That makes perfect sense." But a bigger part of her wanted to type: "Cautious? Protective? From me?"

Kat settled on: I guess.

The steady beating-heart icon was hypnotizing her. She could almost feel as though her own heart were keeping rhythm to the one next to Jeff's profile picture. She waited. He took longer than she expected to reply.

Him: I don't think it's a good idea for us to talk anymore.

The words landed on her like a surprise wave at the beach.

Him: Going back feels like a mistake. I need a fresh start. Do you understand?

For a moment, she truly hated Stacy for butting in and buying her this stupid account. She tried to shake it off, tried to remember that this had been a ridiculous fantasy to begin with, that he had dumped her before, hurt her, had broken her heart, and she would be damned before she would let him do it again.

Her: Yeah, fine, I understand.

Him: Take care of yourself, Kat.

Blink. Heart. Blink. Heart.

A tear escaped her eye and ran down her cheek. Please don't go, she thought, while typing: You too.

The heart on her screen stopped beating. It faded from red to gray to white before vanishing for good.

10

GERARD Remington was losing his mind.

He could almost feel the brain tissue tearing off as though by some bizarre centrifugal force. Most of the time, he was in darkness and in pain, and yet through the haze, a startling clarity had come to him. Perhaps *clarity* was the wrong word. *Focus* might be more apt.

The muscled man with the accent pointed to the path. "You know the way."

He did. This would be Gerard's fourth trip to the farmhouse. Titus would be waiting. Once again, Gerard considered making a run for it, but he knew he'd never get very far. They fed him just enough to keep him alive, no more. Even though he did nothing all day, locked away in that damn underground box, he was exhausted and weak. The trek on this path took all he had. There was nothing left.

Futile, he realized.

He still held out hope for some sort of miracle rescue. His body, yes, that had failed him. His brain, however, was another matter. He kept his eyes open and had started to piece together some basic information about his whereabouts.

Gerard was being held in rural Pennsylvania, a six-hour drive from Logan Airport, the place where they had kidnapped him.

How did he know?

The plain architecture of the farmhouse, the lack of electrical wires (Titus had his own generator), the old windmill, the buggy, the forest green window shades—that all added up to his being on land owned by the Amish. Moreover, Gerard knew that certain color buggies are native to certain areas. Gray, for example, usually indicated Lancaster County in Pennsylvania, thus his conclusion as to his whereabouts.

It made no sense. Or perhaps it did.

The sun shone through the green of the trees. The sky was a blue only a deity could paint. Beauty always found refuge in the ugly. Truth be told, beauty couldn't really exist without the ugly. How can there be light if there is no dark?

Gerard was just about to enter the clearing, when he heard the truck.

For a moment, he let himself believe that someone had come to his rescue. Police cars would follow. There would be sirens. Muscled Man would pull his weapon, but an officer would gun him down. He could almost see it all happening—Titus being arrested, the police starting to comb through the grounds, the whole horrible nightmare being exposed for the world to see, if not comprehend.

Because even Gerard could not fully comprehend it.

But the pickup truck wasn't here to rescue anyone. Just the opposite.

From this distance, he could make out a woman in the back of the truck. She wore a bright yellow sundress. That much he could see. The sundress was so out of place amid this horror that Gerard could actually feel a tear well up in his eye. He pictured Vanessa in a bright yellow sundress like that. He could see her slipping it on, turning toward him, smiling in a way that would thump-thump right into his chest. He could see Vanessa in that bright yellow sundress, and it made him think of everything else beautiful in the world. He thought about growing up in Vermont. He thought about how his father had loved to take him ice fishing when he was little. He thought about how his father had died when Gerard was only eight years old and how that really changed everything, but mostly how it destroyed his mom. He thought about her boyfriends, dirty, horrible men, and how all of them dismissed Gerard as a weird kid or worse. He thought about how he had been bullied in school, the last kid picked for kickball, the laughs and the taunts and the abuse. He thought about how his attic bedroom had become the escape, how he would make it dark and just lie on the bed, how that box underground some-times didn't feel so much different, how, as he grew up, the science lab would start serving the same function. He thought about his mother growing older and losing her looks, and then the men were gone and so she came to live with him, cooking for him, doting on him, being such a large part of his life. He thought about how she had died of cancer two years ago, leaving him completely alone, and how Vanessa had found him and brought beauty—color like in that bright yellow sundress—into his life and how very soon it would all be gone.

The truck did not stop. It vanished in a cloud of dust.

"Gerard?"

Titus never screamed. He never got angry or threatened violence. He didn't have to. Gerard had met men who commanded respect, who walked into a room and immediately took control of it. Titus was like that. His even tone somehow grabbed you by the lapels and made you obey.

Gerard turned toward him.

"Come."

Titus disappeared back into the farmhouse. Gerard followed him.

An hour later, Gerard started back down the path. His gait was unsteady. He began to shake. He didn't want to go back into that damned box. Promises had been made, of course. The way back to Vanessa, Titus had promised him, was to cooperate. He did not know what to believe anymore, but really, did it matter?

Gerard once again considered making a run for it. He once again dismissed it as nonsense.

When he reached the clearing, the Muscled Man stopped playing with his chocolate Lab and gave him an order in what Gerard believed was Portuguese. The dog ran up the path and out of sight. The Muscled Man pointed a gun at Gerard. Gerard had been through this routine before. Muscled Man would keep the gun on him as Gerard entered the box. Muscled Man would close the door and throw on the lock.

Darkness would smother him again.

But there was something different this time. Gerard could see it in the man's eyes.

"Vanessa," Gerard said softly to himself. He had taken to repeating her name, almost like a mantra, something to calm and soothe him, like his mother at the end with her rosary beads.

"This way," Muscled Man said. He pointed with his gun toward the right.

"Where are we going?"

"This way."

"Where are we going?" Gerard said again.

Muscled Man walked up to Gerard and put the gun against his head.

"This. Way."

He started toward the right. He had been here before—it was the spot where he had washed off with the hose and changed into this jumpsuit.

"Keep going."

"Vanessa . . ."

"Yep. Keep walking."

Gerard trekked up past the hose. Muscled Man stayed two steps behind, the gun pointed at Gerard's back.

"Don't stop. Almost there."

Up ahead, Gerard could see a smaller clearing. He frowned, confused. He took one more step, saw it, and froze.

"Keep going."

He didn't. He didn't move. He didn't blink. He didn't even breathe.

To his left—next to a thick oak tree—was a pile of clothes. Lots of clothes, like someone was waiting to do laundry. It was hard to say how many outfits. Ten. Maybe more. He could even see the gray suit he'd been wearing on his way to Logan Airport.

How many of us . . . ?

But his gray suit and even the sheer height of the pile wasn't what drew his eye. That wasn't what made him pull up, stop, and let the truth finally crash over him hard. No, it wasn't the volume of clothes. It was one article of clothing, sitting atop the pile like a cake decoration, that shattered his world into a million pieces.

A bright yellow sundress.

Gerard closed his eyes. His life actually did pass before his eyes—the life he had, the life he almost had—before the blast ushered the darkness back in, this time forever.

11

TWO weeks later, Kat was finishing up some paperwork in the precinct when Stacy stormed in like a Doppler-tracked weather system. Heads turned. Tongues lolled. Most higher-level brain activity ceased. Simply put, nothing lowers a man's IQ like a curvaceous woman. Chaz Faircloth, who was sadly still Kat's partner, straightened his perfectly straightened tie. He started toward her, but Stacy shot him a look that knocked him back a step.

"Lunch at the Carlyle," Stacy said. "I'm buying."

"Deal."

Kat started to sign off her computer.

"So how did your date go last night?" Stacy asked.

"I hate you," Kat said.

"Yet you'll still have lunch with me."

"You said you were buying."

Kat's first three dates from YouAreJustMyType had

been unfailingly polite, nicely dressed, and, well, blah. No sparks, no sizzle, just . . . nothing. Last night—her fourth in the two weeks since Jeff had semi-redumped her—had given her early hope. She and Stan Something—no reason to memorize the last name until she reached the so-far-unreachable Second Date—had been walking on West 69th Street, heading to Telepan restaurant, when Stan asked:

"Are you a Woody Allen fan?"

Kat felt her heart flutter. She loved Woody Allen. "Very much so."

"How about *Annie Hall*? You ever see *Annie Hall*?"

It was only one of her favorite movies of all time. "Of course."

Stan laughed, stopped walking. "You remember that scene when Alvy's going on his first date with Annie and he says something about them kissing before the date so they could relax?"

Kat almost swooned. Woody Allen stops before he and Diane Keaton arrive at the restaurant, kind of like Stan here just did, and says, "Hey, gimme a kiss." Diane Keaton replies, "Really?" Woody says, "Yeah, why not? Because we're just gonna go home later, right, and then there's gonna be all that tension. We've never kissed before and I'll never know when to make the right move or anything. So we'll kiss now and get it over with, and then we'll go eat. We'll digest our food better."

Oh, how she loved that scene. She smiled at Stan and waited.

"Hey," Stan said, doing a meh impression of Woody, "let's go have sex before we eat."

Kat blinked. "Excuse me?"

"Right, I know that's not the exact line, but think

about it. I won't know when to make the right move and how many dates before we jump in the sack and, when you think about it, we might as well start off doing the horizontal mambo because if we aren't good in bed, well, what's the point. You know what I mean?"

She looked for him to start laughing. He didn't. "Wait. You're serious?"

"Sure. We'll digest our food better, right?"

"I can feel my last meal coming up right now," Kat said.

During dinner, she tried to stay on the rather safe topic of Woody Allen movies. It soon became apparent that Stan wasn't a fan, but he had seen *Annie Hall.* "See, here's what I do," Stan confided to her in a low whisper. "I just search on the site for women who love that movie. That line? It didn't work with you, but most of Woody's fans immediately get their legs in the air."

Terrific.

Stacy listened intently to Kat's story about Stan, trying her best not to laugh. "Wow, he sounds like such a douche."

"Yep."

"But you're still being too picky. That guy on the second date. He sounded nice."

"True. I mean, he didn't ruin any of my favorite movies for me."

"I hear a *but.*"

"But he ordered a Dasani. Not a bottle of water. A Dasani."

Stacy frowned. "Let me rephrase: Wow, he sounds like such a Massengill."

Kat groaned out loud.

"You're being too picky, Kat."

"I probably need more time."

"To get over Jeff?"

Kat said nothing.

"To get over a guy who dumped you, what, twenty years ago?"

"Shut up, please." Then: "Eighteen years."

They were just about out the door when Kat heard a voice behind her call her name. They both stopped and turned. It was Chaz.

"Need you for a sec," Chaz said.

"Heading out to lunch," Kat said.

Chaz beckoned her with a finger, all the while keeping his eye on Stacy. Kat sighed and headed up to meet him. Chaz turned his back and pointed with his thumb down toward Stacy. "Who's the Grade A, prime beef, select choice hottie?"

"Not your type."

"She looks like my type."

"She has the capacity to think."

"Huh?"

"What do you want, Chaz?"

"You have a visitor."

"I'm on my lunch hour."

"I told the kid that. Said I'd help him, but he said he'd wait."

"Kid?"

Chaz shrugged.

"What kid?"

"I look like your secretary? Ask him yourself. He's sitting by your desk."

She signaled to Stacy to give her another minute and headed up another level. A teenage boy sat in the chair next to her desk. He sat, well, like a teenager—slouching to the point of nearly melting, as though someone had removed his bones and propped him up. His arm was draped over the back of the chair as if it was something that didn't belong to him. His hair was too long, aiming for boy band or lax bro, but it hung down in his face like a tassel curtain.

Kat approached him. "Can I help you?"

He sat up, pushed the curtain off his face. "You're Detective Donovan."

It was more a statement than a question.

"That's right. What can I do for you?"

"My name is Brandon." He stuck out his hand. "Brandon Phelps."

She shook his hand. "Nice to meet you, Brandon."

"You too."

"Is there something I can help you with?"

"It's about my mom."

"What about her?"

"She's missing. I think you can help me find her."

KAT canceled lunch with Stacy. Then she came back up to her desk and sat across from Brandon Phelps. She asked the first question to come to mind.

"Why me?"

Brandon swallowed hard. "Huh?"

"Why did you come to me specifically? My partner said you wanted to wait for me."

"Yes."

"Why?"

Brandon's eyes darted around the precinct. "I heard you were the best."

A lie. "From?"

Brandon shrugged like a teenager, somehow both lazy and melodramatic at the same time. "Does it matter? I wanted you, not that other guy."

"That's not how it works. You don't get to choose your investigator."

He suddenly looked as though he were about to cry. "You won't help me?"

"I didn't say that." Kat didn't get this, but it didn't feel right. "Why don't you tell me what happened?"

"It's my mom."

"Right."

"She's missing."

"Okay, first things first." Kat took out a pen and paper. "Your name is Brandon Phelps?"

"Yes."

"And your mother's?"

"Dana."

"Phelps?"

"Yes."

"Is she married?"

"No." He started biting a fingernail. "My dad died three years ago."

"I'm sorry," she said, because, well, that was what you said. "Do you have any siblings?"

"No."

"So it's just you and your mom?"

"Right."

"How old are you, Brandon?"

"Nineteen."

"Where do you live?"

"1279 Third Avenue."

"Apartment number?"

"Uh, 8J."

"Phone?"

He gave her his mobile number. She gathered a few more details and then, seeing his growing impatience, Kat said, "And the problem is?"

"She's missing."

"When you say she's missing, I'm not sure exactly what you mean."

Brandon raised his eyebrows. "You don't know what missing means?"

"No, I mean . . ." She shook her head. "Okay, let's start with this: How long has she been missing?"

"Three days."

"So why don't you tell me what happened?"

"Mom said she was going on a trip with her boyfriend."

"Right."

"But I don't think she did. I called her cell. She didn't answer."

Kat tried not to frown. For this she was missing lunch at the Carlyle? "Where was she going?"

"Someplace in the Caribbean."

"Where?"

"She said it was going to be a surprise."

"Maybe the phone service is bad."

He frowned. "I don't think so."

"Or maybe she's busy."

"She said she'd at least text me every day." Then, seeing the look on her face, Brandon added, "We don't do that normally. But this was her first time going away since Dad died."

"Did you try calling the hotel?"

"I told you. She didn't say where she was staying."

"And you never asked?"

He shrugged again. "I figured we'd just text or whatever."

"Have you tried contacting her boyfriend?"

"No."

"Why not?"

"I don't know him. They started dating when I went to college."

"Where do you go to school?"

"I'm at UConn. What difference does that make?"

Fair point. "I'm just trying to put this together, okay? When did your mom start dating this guy?"

"I don't know. She doesn't share that kind of stuff with me."

"But she told you she was going away with him?"

"Yes."

"When?"

"When did she tell me they were going away?"

"Yes."

"I don't know. A week ago, I guess. Look, could you just look into it? Please?"

Kat stared at him. He flinched. "Brandon?"

"Yes?"

"What's going on here?"

His reply surprised her. "You really don't know?"

"No."

Brandon looked at her skeptically.

"Yo, Donovan?"

Kat turned toward the familiar voice. Captain Stagger stood by the stairway. "My office," he said.

"I'm in the middle of—"

"This won't take long."

His tone left no room for debate. Kat looked at Brandon. "Wait here a second, okay?"

Brandon looked off, nodded.

Kat rose. Stagger hadn't waited for her. Kat hurried down the stairs and followed him into his office. Stagger closed the door behind her. He didn't circle back to his desk or delay.

"Monte Leburne died this morning."

She slumped against the wall. "Damn."

"Well, that's not exactly my reaction, but I thought you'd want to know."

For the past two weeks, she had tried repeatedly to get close to him again. It hadn't worked. Now time had run out. "Thanks."

The two of them stood there awkwardly for a few moments.

"Anything else?" Kat asked.

"No. I just thought you'd want to know."

"I appreciate it."

"I assume you've been investigating what he said."

"I have, yes."

"And?"

"And nothing, Captain," Kat said. "I've found nothing."

He nodded slowly. "Okay, you can go."

She started for the door. "Is there going to be a funeral?"

"What, for Leburne?"

"Yes."

"I don't know. Why?"

"No reason."

Or maybe there was. Leburne had a family. They'd changed names and moved out of state, but maybe they'd be interested in the remains. Maybe they'd know something. Maybe, now that dear Monte was dead, they'd want to prove his innocence, at least in one case.

Long shot.

Kat headed out of Stagger's office, trying to sort through her feelings. She just felt numb. So much of her life felt like unanswered questions. She was a cop. She liked closed cases. Something bad happens. You figure out who did it and why. You don't get all the answers. But you get enough.

Her own life suddenly felt like one giant open case. She hated that.

Didn't matter. She could have her little pity party later. Right now, she had to get back and concentrate on Brandon and his missing-mom case. But when she got back up to her floor, the chair in front of her desk was empty. She sat, figuring that maybe the kid had gone to the bathroom or something, when she spotted the note:

HAD TO GO. PLEASE FIND MY MOM. YOU HAVE MY PHONE IF YOU NEED TO REACH ME.—BRANDON

She read the note again. Something about the whole thing—the missing mom, seeking Kat out specifically, all of it really—felt more than wrong. She was missing something here. Kat took a look at her notes.

Dana Phelps.

What harm could it do to take a quick look into the name?

Her desk phone trilled. She picked it up and said, "Donovan."

"Hey, Kat." It was Chris Harrop from Corrections. "Sorry it took so long to get back to you, but like I said, the logs aren't computerized and I had to send a man up to the warehouse in Albany. And then, well, I had to wait."

"Wait for what?"

"Your boy Monte Leburne to die. It is complicated but basically showing you this could be a violation of his rights unless he waives them or you get a court order, blah, blah, you know the deal. But now that he's dead . . ."

"You have the list?"

"I do."

"Could you fax it to me?"

"Fax? What is this, 1996? How about I send it to you via telex? It's in an e-mail. I just sent it. Besides, there's nothing on it that's going to help you."

"What do you mean?"

"The day you asked for, the only person who visited him was his attorney, a guy named Alex Khowaylo."

"That's it?"

"That's it. Oh, and two feds. I got their names here. And an NYPD cop named Thomas Stagger."

12

STAGGER wasn't in his office.

Still standing in front of his office door, Kat typed up a text saying that she needed to talk to him right away. Her fingers shook, but she managed to hit the SEND button. She stood there and stared at the screen for two full minutes.

No reply.

This made no sense. Monte Leburne had been picked up by the FBI, more specifically the feds working RICO, the Racketeer Influenced and Corrupt Organizations Act. NYPD wasn't involved in the arrest at all. The feds suspected him of murdering two members of a rival crime family. A few days later, they'd also uncovered information that Leburne had been the triggerman in the death of her father.

So why had Stagger visited Leburne before that, the day after his arrest?

Kat needed some air. A small twinge sent a reminder that she had also skipped lunch. Kat wasn't good when skipping meals. She tended to lose focus and get grumpy. She hurried down the stairs and asked Keith Inchierca at the front desk to contact her as soon as Stagger came back. Inchierca frowned.

"I look like your secretary?" he said.

"Good one."

"What?"

"Please? It's important, okay?"

He waved at her to go away.

She found a falafel stand on Third Avenue and then, remembering Brandon Phelps's home address, she figured, well, why not? She started walking north. Seven blocks later, she arrived at a fairly unassuming high-rise. On the street level, there was a Duane Reade pharmacy and a store called Scoop, which Kat had wrongly assumed was an ice-cream parlor when, in fact, it was a trendy boutique. The apartment building entrance was on 74th Street. Kat flashed her badge at the doorman.

"I'm here about Dana Phelps," she said. "Apartment 8J."

The doorman stared at her badge. Then he said, "Wrong building."

"You don't have a Dana Phelps here?"

"We don't have a Dana Phelps. We also don't have an apartment 8J. We don't do letters. The apartments on the eighth floor run from 801 to 816."

Kat put her badge away. "Is this 1279 Third Avenue?"

"No, this is 200 East 74th Street."

"But you're on the corner of Third Avenue."

The doorman just stared at her. "Uh, yeah, so?"

"But it says 1279 Third Avenue on this building."

He made a face. "You think, what, I'm lying about the address?"

"No."

"Please, Detective, by all means. Go up to apartment 8J. With my blessing."

New Yorkers. "Look, I'm trying to find apartment 8J at 1279 Third Avenue."

"I can't help you."

Kat headed back outside and turned the corner. The awning did indeed say 200 East 74th Street. Kat moved back to Third Avenue. The 1279 was actually above the entrance to Duane Reade. What the hell? She entered, found the manager, and asked, "Do you have any apartments above you?"

"Uh, we're a pharmacy."

New Yorkers. "I know that, but I mean, how do I get to the apartments above you?"

"You know a lot of people who walk through pharmacies to get to their apartment? The entrance is around the corner on 74th."

She didn't bother with follow-up questions. The answer was now pretty damn apparent. Brandon Phelps, if that was his name, had given her the wrong—or, more likely, a false—address.

BACK AT THE PRECINCT, Google gave Kat some of the answers, but they didn't clarify much.

There was a Dana Phelps with a son named Brandon, but they didn't live on the Upper East Side of Manhattan. The Phelpses resided in a rather tony section of Greenwich, Connecticut. Brandon's father had been a big-time hedge fund manager. Beaucoup bucks. He died when he was forty-one. The obituary gave no cause of death. Kat looked for a charity—people often requested donations made to a heart disease or cancer or whatever cause—but there was nothing listed.

So why had Brandon sought out a specific NYPD cop?

Kat checked out other residences the Phelps might have owned. There was, of course, a chance that a wealthy family from Greenwich might own a place on the Upper East Side, but nothing in Manhattan came up. She ran Brandon's cell phone number through the system. Whoa. It was a prepaid phone. Most rich kids from Greenwich don't use those. Most people who use them either have poor credit ratings or, well, don't want to be traced. Of course, what most people didn't know was that it was rather easy to trace disposable phones. In fact, the U.S. Court of Appeals for the Sixth Circuit had ruled that you could even "ping" a location without getting a warrant. She didn't need to go that far. At least not yet.

For now, she played a hunch. All prepaid phone sales are registered in a data bank. She typed in the number and found out exactly where Brandon had purchased his phone. The answer didn't surprise her. He'd bought it at a Duane Reade, located at, yep, 1279 Third Avenue.

Maybe that explained why he chose that address.

Okay, maybe. But it explained nothing else.

There were other links to explore, but they'd take more time. Brandon Phelps had a Facebook account, but it was set on private. It would probably take only a phone call or two to find out how Brandon's father had died, but really, what was the relevance of that? The kid had come to her because his mother had run off with some guy.

And there was the rub: So what?

This could all be nothing but a stupid hoax. Why was she wasting her time with this nonsense anyway? Didn't she have anything better to do? Maybe, maybe not. Truth was, work was slow today. This was a welcome distraction until Stagger got back.

Okay, she thought. Play it out.

Let's say this was a hoax. Well, for one thing, if this was a joke on Brandon's part, it was almost pathetically lame. The hoax wasn't funny or clever in the slightest. There didn't seem to be much of a punch line or big payoff.

It didn't add up.

Cops loved to buy into their self-created myth that they have some innate ability to "read" people, that they were all human lie detectors, that they could suss out truth from deception from body language or the timbre in a voice. Kat knew that that sort of hubris was complete nonsense. Worse, it too often led to life-altering disaster.

That said, unless Brandon was either a pure sociopath or a recent graduate of the Lee Strasberg school of method acting, the kid truly was distraught about something.

The question was: What?

The answer: Stop wasting time and call him.

She picked up her phone and dialed the number Brandon gave her. Kat half expected him not to answer, to have given up on whatever little game, real or not, he was playing, and hustled his butt back to UConn or Greenwich or wherever. But he answered on the second ring.

"Hello?"

"Brandon?"

"Detective Donovan."

"Right."

"I bet you didn't find my mother yet," he said.

She decided there was no reason to play coy. "No, but I did visit the Duane Reade at 1279 Third Avenue."

Silence.

"Brandon?"

"What?"

"Are you ready to come clean now?"

"Wrong question, Detective."

There was an edge in his tone now.

"What are you talking about?"

"The question is," Brandon said, "are you?"

KAT switched the phone from her right ear to her left. She wanted to take notes. "What are you talking about, Brandon?"

"Find my mom."

"You mean your mom who lives in Greenwich, Connecticut?"

"Yes."

"I'm NYPD. You need to go to the Greenwich police station."

"I did that already. I spoke to a Detective Schwartz."

"And?"

"And he didn't believe me."

"So what makes you think I will? Why come to me? And why all the lies?"

"You're Kat, right?"

"What?"

"I mean, that's what they call you. Kat."

"How do you know that?"

Brandon hung up.

Kat stared at the phone. How had he known she went by Kat? Had he overheard someone in the precinct call her that? Maybe. Or maybe Brandon Phelps just knew a lot about her. He had, after all, come to her specifically, this college kid from Greenwich looking for his mommy. If indeed Dana Phelps was his mommy. If indeed he really was Brandon Phelps. She hadn't found pictures of them online yet.

None of this made any sense. So what to do?

Call him back. Or better yet, ping his location. Pick him up.

For what?

False report maybe. Lying to a police officer. Maybe he was a random psycho. Maybe he had done something to his mother or to Dana Phelps or . . .

She was considering the alternatives when the phone on her desk rang. Kat picked it up. "Donovan."

"This is your secretary calling." It was Sergeant In-chierca. "You wanted to know when the captain came back, right?"

"Right."

"The answer would be 'now.'"

"Thanks."

Just like that, concerns about Brandon and his maybe-missing mom fled. Kat was already out of her seat and rushing down the steps. As she reached his floor, Kat could see Stagger entering his office with two other cops. One was her direct supervisor, Stephen Singer, a guy so skinny he could hide behind a stripper pole. The other was David Karp, who supervised the uniformed cops on the street.

Stagger was about to close the door, but Kat got there just in time, blocking it with her hand.

She forced up a smile. "Captain?"

Stagger stared at the hand on the door as though it had offended him.

"Did you get my message?" Kat asked.

"I'm busy right now."

"This can't wait."

"It's going to have to. I have a meeting with—"

"I got the visitors' logs from the day after Leburne got arrested," she said. Kat kept her eyes on him, looking for a tell. Okay, so she wasn't above reading body language. She just didn't do it with hubris. "I really think I need your help on this."

Stagger's tell might as well have been a neon sign in Vegas. His hands clenched. His face reddened. Everyone, including Kat's displeased supervisor, could see it.

Through clenched teeth, Stagger managed to say, "Detective?"

"Yes?"

"I said I'm busy right now."

The two supervisors, especially Singer, whom she liked and respected, glared at her seeming insubordination. Somewhat stunned, Kat found herself stepping out of his office. He closed the door behind her.

THE text came in ten minutes later. It was from Brandon's prepaid phone:

I'm sorry.

Enough. She picked up the phone and dialed his number. Brandon answered on the first ring. His voice was tentative.

"Kat?"

"What the hell is going on, Brandon?"

"I'm at the Hunter College Bookstore on the corner. Can you meet me?"

"I'm really tired of being jerked around here."

"I'll explain everything. I promise."

She sighed. "On my way."

Brandon was sitting on a bench outside, on the corner of Park Avenue. He fit in here, surrounded by other kids his age rushing back and forth with backpacks and hoodies and exhaustion. He huddled into himself as though he were cold. He looked young and scared and fragile.

She sat down next to him. She didn't ask anything. She just looked at him. This was his call. Let him be the first to speak. It took some time. He stared down at his hands for a while. She rode out his silence.

"My dad died of cancer," Brandon began. "It was slow. Just ate him up. Mom never left his side. He and Mom were high school sweethearts. They were good together, you know? I mean, I go over to my friends' and their folks are, like, always in different rooms. My folks weren't like that. When Dad died, I was devastated, sure. But not like Mom. It was like half of her died."

Kat opened her mouth, closed it. She had a million questions, but they'd keep.

"Mom always calls. I know how that sounds. But I mean, *always*. That's the thing that got me suspicious. See, all we really have is each other. And she's, like, terrified of losing someone else. So she reaches out all the time, just, I don't know, just to make sure I'm still alive."

He looked off.

Finally, Kat broke the silence. "She's been lonely, Brandon."

"I know."

"And now she's away with another man. You understand that, right?"

He didn't say anything.

"Is this guy her first boyfriend since . . . ?"

"Not really, no," he said. "But, I mean, it's the first time she's gone away with someone."

"Maybe that's it, then," Kat said.

"What's it?"

"Maybe she's afraid of how you'll react."

Brandon shook his head. "She knows I want her to find somebody."

"Do you? You just said all you have is each other. Maybe that was true. But maybe that's changing now. Just imagine how hard this is for her. Maybe she needs to pull away a little."

"That's not it," Brandon insisted. "She always calls."

"I get that. But maybe, well, maybe not right now. Do you think she's in love?"

"Mom? Probably." Then: "Yeah, she's in love with this guy. She wouldn't go away with a guy she didn't love."

"Love makes us all forgetful, Brandon. It makes us all a little self-involved."

"That's not it either. Look, this guy? He's a total player. She doesn't get that."

"A player?" Kat smiled at him, maybe understanding a little. He was being protective. It was sweet, in its own way. "Then maybe your mom will end up with a broken heart. So what? She's not a child."

Brandon shook his head some more. "You don't understand."

"What happened when you went to the cops in Greenwich?"

"What do you think? They said the same thing you did."

"So why did you come to me? That's the part I still don't understand."

He shrugged. "I thought you'd get it."

"But why me? I mean, how do you even know me? And how do you know people call me Kat?" She tried to catch his eye. "Brandon?" He wouldn't let her. "Why do you think I can help you?"

He didn't reply.

"Brandon?"

"You really don't know?"

"Of course I don't."

He said nothing.

"Brandon? What the hell is going on?"

"They met online," Brandon said.

"What?"

"My mom and her boyfriend."

"Lot of people meet online."

"Yeah, I know, but—" Brandon stopped. Then he muttered, "Perky and cute."

Kat's eyes widened. "What did you say?"

"Nothing."

She flashed to her YouAreJustMyType profile. The heading Stacy had chosen for her: Cute and perky!

"Are you . . ." She felt a sudden chill. "Wait. Are you stalking me online or something?"

"What?" Brandon sat up straight. "No! Don't you get it?"

"Get what?"

He reached into his pocket. "This is the guy my mom went away with. I got it off the website."

Brandon handed her the photograph. When Kat saw the face, her heart yet again plummeted down a mine shaft.

It was Jeff.

13

WHEN Titus first started out, this was how he found the girls:

He wore a suit and tie. Let his competition wear sweats or low-slung jeans. He carried a briefcase. He wore horn-rimmed glasses. He kept his hair short and neat.

Titus always sat on the same bench in the Port Authority bus station, second floor. If some homeless guy was sleeping there, he gave it up pretty fast when he saw Titus coming. Titus didn't have to say anything. The locals just knew to stay clear. This was Titus's bench. It gave him a perfect bird's-eye view of the south terminal gates 226 through 234 on the level below him. He could see the passengers get off the bus, but they couldn't see him.

He was, he knew, a predator.

He watched the girls depart, like a lion waiting for the limping gazelle.

Patience was key.

Titus didn't want the girls from the bigger cities. He waited for the buses from Tulsa or Topeka or maybe Des Moines. Boston was no good. Neither was Kansas City or St. Louis. The best were the runaways from the so-called Bible Belt. They came in with a mixture of hope and rebellion in their eyes. The more rebellion—the more you wanted to stick it to Daddy—the better. This was the big city. This was where dreams were made.

The girls came in demanding change and excitement—something *had* to happen for them. But in truth, they were already hungry and scared and exhausted. They lugged a too-heavy suitcase, and if they had a guitar that made it better. Titus didn't know why. But if he found one with a guitar, it always upped his chances.

Titus never forced it.

If the setup wasn't ideal—if the girl wasn't the perfect prey—he let it go. That was the key. Patience. You throw out enough nets—you watch enough buses come in— you would eventually find what you needed.

So Titus waited on that bench, and when he saw a girl who looked ripe, he made his move. Most times, it didn't work out. That was okay. He had a good rap. His mentor, a violent pimp named Louis Castman, had mentored him well. You talked politely. You made requests or sugges-tions, never commands or demands. You manipulated the girls by making them believe they were in charge.

You wanted them pretty, of course, but that wasn't a prerequisite.

Most times, Titus used the model rap. He had made up good business cards on heavy stock, not the cheap, flimsy stuff. Spend money to make money. The cards were embossed. They read ELITISM MODEL AGENCY in fine calligraphy. They had his name on it. They had a business line, a home line, and a mobile phone number (all three numbers forwarded to his mobile). It had a legitimate address on Fifth Avenue, and if the girls mistook Elitism for Elite, well, so be it.

He never pressed. He was commuting, he would tell the girls, from his home in Montclair, a wealthy New Jersey suburb, and happened to spot her and thought she might do well in the modeling business "if she didn't already have representation." He pretended to be above horning in on a competitor. At the end of the day, the girls wanted to believe. That helped. They had all heard stories about models or actresses being discovered at the local mall or at Dairy Queen or waitressing.

Why not a bus terminal in Manhattan?

He told them they'd need a portfolio. He invited them for a model shoot with a top fashion photographer. This was where some balked. They had heard this line before. They wanted to know how much it would cost. Titus would chuckle. "Here's a tip," he would tell them. "You don't pay a real agency—they pay you."

If they seemed too suspicious or worried, he would cut them loose and return to his bench. You had to be willing to cut them loose at any point. That was the key. If, for example, they weren't runaways, if they were just here for a short vacation, if they stayed in constant touch with a family member . . . any of those, and he simply moved on.

Patience.

For those who made the cut, well, it depended.

Louis Castman enjoyed inflicting pain. Titus did not.

It wasn't that violence bothered him—Titus could take it or leave it. He just always sought the most profitable avenue. Still Titus had followed Castman's methods: You invite the girls to be photographed. You take some pictures—Castman actually had an eye for it—and then you attack them. Simple as that. You put a knife to her throat. You take away her phone and wallet. You cuff her to the bed. Sometimes you rape her.

You always drug her.

This would go on for days. One time, with a particularly beautiful, strong-willed girl, they kept her like that for two full weeks.

The drugs were expensive—heroin was Titus's favorite—but that was yet another business expense. Eventually, the girl would get hooked. It never took much time. Heroin was like that. You let the genie out of the bottle, it never got put back in. For Titus, that was usually enough. Louis, on the other hand, liked to film the rapes, set the girl up so it looked consensual, and then, just to remove any last shred of hope the girl had, he would threaten to send the tapes to their often religious, traditional parents.

In many ways, it was the perfect setup. You find girls who start out already scarred, already on the run, with bad daddy issues or maybe escaping abuse. They are, yes, wounded gazelles. You take those girls and then you strip away whatever else might be left. You hurt them. You make them afraid. You get them addicted to a drug. And then, when all hope is gone, you give them a savior.

You.

By the time he put them out on the street or into a higher-end brothel—Titus worked both—they would do anything to please him. A few ran back home—a business expense—but not too many. Two girls even managed to make their way to the police, but it was their word against his, with no evidence, and by then, they were crack (or heroin) whores, and really, who believed them or cared?

That was all behind him now.

Right now, Titus was finishing up his afternoon walk. He enjoyed this time, out alone in the woods behind the barn, surrounded by the lush green of foliage and the deep blue of the sky. This surprised him. He'd been born in the Bronx, ten blocks north of Yankee Stadium. While he was growing up, his idea of outdoor space had been the fire escape. He knew only the hustle and noise of the city, believed that it was part of him, in his blood, that he had been not only fully acclimated to brick and mortar and concrete but could not live without it. Titus had been one of eight children living in a run-down two-bedroom walk-up on Jerome Avenue. It was impossible for him to remember a time when he was alone or could bask for more than a moment or two in silence. There was little tranquillity in his life. It wasn't a question of craving it or not. It was simply an unknown.

When he had first visited the farm, Titus thought there was no way he could survive the stillness. Now he had come to love the solitude.

He found his way into the smaller clearing, where Reynaldo, an overmuscled but loyal worker, kept guard. Reynaldo, who was playing fetch with his dog, nodded at Titus. Titus nodded back. The original Amish owner had built root cellars out here. A root cellar was merely a hole in the ground with a door as cover—an underground storage unit to help preserve food at cooler temperatures. They were virtually undetectable if you weren't looking for them.

The property had fourteen of them.

He strolled past the pile of clothes. The bright yellow sundress was still on top.

"How is she?"

Reynaldo shrugged. "The usual."

"Do you think she's ready?"

It was a dumb question. Reynaldo wouldn't know. He didn't even bother responding. Six years ago, Titus had met Reynaldo in Queens. Reynaldo had been a skinny teen working the gay trade and getting beaten twice weekly. Titus realized that the kid wouldn't survive more than another month. The only thing Reynaldo had resembling a family or friend was Bo, a stray Labrador retriever he'd found near the East River.

So Titus "saved" Reynaldo, gave him drugs and confidence, made him useful.

The relationship had started as yet another classic ruse, as with the girls. Reynaldo became his most obedient lackey and muscle. But something had changed over the years. Evolved, if you will. Strange as it might seem, Titus had feelings for Reynaldo. No, not like that.

He considered Reynaldo family.

"Bring her to me tonight," Titus said. "Ten o'clock."

"Late," Reynaldo said.

"Yes. That a problem?"

"No. Not at all."

Titus stared at the bright yellow sundress. "One more thing."

Reynaldo waited.

"The pile of clothes. Burn them."

14

IT was as though Park Avenue froze.

In Kat's periphery, she could still see the students trudge by, still hear the occasional laugh and car horn, but all of it was suddenly so far away.

Kat held the picture in her hand. It was that shot of Jeff on the sand, the broken fence behind him, the waves crashing in the distance. Maybe it was the beach scene, but it now felt as though seashells were pressed against both her ears. Kat felt adrift, numbly holding the photograph of her old fiancé, staring at it as though it might suddenly explain everything to her.

Brandon stood. For a moment, she worried that he might sprint off, leaving her with this damn picture and too many questions. She reached out and grabbed his wrist. Just to make sure. Just to make sure that he didn't vanish.

"You know him, right?" he asked.

"What the hell is going on, Brandon?"

"You're a cop."

"Right."

"So before I reveal anything, you have to give me immunity or something."

"What?"

"It's why I didn't tell you before. What I did. It's like the Fifth Amendment or something. I don't want to incriminate myself."

"Coming to me," Kat said. "It wasn't a coincidence."

"It wasn't."

"How did you find me?"

"That's the part I'm not sure I should tell you," he said. "I mean, the Fifth Amendment and all that."

"Brandon?"

"What?"

"Cut the crap," Kat said. "Tell me what the hell is going on. Tell me now."

"Suppose," he said slowly, "the way I found you, it was kind of, well, illegal."

"I don't care."

"What?"

Kat gave him a dagger stare. "I'm about to take out my gun and jam it in your mouth. What the hell is going on, Brandon?"

"Just tell me one thing first." He pointed to the picture in her hand. "You know him, right?"

Her eyes dropped back to the picture. "I did."

"So who is he?"

"An old boyfriend," she said softly.

"Yeah, I got that. I mean—"

"What do you mean, you got that?" She looked at

him. Something crossed his face. How had he found her? How would he know that Jeff was her old boyfriend? How would . . .

The answer suddenly became obvious. "Did you hack into a computer or something?"

She could see by the look on his face that she had hit pay dirt. It made sense now. Brandon didn't want to come to a cop admitting he had broken the law. So he came up with this story about hearing that she was a good detective.

"It's okay, Brandon. I don't care about any of that."

"You don't?"

Kat shook her head. "Just tell me what's going on, okay?"

"You promise it's just between us?"

"I promise."

He took a deep breath, let it out. His eyes were filling up with tears. "At UConn, I'm a computer science major. My friends and me, we're good with programming and designing, that kind of stuff. So it wasn't hard. I mean, it's just a dating website. The sites with the serious fire-walls and security? They deal with higher-ticket items. Only thing you can get off a dating site is maybe credit card info. So that they keep secure. The rest of the site? Not so much."

"You hacked into YouAreJustMyType.com?"

Brandon nodded. "Like I said, not the financial stuff. That would take forever. But the other pages, well, it took us maybe two hours to get it. The files keep records of everything—who you click on, who you communicate with, what times, who you message. Even instant messages. The website keeps logs on all that."

Kat saw it now. "And you saw mine with Jeff."

"Yeah."

"And that's how you knew my name. From our instant messages."

He stayed silent. But it all made sense to her now. She handed him back the photograph.

"You should go home, Brandon."

"What?"

"Jeff's a good guy. Or at least, he was. They found each other. Your mom is a widow. He's a widower. Maybe it's real. Maybe they're in love. Either way, your mother is a grown woman. You shouldn't go spying on her."

"I wasn't spying on her," he said, defensive now. "I mean, not at first. But when she didn't call me—"

"She's away with a man. That's why she didn't call you. Grow up."

"But he doesn't love her."

"How do you know?"

"He called himself Jack. Why did he do that if his name is Jeff?"

"Lots of people use aliases online. That doesn't mean anything."

"And he talked to a lot of other women."

"So? That's the point of the site. You talk to a lot of potential partners. You're trying to find a needle in a haystack."

Jeff talked, she thought, to me even. Of course, he didn't have the balls to tell her he had already found someone new. No, instead he gave her that crock about being protective and needing a fresh start. Meanwhile, he had already hooked up with another woman.

Why not just say so?

"Look," Brandon said, "I just need to know his real name and address. That's all."

"I can't help you, kid."

"Why not?"

"Because this isn't my business." She shook her head and added, "Man, you have no idea how much this isn't my business."

Her cell phone buzzed. She checked the message and saw it was from Stagger:

Bethesda fountain. Ten minutes.

Kat rose from the bench. "I gotta go."

"Where?"

"Also not your business. This is over, Brandon. Go home."

"Just tell me his name and address, okay? I mean, what's the harm? Just his name."

Part of her thought that telling him was a mistake. Part of her was still a little hurt that Jeff had pushed her aside. What the hell? The kid did have a right to know who his mom was shtupping, didn't he?

"Jeff Raynes," she said, spelling it with the *y* for him. "And I don't have a clue or a care where he lives."

BETHESDA Fountain was the heartbeat of Central Park. The towering angel statue crowning the fountain holds lilies in one hand while blessing the water in front of her with the other. Her stone face is serene to the point of boredom. The water she eternally blesses is called simply the Lake. Kat always liked that name. The Lake. Nothing fancy. Call it what it is.

Beneath the angel were four cherubs representing Temperance, Purity, Health, and Peace. The fountain had been there since 1873. In the sixties, hippies occupied it day and night. The first scene in *Godspell* was filmed there. So was a key scene in *Hair*. In the seventies, Bethesda Terrace became the focal point of drug trafficking and prostitution. Kat's father had told her that even cops were scared of the terrace back in those days. It was hard to imagine now, especially on a summer day like this, that the place was ever anything but paradise.

Stagger sat on a bench overlooking the Lake. Tourists speaking every language imaginable floated by in boats, struggling with the oars before giving up and letting the nearly nonexistent current take them. On the right, a large swarm had gathered for the street performers (or were they park performers?) called the Afrobats. The Afrobats were black teens who did a show combining acrobatics, dancing, and comedy. Another street performer carried a sign that read: $1 A JOKE. LAUGHTER GUARANTEED. People statues— that is, people who stood still and pretended they were statues and posed for pictures with tourists; who was the first person to do this?—dotted the landing. There was a guy who looked like your favorite uncle enthusiastically playing the ukulele, and another guy wearing a ratty bathrobe pretending to be a Hogwarts wizard.

The black baseball cap on Stagger's head made him look like a little boy. His gaze skimmed along the waterway like a flat stone. It was, in many ways, a typical Manhattan scene—you are surrounded and yet you find solace; you find isolation in the tornado of people. Stagger stared out at the water, looking bewildered, and Kat wasn't sure what she felt.

He never turned as she approached. When Kat was standing above him, she waited a moment and then she simply said, "Hey."

"What the hell is wrong with you?" He kept his eyes on the water when he spoke.

"Excuse me?"

"You don't just go busting into my office like that."

Stagger finally turned toward her. If the eyes had been calm looking out at the water, that calm was gone now.

"I didn't mean any disrespect."

"Bullshit, Kat."

"It was just that I finally got Leburne's visitor logs."

"And, what, you desperately needed my take on them?"

"Yes."

"You couldn't even wait until my meeting was over?"

"I thought . . ." Behind them, the crowd roared with laughter at the Afrobats' joke about robbing them. "You know how I am about this case."

"Obsessed."

"It's Dad, Stagger. How do you not get that?"

"Oh, I get it, Kat." He turned back to the water.

"Stagger?"

"What?"

"You know what I found, don't you?"

"Yeah." A slow smile came to his face. "I know."

"So?"

His eyes found a boat and stayed on it.

"Why would you visit Leburne the day after he was arrested?" she asked.

Stagger said nothing.

"The feds arrested him, not NYPD. You had nothing to do with it. You weren't even working my dad's case, since he was your partner and you found the body. So why were you there, Stagger?"

He looked almost amused by her question. "What's your theory, Kat?"

"Truth?"

"Preferably."

"I don't have a theory," she said.

Stagger faced her. "Do you think that I had something to do with what happened to Henry?"

"No. Of course not."

"Then?"

She wished she had a better answer: "I don't know."

"Do you think I hired Leburne or something?"

"I don't think Leburne had anything to do with it. I think Leburne was just a fall guy."

He frowned. "Come on, Kat. Not that again."

"Why were you there?"

"And again, I reply, Why do you think?" Stagger closed his eyes for a second, took a deep breath, turned back toward the Lake. "I see now why we never let people with personal connections handle a case."

"Meaning?"

"You not only have no objectivity—you barely have any clarity."

"Why were you there, Stagger?"

He shook his head. "It couldn't be more obvious."

"Not to me."

"My point exactly." His eyes locked on the boat, watching teens flail furiously and incompetently with the oars. "Go back for a second. Think it through. At the time of his murder, your father was coming close to bringing down one of the leading crime figures in the city."

"Cozone."

"Of course, Cozone. Suddenly, he gets executed. What was our theory at the time?"

"It wasn't *my* theory."

"No offense, Kat, but you weren't a cop. You were a sprightly little coed at Columbia. What was our official theory?"

"The official theory," Kat said, "was that my father was a threat to Cozone and so Cozone eliminated him."

"Exactly."

"But Cozone knew better than to kill a cop."

"Don't let the bad guys fool you with their so-called rules. They do what they think is best for long-term profit and survival. Your father was an impediment to both."

"So you think Cozone hired Leburne to kill my father. I know this. It still doesn't explain why you visited Leburne."

"Sure it does. The feds arrested one of Cozone's most active hit men. Of course we immediately followed up that lead. How can you not see that?"

"Why you?"

"What?"

"Bobby Suggs and Mike Rinsky were the lead cops on the case. So why did you go?"

He smiled again, but there was no joy in it. "Because I was like you."

"Meaning?"

"Meaning your father was my partner. You know what he meant to me."

Silence.

"I wasn't in the mood to wait while NYPD and FBI dealt with their pissing contest over territory and jurisdiction. It would give Leburne time to lawyer up or whatever. I wanted in. I was impetuous. I called a friend with the bureau and asked a favor."

"So you went to interrogate Leburne?"

"Pretty much, yeah. I was a dumb young cop trying to avenge his mentor before it was too late."

"What do you mean, too late?"

"Like I said, I was worried he would lawyer up. But even more than that, I worried Cozone would take him out before he could talk."

"So you spoke to Leburne?"

"Yes."

"And?"

Stagger shrugged. Again, with the baseball cap and the shrug, she could imagine what he had looked like in grade school. Kat gently put her hand on his shoulder. She wasn't sure why. Maybe to remind him that they were on the same side. Maybe to offer an old friend some degree of comfort. Stagger had loved her father. Not like her of course; death doesn't stay with friends or coworkers. They grieve and move on. Death only stays with the family. But his anguish was real.

"And I got nowhere," Stagger said.

"Leburne denied it?"

"He just sat across from me and said nothing."

"And yet later, Leburne confessed."

"Of course. His lawyer made a deal. Kept the death penalty off the table."

The Afrobats closed with their big finale—one of them leapt over spectators who had volunteered. The crowd erupted in applause. Kat and Stagger watched the crowd slowly disperse.

"So that's it," Kat said.

"That's it."

"You never told me."

"True."

"Why?"

"What should I have said, Kat? That I visited a suspect and got nowhere?"

"Yes."

"You were a college student on your way to getting married."

"So?"

There was maybe more edge in her voice than she intended. Their eyes met, and something passed through them. He turned away.

"I don't like the implication, Kat."

"I'm not implying anything."

"Yeah, you are." He stood. "You're not good with the passive-aggressive. It isn't you. So let's put it all on the table, okay?"

"Okay."

"Leburne claimed to the very end that he alone decided that your father had to be killed. We both know it's a lie. We both know Cozone ordered the hit and that Leburne protected him."

Kat said nothing.

"We spent years trying to get him to recant and tell us the truth. He didn't. He went to his grave without turning, and now, well, we don't know how to get justice for your father. It is frustrating and it makes us desperate."

"Us?"

"Yes."

Kat frowned. "Now who's being passive-aggressive?"

"You don't think I hurt too?"

"Oh, I think you hurt. You want to put it all on the table? Let's do that. Yes, for years, I worked under the theory that Cozone ordered a hit and Leburne carried it out. But I never really bought it. It never quite rang true to me. And when Leburne—with no reason to lie—told that nurse that he had nothing to do with it, I believed him. You can say he was drugged or lying, but I was there. His words finally rang true. So yeah, I want to know why you visited him before anyone else. Because, putting my cards on the table, I don't believe you, Stagger."

Something behind his eyes exploded. He fought hard to keep his tone level. "So tell me, Kat. Why did I go up there?"

"I don't know. I wish you'd tell me."

"You're calling me a liar?"

"I'm asking you what happened."

"I already told you," he said, pushing past her. He turned. There was indeed anger in his eyes, but there was something else there. Anguish. And maybe even fear. "You have some vacation days coming. I already checked. Take them, Kat. I don't want to see you in my precinct until I put in for your transfer."

15

KAT grabbed her laptop and headed over to O'Malley's Pub. She sat on her father's old stool. Pete the bartender ambled over to her. Kat was examining the bottom of her dusty shoes.

"What?" he asked.

"Did you guys put down more sawdust than usual?"

"New guy. He overdid the concept of dive chic. What'll you have?"

"Cheeseburger medium rare, fries, a Bud."

"You want an angiogram after that?"

"Good one, Pete. Next time, I'll sample one of your gluten-free vegan entrées."

The crowd was a mix. At the corner tables, a few masters of the universe were having postwork cocktails. The bar had the few loners all bars need: those guys who sat quietly peering into their glasses, shoulders hunched, longing for nothing other than the numbness the amber liquid could provide.

She had pushed too hard with Stagger, but subtle wasn't going to play here. Still, she didn't know what to make of Stagger. She didn't know what to make of Brandon. She didn't know what to make of Jeff.

So now what?

Curiosity got the better of her. She flipped open her laptop and started doing a search on Brandon's mom and Jeff's new lover, Dana Phelps, mostly under images and on social networks. Kat told herself that she was just following up, fully closing the case, making sure, per her one worry, that the kid she'd met was indeed Brandon Phelps, the son of Dana, and not some con man or worse.

With ten empty stools, a guy with a soul patch and frosted tips in his hair sat right next to her. He cleared his throat and said, "Hello, little lady."

"Yeah, hi."

She found the first picture of Dana on a site that covered "Connecticut Society Happenings," one of those places that takes pictures of rich people at parties so fancy, they are called balls, and these rich people, with so much in their lives, can't wait to click on the site to see if their picture is on it.

Last year, Dana Phelps had hosted a gala in support of an animal shelter. It didn't take long to see why Jeff had been drawn to her.

Dana Phelps was a stunner.

She wore a long silver gown that draped and clung in a way Kat would never experience. Dana Phelps oozed class. She was tall and blond and pretty much everything Kat was not.

Bitch.

Kat chuckled out loud. Frosted Tips took this as an invitation. "Something funny?"

"Yeah, your face."

Pete frowned at the lameness of the retort. Kat shrugged. He had a point, but it worked. Frosty took a hike. She drank some more, trying to give off a leave-me-be vibe. It worked for the most part. She did an image search on Brandon Phelps, and yes, he was indeed the skinny, stringy-haired kid who had visited her. Damn. It would have been easier if he'd just been lying about his identity or something.

Kat was starting to feel tipsy, the kind of tipsy when you drunk-text an old boyfriend, except, of course, she had no idea what Jeff's phone number was. She chose instead to do the next best thing ex-lovers do—cyber-stalk him. She put his name into several search engines, but there was nothing on him. Absolutely nothing. She knew that was going to happen—this wasn't her first time drunk-Googling him—but it still surprised her. A few Internet advertisements popped up and offered to find Jeff or, better yet, see if he had a criminal record.

Pass.

She decided to head back to Jeff's profile page on YouAreJustMyType.com. It was probably closed down now, what with his jetting off to some exotic locale with a statuesque blonde. They were probably walking the beach right now, hand in hand, Dana wearing a silver bikini, the moon reflecting on the water.

Bitch.

Kat clicked on Jeff's profile page. It was still there. She checked the status. It still read: Actively Looking. Hmm. No big deal. He had probably not remembered to turn it off. He'd probably been so excited about getting High

Society Blonde in the sackola that he couldn't be bothered with niceties like clicking a button to let other potential suitors know he was off the market. Or maybe
handsome Jeff had a backup plan, a Plan B, in case Dana
didn't pan out (or put out) in the way he hoped. Yeah, ol'
Jeff could have a bunch of women waiting with bated
breath, just in case he needed a substitute or . . .

Her cell phone mercifully knocked her out of her stu-
por. She answered it without checking the caller ID.

"There's nothing."

It sounded like Brandon.

"What?"

"On Jeff Raynes. There is absolutely nothing."

"Oh, I could have told you that."

"You've searched?"

"Drunk-Googled."

"What?"

She was slurring her words. "What do you want,
Brandon?"

"There's nothing on Jeff Raynes."

"Yes, I know. Didn't we cover this already?"

"How can that be? There is something on everyone."

"Maybe he keeps a low profile."

"I checked through all the databases. There're three
Jeff Raynes in the United States. One in North Carolina.
One in Texas. One in California. None of them is our
Jeff Raynes."

"What do you want me to say, Brandon? There are
plenty of people who keep a low profile."

"Not anymore. I mean, seriously. No one is this low
profile. Don't you see? Something isn't right."

The jukebox started playing "Oh Very Young" by
Cat Stevens. The song depressed her. Cat—her sorta

namesake—sang about how you want your father to last forever but "you know he never will," that this man you loved would fade away like his best jeans, denim blue. Man, that lyric always hit her hard.

"I don't know what I can do about it, Brandon."

"I need one more favor."

She sighed.

"I checked my mom's credit cards. There is only one hit in the past four days. She took out money from an ATM the day she vanished."

"She didn't vanish. She—"

"Fine, whatever, but the ATM was in Parkchester."

"So?"

"So we go to the airport via the Whitestone Bridge. Parkchester is at least an exit or two out of the way. Why would she go out of her way?"

"Who knows? Maybe she missed her turn. Maybe she wanted to stop at some fancy lingerie boutique you don't know about and buy something sexy for the trip."

"Lingerie boutique?"

Kat shook her head, tried to clear it. "Listen to me, Brandon. I have no jurisdiction anyway. You need to go to that cop you spoke to in Greenwich. What's his name . . ."

"Detective Schwartz."

"Right, him."

"Please. Can't you do it?"

"Do what?"

"Look into the ATM charge."

"What do you think I'll find, Brandon?"

"Mom never uses her ATM card. I mean, like, never. I don't even think she knows how. I always got cash for her. Can't you—I don't know—check the surveillance video or something?"

"It's late," Kat said, remembering her own rule about doing too much thinking while drinking. "Let's talk in the morning, okay?"

She hit the END button before he could respond. With a quick nod for Pete to put it on her tab, Kat headed out into the fresh air. She loved New York. Friends tried to get her to see the joys of the woods or the beach and yeah, sure, maybe for a few days, but hiking bored her. Plants, trees, greens, fauna could be interesting, but what was more interesting than faces, outfits, headwear, shoes, storefronts, street vendors, whatever?

There was a crescent moon tonight. When she was a little girl, the moon had fascinated her. She stopped and stared and felt the tears pushing into her eyes. A memory blindsided her. When she was six years old, her father had put a ladder in the yard. He led her outside and pointed to the ladder and told her that he'd just put the moon up there, especially for her. She believed him. She believed that was how the moon got up to the sky at night until she was much too old to believe such a thing.

Kat had been twenty-two when her father died—too young, for sure. But Brandon Phelps had lost his father when he was only sixteen.

Was it any wonder he clung so strongly to his mother?

It was late when Kat reached her apartment, but it wasn't as though police stations kept hours. She looked up the phone number of the Greenwich Police Department and called, giving her NYPD title and figuring she would leave a message for Detective Schwartz, but the dispatcher threw her a curve.

"Hold on. Joe is here. I'll connect you."

Two rings later: "This is Detective Joseph Schwartz. How may I help you?"

Polite.

Kat gave her name and rank. "A young man named Brandon Phelps came to see me today."

"Wait. Didn't you say you were NYPD?"

"Yes."

"So Brandon visited you in New York City?"

"Right."

"Are you a friend of the family or something?"

"No."

"I don't understand."

"He thinks his mother is missing," Kat said.

"Yeah, I know."

"So he wanted me to look into it."

Schwartz sighed. "Why the hell would Brandon go to you?"

"You sound like you know him."

"Of course I know him. You said you're NYPD, right? Why did he go to you?"

Kat wasn't sure how much she wanted to go into Brandon's illegal hacking activities or the fact that she was frequenting a dating site. "I'm not sure, but he said he first asked you for help. Is that true?"

"It is."

"I know his claim seems crazy," Kat continued, "but I'm wondering whether we can do something to put his mind at ease."

"Detective Donovan?"

"Call me Kat."

"Okay, call me Joe. I'm trying to think how to put

this. . . ." He took a moment. Then: "I would say that you haven't been told the full story."

"So why don't you fill me in?"

"I have a better idea, if you don't mind," he said. "Why don't you take a drive up to Greenwich in the morning?"

"Because it's far."

"It's only forty minutes from midtown. I think it might benefit both of us. I'm here until noon."

KAT would have driven up, there and then, but she'd had too much to drink. She slept fitfully and, figuring she would wait until after the traffic eased, headed over to yoga class. Aqua, who was always there before the first student arrived, never showed. The students mumbled, concerned. One student, a too-skinny older woman, decided to lead the class, but it didn't take. The students slowly dispersed. Kat waited around a few more minutes, hoping Aqua would show. He didn't.

Figuring most of the traffic had cleared out, Kat rented a Zipcar at nine fifteen. The ride, as advertised, took forty minutes.

Look up "tony" in your figurative dictionary (the adjective, not the name) and lush and flush Greenwich, Connecticut, pops up. If you ran a hedge fund exceeding a billion dollars, it was pretty much a federal law that you had to live in Greenwich, Connecticut. Greenwich had the wealthiest residents per capita of anywhere in the United States, and it looked it.

Detective Schwartz offered Kat a Coke. She accepted it and sat on the other side of his Formica desk. Everything here in the station looked sleek and expensive and unused. Schwartz had a handlebar mustache, complete with the barbershop-quartet waxed tips. He wore a dress shirt with suspenders.

"So tell me how you're involved in this case," Schwartz said.

"Brandon came to me. He asked for my help."

"I still don't get why."

Kat was still not ready to tell him everything. "He said it was because you guys didn't believe him."

Schwartz gave her skeptical cop eyes. "And he thought, what, a random cop in New York City would?"

She tried to steer him away from all this. "He came to you guys, right?"

"Yes."

"And you said something on the phone about knowing him from before?"

"Something like that, yes." Joe Schwartz leaned in a little closer. "This is a small town—you know what I mean? I mean, it's not a small town but it's a small town."

"You're asking for my discretion."

"Yes."

"You got it."

He leaned back and put his hands flat on the desk. "We in the police department are a little too familiar with Brandon Phelps."

"Meaning?"

"What do you think I mean?"

"I checked," Kat said. "Brandon has no record."

Schwartz spread his hand. "I guess you missed the part where I said this was a small town."

"Ah."

"Ever see the movie *Chinatown*?" he asked.

"Sure."

He cleared his throat and tried to imitate Joe Mantell. " 'Forget it, Jake. It's Greenwich.' Don't get me wrong. He's only been arrested for petty crap. He broke into the high school a few times, drives too fast, vandalism, deals a little pot—you get the drift. And to be fair, none of this happened before his old man died. We all knew and liked the father, and the mother, well, Dana Phelps is good people. Salt of the earth. Will do anything for you. But the kid . . . I don't know. There's always been something off about him."

"Off how?"

"No big deal, really. I got a son Brandon's age. Brandon didn't fit in, but this isn't an easy town."

"But he came to you a few days ago. He told you he was worried about his mother."

"Yep." There was a paper clip on his desk. Schwartz picked it up and started bending it back and forth. "But he also lied to us."

"How?"

"What did he tell you about his mother's supposed disappearance?"

"He said she met a guy online, that she went away with him, that she always contacted him but hadn't."

"Yeah, he told us that too," Schwartz said. "But that's not the truth." He dropped the paper clip and opened his desk drawer. He took out some kind of protein bar. "Want one? I got plenty."

"No, thanks. So what is the truth?"

He started rifling through a stack of papers. "I put it here because I knew you were . . . Wait. Here it is. Brandon's cell phone records." He handed her the sheets. "See the yellow?"

She saw two texts highlighted in yellow. They'd both come from the same phone number.

"Brandon received two texts from his mother. One came two nights ago, the other early yesterday morning."

"This is his mother's cell phone?"

"Yep."

Kat could feel her face start to redden. "Do you know what they say?"

"When he was here last, I only had a record of the first one. I confronted him about it, so he showed it to me. It said something like 'Arrived, having a great time, miss you.' Something like that."

Kat kept her eyes on the sheet of paper. "How did he explain it?"

"He said his mother hadn't sent it. But it's her number. You can see it right there, plain as day."

"Did you call the mom's number?"

"We did. No answer."

"Do you find that suspicious?"

"No. To put it crudely, we figure she's on some island, maybe getting laid for the first time in three years. Why, you don't agree?"

"No," she said. "I do. I was just playing devil's advocate."

"Of course, that isn't the only explanation."

"What do you mean?"

"I mean," Schwartz said with a shrug, "Dana Phelps could very well be missing."

Kat waited for him to say more. Schwartz waited longer. Finally, Kat asked, "Did Brandon tell you about the ATM charge?"

"Interestingly enough, no."

"He may not have known about it when he saw you."

"That's one theory."

"You have another?"

"I do. Or let's say, I did. See, that's the main reason I wanted you to take the ride up here."

"Oh?"

"Put yourself in my shoes. A troubled teenager comes to me. He claims his mother is missing. From the texts, we know his story is a lie. We find out some money was taken out of an ATM. So if there was foul play, who would be your number one suspect?"

She nodded. "The troubled teenager."

"Bingo."

Kat had thought of that in passing but hadn't really gone there. Of course, she hadn't known about the kid's past—then again, Joe Schwartz didn't know that Brandon had broken into YouAreJustMyType or her own connection to the case. On the other hand, Brandon had lied to her about the texts. She knew that now. So what exactly was he up to?

Kat said, "You thought that maybe Brandon harmed his own mother?"

"I wasn't ready to go that far. But I didn't think that she had vanished, either. So I took the precaution of taking one extra step."

"What was that?"

"I asked for the ATM surveillance video. I thought maybe you'd want to see it too." He flipped the computer monitor around on his desk so she could see the screen. Schwartz hit a few keys. The monitor came to life. The video was a split screen, two camera angles. That was the latest technology. Too many people knew about the camera on the front of the machine and would cover it with their hand. So the picture on the left was exactly that—

one of those fish-eye views of an ATM machine. The second shot, the one on the right of the screen, had been shot from above, like you see in every convenience store heist. Kat understood that installing a camera near the ceiling was easier, but it was almost always useless. Criminals wore baseball caps or kept their chins tucked. Shoot from below, not above.

The videos were in color, not black-and-white. That was getting more and more common. Schwartz took hold of his mouse. "Ready?"

She nodded. He clicked the PLAY button.

For a few seconds, there was nothing. Then a woman came into view. There was no doubt about it. It was Dana Phelps.

"She look in much distress to you?"

Kat shook her head. Even on the surveillance camera, Dana looked rather beautiful. More than that, she looked ready to go on a vacation with a new lover. Kat couldn't help feel a pang of something akin to envy. Dana's hair looked as though it had just been professionally done. Her nails—Kat could see them up close when they were tapping the keys—were freshly manicured. Her outfit too looked ideal for a romantic trip to the Caribbean:

A bright yellow sundress.

16

AQUA was pacing in front of Kat's apartment building.

His pace was done in tight two-steps-spin-180, two-steps-spin-180 formation. Kat stopped on the corner and watched for a moment. Something was clutched in his hand. Aqua kept looking at it—was it a sheet of paper? He kept talking to it—no, Kat thought, more like arguing or even pleading with it.

People gave Aqua wide berth, but this was New York. Nobody overreacted. Kat started toward him. Aqua hadn't been to her apartment for more than a decade, so why now? When she was about ten feet away from him, she could see what was on the sheet of paper he had bunched up in his right hand.

It was the picture of Jeff she had given to him over two weeks ago.

"Aqua?"

He stopped midstride and spun toward her. His eyes were wide and just past the northern border of sanity. She had seen him talk to himself before, had witnessed a few of his paces and tantrums, but she had never seen him look so . . . Was it agitated? No. It seemed more than that. It seemed pained.

"Why?" Aqua cried, holding up Jeff's picture.

"Why what, Aqua?"

"I loved him," he said, his voice a wounded wail. "You loved him."

"I know we did."

"Why?"

He started sobbing. Pedestrians now gave him wider berth. Kat moved closer. She opened her arms and Aqua fell right in, putting his head against her shoulder and continuing to cry.

"It's okay," she said softly.

Aqua kept at it, his body racked by each new sob. She shouldn't have shown him the photograph. He was beyond fragile. He needed routine. He needed sameness, and here she had gone and given him a picture of someone he cared deeply about and never saw anymore.

Wait. How did she know Aqua never saw Jeff anymore?

Eighteen years ago, Jeff had broken up with her. That didn't mean he had given up all his friends and connections, did it? He and Aqua could still be in touch, still doing what friends do, hang out, grab a beer, watch a game. Except, of course, it wasn't as though Aqua had a computer or a phone or even an address.

But could they still be in touch?

It seemed doubtful. Kat let him have his cry there on the street. He pulled himself together, but it took some time. She patted his back and cooed soothing words. She had done this for Aqua before, especially after Jeff left, but it had been a long, long time. In those days, she had both taken pity on him and been angered by his reaction. Jeff had dumped her, not him. Shouldn't Aqua be the one comforting her?

But, man, she missed this connection. She had long ago mourned the loss of this friend, accepting the yoga-teacher relationship as being the only one he could reasonably be expected to give. Right now, holding him like this, she fell back and yet again felt the pang for all she had lost eighteen years ago.

"Are you hungry?" she asked him.

Aqua nodded, lifting his head. His face was covered with tears and snot. So was Kat's blouse. She didn't care. She started welling up too, not just for the loss of Jeff or what she and Aqua once had, but just from physically comforting someone she cared about. It had been so long. Much too long.

"A little hungry, I guess," Aqua said.

"Do you want to get something to eat?"

"I should go."

"No, no, let's get something to eat, okay?"

"I don't think so, Kat."

"I don't understand. Why did you come here in the first place?"

"Class tomorrow," Aqua said. "I need to prepare."

"Come on," she said, holding on to his hand, trying to keep the plea from her voice. "Stay with me a little while, okay?"

He didn't respond.

"You said you're hungry, right?"

"Right."

"So let's get something to eat, okay?"

Aqua wiped his face with his sleeve. "Okay." They started down the block, arm in arm, a rather bizarre-looking couple, she guessed, but again, this was New York. They walked in silence for a while. Aqua stopped crying. Kat didn't want to push him, but then, she couldn't just leave it alone.

"You miss him," she said.

Aqua squeezed his eyes shut as if wishing the words away.

"It's okay. I understand."

"You don't understand anything," Aqua said.

She wasn't sure how to respond to that, so she went with "So explain it to me."

"I miss him," Aqua said. Then he stopped, turned, and faced her full-on. When he looked at her, the wide-eyed look had been replaced with something akin to pity. "But not like you, Kat."

He started to walk away. She hurried to catch up.

"I'm fine," Kat said.

"It should have been."

"What should have been?"

"You and Jeff," Aqua said. "It should have been."

"Yeah, well, it didn't happen."

"It is like you two were traveling down separate roads for your whole lives—two roads that were destined to become one. You have to see that. Both of you."

"Well, clearly not both of us," she said.

"You travel down those life roads. You choose journeys, but sometimes you are forced to take another route."

She really wasn't in the mood for the yoga woo-woo right now. "Aqua?"

"Yes?"

"Have you seen Jeff?"

He stopped again.

"I mean, since he left me. Have you seen him?"

Aqua tightened his grip on her arm. He started to walk again. She stayed with him. They made the right on Columbus Avenue and headed north.

"Twice," he said.

"You've seen him twice?"

Aqua looked up toward the sky and closed his eyes. Kat let him take his time. He used to do this back at school too. He would talk about the sun on his face, how it relaxed and centered him. For a while, it had even seemed to work. But that face was weathered now. You could see the bad years in the lines around his eyes and mouth. His "mocha latte" skin had taken on the leathery cracking of those who live on the streets too long.

"He came back to the room," Aqua said. "After he ended it with you."

"Oh," she said. Not the answer she'd hoped for.

Because of how he was, Aqua had always been in a single on campus. The school tried him with a roommate, but it never worked out. Some were freaked out by the cross-dressing, but the real problem was that Aqua never slept. He studied. He read. He worked in the lab, the school cafeteria—and at night, he had a job in a fetish club in Jersey City. Sometime in his junior year, Aqua lost his single room. Housing insisted on putting him with three other students. There was no way that would work out. At the same time, Jeff had found a two-bedroom on 178th Street. Serendipity, Jeff had called it.

Aqua was tearing up again. "Jeff was destroyed, you know."

"Thanks. That means a lot eighteen years later."

"Don't be like that, Kat."

Aqua might have been confused, but he hadn't missed the sarcasm.

"So when was the second time you saw him?" Kat asked.

"March twenty-first," he said.

"What year?"

"What do you mean, what year? This year."

Kat pulled up. "Wait. Are you telling me you saw Jeff six months ago for the first time since we broke up?"

Aqua started to fidget.

"Aqua?"

"I teach yoga."

"Yeah, I know."

"I'm a good teacher."

"The best. Where did you see Jeff exactly?"

"You were there."

"What are you talking about?"

"You took my class. On March twenty-first. You aren't my best student. But you try. You are conscientious."

"Aqua, where did you see Jeff?"

"At class," Aqua said. "March twenty-first."

"This year?"

"Yes."

"Are you telling me that Jeff took your class six months ago?"

"He didn't take the class," Aqua said. "He stayed behind a tree. He watched you. He was in so much pain."

"Did you talk to him?"

Aqua shook his head. "I taught class. I thought perhaps he spoke to you."

"No," she said. Then, remembering that she wasn't

dealing with the most dependable mind in the free world, she tried to let it go. There was no way Jeff had been in Central Park six months ago, watching their class from behind a tree. It made no sense.

"I'm so sorry, Kat."

"Don't worry about it, okay?"

"It changed everything. I didn't know it would."

"It's okay now."

They were half a block from O'Malley's. In the old days, they would all hang out here—Kat, Jeff, Aqua, a few other friends. You would think O'Malley's would have been a rough place for a biracial cross-dresser back then. It was. In the beginning, Aqua dressed like a man at O'Malley's, but that didn't really stop the sneers. Dad would just shake his head. He wasn't as bad as most from the neighborhood, but he still had no patience for "fruits."

"Gotta stop hanging around those types," Kat's father would tell her. "They ain't right."

She would shake her head and roll her eyes at him. At all of them. People often referred to these cops now as "old school." True enough. But it wasn't always a compliment. They were narrow and insulated. Excuses could be made (and were), but in the end, they were bigots. Lovable bigots maybe. But bigots nonetheless. Gays were treated with derision, but to a lesser extent, so was pretty much every other group or nationality. It was part of the lexicon. If someone negotiated with you too hard, you complained that they "Jewed" you down. Any activity not deemed macho was for "fags." A ballplayer choked because he was playing like an N-word. Kat didn't excuse it, but when she was younger, she didn't really let it get to her either.

To his credit (or maybe patience?), Aqua hadn't seemed to care. "How do you think we get views to evolve?" he'd say. He took it as a challenge even. Aqua would breeze into O'Malley's, either not caring about—or, more likely, making himself ignore—the sneers and snickers. After a while, most of the cops moved on, got bored, barely looking twice when Aqua strolled in. Dad and his buddies kept their distance.

It pissed Kat off, especially coming from her father, but Aqua would shrug and say, "Progress."

As they reached the pub door, Aqua pulled up short. His eyes went wide again.

"What is it?" Kat asked.

"I have to teach class."

"Right, I know. That's tomorrow."

He shook his head. "I need to prepare. I'm a yogi. A teacher. An instructor."

"And a good one."

Aqua kept shaking his head. There were tears in his eyes now. "I can't go back."

"You don't have to go anywhere."

"He loved you so much."

She didn't bother asking who he meant. "It's okay, Aqua. We are just going to grab a bite to eat, okay?"

"I'm a good teacher, aren't I?"

"The best."

"So let me do what I do. That's how I help. That's how I stay centered. That's how I contribute to society."

"You have to eat."

The door to O'Malley's had a neon sign for Budweiser in the window. She could see the red light reflecting in Aqua's eyes. She reached for the handle and pulled the door open.

Aqua screamed. "I can't go back!"

Kat let go of the door. "It's okay. I get it. Let's go somewhere else."

"No! Leave me alone! Leave him alone!"

"Aqua?"

She reached out for him, but he pulled away. "Leave him alone," he said, his voice more a hiss this time. Then he ran down the street, back toward the park.

17

STACY met her at O'Malley's an hour later.

Kat told her the entire story. Stacy listened, shook her head, and said, "Man, all I wanted to do was help you get laid."

"I know, right?"

"No good deed goes unpunished." Stacy stared a little too hard at her beer. She started peeling off the label.

"What is it?" Kat asked.

"I, uh, took the liberty of doing some of my own investigating on this."

"Meaning?"

"I ran a full check on your old fiancé, Jeff Raynes."

Kat took a quick swallow. "What did you find?"

"Not much."

"Meaning?"

"After you two broke up, do you know where he went?"

"No."

"You weren't curious?"

"I was curious," Kat said. "But he dumped my ass."

"Yeah, I get it."

"So where did he go?"

"Cincinnati."

Kat stared straight ahead. "That makes sense. He was from Cincinnati."

"Right. So anyway, about three months after you two broke up, he got into a bar fight."

"Jeff did?"

"Yes."

"In Cincinnati?"

Stacy nodded. "I don't know the details. The cops came. He was arrested for a misdemeanor. He paid a fine and that was that."

"Okay. And then?"

"And then nothing."

"What do you mean?"

"There is nothing else on Jeff Raynes. No credit card charges. No passport. No bank accounts. Nothing."

"Wait. This is preliminary, right?"

Stacy shook her head. "I ran it all. He's gone with the wind."

"That can't be. He's on YouAreJustMyType."

"But didn't your friend Brandon say he used a different name?"

"Jack. And you know what?" Kat slapped her hands down on top of the bar. "I don't really care anymore. That's in my past."

Stacy smiled. "Good for you."

"I've had enough of old ghosts for one night."

"Hear, hear."

They clinked beer bottles. Kat tried her best to dismiss it.

"His profile said he was a widower," Kat said. "That he had a kid."

"Yeah, I know."

"But you didn't find that."

"I didn't find anything after that bar fight almost eighteen years ago."

Kat shook her head. "I don't get it."

"But you don't care, right?"

Kat gave a firm nod. "Right."

Stacy glanced around the bar. "Is it me or is this place extra douchey tonight?"

Stacy was trying to distract her, Kat thought, but that was okay. And no, it wasn't just Stacy. O'Malley's seemed to be a verifiable United Nations of Douche Baggery on this fine evening. A guy in a cowboy hat tipped the brim toward them and actually muttered, in a Brooklyn accent no less, "Howdy, ma'am." Dancing guy—there is one in every bar who has to do the robot or moonwalk while his buddies egg him on—was working his stuff by the jukebox. One guy wore a football jersey, a look Kat disliked on men but loathed on women, especially the ones who cheer too loudly, trying too hard to prove their fandom is legitimate. It always came off as too desperate. Two steroid-inflated, overwaxed muscleheads preened in the bar's center—those guys never went to the dark corners. They wanted to be seen. Their shirts were always the same size—Too Small. There were hipster hopefuls who smelled like pot. There were guys with tattoo sleeves.

There was the sloppy drunk who had his arm over another guy he'd just met, telling him that he loved him and that even though they had just met that night, they'd be best friends forever.

One biker wannabe wearing black leather and a red bandanna—always a no—made his approach. He had a quarter in his palm. "Hey, babe," he said, looking directly between the two women. Kat figured that this was a take-two-shots-with-one-line-type deal.

"If I flip a coin," Bandanna continued, arching an eyebrow, "will I get head?"

Stacy looked at Kat. "We have to find a new place to hang out."

Kat nodded. "It's dinnertime anyway. Let's eat someplace good."

"How about Telepan?"

"Yum."

"We'll get the tasting menu."

"With the wine pairing."

"Let's hurry."

They were outside and walking fast when Kat's cell phone sounded. The call was coming from Brandon's regular cell phone now—no need for disposables anymore. She debated letting it go—right now, all she wanted was Telepan's tasting menu with wine pairings—but she answered it anyway.

"Hello?"

"Where are you?" Brandon asked. "We need to talk."

"No, Brandon, we don't. Guess where I went today."

"Uh, where?"

"The Greenwich police station. I had a little chat with our friend Detective Schwartz. He told me about a text you received."

"It's not what you think."

"You lied."

"I didn't lie. I just didn't tell you about the texts. But I can explain that."

"No need. I'm out of this, Brandon. Nice meeting you and all. Good luck in the future."

She was about to thumb the END button, when she heard Brandon say, "I found out something about Jeff."

She put the phone to her ear. "That he got in a bar fight eighteen years ago?"

"What? No. This is more recent."

"Look, I don't really care." Then: "Is he with your mother?"

"It's not what we thought."

"What isn't what we thought?"

"None of it."

"What do you mean?"

"Jeff, for one thing."

"What about him?"

"He isn't what you think. We need to talk, Kat. I need to show this to you."

REYNALDO made sure that the blond woman—he didn't need to know any of their names—was secure before he headed up to the same path toward the farmhouse. Night had fallen. He used his flashlight to find his way.

Reynaldo had discovered out here, at the age of nineteen, that he was afraid of the dark. The *dark* dark. Real dark. In the city, there was no real dark. If you were outside, there were always streetlights or lights from windows or storefronts kept lit. You never knew pure black darkness. Here, out in the woods, you could not see your hand in front of your face. Anything could be out there. Anything could be lurking.

When he reached the clearing, Reynaldo could see the porch lights on. He stood and looked at the serene surroundings. He had never really seen anything like this farm in real life before they came out here. In movies, sure, but he hadn't believed that places like this existed, any more than he believed the Death Star in *Star Wars* existed. It was make-believe, these farmlands where kids could walk for miles and play in sandlots and come home to Ma and Pa and do their chores. Now he knew the land was real. The happy stories, however, were still the stuff of make-believe.

He had his orders, but first he headed to the barn to check on his chocolate Labrador retriever, Bo. As always, Bo ran out and greeted him as though he hadn't seen him in a year. Reynaldo smiled, scratched behind his ears, and made sure Bo's water bowl was full.

When he was finished taking care of his dog, Reynaldo made his way to the farmhouse. He opened the door. Titus was there with Dmitry. Dmitry was Titus's computer whiz kid with the bright-colored shirts and knit cap. Titus had decided to decorate as the Amish did. Reynaldo did not know why. The furniture was all quality woodwork—sturdy, heavy, plain, unadorned. There was nothing fancy. It all gave off an aura of quiet strength.

There were a bench and free weights in one of the upstairs bedrooms. They had originally set it up in the cellar, but after a while, no one wanted to go into anything underground. So they moved it up.

Reynaldo lifted weights every day, no matter what. He also had a steady concoction of performance-enhancing drugs in the fridge and cabinet. Most he self-administered with a needle in the upper thigh. Titus supplied them for him.

Six years ago, Titus had found Reynaldo in a garbage dump. For real. Reynaldo had been working a corner in Queens, undercutting the other hustlers by charging only fifteen dollars a pop. A john didn't beat him on that day. His competition did. They'd had enough of his horning in on their territory. So when Reynaldo got out of the car—his sixth car that night—two of them jumped him and beat him senseless. Titus had found him there lying on the ground, bleeding. The only thing Reynaldo could feel was Bo licking his face. Titus had cleaned him up. He had taken him to a gym and taught him about lifting and 'roiding and not being anyone's bitch anymore.

Titus had done more than save his life. He had given Reynaldo a real one.

Reynaldo started toward the stairs.

"Not yet," Titus said to him.

Reynaldo looked back at him. Dmitry kept his face in the computer, concentrating a little too hard on the screen.

"Problem?" Reynaldo asked.

"Nothing that can't be solved."

Reynaldo waited. Titus walked over to him and handed him a gun.

"Wait for my signal."

"Okay."

Reynaldo jammed the gun into his waistband, covering it with his shirt. Titus inspected it for a second and then nodded his approval. "Dmitry?"

Dmitry looked up over his pink-tinted glasses, startled. "Yes?"

"Go get something to eat."

Titus didn't have to tell him twice. Dmitry was out of
the room in seconds. Reynaldo and Titus were alone
now. Titus stood in the doorway. Reynaldo could see a
flashlight bouncing about in the woods. It came into the
clearing and up the steps.

"Hey, guys."

Claude was in his fancy black suit. Titus had two guys
working transportation. Claude was one of them.

"So what's up?" Claude asked with a big smile. "Do
you need me to pick up another package already?"

"Not yet," Titus said in that soothing voice that even
made the hairs on the back of Reynaldo's neck stand up.
"We need to talk first."

Claude's smile started to falter. "Is there a problem?"

"Take off your jacket."

"Excuse me?"

"It's a beautiful suit. It's a warm night. There's no
need for it. Please take it off."

It took effort, but Claude managed a casual shrug.
"Sure, why not?"

Claude took off his suit jacket.

"The pants too."

"What?"

"Take them off, Claude."

"What's going on? I don't understand."

"Humor me, Claude. Take off the pants."

Claude sneaked a glance at Reynaldo. Reynaldo just
stared back.

"Okay, why not?" Claude said, still trying to pretend

that nothing was wrong. "I mean, you're both in shorts. I might as well be too, right?"

"Right, Claude."

He slipped off his pants and handed them to Titus. Titus hung them neatly across the back of a chair in the far corner. He turned again toward Claude. Claude stood there in his dress shirt, tie, boxers, and socks.

"I need you to tell me about the last delivery."

Claude's smile flickered, but managed to stay on. "What's there to tell? It went smoothly. She's here, right?"

Claude forced up a chuckle. He spread his hands, looking at Reynaldo again for some kind of support. Reynaldo stayed still as a stone. He knew how this was going to end. He just wasn't yet sure of the route.

Titus stepped closer, so he was only inches away from Claude. "Tell me about the ATM."

"The what?" Then seeing that wasn't going to play: "Oh. That."

"Tell me."

"Okay, look, it's cool. I know you have rules, Titus, and you know I'd never break them unless, well, I absolutely had to."

Titus stood there, patient, all the time in the world.

"So, okay, right. I started driving and then I realized like an idiot—well, not *like* an idiot. An idiot. I was an idiot. No like about it. A forgetful idiot. See, I left my wallet at home. Stupid, right? So anyway, I can't make the journey without any cash, right? I mean, it's a long ride. You get that, don't you, Titus?"

He stopped and waited for Titus to respond. Titus did not.

"So, okay, yes, we stopped at an ATM. But don't

worry. I kept it in state. I mean, we were still within twenty miles of her house. I never got out of the car, so there was no way the surveillance camera could see me. I just kept the gun on her. I told her if she did anything, I'd go after her kid. She got the money—"

"How much?"

"What?"

Titus smiled at him. "How much money did you have her take out?"

"Uh, the max."

"And how much was that, Claude?"

The smile flickered one more time and went out. "A thousand dollars."

"That's a lot," Titus said, "of cash to need for a journey."

"Well, hey, come on. I mean, she was taking money out anyway. Why not get the max? Am I right?"

Titus just looked at him.

"Oh, right, stupid me. You're wondering why I didn't tell you. I was going to, I swear. I just forgot."

"You're pretty forgetful, Claude."

"Look, in the larger scheme of things, it's a pretty small amount."

"Precisely. You put all of us at risk for petty cash."

"I'm sorry. Really. Here, I have the money. It's in my pants pocket. Go see. It's yours, okay? I shouldn't have done it. It won't happen again."

Titus moved back across the room to the chair where he'd hung the trousers. He reached into the pocket and pulled out the bills. Titus looked pleased. He nodded—the signal—and put the money in his own pocket.

"Are we good?" Claude asked.

"We are."

"Okay, great. Can I, uh, put my clothes back on?"

"No," Titus said. "The suit is expensive. I don't want to get bloodstains on it."

"Bloodstains?"

Reynaldo was right behind Claude now. Without a word or warning, he pressed the barrel of the gun against Claude's head and pulled the trigger.

18

BRANDON was waiting on a bench by Strawberry Fields near 72nd Street. Two guys competed for attention (and handouts) by strumming guitars and singing Beatles songs. One went with the obvious, "Strawberry Fields Forever," but he wasn't doing nearly as brisk a business as the guy in the Eggman T-shirt singing "I Am the Walrus."

"Let me explain that text," Brandon said. "The one Detective Schwartz said my mom sent."

Kat waited. Stacy was there too. Kat was already feeling too close to this. She wanted someone with a little distance to give her perspective.

"Wait. I'll show you." He hunched over and started fiddling with his phone. "Here, read it for yourself."

Kat took his phone and read the message:

Hi. Arrived safely. So excited. Miss you!

Kat handed it to Stacy. She read it and handed it back to Brandon.

"It came from your mother's phone," Kat said.

"Right, but she didn't send it."

"What makes you think that?"

Brandon almost looked insulted by the question. "Mom never says 'miss you.' I mean never. She always finishes with 'love you.'"

"You're kidding, right?"

"I'm dead serious."

"Brandon, how often has your mother gone away on her own like this?"

"This is the first time."

"Right, so naturally she might use 'miss you' at the end, no?"

"You don't get it. Mom always signed her texts with *x*'s and *o*'s and with the word *Mom*. It was like a running joke. She always announced herself. Like if she called me and even though I had caller ID and knew her voice better than my own, she would always say, 'Brandon, it's Mom.'"

Kat looked at Stacy. Stacy gave a small shrug. The kid always had an answer.

"I also saw the surveillance video," Kat said.

"What surveillance video?"

"Of the ATM."

His eyes widened. "Whoa, you saw it? How?"

"Detective Schwartz was more thorough than I would have been. He got the tape."

"So what did it show?"

"What do you think it showed, Brandon?"

"I don't know. Was my mother on it?"

"Yes."

"I don't believe you."

"You think I'm lying?"

"What was she wearing?"

"A yellow sundress."

She saw his face fall. The guy in the Eggman T-shirt finished singing "I Am the Walrus." There was a smattering of applause. The guy bowed deeply and then started singing "I Am the Walrus" again.

"She looked fine too," Kat said. "Your mother is a very beautiful woman."

Brandon waved away the compliment about his mother. "Are you sure she was alone?"

"Definitely. The camera has views from down low and overhead. She was by herself."

Brandon fell back in his seat. "I don't understand." Then: "I don't believe you. You just want me to stop. You could have known about the yellow dress some other way."

Stacy frowned and finally spoke up. "Come on, kid."

He kept shaking his head. "It can't be."

Stacy slapped him on the back. "Be happy, kid. She's alive and well."

He shook his head some more. He stood and began to pace, cutting across the tiles that made up the Imagine mosaic. A tourist yelled, "Hey!" because he had ruined their picture. Kat hurried after him.

"Brandon?"

He stopped pacing.

"You said you found something about Jeff."

"His name isn't Jeff," Brandon said.

"Right. You said he called himself Jack online?"

"That's not his name either."

Kat sneaked a glance at Stacy. "I'm not following."

He took his laptop out of his backpack. He flipped it open. The screen came to life. "It was like I said before. I Googled him and found nothing. But, well, I don't know why I didn't think of it before. It should have come to me right away."

"What should have?"

"Do you know what an image search is?" Brandon asked.

She had just done one on his mother, but there was no reason to tell him that. "It's when you search for someone's picture."

"No, not that one," he said, a hint of impatience in his voice. "That's pretty common. You want to find, say, a picture of yourself online, so you click IMAGE and you type in your name. What I'm talking about is a bit more sophisticated."

"Then no, I don't know," Kat said.

"Instead of searching for text, you search for a particular image," Brandon said. "So, for example, you upload a picture onto the website, and it searches for anyplace else where that picture might exist. More sophisticated software can even find a person's face in other photographs. Stuff like that."

"So you uploaded, what, a picture of Jeff?"

"Exactly. I saved the images from his profile page on YouAreJustMyType.com and then I put them in the Google image search."

"So," Kat said, "if any of those pictures were somewhere else on the web . . ."

"The image search would find them."

"And that's what happened?"

"Not at first. At first it came back with no hits. But here's the thing. Most search engines only look through what is currently on the web. You know how parents are always trying to scare us kids by telling us that anything on the web is on it forever?"

"Yes."

"Well, that's true. It becomes a cached file. This is getting more technical, but when you delete something, it isn't really gone. It's like you're painting your house. You're just painting over the old color. The old color is still there if you take the time to scrape off the new paint." He thought about that. "That's not really a perfect analogy, but you get the point."

"So you scraped off the new paint?"

"Something like that. I found a way to search through deleted pages. A buddy of mine who runs the computer lab at UConn wrote the program. It's still beta."

"What did you find?"

Brandon spun the computer toward her. "This."

It was a Facebook page. The profile picture was the same photograph Jeff had used for YouAreJustMyType.

But the name listed on the top was Ron Kochman.

There was nothing much on the page. The exact same photographs had been posted. There were no posts, no activity, since the day the page had been created four years ago. So the pics were four years old. Well, maybe that explained why Jeff aka Jack aka Ron looked so damned young and handsome. The last four years, Kat thought, had probably aged him a ton.

Yeah, right.

But of course, the greater question remained: Who the hell was Ron Kochman?

"May I take a hopeful shot in the dark?" Stacy said to her.

"Sure."

"Are you certain that's your old fiancé and not some guy who looks like him?"

Kat nodded. "It's a possibility."

"No, it's not," Brandon said. "You instant-messaged him, remember? He knew you. He told you that he needed a fresh start."

"Yeah," Kat said, "I know. Plus, Stacy knows better too. Don't you, Stacy?"

"I do," she said.

"How?" Brandon asked.

Kat ignored him for now, trying to put it together with Stacy. "So eighteen years ago, Jeff moves to Cincinnati. He gets in a bar fight. He changes his name to Ron Kochman—"

"No," Stacy said.

"Why no?"

"You must think I'm the worst private detective on God's green earth. I checked through the databases. If Jeff changed his name to Ron Kochman, he didn't do it legally."

"But you don't have to do it legally," Kat said. "Anyone can change their name."

"But if you want a credit card or a bank account . . ."

"Maybe he didn't want one."

"That doesn't really add up, though, does it? You think, what, Jeff changed his name to Ron? Got married. Had a kid. His wife died. Then he went on YouAreJustMyType to look for dates?"

"I don't know. Maybe."

Stacy thought about it. "Let me run a full background check on Ron Kochman. If he was married or has a child, I'll find something."

"That's a great idea," Brandon said. "I started doing

Google searches on him, but I didn't find much. Just some articles he wrote."

Kat felt her heart go thump-thump. "Articles?"

"Yeah," Brandon said. "Seems Ron Kochman is a journalist."

KAT spent the next hour reading his articles.

There was no doubt in her mind. Ron Kochman was Jeff Raynes. The style. The vocabulary. "Ron" always had a great lead sentence. He pulled you in slowly but consistently. Even the inane was woven into a rich narrative. The articles were always well researched, backed up by several independent sources, thoroughly investigated. Ron worked freelance. There were pieces with his byline in almost every major news publication, both in print and on the web.

Some of those publications featured photographs of their contributors on the editor's page. There was none of Ron Kochman. In fact, no matter how much she searched, she couldn't find one article on Ron Kochman. His biography merely listed some writing credits—no mention of a family or residence, nothing about his education or background or even credentials. He didn't have an active Facebook or Twitter account or any of the now standard promotional tools all journalists employ.

Jeff had changed his name to Ron Kochman.

Why?

Brandon was in her apartment, working feverishly on his laptop. When she stood up, he asked, "Is Ron your old fiancé, Jeff?"

"Yes."

"I checked some databases. So far, I haven't been able to find when or how he changed his name."

"It would be hard to find, Brandon. It isn't illegal to change your name. Leave that to Stacy, okay?"

He nodded, his long hair falling into his face. "Detective Donovan?"

"Call me Kat, okay?"

His eyes stayed on his shoes. "I need you to understand."

"Understand what?"

"My mom. She's a fighter. I don't know how else to put it. When my dad got sick, he gave up right away. But my mom . . . she's like a force of nature. She pulled him through for a long time. That's her way."

He finally looked up.

"Last year, Mom and I took a trip to Maui." Tears filled his eyes. "I swam too far out. I'd been warned. There was a riptide or something. Stay close to shore. But I didn't listen. I'm a tough guy like that, you know?" He gave her a half smile, shook his head. "So anyway, I got caught in the riptide. I tried to swim against it, but there was no way. I was done. It kept dragging me down and farther out. I knew it was just a matter of time. And then Mom was there. She'd been swimming near me the whole time, you know, watching, just in case. She never said anything. That was just her way. So anyway, she grabs me and says to hold on. That's it, she says. Just hold on. And now the tide was pulling us both out. I start panicking, pushing her away. But Mom, she just closed her eyes and held on to me. She just held on to me and wouldn't let me go. Eventually, she steered us toward a small island."

A tear escaped his eye and ran down his cheek.

"She saved my life. That's what she does. She's strong like that. She'd never just let me go. She would have held on no matter what, even if I took her down with me. And now, well, it's my turn to hold on. Do you get that?"

Kat nodded slowly. "I do."

"I'm sorry, Kat. I should have showed you the texts. But if I had, you'd have never listened."

"Speaking of which."

"What?"

"You only showed me the one text. There were two."

He pressed a few buttons on his phone and handed it to her. The text read:

Having a wonderful time. Can't wait to tell you all about it. I have a big surprise too. Phone reception is terrible. Miss you.

Kat handed him back the phone. "Big surprise. Any idea what that means?"

"No."

Her cell phone rang. Talk about the perfect interruption—Kat could see from the caller ID that her mother was calling. "I'll be right back," Kat said.

She ducked into the bedroom, wondering how long her own mother would last in a riptide, and answered. "Hey, Mom."

"Ooh, I hate that," her mother said.

"Hate what?"

Her voice was raspy from too many years of cigarettes. "That you know it's me before you pick up."

"It pops up on the caller ID. I've explained this to you before."

"I know, I know, but really, can't some things remain a mystery? Do we really need to know everything?"

Kat held back the sigh but allowed herself the eye roll.

She could picture her mom in that old kitchen with the linoleum floor, standing up, using one of those old wall-mounted phones that had yellowed from ivory too many years ago. The phone would be tucked under her chin. There would be a half glass of cheap Chablis in her hand, the rest of the jug back in the fridge to keep it cold. A vinyl tablecloth with faux crochet would be covering the kitchen table. A glass ashtray would, Kat had no doubt, be perched atop it. The peeling wallpaper had a flower pattern, though many of the blooms had also turned pale yellow over the years.

When you live with a smoker, everything starts to take on a yellowish hue.

"Are you coming or not?" Mom asked.

Kat could hear the drink in her mother's voice. It was not an unfamiliar sound.

"Coming where, Mom?"

Hazel Donovan—she and Kat's father used to call themselves and sign all their correspondences H&H for Hazel and Henry, as if this were the cleverest thing in the world—didn't bother to hide the sigh.

"Steve Schrader's retirement party."

"Oh, right."

"You get time off for that, you know. The precinct has to do that."

They didn't—Mom had all kinds of weird ideas about the lax rules for cops, all gathered in the era of her father and her husband—but Kat didn't bother correcting her.

"I'm really busy, Mom."

"Everyone will be there. The whole neighborhood. I'm going with Flo and Tessie."

The Trinity of Cop Widows.

Kat said, "I'm working on a pretty big case."

"Tim McNamara is bringing his son. He's a doctor, you know."

"He's a chiropractor."

"So what? They call him doctor. And a chiropractor was so good with your uncle Al. You remember?"

"I do."

"The man could barely move. Remember?"

She did. Uncle Al had gotten worker's comp for a work-related injury at the Orange Mattress factory. Two weeks later, this chiropractor healed him. It was nothing short of a miracle.

"And Tim's son is so handsome. He looks like that guy on *The Price Is Right*."

"Thanks for the invite, Mom, but I'm going to have to pass, okay?"

Silence.

"Mom?"

Now Kat thought that maybe she heard gentle sobs. She waited. Her mother called only late at night—drunk, slurring her words. The call could consist of many things. There might be sarcasm. There might be bitterness or anger. There was always a mother-daughter guilt trip.

But Kat didn't remember ever hearing sobs.

"Mom?" she tried again, her voice softer now.

"He died, didn't he?"

"Who?"

"That man. The one who ruined our lives."

Monte Leburne. "How did you hear?"

"Bobby Suggs told me."

Suggs. One of the two lead detectives on the case. He was retired, living not far from Mom. Mike Rinsky, the other detective, had died three years ago, sudden coronary.

"I hope it was painful," Mom said.

"I think it was. He had cancer."

"Kat?"

"Yes, Mom?"

"You should have been the one to tell me."

Fair point. "You're right. I'm sorry."

"We should have gotten together. We should have sat at the kitchen table like we used to do, like we did when we first heard. Your father would have wanted that."

"I know. I'm sorry. I'll visit soon."

Hazel Donovan hung up then. This was how it always went too. There was never a good-bye. There was just a hang-up.

Dana Phelps had been missing a day or two before her son noticed and started to worry. Kat wondered how long her mother could go missing. Weeks maybe. It wouldn't be Kat who'd notice. It would be Flo or Tessie.

She made a quick call to Joe Schwartz in Greenwich and asked him to e-mail her the ATM video. "Crap," he said. "I don't want to get involved. My captain chewed my ass off for taking it this far."

"I just need the video. That's all. Once Brandon sees his mother, I think it'll help calm him down."

Schwartz took a few moments. "All right, but that's it, okay? And I can't e-mail it to you. I'll e-mail you a secure link. It'll be good for the next hour."

"Thanks."

"Yeah, whatever."

Kat came back out into the living room. "Sorry," she said to Brandon, "I had to take that call."

"Who was it?"

She was about to tell him that it was none of his business but decided to go in another direction. "I want to show you something."

"What?"

She beckoned Brandon toward her computer and checked her e-mail. Two minutes later, the message from Joe Schwartz came up. The subject read: Per your request. The message was only a link.

"What's this?" Brandon asked.

"The ATM video of your mom."

She clicked the link and hit the PLAY button. This time, she watched Brandon's reaction more than the video. When his mother appeared at the ATM, Brandon's face went slack. He never, not for a second, looked away from the screen. He didn't blink.

Kat had seen psychos who could channel Daniel Day-Lewis when it came to lying to the police. But there was no way this kid had hurt his mother.

"What do you think?" Kat asked.

He shook his head.

"What?"

"She looks scared. And pale."

Kat turned back and watched the screen. Scared, pale—hard to say. Everyone looked drawn on an ATM surveillance video. The images were often less flattering than DMV photos. You are concentrating on a small screen and trying to push buttons and there is money involved and you are basically facing a wall. No woman looks her best under those circumstances.

The video continued. Kat watched more carefully this time. It did take Dana three tries to get her PIN right, but that didn't mean much. When the money was dispensed, Dana fumbled with it, but again, those machines sometimes held on to your bills too tightly.

It was when Dana finished up and started to walk away that Kat saw something. She reached out and hit the PAUSE button.

Brandon looked at her. "What?"

It was probably nothing, but then again, no one had studied the video closely. There had been no need. All they wanted to do was confirm that Dana Phelps had taken out the money on her own. Kat hit the slow-motion REWIND button. Dana started walking backward toward the ATM.

There.

Kat had seen movement in the upper right-hand corner of the screen. Something—or someone—was barely there, in the distance. That wasn't too much of a surprise, but whoever it was seemed to move when Dana did.

The video quality had enough pixels for Kat to close in on the figure, clicking the magnifying glass until the dark dot grew into an image.

It was a man in a black suit with a black cap on.

"How would your mother have gone to the airport?" Kat asked.

Brandon pointed to the guy in the black suit. "He wouldn't have taken her."

"Not what I'm asking."

"We always use Bristol Car Service."

"Do you have their phone number?"

"Yeah, hold on." Brandon started tapping his phone. "They picked me up from college a few times, you know, when I wanted to go home for the weekend. Easier than having Mom get me sometimes. Here."

Brandon read out the number. Kat plugged it into her phone and hit SEND. The answering voice gave her two options. Press one for reservations. Press two for dispatch. She went with dispatch. When a man answered, she introduced herself and identified herself as a cop. Sometimes, this made people clam up and demand proof. Most times it opened doors.

When people are both cautious and curious, curious usually wins out.

Kat said, "I'm wondering if a woman named Dana Phelps recently booked a ride to an area airport."

"Oh, sure, I know Mrs. Phelps. She's a regular. Nice lady."

"Did she book a car with you recently?"

"Yeah, maybe a week ago. For Kennedy airport."

"Could I speak to her driver?"

"Oh."

"Oh?"

"Yeah, like, oh, wait. You asked me if she booked the ride to JFK."

"Right."

"She booked it, yeah, but she didn't take it."

Kat switched the phone from her left hand to her right. "What do you mean?"

"Mrs. Phelps canceled, maybe two hours before the ride. I took the call myself. It was kinda funny, actually."

"Funny how?"

"She was apologetic, what with it being so late and all. But she was also, I don't know, all giddy."

"Giddy?"

"Yeah, like laughing or whatever."

"Did she give a reason for canceling so late?"

"Kind of. I mean, I think that's why she was giddy. She said her boyfriend was sending his own black stretch limo to get her. As a surprise or something."

19

HOPING cooler heads would prevail—and needing to make an official police request—Kat showed up at the precinct for work the next day. Her still-partner (ugh) Chaz, resplendent in a suit so shiny Kat reached for her sunglasses, stood by her desk with his fists on his hips. He looked surprised to see her.

"Yo, Kat, need something?"

"No," she said.

"Boss man said you were on leave."

"Yeah, well, I changed my mind. I just need to do one quick thing and then I want to hear what's going on."

Kat sat at her computer. Last night, she had used Google Earth to figure out what nearby surveillance cameras could give her a fuller view of the street near Dana's ATM. She hoped to see what car Dana had gotten into, maybe get a license plate or some other lead.

Chaz peeked over her shoulder. "This about that kid who was in here the other day?"

She ignored him, made the info request, and was prompted for her user name and password. She typed them in and hit RETURN.

ACCESS DENIED

Kat tried again. Same thing. She turned back to Chaz, who stood watching her with his arms crossed.

"What's going on, Chaz?"

"Boss man said you were on leave."

"We don't disable someone's computer access because they take a leave."

"Yeah, well." Chaz shrugged. "You did ask for it, didn't you?"

"Ask for what?"

"You wanted a transfer, so I guess you're getting one."

"I never asked for a transfer."

"That's what the captain told me. Said you put in for a new partner."

"I put in for a new partner. I didn't ask for a transfer."

Chaz looked wounded. "I still don't know why you'd do that."

"Because I don't like you, Chaz. You're crude, you're lazy, and you have no interest in doing the right thing—"

"Hey, I have my own way of working."

She didn't want to get into this now.

"Detective Donovan?"

Kat looked behind her. It was Stephen Singer, her immediate superior.

"You're on voluntary leave."

"No, I'm not."

Singer moved closer. "Voluntary leave is something that no one holds against you. It doesn't show up on your record as, say, insubordinate conduct toward a superior officer."

"I didn't—"

Singer cut her off by raising his hand and closing his eyes. "Enjoy your vacation, Kat. You've earned it."

He walked away. Kat looked at Chaz. Chaz said nothing. She understood what was being said—keep quiet, take the slap, it will all go away. That was the smart move, she guessed. The only move, really. She stood up and reached down to turn her computer off.

"Don't," Chaz said.

"What?"

"Singer said to get out of here. So do it. Now."

Their eyes met. Chaz may have given her the slightest nod—she couldn't be sure—but she didn't shut the computer off. As she headed down the stairs, Kat glanced toward Stagger's office. What the hell was his problem anyway? She knew he was a stickler for rules and regulations, and yeah, maybe she should have more respect, but this felt like overkill.

She checked her watch. Her day was somewhat free now. She changed subways three times on her way down to the Main Street stop on the 7 train in Flushing. The Knights of Columbus hall had wood paneling and American flags and eagles and stars and any other emblem you might loosely associate with patriotism. The hall was, as at every event, boisterous. Knights of Columbus halls, like school gymnasiums, are not meant to be quiet. Steve Schrader, who was retiring at the tender age of fifty-three, stood near a keg, handling the reception line like a groom.

Kat spotted retired detective Bobby Suggs sitting at a corner table overflowing with bottles of Budweiser. He wore a plaid sports coat and gray slacks so polyester they made Kat itch. As Kat started toward him, she glanced at the faces. She knew so many of them. They stopped and hugged her and wished her well. They told her—they always told her this—that she was the spitting image of her dear father, God rest his eternal soul, and asked when she would find a man and start a family. She tried to nod and smile her way through them. It wasn't that easy. Their faces leaned in close to be heard, too close, smothering, as though the pockmarks and burst vessels were going to swallow her whole. A four-piece polka band led by a tuba started up. The room smelled of stale beer and dance sweat.

"Kat? Sweetheart, we're over here."

She turned toward the familiar raspy voice. Mom's face was already flush with drink. She waved Kat toward the table where she sat with Flo and Tessie. Flo and Tessie waved her over too, just in case she didn't know that Mom's wave was indicating she should join them.

Trapped, Kat started toward them. She kissed her mother on the cheek and said hello to Flo and Tessie.

"What?" Flo said. "No kiss for your aunt Flo and Tessie?"

Neither woman was an aunt, just close family friends, but Kat kissed them anyway. Flo had a bad red dye job that sometimes leaned toward purple. Tessie kept her hair a gray that also had a tendency toward purple. Both smelled a little like potpourri on an old couch. The two "aunts" grabbed Kat's face before kissing her cheek. Flo wore heavy ruby red lipstick. Kat wondered how to discreetly wipe it away.

All three widows openly inspected her.

"You're too skinny," Flo said.

"Leave her alone," Tessie said. "You look fine, dear."

"What? I'm just saying. Men like a woman with a little meat on her bones." To emphasize her point, Flo hoisted up her substantial bosom without the slightest sense of embarrassment. Flo was always doing that—adjusting her bosoms as though they were unruly children.

Mom continued to study Kat with not-so-subtle disapproval. "Do you think that hair flatters your face?"

Kat just stared at her.

"I mean, you have such a pretty face."

"You're beautiful," Tessie said, as always the defiant albeit normal one. "And I love your hair."

"Thank you, Aunt Tessie."

"Did you come for Tim's son the doctor?" Flo asked.

"No."

"He's not here yet. But he will be."

"You'll like him," Tessie added. "He's very handsome."

"He looks like that guy on *The Price Is Right*," Flo added. "Am I right?"

Mom and Tessie nodded enthusiastically.

Kat asked, "Which guy?"

"What?"

"You mean the guy who hosts it now or the one who used to host it?"

"Which guy?" Flo repeated. "Never you mind which guy, Miss Picky. What, one of them isn't handsome enough for you?" Flo hoisted up the bosom again. "Which guy?"

"Stop that," Tessie said.

"What?"

"With the booby play. You're going to put someone's eyes out with one of those."

Flo winked. "Only if he's lucky."

Flo was big and bouncy and still wanted to catch a man. She caught their eyes far too often—but it never lasted. Despite a lifetime of evidence to the contrary, Flo was still a hopeless romantic. She fell in love hard and fast, and everyone but Flo could see the oncoming wreck. She and Mom had been best friends since elementary school at St. Mary's. There was a brief period, when Kat was in high school, when the two women didn't talk for maybe six months or a year—a fight over a houseguest or something—but other than that, they were inseparable.

Flo had six grown kids and sixteen grandchildren. Tessie had eight kids and nine grandkids. They had lived hard lives, these women—raising tons of children under the thumbs of uninvolved husbands and an overly involved church. When Kat was nine years old, she came home from school early and saw Tessie crying in their kitchen. Mom sat with her, in the stillness of that midday kitchen, holding Tessie's hand and telling her how sorry she was and how it would all be okay. Tessie just sobbed and shook her head. Nine-year-old Kat wondered what tragedy had befallen Tessie's family—if maybe something had happened to her daughter Mary, who had lupus, or if her husband, Uncle Ed, had lost his job, or if Tessie's hoodlum son Pat had failed out of school.

But it wasn't any of that.

Tessie was sobbing because she'd just learned she was pregnant yet again. She cried and clutched tissues and repeated over and over that she couldn't handle it, and

Mom listened and held her hand and then Flo came over and Flo listened and eventually they all cried.

Tessie's children were grown now. After Ed died six years ago, Tessie, who had never gone any farther than an Atlantic City casino, started traveling extensively. Her first trip had been to Paris three months after Ed's death. For years, Tessie had been taking out language tapes from the Queens Library and teaching herself French. Now she put it to use. Tessie kept her personal travel diaries in leather binders in the den. Tessie never pushed them on anyone—rarely admitted what they were—but Kat loved to read them.

Kat's father had seen it early. "This life," Dad had told her, eyeing Kat's mom standing over an oven. "It's a trap for a girl." The only girls Kat grew up with who stayed in the neighborhood had been knocked up young. The rest, for better or worse, had fled.

Kat turned around, her gaze heading back toward Suggs's table. He was staring straight at her. He didn't look away when she spotted him. Instead, he brought the bottle up toward her in a distant, sad toast. She nodded in return. Suggs took a deep, long swig, his head back, his throat sliding up and down.

"I'll be right back," Kat said, starting toward him.

Suggs rose and met her halfway. He was a short, burly man who walked as though he'd just gotten off a horse. The room was warm now, the weak air-conditioning no match for the crowded hall. Everyone, including both Suggs and Kat, had a thin sheen of sweat on them. They hugged, no words exchanged.

"I guess you heard," Suggs said, releasing her.

"About Leburne? Yeah."

"Not sure what to say here, Kat. 'I'm sorry' doesn't seem appropriate."

"I know what you mean."

"I just wanted you to know I was thinking of you. I'm glad you're here."

"Thanks."

Suggs raised his bottle. "You need a beer."

"That I do," Kat agreed.

There was no bar, just a bunch of coolers and kegs in the corner. Ever the gentleman, Suggs opened the bottle with his wedding band. They clinked bottles and drank. With all due respect to the Bob Barker or Drew Carey look-alike, Kat had traveled here to talk to Suggs. She just wasn't sure how to begin.

Suggs helped her out. "I heard you visited Leburne before he died."

"Yeah."

"What was that like?"

"He said he didn't do it."

Suggs smiled as though she'd just told him a joke that he was pretending he found amusing. "Did he, now?"

"He was on a mess of drugs."

"So I guess he was telling one last lie."

"Just the opposite. They were more like a truth serum. He admitted killing others. But he said that he just took the blame for Dad's murder because he was serving life anyway."

Suggs took a long sip of beer. He was probably in his early sixties. He still had a full head of gray hair, but what always struck her about him—what struck most people about him—was that he had the kindest face. Not handsome or even striking. Just kind. You couldn't help but like a man with that face. Some people look like jack-offs, even though they may be the sweetest people in the world. Suggs was the opposite—you couldn't imagine a man with this face could be anything but trustworthy.

You had to remind yourself that it was just a face.

"I found the gun, Kat."

"I know."

"It was hidden in his house. In a false panel under his bed."

"I know that too. But didn't you ever find that odd? The guy was always so careful. He'd use his weapon and dump it. But suddenly, you find the murder weapon stashed with his unused guns."

The quasi-amused smile stayed on his lips. "You look like your old man. You know that?"

"Yeah, so I hear."

"We had no other suspects or even theories."

"Doesn't mean there weren't any."

"Cozone put out a hit. We had a murder weapon. We had a confession. Leburne had means and opportunity. It was a righteous bust."

"I'm not saying you guys didn't do good work."

"Sure sounds like it."

"There are just some pieces that don't fit."

"Come on, Kat. You know how these things go. It is never a perfect fit. That's why we have trials and defense lawyers who keep telling us, even when the case is completely solid, that there are holes or inconsistencies or that the prosecution's case doesn't"—he made quote marks with his fingers—"fit."

The band stopped playing. Someone took the microphone and began a long-winded toast. Suggs turned and watched. Kat leaned closer to him and said, "Can I ask you one more question?"

He kept his eyes on the speaker. "I couldn't stop you if I still carried my piece."

"Why did Stagger go up to see Leburne the day after he was arrested?"

Suggs blinked a few times before turning his face toward her. "Come again?"

"I saw the visitors' logs," Kat said. "The day after the feds arrested Leburne, Stagger interrogated him."

Suggs mulled it over. "I would say something like 'I think you're mistaken,' but my guess is, you've already confirmed it."

"Did you know about it?"

"No."

"Stagger never told you?"

"No," Suggs said again. "Did you ask him?"

"He said he went up on his own because he was obsessed with the case. That he was impetuous."

"Impetuous," Suggs repeated. "Good word."

"He also said that Leburne didn't talk to him."

Suggs started peeling the label off his beer. "So what's the big deal, Kat?"

"Maybe nothing," she said.

They both stood there, pretending to listen to the speaker.

Then Suggs asked: "When did Stagger visit exactly?"

"The day after Leburne was arrested," Kat said.

"Interesting."

"Why?"

"Leburne didn't even come up on our radar until, what, a week later."

"Yet Stagger was up there first."

"Could have been a good hunch on his part."

"One you and Rinsky missed, I guess."

Suggs frowned. "You really think I'm going to take that bait, Kat?"

"Just saying. It's bizarre, right?"

Suggs made a maybe-yes/maybe-no gesture. "Stagger was gung ho, but he was also pretty good about leaving us alone. He respected that Rinsky and I were running the investigation. The only thing we let him do was run down that fingerprint hit, but by then, we already had Leburne dead to rights."

Kat felt a small tingle in the base of her spine. "Wait, what fingerprint?"

"It was nothing. A dead end."

She put a hand on his sleeve. "Are you talking about the fingerprint found at the murder scene?"

"Yep."

Kat couldn't believe what she was hearing. "I thought you never got a hit on it."

"Not while the case was live. It was no big deal, Kat. We got an ID a few months after Leburne confessed, but the case was already closed."

"So you just let it go?"

He looked crestfallen by her question. "You know Rinsky and me better than that. No stone unturned, right?"

"Right."

"Like I said, Stagger checked it out for us. Turns out it was some homeless guy who offed himself. A dead end."

Kat just stood there.

"I don't like the expression on your face, Kat."

"The fingerprints," she said. "Would they still be in the file?"

"I guess so. I mean, sure. It would be in the warehouse by now, but maybe—"

"We need to run them again," Kat said.

"I'm telling you. It's nothing."

"Then do it for me, okay? As a favor. To shut me up, if nothing else."

Across the room, the speaker finished up. The crowd applauded. The tuba started up. The rest of the band followed.

"Suggs?"

He didn't reply. He left her alone then, winding his way through the crowd. His friends called out to him. He ignored them and headed toward the exit.

20

BRANDON needed to walk it out.

His mom would be proud of that. Like every parent, Brandon's mom bemoaned the time her child spent in front of screens—computers, televisions, smartphones, video games, whatever. It was a constant battle. His dad had understood better. "Every generation has something like this," he'd tell Brandon's mother. Mom would throw her hands up. "So we just surrender? We let him stay in that dark cage all day?" "No," Dad would counter, "but we put it in perspective."

Dad was good at that. Putting things in perspective. Offering a calming influence on friends and family. In this case, Dad would explain it to Brandon like this: Way back when, parents would bemoan the lazy child who always had their nose in a book, telling the child they should get out more, that they should experience life instead of reading about it.

"Sound familiar?" Dad would say to Brandon.

Brandon would nod his head.

Then Dad said, when he was growing up, his parents were always yelling at him to turn off the television and either get outside or—and this was kind of funny when you remember the past—read a book instead.

Brandon remembered how his dad had smiled when he told him that.

"But, Brandon, do you know what the key is?"

"No. What?"

"Balance."

Brandon hadn't really understood what he meant at the time. He'd been only thirteen. Maybe he would have pressed the point if he had known that his father would be dead three years later. But no matter. He got it now. Doing any one thing—even something fun—for too long isn't good for you.

So the problem with taking long walks outside or any of that nature stuff was, well, it was boring. The worlds online may be virtual, but they were constant stimuli in constant flux. You saw, you experienced, you reacted. It never bored. It never got old because it was always changing. You were always engrossed.

Conversely, walking like this—in the wooded area of Central Park called the Ramble—was blah. He looked for birds—according to the web, the Ramble "boasted" (that was the word the website used) approximately 230 bird species. Right now, there were zero. There were sycamores and oaks and plenty of flowers and fauna. No birds. So what was the big deal about walking through trees?

He could, he guessed, understand walking through city streets a little better. At least there was stuff to see—stores and people and cars, maybe someone fighting over a taxi or arguing over a parking spot. Action, at least. The woods? Green leaves and some flowers? Nice for a minute or two, but then, well, Dullsville.

So no, Brandon wasn't walking through this Manhattan woodland because he suddenly had an appreciation for the great outdoors or fresh air or any of that stuff. He did it because walking like this bored him. It bored him silly.

Balance for the constant stimuli.

More than that, boredom was a kind of thinking tank. It fed you. Brandon didn't take walks in the woods to calm himself or get in tune with nature. He did it because the boredom forced him to look inward, to think hard, to concentrate solely on his own thoughts because nothing around him was worthy of his attention.

Certain problems cannot be solved if you are constantly entertained and distracted.

Still, Brandon couldn't help it. He had his smartphone with him. He had called Kat, but the call had gone to her voice mail. He never left messages on voice mail—only old people did that—so he sent her a text to call him when she could. No rush. At least, not yet. He wanted to digest what he had just learned.

He stayed on the winding pathways. He was surprised at how few people he saw. Here he was in the heart of Manhattan, ambling between 73rd and 78th streets (again according to the website—he really had no idea where he was), and he felt virtually alone. He was missing school, but that couldn't be helped. He had let Jayme Ratner, his lab partner, know that he was currently out of commission. She was okay with it. Her last lab partner had had something like a nervous breakdown last semester, so she was just happy he wasn't down at mental health like, it seemed, half their friends were.

His cell phone rang. The caller ID read Bork Investments. He answered.

"Hello?"

A woman's voice asked, "Is this Mr. Brandon Phelps?"

"Yes."

"Please hold for Martin Bork."

The hold music was an instrumental version of "Blurred Lines." Then: "Well, hello, Brandon."

"Hello, Uncle Marty."

"Nice to hear from you, son. How's school?"

"It's fine."

"Wonderful. Do you have plans for the summer?"

"Not yet."

"No rush. Am I right? Enjoy it. That's my advice. You'll be out in the real world soon enough. You hear what I'm saying?"

Martin Bork was nice enough, but all adults, when they start with the life advice, sound like blowhards. "I do, yes."

"So I got your message, Brandon." All business now. "What can I do for you?"

The pathway started down toward the Lake. Brandon got off it and moved closer to the water's edge. "It's about my mother's account."

There was silence at the other end of the line. Brandon pressed on.

"I see she made a pretty big withdrawal."

"How did you see that?" Bork asked.

Brandon didn't like the change in tone. "Pardon?"

"While I won't confirm or deny what you just said, how did you see this supposed withdrawal?"

"Online."

More silence.

"I have her password, if that's what you're worried about."

"Brandon, do you have any questions about your own account?"

He moved away from the Lake and started over the stream. "No."

"Then I'm afraid that I have to go now."

"There's nearly a quarter of a million dollars missing from my mother's account."

"I assure you that nothing is missing. If you have any questions about your mother's account, perhaps it is best if you ask her."

"You talked to her? She approved this transaction?"

"I can't say any more, Brandon. I hope you understand. But talk to your mother. Good-bye."

Martin Bork hung up.

In something of a daze, Brandon stumbled over the old stone arch into a more secluded area. The vegetation was denser up here. He finally spotted a bird—a red cardinal. He remembered reading that the Cherokees believed cardinals were daughters of the sun. If the bird flew up toward the sun, it was good luck. If the bird chose to fly downward, well, obviously the opposite would be true.

Brandon stood transfixed and waited for the cardinal to make his move.

That was why he never heard the man lurking behind him until it was too late.

*   *   *

CHAZ, her soon-to-be ex-partner, called Kat's cell phone. "I got it."

"Got what?"

Kat had just gotten out of the Lincoln Center subway station, which smelled decidedly like piss, and onto 66th Street, which smelled almost as decidedly like cherry blossoms. Kat ♥ New York. A text from Brandon had been waiting for her. She called, but there was no answer, so she left a brief voice mail.

"You were trying to put in a request for a surveillance video," Chaz said. "It came in."

"Hold up. How did that happen?"

"You know how that happened, Kat."

She did, bizarre as it was. Chaz had put in the request for her. The only consistent thing she understood about people was that they are never consistent. "You could get in trouble," Kat said.

"Trouble is my middle name," he said. "Actually, my middle name is Hung Stallion. Did you tell your hot friend I'm rich?"

Yep. Consistent. "Chaz."

"Right, sorry. Do you want me to e-mail you the video?"

"That'd be great, thanks."

"Were you trying to see what car that lady got in?"

"You watched the tape?"

"That was okay, right? I'm still your partner."

Fair point, Kat thought.

"Who is she?"

"Her name is Dana Phelps. That was her son who

came to see me the other day. He thinks she's missing. No one believes him."

"Including you?"

"I'm somewhat more open-minded."

"Could you tell me why?"

"It's a long story," Kat said. "Can it wait?"

"Yeah, I guess."

"So did Dana Phelps get in a car?"

"She did," Chaz said. "More specifically, a black Lincoln Town Car stretch limo."

"Was the driver wearing a black cap and suit?"

"Yes."

"License plate?"

"Well, here's the thing. The bank video didn't pick up his plates. The guy kept the car on the street. Hard enough to figure out the make."

"Damn."

"Well, no, not really," Chaz said.

"How's that?"

Chaz cleared his throat, more for effect than need. "I checked Google Earth and saw that there was an Exxon station two stores down in the direction the guy was driving. I made a few calls. The gas station surveillance video captures the street."

Most people understand on some level that there are a lot of surveillance cameras out there, but very few people really get it. There are forty million surveillance cameras in the United States alone and the number keeps growing. You never go through a day without being recorded.

"Anyway," Chaz said, "the request may take another hour or two, but when we get it, we should be able to spot the license plate."

"Great."

"I'll call you when it comes. Let me know if you need anything else."

"Okay," Kat said. Then: "Chaz?"

"Yeah?"

"I appreciate this. I mean, you know, uh, thanks."

"Can I have your hot friend's phone number?"

Kat hung up. Her phone rang again. The caller ID read Brandon Phelps.

"Hey, Brandon."

But the voice on the other end wasn't Brandon's. "May I ask with whom I'm speaking?"

"You called me," Kat reminded him. "Hey, who is this? What's going on?"

"This is Officer John Glass," the man on the phone said. "I'm calling about Brandon Phelps."

CENTRAL Park's 840 acres is policed by the 22nd Precinct, the city's oldest, better known as the Central Park Precinct. Kat's father had spent eight years there in the seventies. Back then, the officers of the "two-two" were housed in an old horse stable. They still were, in a way, though a sixty-one-million-dollar renovation had given the place maybe too much of a new shine. The precinct now looked more like a museum for modern art than anything to do with law enforcement. In a typically New York City move—that is, you didn't know if it was for real or a joke—the rather impressive glass atrium had been built out of bulletproof glass. The original estimate called for the renovation to cost almost twenty million less, but in what one might also consider classically Manhattan style, the builders had unexpectedly run across old trolley tracks.

The old ghosts never quite leave this city.

Kat hurried to the front desk and asked for Officer Glass. The desk sergeant pointed at a slender black man behind her. Officer Glass was in uniform. She might have known him—Central Park Precinct was pretty close to her own 19th—but she couldn't be sure.

Glass was talking to two elderly gentlemen who looked as though they'd just come from a gin tournament in Miami Beach. One wore a fedora and used a cane. The other wore a light blue jacket and trousers the orange of a mango. Glass was taking notes. As Kat approached, she heard him tell the two old men that they could go now.

"You have our numbers, right?" Fedora asked.

"I do, thank you."

"You call us if you need us," Mango Pants said.

"I'll do that. And again, thanks for your help."

When they started away, Glass spotted her and said, "Hey, Kat."

"We know each other?"

"Not really, but my old man worked here with your old man. Your dad was a legend."

You become a legend, Kat knew, by dying on the job. "So where's Brandon?"

"He's with the doctor in the back room. He wouldn't let us take him to a hospital."

"Can I see him?"

"Sure, follow me."

"How badly was he hurt?"

Glass shrugged. "Would have been a lot worse if it hadn't been for those two reliving their youth." He gestured toward the two old men, Fedora and Mango Pants, slowly exiting the atrium.

"How's that?"

"You know about the Ramble's, uh, flamboyant past, right?"

She nodded. Even the official Central Park website referred to the Ramble as a "gay icon" and a "well-known site for private homosexual encounters throughout the twentieth century." Back in the day, the dense vegetation and poor lighting made it perfect for so-called gay cruising. More recently, the Ramble had become not only the park's premier woodland but something of a historical landmark for the LGBT community.

"Seems those two guys met in the Ramble fifty years ago," Glass said. "So today they decided to celebrate their anniversary by going behind the old bushes and engaging in a little, uh, nostalgia."

"In the daytime?"

"Yep."

"Wow."

"They told me that, at their age, it's hard to stay up late anymore. Or even up, I guess. So anyway, they were whatevering and they heard a commotion. They ran out—I don't want to know in what stage of undress—and saw some 'homeless guy' attacking your boy."

"How did they know he was homeless?"

"That was their description, not mine. It looks like the perp sneaked up on Brandon and punched him in the face. No warning, nothing. One of our witnesses said he saw a knife. The other said he didn't, so I don't know. Nothing was stolen—there was probably no time—but this was either a robbery or some guy off his meds. Maybe an old-fashioned gay basher, though I doubt that. Despite the actions of Romeo and, uh, Romeo, the Ramble isn't known for that anymore, especially not in the daytime."

Glass opened the door. Brandon was sitting on a table, talking to the doctor. There was tape across his nose. He looked pale and skinny, but then again, he always looked that way.

The doctor turned toward Kat. "Are you his mother?"

Brandon smiled at that. For a moment, Kat was insulted, but then she realized that, first off, she was indeed old enough to have a son his age—wow, that was depressing—and second, his actual mom probably looked younger than Kat. Double depressing.

"No. Just a friend."

"I'd like him to go to the hospital," the doctor said to Kat.

"I'm fine," Brandon said.

"His nose is broken, for one thing. I also believe that he probably suffered some sort of concussion in the assault."

Kat looked over at Brandon. Brandon just shook his head.

"I'll look after him," Kat said.

The doctor shrugged his surrender and headed out the door. Glass helped them with the rest of the paperwork. Brandon never saw his attacker. He didn't seem to care much, either. He hurried through the paperwork. "I have something I need to tell you," he whispered when Glass stepped away.

"Let's concentrate first on what just happened, okay?"

"You heard Officer Glass. It was a random attack."

Kat wasn't buying that. Random? Now, when they were in the throes of . . .

Of what?

There was still no evidence to suggest any crimes were taking place. Besides, what other theories were there?

Had the black-suited chauffeur disguised himself as a homeless man and followed Brandon into the Ramble? That made no sense either.

When Glass walked them back into the bulletproof atrium, Kat asked him to let her know the moment they learned anything.

"Will do," Glass promised.

He shook both of their hands. Brandon thanked him, still in a rush to get outside. He sprinted away from the front door. Kat followed him up to the huge body of water—it took up an eighth of the park—called the Jacqueline Kennedy Onassis Reservoir. Yes, for real.

Brandon checked his watch. "There's still time."

"For what?"

"To get down to Wall Street."

"Why?"

"Someone is stealing my mother's money."

21

KAT didn't want to go.

Bork Investments was located in a sleek über-skyscraper on Vesey Street and the Hudson River in Manhattan's Financial District, a stone's throw away from the new World Trade Center. Kat had been a fairly young officer on that bright, sunny morning, but that wasn't much of an excuse. When the first tower was hit at 8:46 A.M., she was sleeping one off only eight blocks away. By the time she woke up and fought through her hangover and got down there, both towers were down and it was too late to do anything about the dead, especially her fellow officers. Many who died had come down on their own from a lot farther away. She hadn't made it in time.

Not that she could have done anything anyway.

No one could in the end. But the survivor's guilt

stayed with her. She attended every cop funeral she
could, standing there in uniform, feeling like a complete
fraud. There were nightmares—almost everyone who
was there that day had them. In life, you can forgive
yourself for a lot, but for reasons that made very little
rational sense, it is very hard to forgive yourself for sur-
viving.

It was a long time ago. She didn't think about it much
anymore, maybe around the anniversary. That outraged
her on another level, the way time does indeed heal
wounds. But since that day, Kat stayed away from this
area, not that there was much reason for her to come
down here anyway. This was the land of the dead, the
ghosts, and the power suits with the big money. There
was nothing here for her. Lots of the boys from her old
neighborhood—yes, some girls too, but far fewer—had
made their way here. As children, they had admired and
feared their cop and firemen fathers and grew up wanting
to be nothing like them. They went to St. Francis Prep
and then to Notre Dame or Holy Cross, ended up selling
junk bonds or derivatives, making a lot of money and
getting as far away from their upbringing and roots as
they could—just as their fathers had run from their fathers, who had toiled in mills or starved in lands far away.

Progress.

We have this sense of continuity and nostalgia in
America, but in truth, every generation runs away from
the one before it. Oddly enough, most of the time, they
run to someplace better.

Judging by his plush office, Martin Bork had run to
someplace better. Kat and Brandon waited in a confer-
ence room with a mahogany table the size of a landing
strip. There was a food spread waiting—muffins, donuts,

fruit salad. Brandon was starving and started wolfing down the food.

"How do you know him again?" Kat asked.

"He's our family financial adviser. He worked with my dad at a hedge fund."

Kat didn't know exactly what a hedge fund was, but the phrase never failed to make her cringe a little. She checked out the view of the Hudson River and New Jersey in the distance. One of those mega cruise ships floated north toward the piers off Twelfth Avenue, in the fifties. Passengers on deck waved. Even though there was no way they could see into this building, Kat waved back.

Martin Bork entered the room and gave a tight "Good afternoon."

Kat had expected Bork to be some fat cat with plump fingers, a tight collar, and a stroke red flush in his skin. Wrong. Bork was short and wiry, almost like a bantam-weight boxer, with olive-toned skin. She guessed his age at a youthful fifty. He wore funky designer glasses that would probably have worked better on a younger guy. There was a smoothness to his face that indicated some kind of cosmetic treatment, and a diamond stud in his left ear that traveled quickly from hip to desperate.

Bork's mouth dropped open when he saw Brandon. "My God, what happened to your face?"

"I'm fine," Brandon said.

"You don't look fine to me." He started toward him. "Did someone hit you?"

"He's fine," Kat assured him, not wanting to get off track here. "Just a minor accident."

Bork looked dubious, but there was nowhere else to go with this. "Let's sit."

He took the seat at the head of the table. Kat and Brandon grabbed the two chairs closest to him. It felt weird, three people at a table that could probably hold thirty.

Bork spoke to Kat first. "I'm not sure why you're here, Miss . . . ?"

"Donovan. Detective Donovan. NYPD."

"Yes, sorry about that. I don't quite understand why you're a part of this, though. Are you here in some official capacity?"

"Not yet," she said. "This is more informal."

"I see." Bork put both hands together in a prayer gesture. He did not bother looking at Brandon. "And I assume that this has something to do with Brandon's call to me earlier today."

"We understand that a quarter of a million dollars had been removed from his mother's account."

"Do you have a warrant, Detective?"

"I do not."

"Then not only am I under no obligation to talk to you, but it would be unethical to say more."

Kat hadn't really thought this through. She had come down here buoyed by Brandon's enthusiasm for his money discovery. Since the ATM withdrawal, there had been no activity on Dana Phelps's credit cards or checking accounts. But yesterday, she had made a "wire transaction"—that was how it was listed on the online statement—for approximately $250,000.

"You know the Phelps family, correct?"

Bork still had the prayer position going. Now he leaned it against his nose as though this were a tough question. "Very well."

"You were friends with Brandon's father."

A shadow crossed his face. His voice was suddenly soft: "Yes."

"In fact," Kat said, weighing her own words before letting them out, "of all the people the Phelpses could have trusted to handle their affairs, you were the one the family chose. That says a great deal not just for your business acumen—let's face it, there is no shortage of supposed geniuses down here—but my guess is that they chose you because they trusted you. Because you cared about their well-being."

Martin Bork let his eyes slide over to Brandon. Brandon just stared back at him. "I care about them very much."

"And you know that Brandon and his mother are close."

"I do. But that doesn't mean that she shares all of her fiduciary matters with him."

"Yes, she does," Brandon said, trying to keep the whine out of his voice. "That's why she gave me the passwords and account numbers. We don't keep secrets like that."

"He has a point," Kat added. "If his mother wanted to transfer money without his knowledge, wouldn't she have used another account?"

"I can't say," Bork said. "Perhaps Brandon should call her."

"Did you?" Kat asked.

"Pardon?"

"Before you made the transaction. Did you call Mrs. Phelps?"

"She called me," he said.

"When?"

"I'm not at liberty to discuss—"

"Could you call her now?" Kat asked. "I mean, just to double-check."

"What's going on here?"

"Just call her, okay?"

"What will that prove?"

"Uncle Marty?" All eyes turned to Brandon. "I haven't heard from her in five days. It's like she just disappeared."

Bork gave Brandon a look that aimed to be sympathetic but landed firmly in the patronizing camp. "Don't you think it's time to cut the apron strings, Brandon? Your mother has been lonely for a long time."

"I know that," Brandon snapped. "Don't you think I know that?"

"I'm sorry." Bork started to rise. "For reasons both legal and ethical, I can't help you."

So much for trying the nice route. "Sit down, Mr. Bork."

He stopped midrise and looked at her, stunned. "Excuse me?"

"Brandon, wait out in the hall."

"But—"

"Go," Kat said.

She didn't need to tell him twice. Brandon was out the door, leaving Kat alone with Martin Bork. Bork was still half standing, his mouth agape.

"I said sit down."

"Are you out of your mind?" Bork asked. "I'll have your badge."

"Yeah, that's a good one. The badge threat. Are you going to call the mayor or my immediate superior? I love both of those lines too." She gestured to the phone. "Call Dana Phelps right now."

"I'm not taking orders from you."

"Do you really think I'm here as a favor to her kid? This is an ongoing investigation into a dangerous series of crimes."

"Then show me a warrant."

"You don't want a warrant, believe me. You see, warrants require judges and then we have to go through everything, every file in your office, every account—"

"You can't do that."

True. It was a bluff, but what the hell? Better to come off a little crazy, a little unhinged. Kat lifted the receiver. "I'm asking you to make one call."

Bork hesitated for a moment. Then he took out his smartphone, found Dana Phelps's mobile number, and dialed it. Kat heard it ring once and then the voice mail picked up. Dana Phelps's happy voice asked the caller to leave a brief message. Bork hung up.

"She's probably on the beach," he said.

"Where?"

"I'm not at liberty to discuss it."

"Your client transferred a quarter of a million dollars out of this country."

"Which is her right."

Realizing he'd said too much, Bork blanched as soon as the words came out of his mouth. Kat nodded at the mistake. So the money had been sent out of the country. She hadn't known that.

"It was completely on the up-and-up," Bork said, his explanation coming fast. "This company has a protocol with a transfer this substantial. Perhaps in the movies, it can be done with just a few clicks on a computer. But not here. Dana Phelps made the request. I personally spoke to her on the phone about it."

"When?"

"Yesterday."

"Do you know where she called from?"

"No. But she called from her own cell phone. I don't understand. What do you think happened here?"

Kat wasn't sure how to answer. "I can't reveal the full extent of my investigation."

"And I can't tell you anything without Dana's permission. She gave me strict instructions to keep this confidential."

Kat cocked her head. "Didn't you find that odd?"

"What? Keeping things confidential?" Bork considered that. "Not in this case."

"How so?"

"It isn't my job to judge. It is my job to honor the request. Now if you'll excuse me . . ."

But Kat still had one major card to play. "I assume you reported this transaction to FinCEN."

Bork stiffened. Pay dirt, Kat thought. FinCEN stood for the Financial Crimes Enforcement Network, a scary division of the Department of the Treasury. FinCEN looks at suspicious financial activity in the hopes of combating money laundering, terrorism, fraud, tax evasion, stuff like that.

"A transaction this big," Kat said. "It has to send up a red flag, don't you think?"

Bork tried to play it cool. "I have no reason to suspect that Dana Phelps has done anything illegal."

"Okay, then you won't mind me calling Max."

"Max?"

"He's my pal with FinCEN. I mean, if everything is on the up-and-up—"

"It is."

"Cool." She took out her cell phone. It was another bluff, but an effective one. There was no Max at FinCEN, but then, how hard would it be to report something like this to the Department of the Treasury? She smiled now, trying again to look a bit unhinged. "I got nothing else, so I might as well—"

"There's no need for that."

"Oh?"

"Dana . . ." He looked at the door. "I'm betraying a trust here."

"You can explain it to me," Kat said, "or you can explain it to Max and his team. Up to you."

Bork started to bite on his manicured thumbnail. "Dana asked for confidentiality here."

"To cover up a crime?"

"What? No." Bork leaned forward and spoke softly. "Off the record?"

"Sure."

Off the record. Did he think she was a reporter?

"Her transaction, I admit, is rather unconventional. We may indeed file an SAR, though I have thirty days to do it."

SAR stood for Suspicious Activity Report. By law, a transaction of this size out of the country should require that the financial institution or individual notify the Department of the Treasury. It isn't written in stone, but the large majority of honest institutions would do it.

"Dana asked for a little time first."

"What do you mean?"

"Again nothing illegal."

"Then?"

He looked toward the corridor. "You can't tell Brandon this."

"Okay."

"I mean it. Dana Phelps specifically requested that no one, especially her son, know about her plans."

Kat leaned in closer. "My lips are sealed."

"I wouldn't be telling you any of this—in fact, I *shouldn't* be—but my job is also to protect my clients and my business. I don't know what Dana would say, but my feeling is that she would not want her confidential wire transfer—one that her child should have never seen, by the way—scrutinized by the Department of the Treasury. Not because it is illegal. But because that could present a host of problems and attention."

Kat waited. Bork wasn't really talking to her right now. He was talking to himself, trying to find a justification to give her information.

"Dana Phelps is buying a house."

Kat wasn't sure what she was expecting him to say, but that wasn't it. "What?"

"In Costa Rica. Five-bedroom beach villa on the Peninsula Papagayo. Stunning. Right on the Pacific Ocean. The man she's traveling with? He proposed."

Kat just sat there. The word *proposed* turned into a stone and dropped down some internal mine shaft. She could see it all—the gorgeous stretch of beach, the coconut trees (were there coconut trees in Costa Rica? Kat didn't know), Jeff and Dana strolling hand in hand, a gentle kiss, lounging together on a hammock as the sun set in the distance.

"You have to understand," Bork continued. "Dana has not had it easy since her husband's death. She raised Brandon by herself. He wasn't an easy kid. His father's death . . . it really affected him. I won't get into more details than that, but now that Brandon's in college, well,

Dana is ready for a life of her own. You can understand that, I'm sure."

Kat's head spun. She tried to push away thoughts of a life in a beach villa and concentrated on the task at hand. What had the last text Dana sent her son said again? Something about having a great time and a big surprise . . .

"Anyway, Dana is getting married. She and her new husband may even decide to move down there permanently. Naturally, this is not news she wants to break to Brandon over the phone. That's why she's been incommunicado."

Kat said nothing, still trying to process. A proposal. A beach villa. Not wanting to tell her son on the phone. Did all that add up?

It did.

"So Dana Phelps, what, wired the money to the homeowner?"

"No, she transferred the money to herself. The real estate transaction involves some complicated local issues that require a level of discretion. It isn't my job to pry further than that. Dana opened a legal account in Switzerland and wired money from another account to fund it."

"She opened a Swiss bank account in her name?"

"Which is perfectly legal." Then: "But no, not in her name."

"Whose name, then?"

Bork was working on that manicured thumbnail again. It was amazing how all men, no matter how successful, still have the little-boy insecurity in them. Finally, he said, "No name."

She understood now. "A numbered account?"

"It isn't as dramatic as it sounds. Most Swiss accounts are numbered. Are you at all familiar with them?"

She sat back. "Pretend I'm not."

"Numbered accounts are pretty much just what you think—they have a number associated with the account instead of a name. This gives you a great deal of privacy— not just for criminals, but even the most honest people who don't want their financial situations known. Your money is safe and secure."

"And secret?"

"To some degree, yes. But not like it used to be. The United States government now can, and does, find out about the account. Everyone looks out for criminal wrongdoing and has to report it. And the secrecy only goes so far. Many people foolishly believe that no one knows whose numbered account belongs to whom. That's ridiculous, of course. Select employees of the bank know."

"Mr. Bork?"

"Yes."

"I'd like the bank name and number."

"It won't do you any good. Even I can't say for sure what name is associated with that number. If you some- how take out a warrant for information, the Swiss bank will tie you up for years. So if you want to prosecute Dana Phelps for some petty crime—"

"I have no interest in prosecuting Dana Phelps. You have my word on that."

"Then what's this all about?"

"Give me the number, Mr. Bork."

"And if I don't?"

She lifted her phone. "I can still call Max."

22

ON the way out, Kat called Chaz and gave him the Swiss bank and account number. She could almost hear his frown over the phone.

"What the hell do you want me to do with it?" Chaz asked.

"I don't know. It's a new account. Maybe we can find out if there's any new activity on it."

"You're joking, right? An NYPD cop asking for information from a major Swiss bank?"

He had a point. This was indeed the long shot of all long shots. "Just send the number to Treasury. I got a source named Ali Oscar. If anyone issues an SAR or whatever in the future, maybe it will get a hit."

"Yeah, okay. Got it."

Brandon was oddly quiet on the subway back uptown. Kat had expected him to be all over her, demanding to know why he had had to leave and what Martin Bork had told her. He hadn't. He sat in the subway car, deflated, shoulders slumped. He let his body sway and rock without putting up the least resistance.

Kat sat next to him. She imagined her own body language wasn't much better. She let the truth sink in slowly. Jeff had proposed. Or should she call him Ron now? She hated the name Ron. Jeff was a Jeff. He wasn't a Ron. Did people really call him that now? Like "Hey, Ron!" Or "Look, there goes Ronnie!" Or "Yo, it's Ronald, the Ronster, Ronamama . . ."

Why the hell choose the name Ron?

Dumb thoughts, but there you go. It kept her mind off the obvious. Eighteen years was a long time. Old Jeff had been so antimaterialistic back in the day, but New Ron was crazy in love with an überrich widow who was buying him a house in Costa Rica. She made a face. Like he was her boy toy or something. Ugh.

When they first met, Jeff was renting this wonderful craphole overlooking Washington Square. His mattress had been on the floor. There was always noise. The pipes shrieked through the walls when they weren't leaking. The place always looked like a bomb had just exploded in it. When Jeff was writing a story, he'd get every photograph he could on the subject and randomly thumbtack them to the walls. There was no organization to the process. The mess, he said, inspired him. It looked, Kat countered, like when the cops on TV break into the killer's hidden room and find pictures of the victims everywhere.

But it felt so right with him. Everything—from the smallest, most mundane activity to the crescendo, if you will, of making love—felt true and perfect with him. She missed that wonderful craphole. She missed the mess and the photographs on the wall.

God, how she had loved him.

They got off on 66th Street near Lincoln Center. There was a chill in the night air. Brandon still seemed lost in his thoughts. She let him stay there. When they got back to Kat's apartment—she really didn't think it would be good for him to be on his own right now—she asked, "Are you hungry?"

Brandon shrugged. "Guess so."

"I'll order a pizza," Kat said. "Pepperoni okay?"

Brandon nodded. He collapsed into a chair and stared at the window. Kat called La Traviata Pizzeria and placed the order. She took the chair across from him.

"You're awfully quiet, Brandon."

"I was just thinking," he said.

"About?"

"My dad's funeral."

Kat waited. When he didn't say anything more, Kat prodded gently. "What about it?"

"I was thinking about Uncle Marty's—that's what I call Mr. Bork—I was thinking about his eulogy. Not so much what he said, though it was really nice, but what I remember most was when it was over, he kinda rushed out of the chapel or whatever you call it. So he finished and he hurried out. I followed him. I don't know. I was still blocking on the whole thing. It was like I was just at some service and I was removed and it had nothing to do with me. Does that make any sense?"

Kat remembered the numbness at her own father's funeral. "Sure."

"Anyway, I found him in some back office. The lights were out. I could barely see him, but I could hear him. I guess he held it together for the eulogy but lost it after. Uncle Marty was on his knees and crying his eyes out. I just stood in the doorway. He didn't know I was watching him. He thought he was alone."

Brandon looked up at Kat.

"Uncle Marty told you that my mother called him, right?"

"Right."

"He wouldn't lie about that."

Not sure what else to say, Kat went with "That's good to know."

"Did he tell you why she moved the money?"

"Yes."

"But you're not going to tell me."

"He said your mother asked for confidentiality."

Brandon kept his eyes on the window.

"Brandon?"

"My mom dated another guy. Not someone she met online. He lived in Westport."

"When was this?"

Brandon shrugged. "Maybe two years after my father died. His name was Charles Reed. He was divorced. He had two kids who lived with their mom in Stamford. He got them on the weekends and some night during the week. I don't know."

"So what happened?"

"Me," Brandon said. "I happened." A strange smile came to his face. "When you visited Detective Schwartz, did he tell you I'd been arrested?"

"He said there had been some incidents."

"Yeah, well, they cut me a lot of slack, I guess. See, I didn't want my mom dating anyone. I kept picturing, you know, this guy taking over for my dad—living in my dad's house, sleeping on his side of the bed, using my dad's closet and drawers, parking his car in my dad's spot. You know what I mean?"

"Of course," Kat said. "Those feelings are natural."

"So that's when I started 'acting out' "—he made finger quotes—"as my therapist used to say. I got suspended from school. I slashed a neighbor's tires. When the police would bring me home, I'd be smiling. I wanted her to suffer. I'd tell my mom it was all her fault. I'd tell her I was doing this because she was betraying my father." He blinked hard and rubbed his chin. "One night, I called her a whore."

"What did she do?"

"Nothing," Brandon said with a faraway chuckle. "She didn't say a word. She just stood there and stared at me. I will never forget the look on her face. Never. But it didn't stop me. I just kept at it until, well, Charles Reed was gone."

Kat leaned toward him. "Why are you telling me this now?"

"Because I blew that for her. He was a nice enough guy, I guess. Maybe he would have made her happy. So I'm asking you, Kat. Am I doing that to her again?" Brandon turned and met her gaze. "Am I screwing this up for my mom, like I did last time?"

Kat tried to step back and look at it like, well, a detective. What did they really have? A mother goes away and doesn't contact her son. If that had been out of character or unusual, hadn't Martin Bork clarified her reasons for that? As for the ATM transaction and surveillance tape, what had Kat really found? A black limousine and a driver waiting for her—which perfectly fit into the explanation Dana Phelps had given her regular limo company: Her boyfriend had sent the limousine for her.

Take another cold, hard step back: What evidence did they have that Dana Phelps was in trouble?

None.

Brandon was a scared kid. He had loved his father and felt that his mother dating other men was a betrayal. Naturally, he would twist what he saw into some kind of conspiracy.

So what was Kat's excuse?

Sure, some of Jeff's behavior might be considered bizarre. But so what? He had changed his name and was living his life. He had made it clear that he didn't want to go back to the past. Kat had been hurt. So, naturally, she too saw conspiracy rather than rejection. The past—her father, her ex-fiancé—was all coming back at her in a rush.

There was nothing more to discuss. It was time to put this behind her. If the man Dana Phelps ran off with had been someone other than Jeff, she would have let this go a long time ago. The problem—a problem she had really never wanted to face—was she had never let Jeff go. Yes, this thought was a corny "ugh," but in her heart (if not her mind) it had been because they were somehow destined to be together, that life would take some weird twists and turns, but somehow—and no, she never consciously thought this—she and Jeff would end up back together. But now, sitting on the floor, eating pizza with Brandon, Kat realized there was probably more to it. Yes, it had been a period of her life of so much upheaval, so much raw, concentrated emotion, but more than that, it had all been cut off before its time. It felt incomplete.

Falling in love, the murder of her father, the breakup,

the capture of the murderer—all of it demanded some sort of closure, but she never got it. In her heart, when she looked past all the ridiculous lies she'd told herself, Kat had never really understood why Jeff ended it. She had never understood why her father was murdered or why she had never believed that Cozone ordered a hit carried out by Leburne. Her life hadn't just taken detours or even gone off the rails. It was as though the rails had vanished beneath her.

A person needs answers. A person needs them to make some kind of sense.

They finished the pizza in record time. Brandon was still groggy from the earlier assault. She blew up the air mattress and gave him some pain meds she had picked up at the twenty-four-hour pharmacy. He fell asleep quickly. She watched him for a while, wondering how he would handle his mother's upcoming big news.

Kat slipped under the covers of her bed. She tried to read, but it was pointless. The words on the page swam by in a meaningless haze. She put the book away and lay in the dark. Concentrate on the possible, she thought. Dana Phelps and "Ron Kochman" were beyond her reach.

The truth about her father's murder, even after eighteen years, still needed to be unearthed. Focus on that.

Kat closed her eyes and fell into a deep black sleep. When her phone rang, it took some time to swim back up to consciousness. She reached blindly for her phone and put it to her ear.

"Hello?"

"Hey, Kat. It's John Glass."

She was still groggy. The digital clock read 3:18 A.M. "Who?"

"Officer Glass from the Central Park Precinct."

"Oh, right, sorry. You know that it's three in the morning, right?"

"Yeah, well, I'm an insomniac."

"Yeah, well, I'm not," Kat said.

"We caught the guy who assaulted Brandon Phelps. Just as we suspected. He's homeless. No ID on him. He won't talk."

"I appreciate the update, but I'm thinking it could have waited until the morning."

"Normally, I'd agree," Glass said, "except for one weird thing."

"What's that?"

"The homeless guy."

"What about him?" Kat asked.

"He's asking for you."

KAT threw on workout clothes, wrote Brandon a note in case he woke up, and jogged north the twenty blocks to the Central Park Precinct. John Glass met her at the front door, still in uniform.

"You want to explain?" he said to her.

"Explain what?"

"Why he asked for you."

"Maybe I should see who he is first?"

He spread his hand. "This way."

Their footsteps echoed through the near-empty bulletproof-glass atrium. From Glass's brief description on the phone, Kat had some idea of who would be waiting for her in the holding cell. When they arrived, Aqua was doing his tight-formation pace. His fingers plucked at his lower lip. It was an odd thing. Kat tried to remember the last time she had seen him in something other than yoga pants or at least women's clothes. She couldn't. But right now, Aqua wore beltless jeans that sagged like an insecure teenager's. His shirt was torn flannel. His oncewhite sneakers were a shade of brown you might achieve if you'd buried them in mud for a month.

"Do you know him?" Glass asked.

Kat nodded. "His real name is Dean Vanech, but everyone calls him Aqua."

Aqua kept pacing, arguing under his breath with some unseen foe. There was no sign that he had heard them enter.

"Any clue why he'd attack your boy?"

"None."

"Who's Jeff?" Glass asked.

Kat's head spun toward him. "What?"

"He keeps muttering about some guy named Jeff."

Kat shook her head, swallowed. "Can I have a few minutes alone with him?"

"Like for an interrogation?"

"He's an old friend."

"So, like his attorney?"

"I'm asking a favor, Glass. We'll do the right thing here. Don't worry."

Glass shrugged a "suit yourself" and left the room. The holding cells were made of Plexiglas rather than bars. The whole precinct was simply too sleek for her—more like a movie set than a real precinct. Kat took a step forward and knocked to get his attention. "Aqua?"

His pace picked up speed, as though he could outrun her.

She spoke a little louder. "Aqua?"

He stopped all at once and turned toward her. "I'm sorry, Kat."

"What's going on, Aqua?"

"You're mad at me."

He started to cry. She would have to take this slow or lose him completely.

"It's okay. I'm not mad. I just want to understand."

Aqua closed his eyes and sucked in a long deep breath. He released it and did it again. Breathing was, of course, a huge part of yoga. He seemed to be trying to center himself. Finally, he said, "I followed you."

"When?"

"After we talked. Remember? You went to O'Malley's. You wanted me to go too."

"But you didn't want to go in," she said.

"Right."

"Why?"

He shook his head. "Too many old ghosts in there, Kat."

"They were good times too, Aqua."

"And now they're dead and gone," he said. "Now they haunt us."

Kat needed him to stay on track here. "So you followed me."

"Right. You left with Stacy." He smiled for a moment. "I like Stacy. She's a gifted student."

Terrific, Kat thought. Even cross-dressing schizophrenic gay men found Stacy intoxicating. "You were following me?" she asked.

"Right. I changed and waited down the street. I wanted to talk to you some more or just—I don't know. I just wanted to make sure you got out of that place okay."

"Out of O'Malley's?"

"Of course."

"Aqua, I go to O'Malley's five days a week." She stopped herself. Track. Stay on track. "So you followed us."

He smiled and sang in his beautiful falsetto, "I am the walrus, koo kook kachoo."

Kat started putting some of it together. "You followed us into the park. To Strawberry Fields. You saw me talking to Brandon."

"Did more than see," he said.

"What do you mean?"

"I dress like this, I'm just another black guy to avoid. All eyes divert. Even yours, Kat."

She wanted to argue the point—defend her lack of prejudice and general goodwill toward all—but again, it was more important to keep him on track. "So what did you do, Aqua?"

"You were sitting on Elizabeth's bench."

"Who?"

He recited it from memory. "'The best days of my life—this bench, chocolate chip ice cream, and Daddy— Miss you always, Elizabeth.'"

"Oh."

She got it now, and despite herself, she welled up. Central Park has an Adopt-A-Bench program to raise funds. For seventy-five hundred dollars, a personalized plaque is installed on the bench. Kat spent many hours reading them, imagining the story behind them. One read ON THIS BENCH, WAYNE WILL ONE DAY PROPOSE MAR-RIAGE TO KIM (did he? Kat always wondered. Did she say yes?). Another favorite, near a dog park, read IN MEMORY OF LEO AND LASZLO, A GREAT MAN, HIS NOBLE HOUND, while yet another simply read REST YOUR TUSH HERE—IT'S ALL GOING TO BE OKAY.

Poignancy is found in the ordinary.

"I heard you," Aqua said, his voice rising. "I heard

you all talking." Something crossed his face. "Who is that boy?"

"His name is Brandon."

"I know that!" he shouted. "You think I don't know that? Who is he, Kat?"

"He's just a college student."

"So what are you doing with him?" He slammed his hands against the Plexiglas. "Huh? Why are you trying to help him?"

"Whoa." Kat stepped back, startled by his sudden aggression. "Don't turn this around, Aqua. This is about you. You attacked him."

"Of course, I attacked him. You think I'm going to let someone hurt him again?"

"Hurt who?" she asked, while a small voice in her head—because this is how crazy life could be—heard Stacy correcting her grammar with a gentle *hurt whom*.

Aqua said nothing.

"Who is Brandon trying to hurt?"

"You know," he said.

"No, I don't." But now she thought that maybe she did.

"I was hiding right there. You were sitting on Elizabeth's bench. I heard every word. I told you to leave him alone. Why didn't you listen?"

"Aqua?"

He closed his eyes.

"Look at me, Aqua."

He didn't.

She had to make him say it. She couldn't put the idea in his head first. "Who do you want us to leave alone? Who are you trying to protect?"

With his eyes still closed, Aqua said, "He protected me. He protected you."

"Who, Aqua?"

"Jeff."

There. Aqua had finally said it. Kat had expected that answer—had braced for it—but the blow still landed with enough force to knock her back a step.

"Kat?" Aqua pushed his face against the glass, his eyes shifting left and right to make sure no one could hear him. "We have to stop him. He's looking for Jeff."

"And that's why you attacked him?"

"I didn't want to hurt him. I just need him to stop. Don't you see?"

"I don't," Kat said. "What are you so afraid he'll find?"

"He never stopped loving you, Kat."

She let that one go. "Did you know that Jeff changed his name?"

Aqua turned away.

"He's Ron Kochman now. Did you know that?"

"So much death," Aqua said. "It should have been me."

"What should have been you?"

"I should have died." Tears ran down his face in free fall. "Then it would all be okay. You'd be with Jeff."

"What are you talking about, Aqua?"

"I'm talking about what I did."

"What did you do, Aqua?"

He kept crying. "It's all my fault."

"You had nothing to do with Jeff breaking up with me." More tears.

"Aqua? What did you do?"

He started to sing. "The gypsy wind it says to me, things are not what they seem to be. Beware."

"What?"

He smiled through the tears. "It's like that old song. You remember. The one about the demon lover. The boyfriend dies and so she marries someone else, but she still loves him, only him, and then one day, his ghost comes back to her and they drive away and burst into flames."

"Aqua, I don't know what you're talking about."

But there was something about the song that was familiar. She just couldn't place it. . . .

"The last lines," Aqua said. "You have to listen to the last lines. After they burst into flames. You have to listen to that warning."

"I don't remember it," Kat said.

Aqua cleared his throat. Then he sang the last lines in his beautiful, rich voice:

"Watch out for people who belong in your past. Don't let 'em back in your life."

23

AQUA shut down after that. He just kept singing the same thing over and over: *"Watch out for people who belong in your past. Don't let 'em back in your life."*

When she Googled the lyrics on her phone, it all came flooding back to her. The song was "Demon Lover" by Michael Smith. They had all seen him live in some dingy venue down in the Village twenty years ago. Jeff had scored the tickets, having seen him perform in Chicago two years earlier. Aqua had come with a fellow cross-dresser named Yellow. The two ended up working a drag-queen act out of a club in Jersey City. When they broke up, Aqua naturally claimed: "Aqua clashes with Yellow."

The lyrics didn't trigger any more information. She found the song online and listened to it. It was eerie and wonderful, more poetry than song, the story of a woman named Agnes Hines who loved a boy named Jimmy Harris, who died young in a car crash and then came back to her years later, after she was married, in that same car. The song's message was clear: Keep past lovers in the past.

So was Aqua's ranting just influenced by a favorite song? Had he simply listened to it and felt that if she kept searching for her demon lover, Jeff, they'd both end up bursting into flames like Agnes and Jimmy? Or was there something more?

She thought about Aqua now, how Jeff's dumping her and returning to Cincinnati had affected him. He had already gotten worse, but Jeff's departure really ran him off the rail. Was he already institutionalized when Jeff left? She tried to think back. No, she thought, it was after.

It didn't matter. None of it mattered, really. Whatever mess Jeff had gotten himself into—she assumed there was a mess because you don't change names for no reason—it was his concern, not hers. Despite his insanity, Aqua was the brightest man she had ever known. It was one of the reasons why she loved his yoga so much—the small truths he spoke during meditation, the little vignettes that rang deep, the offbeat way he had to teach a lesson.

For example, singing an obscure song she had last heard nearly two decades ago.

Aqua's warning, coming from a diseased mind or not, made a lot of sense.

Brandon was awake when she got back from the precinct. He had two black eyes from his broken nose. "Where were you?" he asked.

"How are you feeling?"

"Sore."

"Take some more painkillers or something. Here, I

brought you a couple of cupcakes." She had stopped at Magnolia Bakery on the way from the Central Park Precinct. She handed him the bag. "I have a favor to ask."

"Shoot," Brandon said.

"They caught the man who assaulted you. That's where I was. At the precinct."

"Who is he?"

"That's the favor part. He's a friend of mine. He thought he was protecting me. I need you to drop the charges."

She explained, trying to be as vague as humanly possible.

"I'm still not sure I understand," Brandon said.

"Then do it for me, okay? As a favor."

He shrugged. "Okay."

"I also think it's time we let this go, Brandon. What do you think?"

Brandon pulled a cupcake apart and slowly ate half. "Can I ask you something?"

"Sure."

"On TV, they always talk about cop intuition or playing a hunch."

"Right."

"Do you ever do that?"

"All cops do. Hell, all people do. But when the hunch flies in the face of the facts, it more often than not leads to mistakes."

"And you think my hunch flies in the face of the facts?"

She thought about that. "No, not really. But it doesn't match up with the facts, either."

Brandon smiled and took another bite. "If it matched up with the facts, it wouldn't be a hunch, would it?"

"Good point. But I still go with the Sherlock Holmes axiom."

"What's that?"

"I'm paraphrasing, but basically Sherlock warned that you should never theorize before you have the facts because then you twist the facts to suit the theory instead of twisting the theory to suit the facts."

Brandon nodded. "I like that."

"But?"

"But I'm still not buying it."

"What about all that talk about not ruining it for your mom?"

"I won't. If this is true love, I'll let it be."

"It's not your place to say what kind of love it may be," Kat said. "Your mom is allowed to make her own mistakes, you know. She's allowed to get her heart broken by him."

"Like you?"

"Yeah," Kat said. "Like me. He was my demon lover. I need to leave him in my past."

"Demon lover?"

She smiled and grabbed a carrot cupcake with cream cheese icing and walnuts. "Never mind."

IT felt good to let it go. For about twenty minutes. Then Kat got two calls.

The first was from Stacy. "I have a lead on Jeff Raynes aka Ron Kochman," she said.

Too late. Kat didn't want to know. It didn't matter anymore. "What?"

"Jeff didn't change his name legally."

"You're sure?"

"Definitely. I even called all fifty state offices. It's a fake ID. Well done. Professional. A complete makeover. I even wonder if he was put into Witness Protection or something."

"Could that be it? Witness Protection, I mean."

"Doubtful. Guys in WP shouldn't be advertising themselves on dating services, but it's a possibility. I'm checking with a source. What I can tell you without question is that Jeff didn't change his name legally nor does he really want to be found. No credit cards, no bank accounts, no residence."

"He's working as a journalist," Kat said. "He has to be paying taxes."

"That's what I'm following up on now—my source with the IRS. I hope to get an address soon. Unless."

"Unless what?"

"Unless you want to call me off," Stacy said.

Kat rubbed her eyes. "You were the one who told me that Jeff and I might have the fairy-tale ending."

"I know, but do you ever really read fairy tales? Little Red Riding Hood? Hansel and Gretel? There's a lot of bloodshed and hurt."

"You think I should leave it alone, don't you?"

"Hell, no," Stacy said.

"But you just said—"

"Who cares what I just said? You can't leave this alone, Kat. You're not good with loose ends. And right now? Your fiancé is a major loose end. So screw it. Let's figure out what the hell happened to him, so once and for all, you can move past this dickwad who was dumb enough to dump your shapely ass."

"Well, when you put it like that," Kat said. Then: "You're a good friend."

"The best," Stacy agreed.

"But you know what? Let it go."

"Really?"

"Yeah."

"You sure?"

No, Kat thought. God, no. "Positive."

"Look at you, being all Miss Brave and whatnot," Stacy said. "Drinks tonight?"

"They're on me," Kat said.

"Love you."

"Love you too."

Brandon had felt well enough to leave after the cupcake. So Kat was alone, getting undressed and turning on the shower—she had a full day of binge-TVing in bed planned—when the second call came in.

"Are you home?"

It was Stagger. He didn't sound pleased.

"Yes."

"I'll be there in five minutes," Stagger said.

It took less. Stagger must have made the call standing right outside her building. She didn't greet him when he entered. He didn't greet her back. He stormed in and said, "Guess who just called me."

"Who?"

"Suggs."

Kat said nothing.

"You went to Suggs, for crying out loud?"

It was funny. Last time she saw him, Kat had thought how much Stagger still looked like a little boy. Now she thought the opposite. He looked old. His hair was receding, growing flimsy and flyaway. His jowls sagged. There was a belly now, not a big one, but there was still the feeling of age and softness. His children, she knew, weren't babies anymore. The trips to Disney were being slowly replaced with college visits. That, she realized, could have been her life. If she and Jeff had married, would she have joined the force? Would she right now be some aging soccer mom raising her family in some shiny-brick McMansion in Upper Montclair?

"How could you do that, Kat?"

"You're kidding, right?"

Stagger shook his head. "Look at me. Okay? Really look at me." He came close and put his hands on her shoulders. "Do you really think I would hurt your father?"

She did as he asked and then replied, "I don't know."

Her words hit him like a slap across the face. "Are you serious?"

"You're lying, Stagger. We both know it. You're covering something up."

"And so, what, you think I had something to do with your father's murder?"

"I just know you're lying. I know you've been lying for years."

Stagger closed his eyes and took a step back. "You got anything to drink?"

She headed over to the bar and held up a bottle of Jack Daniel's. He nodded and said, "Neat." She poured him a glass and figured, What the hell? Then she poured herself one too. They didn't clink glasses. Stagger brought the glass quickly to his lips and took a deep gulp. She stared at him.

"What?" he said.

"I don't think I've ever seen you drink."

"I guess we're both full of surprises."

"Or we don't know each other very well."

"That may be true," he said. "Our relationship, as it

were, was really based on your father. When he was gone, so was our connection. I mean, I'm your boss now, but it isn't as though we communicate much."

Stagger took another gulp. She took her first sip.

"Then again," he went on, "when you form a bond in tragedy, when you have a history like ours . . ." He turned and gazed at her door as though it had just materialized. "I remember everything about that day. But the part I remember most was when you first opened that door. You had no idea I was about to destroy your world."

He turned back toward her. "Can't you just let this go?"

She took a deep sip. She didn't bother answering.

"I haven't lied to you," Stagger said.

"Sure you have. You've been lying to me for eighteen years."

"I've been doing what Henry would have wanted."

"My father is dead," Kat said. "He doesn't get a say in this anymore."

Another deep gulp. "It isn't going to bring him back. And it isn't going to change the facts. Cozone ordered the hit. Monte Leburne carried it out."

"How were you onto Leburne so fast?"

"Because I already had an eye out for him."

"Why?"

"I knew Cozone had killed your dad."

"And Suggs and Rinsky missed it?"

He took another swig, emptying his glass. "They were like you."

"How so?"

"They didn't think Cozone would kill a cop."

"But you thought differently."

"Yep."

"Why?"

He poured himself another glass. "Because Cozone didn't view your father as a cop."

She made a face. "What did he view him as?"

"An employee."

A hot flush hit her face. "What the hell are you talking about?"

He just looked at her.

"Are you saying he was on the take?"

Stagger poured himself another. "More than that."

"What the hell is that supposed to mean?"

Stagger looked around the apartment as though for the first time. "Nice digs, by the way." He tilted his head. "How many cops do you know can buy a place on the Upper West Side outright?"

"It's small," she said, hearing the defensiveness in her voice. "He got a deal from a guy he helped."

Stagger smiled, but there was no joy in it.

"What are you trying to say here, Stagger?"

"Nothing. I'm trying to say nothing."

"Why did you visit Leburne in prison?"

"Why do you think?"

"I don't know."

"Then let me spell it out for you. I knew Leburne had killed your father. I knew Cozone had ordered it. You still don't see?"

"No, I don't."

He shook his head in disbelief. "I didn't visit Leburne to get him to confess," he said. "I went up there to make sure that he didn't tell why."

Stagger downed the entire glass.

"That's crazy," Kat said, even as she felt the floor beneath her start to shift. "What about that fingerprint?"

"Huh?"

"The fingerprint found at the scene. You checked it out for Suggs and Rinsky."

He closed his eyes. "I'm leaving."

"You're still lying," she said.

"It was just some homeless guy's print."

"That's crap."

"Let it go, Kat."

"Your whole theory makes no sense," she said. "If my father was on the take, why would Cozone kill him?"

"Because he wasn't going to be on the take much longer."

"What, he was going to turn on him?"

"I've said enough."

"Whose fingerprint was at the scene?" she asked.

"I told you. Nobody's."

Stagger slurred his words now. She'd been right about not seeing him drink before. It wasn't that she didn't know him. He simply wasn't a drinker. The alcohol was hitting him fast.

He started for the door. Kat stepped in his way.

"You're still not telling me everything."

"You wanted to know who killed your father. I told you."

"You still didn't explain what really happened."

"Maybe I'm not the one you should be asking," he said.

"Who, then?"

A strange look—something drunk, something gleeful—came to his face. "Didn't you ever wonder why your dad would disappear for days at a time?"

She stopped, stunned. For a moment, she just stood there, blinking helplessly, trying to get her bearings. Stagger took advantage, moving toward the door, putting his hand on the knob, opening it.

"What?" she managed.

"You heard me. You want to start getting to the truth, but you just bury your head in the sand. Why was Henry always vanishing? Why didn't anyone in your house ever talk about that?"

She opened her mouth, closed it, tried again. "What the hell are you saying, Stagger?"

"It isn't for me to say anything, Kat. That's what you're not getting here. I'm not the one you should be talking to."

24

KAT took the B to the E and then picked up the 7 train out to her old neighborhood in Flushing. She headed down Roosevelt Avenue toward Parsons Boulevard, walking toward her house without conscious thought, as you do with the places of your childhood. You just know every step. She had lived in Manhattan longer, knew the Upper West Side better in some ways, but it never felt like this. Not home exactly. This was stronger than that. This neighborhood felt like a part of her. It felt as though some of her DNA was in the blue clapboards and off-white Cape Cods and cracked pavement and small patches of lawn, like she'd been beamed away à la *Star Trek* but a few of her particles got left behind. Part of her would always be at Thanksgiving at Uncle Tommy and Aunt Eileen's, sitting at the "kids' table," which was a Ping-Pong table with a king-size sheet doubling as a tablecloth. Dad always carved the turkey—no one else was allowed to touch it. Uncle Tommy poured the drinks. He wanted the kids to have wine too. He'd start off with a spoonful and stir it into your Sprite, making it somewhat stronger as you got older until you reached an age where you left the Ping-Pong table altogether and got a full glass of wine. Uncle Tommy retired after thirty-six years of working as an appliance repairman for Sears, and he and Aunt Eileen moved down to Fort Myers, Florida. Their old house was now owned by a Korean family who'd knocked out the back wall and built an addition and slapped on aluminum siding because, when Uncle Tommy and Aunt Eileen lived there, the paint was flaking like it had a bad case of dandruff.

But make no mistake. Kat's DNA was still there.

The houses on her block had always been crowded together, but with all the bloated additions, they were even more so. TV antennas still stood atop most roofs, even though everyone had gone to either cable or a satellite dish. Virgin Mary statuary—some stone, most plastic—overlooked tiny gardens. Every once in a while, you'd see a house that had been totally razed in favor of shoehorning in some over-the-top faded-brick McMansion with arched windows, but they always looked like a fat guy squeezing into too small a chair.

Her phone buzzed as she reached her old house. She checked and saw the text was from Chaz:

Got license plate off gas station video.

She quickly typed back: Anything interesting?

Black Lincoln town car registered to James

Isherwood, Islip, New York. He's clean. Honest
citizen.

She wasn't surprised. Probably the name of an innocent limo driver hired by Dana's new boyfriend. Another
dead end. Another reason to put Dana and Jeff behind
her.

The back door off the kitchen was unlocked, as always. Kat found her mother sitting at the kitchen table
with Aunt Tessie. There were grocery store coupons
spread out on the table and a deck of playing cards. The
ashtray was filled with lipstick-tainted cigarette butts.
The same five chairs from her childhood still circled the
table. Dad's chair had arms on it, thronelike; the rest
didn't. Kat had sat between her two brothers. They too
had abandoned this neighborhood. Her older brother,
Jimmy, graduated from Fordham University. He lived
with his wife and three kids in a garish mansion on Long
Island, in Garden City, and worked on a crowded floor
as a bonds trader. He had explained to her a hundred
times what exactly he did, but she still didn't get it. Her
younger brother, Farrell, had gone to UCLA and stayed
there. He supposedly filmed documentaries and got paid
to write screenplays that never got made.

"Two days in a row," Mom said. "This has to be a
world and Olympic record."

"Stop it," Tessie scolded. "It's nice she's here."

Mom waved a hand of dismissal. Tessie rose and gave
Kat a kiss on the cheek. "I have to run. Brian's visiting
and I always make him my famous tuna fish sandwich."

Kat kissed her back. She remembered tuna fish at
Aunt Tessie's. Tessie's secret: potato chips. She sprinkled

them on top of the tuna. They added crunch and flavor if not nutritional value.

When they were alone, Mom asked, "You want some coffee?"

She pointed to her old coffee percolator. A tin of Folgers sat next to it. Kat had bought her a stainless steel Cuisinart coffee pod machine last Christmas, but Mom said it didn't "taste right," meaning, in her case, that it tasted good. Mom was like that. Anything more expensive wouldn't work for her. If you bought a twenty-dollar bottle of wine, she preferred the one that cost only six. If you got her a brand-name perfume, she preferred the knockoff she'd get at the drugstore. She bought all her clothes at Marshalls or T.J.Maxx and only off the sale rack. Part of this was because she was frugal. Part of it was something much more telling.

"I'm fine," Kat said.

"You want me to fix you a sandwich? I know nothing I'd make could ever be as good as Aunt Tessie's tuna, which is really just Bumble Bee, but I have some nice sliced turkey from Mel's."

"That would be great."

"You still like it with white bread and mayonnaise?"

Kat didn't, but it wasn't as if her mom had a seven-grain option on hand. "Sure, whatever."

Mom lifted herself slowly, making a production of it, using the back of the chair and the table to assist her. She wanted Kat to comment. Kat didn't bother. Mom opened the refrigerator—an old Kenmore model Uncle Tommy got them at cost—and pulled out the turkey and mayo.

Kat debated how to play this. There was too much history between them for games or subtlety. She decided to dive right in.

"Where did Dad go when he used to disappear?"

Mom had her back to her when Kat asked. She'd been reaching into the bread drawer. Kat looked to see her reaction. There was the briefest pause—nothing more.

"I'm going to toast the bread," Mom said. "It tastes better that way."

Kat waited.

"And what are you talking about, disappear? Your father never disappeared."

"Yeah, he did."

"You're probably thinking of his trips with the boys. They'd go hunting up in the Catskills. You remember Jack Kiley? Sweet man. He had a cabin or a lodge or something like that. Your father loved to go up there."

"I remember him going up there once. He used to vanish all the time."

"Aren't we dramatic?" Mom said, arching an eyebrow. "Disappear, vanish. You make it sound like your father was a magician."

"Where did he go?"

"I just told you. Don't you listen?"

"To Jack Kiley's cabin?"

"Sometimes, sure." Kat could hear the growing agitation in her mother's voice. "There was also a fishing trip with Uncle Tommy. I don't remember where. Somewhere on the North Fork. And I remember he went on a golf trip with some of the guys at work. That's where he was. He went on trips with his friends."

"I don't remember him ever taking you on trips."

"Oh, sure he did."

"Where?"

"What difference does it make now? Your father liked

blowing off steam with the guys. Golfing trips, fishing trips, hunting trips. Men do that."

Mom was spreading the mayo hard enough to scrape paint.

"Where did he go, Mom?"

"I just told you!" she shouted, dropping the knife. "Damn, look what you made me do."

Kat started to get up to retrieve the knife.

"You just stay in your seat, little missy. I got it." Mom picked up the knife, tossed it in the sink, grabbed another. Five vintage McDonald's glasses from 1977—Grimace, Ronald McDonald, Mayor McCheese, Big Mac, and Captain Crook—sat on the windowsill. The complete set had six. Farrell had broken the Hamburglar when he threw a Frisbee indoors when he was seven years old. Years later, he bought Mom a replacement vintage Hamburglar on eBay, but she refused to put it up with the others.

"Mom?"

"What?" She started on the sandwich again. "Why on earth would you be asking me all this now anyway? Your father, God rest his soul, has been dead for nearly twenty years. Who cares where he went?"

"I need to know the truth."

"Why? Why would you bring this up, especially now that the monster who murdered him is finally dead? Put it to bed. It's over."

"Did Dad work for Cozone?"

"What?"

"Was Dad on the take?"

For a woman who needed help getting up, Mom moved now with dizzying speed. "How dare you!" She twirled and, without any hesitation, slapped Kat across the left cheek. The sickening sound of flesh on flesh was loud, almost deafening in the stillness of the kitchen. Kat felt tears come to her eyes, but she didn't turn away or even reach up to touch the red.

Mom's face crumbled. "I'm so sorry. I didn't mean . . ."

"Did he work for Cozone?"

"Please stop."

"Is that how he paid for the apartment in New York City?"

"What? No, no. He got a good deal, remember? He saved that man's life."

"What man?"

"What do you mean, what man?"

"What man? What was his name?"

"How am I supposed to remember?"

"Because I know Dad did a lot of good work as a cop, but I don't remember him saving any real estate magnate's life. Do you? Why did we just accept that story? Why didn't we ask him?"

"Ask him," Mom repeated. She retied her apron strings, pulling the ends a little too hard. "You mean, like you are now? Like an interrogation? Like your father was some kind of liar? You'd do that to that man—to your father? You'd ask him questions and call him a liar in his own home?"

"That's not what I mean," Kat said, but her voice was weak.

"Well, what do you mean? Everyone exaggerates, Kat. You know that. Especially men. So maybe your father didn't save the man's life. Maybe he only—I don't know—caught a burglar who robbed him or helped him with a parking ticket. I don't know. Your father said he saved his life. I didn't question his word. Tessie's husband, Ed? He used to limp, remember? He told everyone it was from shrapnel in the war. But he was clerical because of his eyesight. He hurt his leg falling down subway stairs when he was sixteen. You think Tessie went around calling him a liar every time he told that story?"

Mom brought the sandwich to the table. She started to cut it diagonally—her brother had preferred it that way—but Kat, ever the contrarian, had insisted sandwiches be cut to make two rectangles. Mom, again out of habit, remembered, angled the knife, cut it in two perfect halves.

"You've never been married," Mom said softly. "You don't know."

"Know what?"

"We all have our demons. But men? They have them much worse. The world tells them that they are the leaders and great and macho and have to be big and brave and make a lot of money and lead these glamorous lives. But they don't, do they? Look at the men in this neighborhood. They all worked too many hours. They came home to noisy, demanding homes. Something was always broken they needed to fix. They were always behind on the house payments. Women, we get it. Life is about a certain kind of drudgery. We are taught not to hope or want too much. Men? They never get that."

"Where did he go, Mom?"

She closed her eyes. "Eat your sandwich."

"Was he doing jobs for Cozone?"

"Maybe." Then: "I don't think so."

Kat pulled the chair out for her mother to sit. Mom sat as though someone had cut her knees out from beneath her.

"What was he doing?" Kat asked.

"You remember Gary?"

"Flo's husband."

"Right. He used to go to the track, remember? He kept losing everything they had. Flo would cry for hours. Your uncle Tommy, he drank too much. He was home every night, but rarely before eleven o'clock. He'd stop at the pub for a quick one and then it would be hours later. The men. They all needed something like that. Some drank. Some gambled. Some whored. Some, the lucky ones, found the church, though they could kill you with their sanctimonious baloney. But the point is, with men, real life was never enough. You know what my dad, your grandfather, used to say?"

Kat shook her head.

"'If a man had enough to eat, he'd want to grow a second mouth.' He also had a dirty way of saying it, but I won't repeat it here."

Kat reached out and took her mother's hand. She tried to remember the last time she had done that—reached out to her very own mother—but no memory came to her.

"What about Dad?"

"You always thought it was your father who wanted you to get out of this life. But it was me. I was the one who didn't want you stuck here."

"You hated it that much?"

"No. It was my life. It's all I have."

"I don't understand."

Mom squeezed her daughter's hand. "Don't make me face what I don't need to face," she said. "It's over. You can't change the past. But see, you can shape it with your memories. I get to choose which ones I keep, not you."

Kat tried to keep her voice gentle. "Mom?"

"What?"

"Those don't sound like memories. They sound like illusions."

"What's the difference?" Mom smiled. "You lived here too, Kat."

Kat sat back in her chair. "What?"

"You were a child, sure, but a smart child, very mature for your age. You loved your father unconditionally, yet you saw him vanish. You saw through my fake smiles and all that sweetness when he came home. But you looked away, didn't you?"

"I'm not looking away now." Kat reached out her hand again. "Please tell me where he went."

"The truth? I don't know."

"But you know more than you're telling me."

"He was a good man, your father. He provided for you and your brothers. He taught you right from wrong. He worked long hours and made sure that you all got a college education."

"Did you love him?" she asked.

Mom started busying herself, rinsing a cup in the sink, putting the mayo back in the fridge. "Oh, he was so handsome when we met, your father. Every girl wanted to date him." There was a faraway look in her eye. "I wasn't so bad back then either."

"You're not so bad now."

Mom ignored the remark.

"Did you love him?"

"The best I could," she said, blinking until the faraway look was no more. "But it's never enough."

25

KAT started back toward the 7 train. School must have been letting out. Kids with giant backpacks shuffled by, their eyes down, most playing with their smartphones. Two girls from St. Francis Prep walked by in their cheerleader uniforms. To the shock of all who knew her, Kat had tried out for cheerleading her sophomore year. Their main cheer was the old standby: "We're St. Francis Prep, we don't come any prouder, and if you can't hear us, we'll shout it a little louder." Then you repeat the cheer louder and then louder still until it all felt a tad inane. The other cheer—she smiled at the memory—was when your team made a mistake. They'd do a quick clap while shouting, "That's all right. That's okay. We're gonna beat you any-way." A few years ago, Kat had gone to a game and noticed that they changed the cheer from "we're gonna beat you" to the more politically correct "we're gonna win."

Progress?

Kat was just in front of Tessie's house when her cell phone rang. It was Chaz.

"You got my text?"

"About the license plate? Yeah, thanks."

"Dead end?"

"Yeah, I think so."

"Because," Chaz said, "there was one thing about the license plate that bothered me."

Kat squinted into the sun. "What?"

"The registration was for a black Lincoln Town Car. Not a stretch. Do you know anything about stretches?"

"Not really, no."

"They are all custom-made. You take a regular car, you strip the interior, and then you literally slice it in half. Then you pull it back, install the prefab exterior, rebuild the interior with a bar or TV or whatever."

More kids ambled past her, heading home from school. Again she thought back to her own days, when school dismissal was boisterous. None of these kids said a word. They just stared at their phones.

"Okay," Kat said, "so?"

"So James Isherwood's registration didn't read 'stretch.' It could be an oversight, no big deal. But I decided to take a deeper look. The car also doesn't have a livery license. Again, that isn't a huge deal. If the car was privately owned, that wouldn't be necessary. But the boyfriend's name isn't Isherwood, correct?"

"Correct," Kat said.

"So I looked some more. No harm, right? I called Isherwood's house."

"And?"

"He wasn't home. Let me cut to the chase, okay? Isherwood lives in Islip, but he works for an energy company headquartered in Dallas. He flies out there a lot. That's where he is now. So, see, he parked his car in long-term parking."

A dark, cold shiver eased its way down the back of Kat's neck. "And someone stole his license plate."

"Bingo."

Amateurs steal cars to commit crimes. That was messy. Stolen cars are immediately reported to the police. But if you swipe a license plate, especially a front one from some long-term garage, it could be days or weeks before the theft is reported. Even then, it is harder to spot a license plate than an entire car. With a stolen car, you can be on the lookout for a specific make and model. With a stolen license plate, especially if you're smart enough to steal it off a car with a similar make . . .

Chaz said, "Kat?"

"We need to find out everything we can about Dana Phelps. See if we can ping her phone location. Get her recent texts."

"This isn't our jurisdiction. They live in Connecticut."

The front door of Tessie's house opened. Tessie stepped outside.

"I know," Kat said. "Tell you what. E-mail all you got to a Detective Schwartz at the Greenwich Police Department. I'll contact him later."

Kat hung up the phone. What the hell was going on? She debated calling Brandon, but that seemed premature. She needed to think it through. Chaz was right—this wasn't their case. That was clear. Plus, Kat had her own issues right now, thank you very much. She would pass it on to Joe Schwartz and leave it at that.

Tessie was making her way toward her. Kat flashed back to when she was nine years old, hiding behind the kitchen door, listening to Tessie cry about being pregnant. Tessie was one of those people who kept it all hidden with a smile. She had eight kids in twelve years in an era when husbands would sooner drink from a septic tank than change a diaper. Her children were scattered around the country now as though tossed by a giant hand. Some kept moving. Usually at least one still stayed at their childhood home. Tessie didn't care. She didn't like the company or dislike it. Motherhood was over for her, at least the labor-intensive part. They could stay or they could leave. She might make the occasional tuna fish sandwich for Brian or she might not. It didn't matter to her.

"Is everything okay?" Tessie asked.

"Fine."

Tessie looked doubtful. "Sit with me a minute?"

"Sure," Kat said. "I'd like that."

Tessie had always been Kat's favorite of Mom's friends. During Kat's childhood, despite the chaos and exhaustion, Tessie had always found time to chat with her. Kat had worried that she was yet another burden or obligation, but somewhere along the way, she realized that wasn't the case, that Tessie enjoyed their time together. Tessie had trouble communicating with her own daughters, and Kat, of course, had the same issue with her mother. Some might call their rapport special—that Tessie should have been Kat's mom or something like that—but more likely, it was just that they weren't related and could both relax.

Maybe familiarity—accent on the *familia*—did indeed breed contempt.

Tessie's house was a tired Tudor. It was spacious enough, but when it had housed ten, it had seemed as though the walls were buckling from the onslaught. There was a fence across the driveway. Tessie opened it so they could head into the backyard, where she kept her small garden.

"Bad year again," Tessie said, pointing toward the to-mato plants. "This global warming or whatever keeps messing with my timing."

Kat sat on the bench.

"Do you want something to drink?"

"No, thanks."

"Okay, then," Tessie said, spreading her arms. "Tell me."

So Kat did.

"Little Willy Cozone," Tessie said, with a shake of her head when Kat finished. "You know he's from the neigh-borhood, right? Grew up on Farrington Street near the car wash."

Kat nodded.

"My older brother, Terry, graduated from Bishop Reilly with him. Cozone was a scrawny kid. Threw up in first grade at St. Mary's. Vomited all over the nun, right in the middle of class. Stunk up the whole room. The kids started picking on him after that. Called him Stinky or Smelly or something. Real original." She shook her head. "You know how he stopped it?"

"Stopped what?"

"Being picked on."

"No. How?"

"Cozone beat a kid to death when he was in fifth grade. Took a hammer to school and bashed his head in. Pried open the back of the skull with the claw part."

Kat tried not to make a face. "I didn't see that in the files."

"The records were sealed, or maybe they never con-victed him. I don't know. It was kept pretty hush-hush."

Kat just shook her head.

"When Cozone was around, well, pets used to disappear from this neighborhood, if you know what I'm saying. They'd find like a paw or something in the trash. That would be it. You know he lost his whole family to violence."

"Yes," Kat said. "And all this, I mean, that's why I don't believe my dad worked for him."

"I don't know one way or the other," Tessie said.

Tessie started busying herself with the garden, retying the plants to the stakes.

"What do you know, Tessie?"

She inspected a tomato, still on the vine. It was both too small and too green. She let it go.

"You were around," Kat said. "You knew about my father's vanishing acts."

"I did, yes. Your mother used to pretend it was all okay. Even to Flo and me, she'd lie."

"Do you know where he went?"

"Not specifically, no."

"But you had some idea."

Tessie stopped fiddling with the tomatoes and stood up straight. "I'm of two minds on this."

"That being?"

"The obvious. It's none of my business. It's none of your business. And it all happened a long time ago. We should respect your mother's wishes."

Kat nodded. "Understandable."

"Thank you."

"What's the other mind?"

Tessie sat down next to her. "When you're young, you think you have all the answers. You're right wing or you're left wing and the other side is a bunch of idiots.

You know. When you get a little older, though, you start to more and more see the grays. Now I understand that true idiots are the ones who are certain they have the answers. It is never that simple. Do you know what I mean?"

"I do."

"I'm not saying there's no such thing as right or wrong. But I'm saying what may work for some doesn't work for others. You talked before about your mother confusing memories with illusion. But that's okay. That's how she survives. Some people need illusions. And some people, like you, need answers."

Kat waited.

"You also need to weigh the hurts," Tessie said.

"What do you mean?"

"If I tell you what I know, it is going to hurt you. A lot, probably. I love you. I don't want to hurt you."

Kat knew that Tessie, unlike Flo or even Mom, did not lean toward the melodramatic. It was not a warning to take lightly. "I can take it," Kat said.

"I'm sure you can. Plus, I have to weigh that hurt against the dull ache you feel from always wondering, from never knowing. There's a pain in that too."

"A greater pain, I'd argue," Kat said.

"And I don't disagree." Tessie let loose a long breath. "There is one more problem."

"I'm listening."

"My information. It is all based on rumors. A friend of Gary's—you remember Gary?"

"Flo's husband."

"Right. So a friend of Gary's told Gary and Gary told Flo and Flo told me. So for all I know, it's a load of garbage."

"But you don't think it is," Kat said.

"Right, I don't think it is. I think it's the truth."

Tessie seemed to be bracing herself.

"It's okay," Kat said in the gentlest voice she could muster. "Tell me."

"Your father had a girlfriend."

Kat blinked twice. Tessie had warned that this revelation would hurt. It would, Kat supposed, but right now, it was as though the words were skimming the surface, not yet penetrating the skin.

Tessie kept her eyes on Kat. "I would say it's no big deal—hell, I'd bet more than half the married men in this town had girls—but there were a few things that made this case different."

Kat swallowed, trying to sort her thoughts. "Like what?"

"You sure you don't want a drink?"

"No, Aunt Tessie, I'm fine." Kat straightened her back and fought through it. "What made my father's case different?"

"For one thing, it seemed to be ongoing. Your father spent quite a bit of time with her. Most guys, it's one night, one hour, a strip club, maybe a short fling with a girl at work. This wasn't like that. This was more serious. That's what the rumors were, anyway. That's why he'd disappear. They traveled together, I guess. I don't know."

"Mom knew?"

"I don't know, honey." Then: "Yes, I think so."

"Why didn't she leave him?"

Tessie smiled. "And go where, sweetheart? Your mother was raising three children. He was the provider and the husband. We didn't have options back then. Plus, well, your mother loved him. And he loved her."

Kat snorted. "You're kidding, right?"

Tessie shook her head. "See, you're young. You think things are simple. My Ed had girlfriends too. You want to know the truth? I didn't care. Better her than me—that's what I thought. I had all these kids and was always pregnant—I was happy he was leaving me alone, if you want to know the truth. You don't imagine feeling that way when you're young, but you do."

So that was it, Kat thought. Dad had a girlfriend. A whole bunch of emotions ricocheted through her. Per her yoga training, she saw the emotions, but for right now, because she needed to stay focused, she simply let them go.

"There's something else," Tessie said.

Kat raised her head and looked at her.

"You have to remember where we live. Who we are. What the times were like."

"I don't understand."

"Your father's girlfriend," Tessie said. "Well, again this is what Gary's friend said. See, a married man with another woman? No surprise, right. No one would have said boo. Gary's friend wouldn't have even noticed, except he said that this girlfriend was, um, black."

Again Kat blinked, not sure what to make of it. "Black? You mean like African-American?"

Tessie nodded. "Rumor—and again, this is just rumor probably fueled by racism—but someone thought she was some prostitute he busted. That was how they met or something. I don't know. I doubt that."

Kat felt dizzy. "Did my mother know?"

"I never told her, if that's what you're asking."

"That's not what I'm asking." Then Kat remembered something. "Wait. Flo told her, didn't she?"

Tessie didn't bother to confirm or deny. Now, finally, Kat knew another truth—why there had been a yearlong silence between Flo and Mom. Flo had told Mom about the black prostitute, and Mom had promptly gone into denial.

But as emotionally wrenching as this was—Kat still didn't know how she felt other than sad—it also seemed irrelevant to the issue at hand. She could cry about it later. For now, Kat needed to figure out if any of this had anything to do with her father's murder.

"Do you know the woman's name?" Kat asked.

"Not really, no."

Kat frowned. "Not really?"

"Let it go, honey."

"You know I can't," Kat said.

Tessie looked everywhere but at Kat. "Gary said her street name was Sugar."

"Sugar?"

She shrugged. "I don't know if that's true or not."

"Sugar what?"

"I don't know."

The blows just kept coming. Kat wanted to curl up in a ball and ride them out, but she didn't have that luxury. "Do you know what happened to Sugar after my father's murder?"

"No," Tessie said.

"Did she—"

"That's all I know, Kat. There's nothing more." Tessie started back on the plants again. "So what are you going to do now?"

Kat thought about it. "I'm not sure."

"You know the truth now. Sometimes that's enough."

"Sometimes," Kat agreed.

"But not this time?"

"Something like that," Kat said.

"The truth may be better than lies," Tessie said. "But it doesn't always set you free."

Kat understood that. She didn't expect to be free. She didn't expect to be happier even. She just expected . . .

What exactly?

There was nothing to be gained here. Her mother would be hurt. Stagger, who probably did this out of loyalty to her father, could be open to tampering with charges if he convinced Monte Leburne to stay quiet or change his testimony. Kat knew the truth now. Enough anyway.

"Thank you, Aunt Tessie."

"For what?"

"For telling me."

"I don't think a 'you're welcome' fits here," Tessie said, bending down and picking up the spade. Then: "You're not going to leave it alone, are you, Kat?"

"No, I'm not."

"Even if it hurts a lot of people."

"Even if."

Tessie nodded, digging the spade deep into the fresh soil. "It's getting late, Kat. I think maybe it's time you headed back home."

THE revelation began to sink in during the subway ride home.

It was easy to feel angry and betrayed and disgusted.

Her father had been her hero. Kat got, of course, that he wasn't perfect, but this was the man who climbed up a ladder and hung up the moon for her. She had honestly believed it—that her father had taken the ladder out of the garage and put up the moon just for her benefit—but, of course, when you stop and think about it, that had been a lie too.

Sometimes she imagined that her father used to disappear because he was saving lives, working undercover, doing something grand and brave. Now Kat knew that he had abandoned and terrified his entire family to shack up with a hooker.

So that would be the easy way for her emotions to go—in the direction of disgust, anger, betrayal, maybe even hate.

But as Tessie had warned her, life was rarely that simple.

Her overwhelming emotion was sadness. There was sadness for a father who was so unhappy at home that he ended up living a lie. There was sadness too for Kat's mother for all the obvious reasons, for also being forced to live the lie, and when she looked at it carefully, maybe there was sadness because this news didn't shock Kat as much as she might now claim. Maybe Kat had subconsciously suspected this kind of ugliness. Maybe this had been the root cause for her tense relationship with her mother—a stupid, subconscious belief that somehow Mom didn't do enough to make Dad happy and so he would go away and Kat would be scared that he would never come back and it would be Mom's fault.

She also wondered whether Sugar, if that was her name, had made her father happy. There had been no passion in his marriage. There had been respect and companionship and partnership, but had her father found something approaching romantic love with this other woman? Suppose he had been happy with this other, forbidden woman. How should Kat feel about that? Should she feel anger and betrayal—or some form of joy that Dad had found something to cherish?

She wanted to go home and lie down and cry.

Her phone didn't work until she was out of the subway tunnel. There were three missed calls from Chaz's cell phone. Kat called him back as soon as she was at street level.

"What's up?" she asked.

"You sound like crap."

"Rough day."

"It may get rougher."

"What do you mean?"

"I got something on that Swiss bank account. I think you'll want to see this."

26

TITUS got tired of the prostitution ring.

The world was getting dangerous, tricky, and even boring. Whenever you had a good thing going, too many dumb people with overly violent tendencies had a habit of getting involved. The Mob moved in and wanted a piece. Lazy men saw this as easy money—abuse a desperate girlfriend, make her do what you want, collect the cash. His mentor, Louis Castman, had long since disappeared, retiring, Titus figured, to some island in the South Pacific. The Internet, which made so many retail businesses and go-betweens obsolete, had made the pimp that much less valuable. The whore-to-john connection became much more streamlined with the web or with larger consolidators who swallowed the smaller pimps in the same way that Home Depot swallowed the mom-and-pop hardware store.

Prostitution had become too small-time for Titus. The risks had started to outweigh the benefits.

But like any business, when one aspect became obsolete, the top entrepreneurs found new avenues. Technology might have hurt the street business, but it also opened up new worlds online. For a while, Titus became one of those consolidators, but it became too rote, too distant, sitting behind a computer and making appointments and transactions. He moved on and ran online cons with some backers in Nigeria. No, he didn't run the easy-to-spot spam e-mails about helping someone who owed or wanted to give away money. Titus had always been about seduction—about sex, about love, about the interplay between them. For a while, his best "romantic scam" was to pretend that he was a soldier serving in Iraq or Afghanistan. He would set up fake identities for his soldiers on social media sites and then start to romance single women he would meet online. Eventually, he would "reluctantly" ask for help so he could purchase a laptop, or airfare so they could meet in person, or maybe he would need money for rehabilitation after a war-related injury. When he needed quick cash, Titus would pretend he was a soldier being deployed and needing to sell a vehicle on the cheap, sending prospective buyers bogus registration and information and having them wire the money to third-party accounts.

There were problems with these scams, however. First, the money was relatively small and took a great deal of effort. People were dumb, but alas, they were getting shrewder. Second, as with anything profitable, too many amateurs heard about it and rushed into the business. The Army Criminal Investigation began issuing warnings and going after the perpetrators in a more serious manner. For his partners in western Africa, that wasn't a big problem. For Titus, it could very well be.

But more than that, it was again small-time with the lowest-case *s* imaginable. Titus, like any businessman, was looking for ways to expand and capitalize. These cons had been a step up from his earlier pimping days, but how big a step? He needed a new challenge—something bigger, faster, more profitable, and completely safe.

Titus had used up almost his entire life savings to get his new venture off the ground. But it was paying off big-time.

Clem Sison, the new chauffeur, came into the farmhouse. He was wearing Claude's black suit. "How do I look?"

It was a little baggy in the shoulders, but it would do. "You understand your training."

"Yes."

"No deviations from the plan," Titus said. "Do you understand?"

"Sure, of course. She comes straight here."

"Then go get her now."

CHAZ'S shift was over, so Kat met him at his apartment in the ritzy Lock-Horne Building on Park Avenue and 46th Street. Kat had come to an office party here two years ago when Stacy was dating the playboy who owned the building. The playboy, whose name was Wilson or Windsor or something else overtly preppy, was brilliant and rich and handsome and now, if rumors were true, had lost his mind à la Howard Hughes and become a complete recluse. Recently, the building had converted some office floors into residential space.

That was where Chaz Faircloth lived. Quick albeit obvious conclusion: Coming from great wealth was nice.

When Chaz opened the door, his white shirt was opened a button more than it should have been, revealing pecs so waxed they made a baby's butt look like it had a five-o'clock shadow. He smiled with the perfect teeth and said, "Come in."

She glanced around the apartment. "Label me surprised."

"What?"

Kat had expected a man cave or bachelor pad and instead found the place almost too classily decorated with old wood and antiques and tapestries and Oriental rugs. Everything was rich and expensive yet understated.

"The decor," Kat said.

"You like?"

"I do."

"I know, right? My mom decorated the place with family heirlooms and whatnot. I was going to change it up, you know, make it more me, but then I found that chicks actually love this stuff. Makes me look more sensitive and stuff."

So much for the surprise.

Chaz moved behind the bar and picked up a bottle of Macallan Scotch 25 Year. Kat's eyes went wide.

"You're a Scotch drinker," he said.

She tried not to lick her lips. "I don't think I should right now."

"Kat?"

"Yeah?"

"You're staring at that bottle like I stare at ample cleavage."

She frowned. "Ample?"

Chaz smiled with the even teeth. "Have you ever had the twenty-five?"

"I had the twenty-one once."

"And?"

"I almost asked it for a ring."

Chaz grabbed two whiskey glasses. "This sells for about eight hundred dollars a bottle." He poured both and handed one to her. Kat held the glass as if it were a baby bird.

"Cheers."

She took a single sip. Her eyes closed. She wondered whether it was possible to drink this and keep your eyes open.

"How is it?" he asked.

"I may shoot you just so I can take the bottle home."

Chaz laughed. "I guess we should get on with it."

Kat almost shook her head and told him it could wait. She didn't want to hear about the Swiss bank account. The realization of what her life had been—what her parents' lives had been—was beginning to burrow through her mental blockades. Every house on every street is really just a family facade. We look at it and think we know what's going on inside, but we never really have any idea. That was one thing, sure—to be fooled that way. She could get past that. But to be on the inside, to live behind the facade and still realize she had no idea of the unhappiness, the broken dreams, the lies and delusions being played out right in front of her, made Kat just want to sit on this perfect leather couch and sip this primo beverage and let it all slip into the wonderful numb.

"Kat?"

"I'm listening."

"What's going on with you and Captain Stagger?"

"You don't want to get in the middle of that, Chaz."

"Are you coming back soon?"

"I don't know. It's not important."

"You sure?"

"Positive," Kat said. It was time to change subjects. "I thought you wanted to see me about the numbered Swiss bank account."

"I did, yes."

"Well?"

Chaz put the glass down. "I did what you asked. I reached out to your contact at the Department of Treasury. I just asked him if he could put the account on their watch list. The list is huge, by the way. I guess the IRS is going hard after the secret Swiss accounts, and the Swiss are fighting back. Unless there is a strong hint of terrorism, they're pretty backlogged, so I don't think they've picked up on this yet."

"Picked up on?"

"You said the account was new, right?"

"Right. Supposedly Dana Phelps just opened it."

"When exactly?"

"I don't know. From what her financial guy said, I'd assumed that she set it up two days ago when she transferred the funds into it."

"That can't be," Chaz said.

"Why not?"

"Because someone already issued a Suspicious Activity Report on it."

Kat put the glass down. "When?"

"A week ago."

"Do you know what the report said?"

"A Massachusetts resident transferred over three hundred thousand dollars into that same account."

Chaz opened up the laptop sitting on the coffee table and began to type.

"Do you have the name of the person who made the transfer?" Kat asked.

"No, it was left out of the report."

"Do you know who issued the SAR?"

"A man named Asghar Chuback. He's a partner at an investment firm called Parsons, Chuback, Mitnick and Bushwell Investments and Securities. They're located in Northampton, Massachusetts."

Chaz spun the laptop toward her. The Parsons, Chuback, Mitnick and Bushwell web page was the digital equivalent of thick ivory stock and embossed logos—rich, fancy, upper class—the kind of design that told those without eight-figure portfolios not to bother.

"Did you tell Detective Schwartz about this?" Kat asked.

"Not yet. Frankly, he didn't seem all that impressed with the stolen license plate."

There were links on the site for wealth management, institutional services, global investments. There was a lot of talk about privacy and discretion. "We'll never get them to talk to us," Kat said.

"Wrong."

"How so?"

"I thought the same thing, but I made the call anyway," Chaz said. "He's willing. I made you an appointment."

"With Chuback?"

"Yep."

"For when?"

"Anytime tonight. His secretary said he's working with the overseas market and will be there all night.

Weird, but he seems anxious to talk. The ride should take about three hours." He snapped the laptop closed and stood. "I'll drive."

Kat didn't want that. Yes, she trusted Chaz and all, but she still hadn't told him all the details, especially about the personal Jeff-Ron connection. That wasn't the kind of thing you wanted around the precinct. Plus, much as he might be getting better, three hours in a car with Chaz—six hours round-trip—was something she wasn't yet ready to handle.

"I'll drive myself up," she said. "You stay here in case we need some kind of follow-up."

She expected an argument. She didn't get one.

"Okay," he said, "but it'll be faster if you just take my car. Come on. The garage is around the corner."

MARTHA Paquet carried her suitcase to the door. The suitcase was old, predating the invention of the rolling ones, or maybe Harold had been too cheap, even back then. Harold hated to travel, except twice a year when he did a "Vegas run" with his drinking buddies, the kind of trip that caused cringing winks and snickers from all upon their return. For those outings, he used a fancy Tumi carry-on—it was only for his use, he said—but he'd taken that, and pretty much everything else of value in their condo, years ago, before the final divorce. Harold didn't wait for the courts. He rented a U-Haul, took everything he could from the condo, and told her, "Try to get it back, bitch."

Long time ago.

Martha looked out the window. "This is crazy," she said to her sister, Sandi.

"You only live once."

"Yes, I know."

Sandi put her arm around her. "And you deserve this. Mom and Dad would so approve."

Martha arched her eyebrow. "Oh, I doubt that."

Her parents had been deeply religious people. After years of domestic abuse at the hands of Harold—no reason to go into that—Martha had ended up moving back here to help Dad take care of her terminally ill mom. But as it often plays out, Dad, the healthy one, had died of a sudden heart attack six years ago. Mom had finally passed last year. Mom had firmly believed she was going to Paradise with Dad—claimed she couldn't wait for that day—but that hadn't stopped her from fighting and scraping and enduring agonizing treatments to hang on to this mortal coil.

Martha had stayed with her mother the whole time, living in this house as her nurse and companion. She didn't mind. There was no talk of sending Mom to hospice or a nursing home or even hiring someone. Her mother wouldn't hear of it, and Martha, who loved her mother dearly, would never have asked.

"You put your life on hold long enough," Sandi reminded her. "You're due for some fun."

She was, she guessed. There had been attempts at relationships after the divorce, but her caring for Mom, not to mention her own wariness after Harold, got in the way. Martha never complained. It wasn't her way. She was glad for her lot in life. She didn't ask or expect more. That wasn't to say she didn't long.

"It only takes one person to change your life," Sandi said. "You."

"Right."

"You can't start the next chapter of your life if you keep rereading the last one."

Sandi meant well with all her little life aphorisms. She posted them on her Facebook wall every Friday, often accompanied by a picture of flowers or perfect sunsets, stuff like that. She called them Sandi's Sayings, though, of course, she had written none of them.

A black limousine pulled up in front of the house. Martha felt something catch in her throat.

"Oh, Martha, that car is beautiful!" Sandi squealed.

Martha couldn't move. She stood there as the chauffeur got out and started toward her door. A month ago, after much prodding from Sandi, Martha had signed up for an Internet dating service. To her surprise, she almost immediately had begun an online flirtation with a wonderful man named Michael Craig. It was crazy when she thought about it—so unlike her—and she had scoffed at the whole idea, how juvenile it was, how the kids today wouldn't know what a real relationship was if it bit them on the ass because they spend all their time on screens and never see the person face-to-face and blah blah blah.

So how did she fall into this?

The truth was, there were advantages to starting online. It didn't matter what you looked like (other than in photographs). Your hair could be messed up, your makeup all wrong, something stuck in your teeth—it didn't matter. You could relax and not try so hard. You never saw disappointment on your suitor's face and always assumed he was smiling at what you said and did. If it didn't work out, you wouldn't have to worry about seeing him at the grocery store or local strip mall. It gave it enough distance so you could be yourself and let your guard down.

It felt safe.

How serious could it get, after all?

She suppressed a smile. The relationship had heated up—no reason to go into details—and was moving into more and more intense areas, until finally, Michael Craig wrote in an IM: Let's chuck it all and meet!

Martha Paquet remembered sitting at the computer in full-blush mode. Oh, how she longed for real contact, for the kind of physical intimacy with a man she had always imagined. She had been lonely and afraid for so long, and now she had met someone—but did she dare take the next step? Martha expressed her reluctance to Michael. She didn't want to risk losing what they had—but then again, as he himself finally said in his own understanding way, what did they have?

Nothing when you thought about it. Smoke and mirrors. But if they met in person, if the chemistry was anything like it was online . . .

But suppose it wasn't? Suppose—and this must happen more times than not—suppose it all fizzled away when they finally met face-to-face. Suppose she ended up being, as she expected she would, a complete disappointment.

Martha wanted to postpone. She asked him to be patient. He said he would be, but relationships don't work like that. Relations can't remain stagnant. They are either getting better or getting worse. She could feel Michael starting to pull back ever so slowly. He was a man, she knew. He had needs and wants, just as she did.

Then, odd as this may now seem, Martha had visited her sister's Facebook page and seen the following aphorism posted against a photo of waves crashing on the shore:

"I don't regret the things I've done. I regret the
things I didn't do when I had the chance."

No one was credited with the quote, but it hit Martha
right where she lived. She had been right in the first
place: An online relationship isn't real. It could work as
an introduction maybe. It could be intense. It could
bring pleasure and pain, but you can live in a fake reality
only for so long. In the end, it was role-playing.

There seemed little to lose and so much to gain.

So yes, as Martha stood by the door watching the
chauffeur make his approach, she was both terrified and
excited. There was also another damn quote on Sandi's
wall, something about taking risks and doing one thing
every day that scares you. If that was in any way the
meaning of life, Martha had managed to never live even
a single moment.

She had never been so scared. She had never felt so
alive.

Sandi threw her arms around her. Martha hugged her
back.

"I love you," Sandi said.

"I love you too."

"I want you to have the best time in the whole world—
you hear me?"

Martha nodded, afraid that she'd cry. The chauffeur
knocked on the door. Martha opened it. He introduced
himself as Miles and took her suitcase.

"This way, madam."

Martha followed him out to the car. Sandi came too.
The chauffeur put her suitcase in the trunk and opened
the door for her. Sandi hugged her again.

"Call me for anything," Sandi said.

"I will."

"If it doesn't feel right or you want to go home . . ."

"I'll call you, Sandi. I promise."

"No, you won't because you'll be having too much fun." There were tears in Sandi's eyes. "You deserve this. You deserve happiness."

Martha tried very hard not to cry. "I'll see you in two days."

She slipped into the back. The driver closed the door. He got into the front seat and drove her toward her new life.

27

CHAZ drove a Ferrari 458 Italia in a color he insisted on calling fly yellow.

Kat frowned. "Label me unsurprised."

"I call it the Chick Trawler," Chaz told her, handing her a Superman key chain.

"A better name might be the Overcompensation."

"Huh?"

"Never mind."

Three hours later, when the female GPS voice said, "You have arrived at your destination," Kat was sure it was some kind of mistake.

She double-checked the address. This was the place—909 Trumbull Road. Northampton, Massachusetts. Home, according to both the web and online yellow pages, of Parsons, Chuback, Mitnick and Bushwell Investments and Securities.

Kat parked on the street between a Subway and a beauty salon called Pam's Kickin' Kuts. She had expected the office to be something akin to Lock-Horne Investments and Securities, albeit on a small-town scale, but this place looked more like a weathered Victorian B&B, what with the salmon pink door and the browning ivy climbing a white lattice.

An old lady in a housedress rocked on the lemonade porch. Her legs had varicose veins that could have doubled as garden hoses.

"Help you?" she said.

"I'm here to see Mr. Chuback."

"He died fourteen years ago."

Kat wasn't sure what to make of that. "Asghar Chuback?"

"Oh, right, Chewie. You say mister, I think of his dad. You know what I mean? To me, he's just my Chewie." She had to rock the chair a bit to make her way to a standing position. "Follow me."

A fleeting wish that she had brought Chaz with her as backup whisked through her. The old lady brought her inside and opened the basement door. Kat didn't reach for her gun, but she was very aware of where it was and rehearsed in her head, as she often did, how she'd pull it out.

"Chewie?"

"What, Ma? I'm busy down here."

"Someone here to see you."

"Who?"

The old lady looked at Kat. Kat shouted, "Detective Donovan, NYPD."

A big mountain of a man lumbered over to the bottom of the basement stairs. His receding hair was pulled back into a tiny ponytail. His face was wide and sweaty.

He wore baggy cargo shorts and a T-shirt that read TWERK TEAM CAPTAIN.

"Oh, right. Come on down."

The old lady said, "Would you care for an Orangina?"

"I'm good," Kat said, descending the stairway. Chuback waited for her. He wiped his hands on his shirt before shaking her hand with a meaty paw. "Everyone calls me Chewie."

He was thirty, maybe thirty-five, with a bowling-ball gut and thick pale legs like marble pillars. There was a Bluetooth jammed into his ear. The basement looked like Mike Brady's office with wood paneling and clown paintings and tall filing cabinets. The desk area was made up of workbenches, three of them forming a U, all loaded up with a dizzying variety of screens and computers. There were two huge leather chairs on large white pedestals. The arms of the chairs were covered with colorful buttons.

"You're Asghar Chuback," Kat said.

"I prefer being called Chewie."

"Senior partner at Parsons, Chuback, Mitnick and Bushwell?"

"That's me."

Kat glanced around. "And who are Parsons, Mitnick, and Bushwell?"

"Three guys I played basketball with in fifth grade. I just use their names for the masthead. Sounds fancy, though, right?"

"So the entire investment firm . . ."

"Is me, yep. Hold on a second." He tapped the Bluetooth. "Yeah, right, no, Toby, I wouldn't sell it yet. Have you seen the commodities in Finland? Trust me on this. Okay, I'm with another client. Let me call you back."

He tapped the Bluetooth to hang up.

"So," Kat asked, "was your mom the secretary my partner spoke with?"

"No, that was me too. I have a voice changer on the phone. I can also be Parsons, Mitnick, or Bushwell if a client wants a second opinion."

"That's not fraud?"

"I don't think so, but the truth? I make my clients so much money they don't much care." Chewie pulled joysticks and gaming consoles off the two large chairs. "Have a seat."

Kat stepped onto the pedestal and sat. "Why does this chair look familiar to me?"

"They're Captain Kirk's chairs from *Star Trek*. Replicas, sadly. I couldn't buy the original. You like? Truth? I'm not a *Star Trek* guy. *Battlestar Galactica* was so my thing, but these chairs are pretty comfy, right?"

Kat ignored the question. "You recently issued a Suspicious Activities Report on a certain Swiss bank account—is that correct?"

"It is, but why are you here?"

"Pardon?"

"You're NYPD, right? SARs go to the Financial Crime Enforcement Network. That's the jurisdiction of the United States Department of Treasury, not the city police department."

Kat used the armrests, careful not to hit any of the buttons. "The account has come up in a case I'm investigating."

"In what way?" he asked.

"That's not something I'm willing to discuss."

"Oh, that's too bad." Chuback rose from his chair and stepped down from the pedestal. "Let me show you out."

"We aren't done here, Mr. Chuback."

"Chewie," he said. "And yes, I think we are."

"I could report this whole operation."

"Go ahead. I'm a licensed financial adviser working in conjunction with an FDIC-insured banking institution behind me. I can call myself whatever I want. I filled out the Suspicious Activity Report because I am law-abiding and had concerns, but I'm not about to betray my clients or their financial confidences blindly."

"What kind of concerns?"

"I'm sorry, Detective Donovan. I need to know what you're after here, or I'm going to have to ask you to leave."

Kat debated how to play it, but a grown man named Chewie had given her little choice. "I'm investigating another case where someone deposited a large sum of money in a numbered Swiss bank account."

"And it was the same account I reported?" Chuback asked.

"Yes."

He sat back down and drummed his fingers over the multicolored Captain Kirk lights. "Hmm."

"Look, as you pointed out, I'm not with the Department of Treasury. If your client is money laundering or evading taxes, I don't care."

"What are you investigating exactly?"

Kat decided to go for it. Maybe it would shock him into some kind of admission. "A missing woman."

Chuback went slack-jawed. "Are you serious?"

"I am."

"And you think my client is somehow involved?"

"I don't have a clue, quite frankly. But that's what I'm after. I don't care about financial improprieties. If you're willing to protect a client who may be involved in some kind of kidnapping—"

"Kidnapping?"

"—or abduction. I don't know—"

"I'm not, no. Are you serious?"

Kat leaned forward. "Please tell me what you know."

"This whole thing," Chuback said. "None of it adds up." He pointed to the ceiling. "I have security cameras everywhere in this room. They're recording everything we say. I want your word—and I realize that your power is limited—that you'll help my client rather than aggressively prosecute him."

Him. So at least she knew the gender now. She didn't bother hemming and hawing. The recording would be meaningless in a court of law anyway. "You have it."

"My client's name is Gerard Remington."

She scoured her memory banks, but the name meant nothing to her. "Who is he?"

"A pharmaceutical chemist."

Still nothing. "So what happened exactly?"

"Mr. Remington instructed me to transfer the bulk of his account to that Swiss bank account. That's not illegal, by the way."

Again with the illegal. "So why did you report it?"

"Because the activity could indeed be considered suspicious. Look, Gerard isn't just a client. He's also my cousin. His mom and my mom—that's the lady who showed you in—were sisters. His mom died a long time ago, so we're pretty much all the family he has. Gerard is a bit, well, he's on the spectrum, as they say. If he were younger, someone would have categorized him as autistic or having Asperger's or something like that. He's a genius in many ways—he's a helluva scientist—but socially he is inept." Chuback spread his arms and smiled. "And yes, I realize how strange that sounds coming from a grown man who lives with his mother and sits in *Star Trek* chairs."

"So what happened?"

"Gerard called me and asked me to wire money into this Swiss bank account."

"Did he say why?"

"No."

"What did he say exactly?"

"Gerard said that it was his money and that he didn't have to give me a reason. I pressed a little more. He said he was starting a new life."

A cold blast ran down her neck. "What did you make of that?"

Chuback rubbed his chin some more. "I thought it was bizarre, but when it comes to people's money, well, bizarre is almost the norm. I also have a fiduciary responsibility to him. If he asks for confidentiality, I have to honor it."

"But you didn't like it," Kat said.

"No, I didn't. It was out of character for him. But there wasn't much I could do."

Kat saw where this was heading. "Of course, you also have a fiduciary responsibility to the law."

"Exactly."

"So you filled out the SAR, half hoping someone might investigate."

He shrugged, but Kat could see that she had hit bone. "And here you are."

"So where is Gerard Remington now?"

"I don't know. Overseas somewhere."

Kat felt another frosty skin prick. Overseas. Like Dana Phelps. "By himself?"

Chuback shook his head, turned around, and hit his keyboard. The screens all came to life, showing what Kat assumed was his screen saver: a curvaceous woman who looked as though she'd just stepped out of the pornographic dream of a fifteen-year-old boy—or to say the same thing in a slightly different way, the sort of evocative image you see almost every time you go on the Internet. The woman's smile was come-hither. Her lips were full. Her bosom was large enough to qualify for financial aid.

Kat waited for him to press another button, so the screen-saving bimbo would disappear. But he didn't. Kat looked at Chuback. Chuback nodded.

"Wait. Are you saying your cousin went away with her?"

"That's what he told my mother."

"You're kidding, right?"

"That's what I said. I mean, Gerard's a nice guy and all, but a chick who looks like this? Way out of his league. See, my cousin can be rather naive. I was concerned."

"Concerned in what way?"

"At first, I thought that maybe he was being conned. I'd read about guys who meet girls online who get them to carry drugs to South America or do something stupid. Gerard would be the perfect mark."

"And you don't think that anymore?"

"I don't know what to think," Chuback said. "But when he made the transfer, he told me that he's very much in love. He wants to start a new life with her."

"And that didn't sound like a con to you?"

"Of course it did, but what could I do about it?"

"Report it to the police."

"And say what? My weird client wants me to transfer

his money to a Swiss bank account? Come on. Plus, there was still financial confidentiality."

"He swore you to secrecy," Kat said.

"Right, and in my business, that's like confessing to a priest."

Kat shook her head. "So you did nothing."

"Not nothing," he said. "I filled out an SAR. And now here you are."

"Do you know the woman's name?"

"Vanessa something."

"Where does your cousin live?"

"It's about a ten-minute drive."

"Do you have a key?"

"My mom does."

"Then let's go."

CHUBACK unlocked the door and ducked inside. Kat followed, her eyes scanning ahead. Gerard Remington's home was indecently neat and clean and organized. It looked more like something behind glass—something for show—than a true human habitat.

"What are you looking for?" Chuback asked.

It used to be that you would start opening drawers and closets. Now searches were often simpler. "His computer."

They searched the desk. Nothing. They searched the bedroom. More nothing. Not under the bed or on the night table.

"He only has a laptop," Chuback said. "He may have taken it with him."

Damn.

Kat started going old-school—that is, opening draw-

ers and closets. Even they were impossibly neat. The
socks were rolled, four sets in each row, four rows. Everything was folded. There were no loose papers or pens or
coins or paper clips or matchbooks—nothing was out of
place.

"What do you think is going on?" Chuback asked.

Kat didn't want to speculate. There was no actual evidence that any crime had been committed, other than
maybe fuzzy monetary laws on moving sums of money
to a foreign account. There were oddities, of course, and
activities that one might deem suspicious, but right now,
what could she do with that?

Still she had some contacts at the FBI. If she learned
a little more, she might be able to run it by them, get
them to take a more serious look into it, though, again,
what would they find?

She had a thought. "Mr. Chuback?"

"Call me Chewie," he said.

"Right, Chewie. Can you e-mail me that picture of
Vanessa?"

He winked. "You into that kind of thing?"

"Good one."

"Lame, right? But hey, he's my cousin," he said as
though that explained everything. "I'm weirded out here
too."

"Just send it to me, okay?"

There was only one framed photograph on Gerard's
desk. A black-and-white shot taken in the winter. She
picked it up and took a closer look.

Chuback came up behind her. "The little kid is Gerard. And the guy is his father. He died when Gerard was
eight. I guess they liked to ice fish or something."

They were both dressed in parkas with big, fur

bomber hats. There was snow on the ground. Little Gerard held up a fish, a huge smile spread across his face.

"You want to hear something weird?" Chuback said. "I don't think I ever saw Gerard smile like that."

Kat put down the photograph and started checking the drawers again. The bottom drawer contained files, again neatly labeled in a handwriting that could have been a computer font. She found the bills for his Visa card and pulled out the most recent.

"What are you looking for?" Chuback asked.

She started to scan down the row. The first charge that stuck out was for $1,458 to JetBlue Airways. The charge gave no further details—where he planned on traveling or when—but she could trace that back pretty easily. She snapped a photograph of the charge and e-mailed it to Chaz. He could look into it. JetBlue, Kat knew, didn't offer first class, so odds were, that amount was for two round-trip tickets.

For Gerard and the buxom Vanessa?

The rest of his charges seemed normal. There was the cable company and his cell phone (she might need that information), electric, gas, the usual. Kat was about to put the bill back in the drawer, when she saw it near the bottom.

The payee was a company called TMJ Services.

That didn't strike her as anything unusual. She probably would have passed it by except for the amount.

$5.74.

And then she thought about the name. TMJ. Now reverse the order of those initials. TMJ becomes JMT. How discreet.

JMT billing for $5.74.

Like Dana Phelps, like Jeff Raynes, like Kat Donovan

herself, Gerard Remington had been using YouAreJust-
MyType.com.

WHEN Kat was back in the fly yellow Ferrari, she called
Brandon Phelps.

He answered with a tentative "Hello?"

"How are you, Brandon?"

"I'm okay."

"I need a favor."

"Where are you?" he asked.

"I'm driving back from Massachusetts."

"What's up there?"

"I'll fill you in in a little while. But right now, I'm
sending you a photograph of a rather robust woman."

"Huh?"

"She's in a bikini. You'll see. Remember that image-
search thing you did on the pictures of Jeff?"

"Yes."

"I want you to do the same thing with her picture.
See if she's online anywhere. I need a name, address,
whatever you can get on her."

"Okay," he said slowly. Then: "This doesn't have anything to do with my mother, does it?"

"It might."

"How?"

"It's a long story."

"Because if you're still looking for my mother, I think
you should probably stop."

That surprised her. "Why?"

"She called me."

"Your mother?"

"Yes."

Kat pulled the Ferrari off onto the shoulder. "When?"

"An hour ago."

"What did she say?"

"She said that she'd just gotten e-mail access and saw all my e-mails and that everything was fine. She said that I should stop worrying, that she was really happy and might even stay a few days longer."

"What did you say?"

"I asked her about the money transfer."

"What did she say?"

"She kinda got angry. She said it was personal and that I had no right to be poking through her stuff."

"Did you tell her that you'd gone to the police?"

"I told her about Detective Schwartz. I think she called him after me. I didn't tell her about you, though."

Kat wasn't sure what to make of all this.

"Kat?"

"Yeah?"

"She said that she'd be home soon and that she had a big surprise for me. Do you know what it is?"

"I might."

"Does it have something to do with your old boyfriend?"

"It might."

"My mom asked me to leave it alone. I think maybe what she's doing with the money isn't completely legal and that asking around will get her in some kind of trouble."

Kat sat in the car, frowning. Now what? There had been so little evidence of any wrongdoing before. Now that Dana Phelps had called her son and probably Detective Schwartz, there was literally nothing here but a bizarre, paranoid conspiracy theory coming from an NYPD detective who had recently been given a leave by her superior because, well, she had voiced another bizarre, paranoid conspiracy theory.

"Kat?"

"Will you do that image search for me, Brandon? That's all I'm asking right now. Run that search."

There was a brief hesitation. "Yeah, okay."

Another call was coming in, so Kat said a quick good-bye and took it.

Stacy said, "Where are you?"

"I'm in Massachusetts, but I'm heading back home. Why?"

"I found Jeff Raynes."

28

TITUS was lying on the grass, staring up into the perfect night sky. Before he had moved to this farm, he half believed that stars and constellations were the stuff of fairy tales. He wondered whether the stars simply didn't shine in the big city or if he had just never taken the time to lie down like this, his fingers interlaced behind his head, and look up. He'd found a constellations map online and printed it out. For a while, he would bring it out here with him. He didn't need it now.

Dana Phelps was back in her box.

She was tougher than most, but in the end, when the lies and distortions and threats and confusion do not guarantee cooperation, all Titus had to do was hold up a picture of a child, and a parent fell in line.

Dana had made the call. Eventually, they always do. There had been one man who tried to warn the caller.

Titus had cut him off immediately. He had debated killing the man right then and there, but instead, he let Reynaldo work on him with the old Amish pruning saw in the barn. The blade was dull, but that just made Reynaldo enjoy himself more. Three days later, Reynaldo brought him back. The man begged on his knees to cooperate. He would have clasped his hands in prayer position, but all his fingers were gone.

And so it goes.

Titus heard the footsteps. He kept his eyes on the stars until Reynaldo loomed over him.

"Is everything okay with the new arrival?" Titus asked.

"Yes. She's in her box."

"Did she pack her laptop?"

"No."

Not surprising. Martha Paquet had been more reticent than others. Her getaway to this farm hadn't been a week to some reclusive warm-weather locale. They had instead broken her in with something more digestible—two nights at a bed-and-breakfast in Ephrata, Pennsylvania. It had seemed at first as though Martha wouldn't take them up on it—no matter, you just cut the bait and move on—but she eventually acquiesced.

Having her laptop would have been helpful. Most people have their lives on theirs. Dmitry could go through it and find bank accounts and passwords. They would check her smartphone, but he didn't like to leave it on too long—though unlikely, a phone that was powered on could be traced. That was why he not only took the phones but removed the batteries.

The other difficulty was, of course, that Titus had less time to work with her. She didn't have much family, just a sister who had been encouraging Martha to take this chance. The sister might buy it if Martha decided to stay a few extra days, but there was still a small degree of urgency.

Sometimes, when they first arrived at the farm, Titus liked to keep them locked in the underground box for hours or even days. It softened them up. But other times—and Titus was still experimenting here—it was best to get on with it and use the shock to his advantage. Eight hours ago, Martha Paquet had left her house, believing she was on her way to find true love. Since then, she had been locked in a car, assaulted when she got out of hand, stripped of her clothes, and buried in a dark box.

Hopelessness was much more potent when it started out as hope. Think about it: If you want to drop something so it lands hard and cracks, you first have to lift it up as high as possible.

Put more simply, there has to be hope in order to take it away.

Titus stood in one fluid motion. "Send her up the path."

He made his way back to the farmhouse. Dmitry was waiting for him. He had the computer up. Dmitry was computer savvy, but his expertise didn't factor into this work all that much. It was Titus's job to get their account numbers, their e-mails, their passwords—all the information. Once you had that, all you needed to do was plug them into the proper prompts.

Reynaldo would be pulling Martha Paquet out of her box now. He would make her hose off and then give her the jumpsuit. Titus checked the time. He still had about ten minutes. He grabbed a snack from the kitchen—he loved rice crackers with almond butter—and put a kettle of boiling water on the stove.

There were various ways for Titus to bleed his "guests" dry. For the most part, he tried to do it slowly so no one, to keep with the metaphor, applied a tourniquet too early. Over the first few days, he would have them transfer amounts close to ten thousand dollars to various accounts he had set up overseas. The moment any money arrived, Titus transferred it to another account, then another, then another. In short, he made it virtually impossible to track.

Just like in the old days when he watched a girl getting off a bus at the Port Authority, Titus knew that patience was key. You had to wait, letting some targets go by, so that you could find ones more ideal. With the buses, Titus would hope to encounter maybe one or two potential marks per week. But the Internet made the possibilities endless. He could hunt from a steady pool of targets on various dating sites. Many were deemed worthless immediately, but that was okay because there were so many more out there. It took time. It took patience. He wanted to make sure they didn't have much family. He wanted to make sure that a lot of people wouldn't miss them. He wanted to make sure they had adequate funds to make the enterprise profitable.

Sometimes the mark bit. Sometimes they didn't. *C'est la vie*.

Take Martha for example. She had inherited money recently from her deceased mother. She told only her sister about Michael Craig. Since their rendezvous was over a weekend, there was no reason for Martha even to tell her bosses at NRG. That would have to change, of course, but once Titus got her e-mail password, it would be easy for "Martha" to inform her employer that she had decided to take a few days off. With Gerard Remington, it was even easier. He had planned a full ten-day vacation-cum-honeymoon with Vanessa. He had notified the pharmaceutical company that he was taking some of his much accrued vacation time. Gerard was a lifelong bachelor and had virtually no family. Transferring the bulk of his account was easy to explain, and while his financial adviser had asked plenty of questions, there was really no serious issue.

Once that was done—once Titus had taken as much as he could from Gerard or any mark—they were useless to him. They were the rind of a just-eaten orange. He obviously couldn't let them go. That would be far too risky. The safest and neatest solution? Make the person disappear forever. How?

Put a bullet in their brains and bury them in the woods.

A live person leaves a lot of clues. A dead body leaves some clues. But with a person simply missing, supposedly alive and seeking contentment, there were virtually no clues. There was nothing for anyone, especially over-worked law enforcement officers, to investigate.

Eventually, family members might wonder and worry. They might, weeks or months later, go to the authorities. The authorities might investigate, but in the end, these "missing" people were consenting adults who had claimed they wanted to start anew.

There were no signs of foul play. The adults in question had given reasonable explanations for their supposed disappearance—they'd been sad and lonely and had fallen in love and wanted to start a new life.

Who couldn't relate to that fantasy?

On the rare occasion that someone might not buy it—

that some ambitious law enforcement officer or family member might want to investigate further—what would they find? The trail was weeks old. It would never lead to an Amish farm in rural Pennsylvania, one that was still registered to Mark Kadison, an Amish farmer, who had sold the land for cash.

Titus stood in the doorway. In the darkness, he saw the familiar movement on his left. A few seconds later, Martha shuffled into view.

Titus was always careful. He kept his crew small and paid them well. He didn't make mistakes. And when a mistake was made, like Claude's idiotic petty greed with the ATM, Titus cut all ties and removed the threat. It was harsh perhaps, but everyone who worked here understood the rules from day one.

Martha took another step. Titus put on a warm smile and beckoned for her to follow him inside. She made her way toward the porch, hugging herself, shivering from either cold or fear, though more likely a toxic combination of both. Her hair was wet. Her eyes had that look Titus had seen plenty of times before—like two shattered marbles.

Titus sat in the big chair. Dmitry sat by his computer, wearing, as always, his knit cap and dashiki.

"My name is Titus," he said in his soothing voice when she entered. "Please sit down."

She did so. Many of them started to ask questions at this point. Some, like Gerard, clung to the belief that their newly found loved one was still out there. Titus could use that, of course. Gerard had refused to cooperate until Titus threatened to hurt Vanessa. Others saw immediately what was going on.

That seemed to be the case with Martha Paquet.

Titus looked toward Dmitry. "Ready?"

Dmitry adjusted his tinted glasses and nodded.

"We have some questions for you, Martha. You are going to answer them."

A lone tear ran down Martha's cheek.

"We know your e-mail address. You wrote to Michael Craig often enough. What is the account's password?"

Martha said nothing.

Titus kept his voice low and measured. There was no need to shout. "You're going to tell us, Martha. It is just a question of time. With some people, we keep them in that box for hours or days or even weeks. With some people, we turn on the kitchen stove and hold their hand against the burner until we can't stand the smell. I don't like to do that. If we leave too many scars on a person, it means we will need to get rid of the evidence eventually. Do you understand?"

Martha stayed still.

Titus rose and moved toward her. "Most people—and yes, we've done this quite a few times—understand exactly what is going to happen here. We are going to rob you. If you cooperate, you will go home somewhat poorer but in perfect health. You will continue to live your life as though nothing ever happened."

He sat on the arm of her chair. Martha blinked and shuddered.

"In fact," Titus continued, "three months ago, we did this with someone you know. I won't mention her name because that's part of the deal. But if you think hard enough, you might figure it out. She told everyone she was going away for the weekend, but really, she was here. She gave up all the information we needed right away and we sent her home."

This almost always worked. Titus tried not to smile as he saw the wheels in Martha's head start to work. It was a lie, of course. No one ever left the farm. But again, it wasn't merely about tearing someone down. You had to give them hope.

"Martha?"

He put his hand gently on her wrist. She almost screamed.

"What's the password on your e-mail?" he asked with a smile.

And Martha gave it to him.

29

SINCE Kat had to return the Chick Trawler anyway, she and Stacy decided to meet up in the lobby of the Lock-Horne Building. Stacy wore a black turtleneck, sprayed-on blue jeans, and cowboy boots. Her hair cascaded down in ideal just-mussed waves, as if she simply got out of bed, shook her head, and voilà, perfection.

If Kat didn't love Stacy, she'd hate her so much.

It was near midnight. Two women, one petite and lovely, the other huge and dressed flamboyantly, exited an elevator. Outside of them, the only person in the lobby was a security guard.

"Where should we talk?" Kat asked.

"Follow me."

Stacy showed her ID to the security guard, who pointed to an elevator alone on the left. The interior was velvet lined with a padded bench. There were no buttons to press. No lights told them what floor they were approaching. Kat looked a question at Stacy. Stacy shrugged.

The elevator stopped—Kat didn't have a clue on what floor—and they stepped onto an open-space trading floor. Dozens, maybe hundreds, of desks were laid out in neat rows. The lights were out, but the computer screens provided enough illumination to give the whole place a sinister glow.

"What are we doing here?" Kat whispered.

Stacy started down the corridor. "You don't have to whisper. We're alone."

Stacy stopped in front of the door with a keypad. She typed in a code and the door unlocked with an audible click. Kat entered. It was a corner office with a pretty great view up Park Avenue. Stacy flicked on the lights. The office was done in early American Elitism. Rich burgundy leather chairs with gold buttons sat atop a forest green Oriental carpet. Paintings of foxhunts hung on dark wood paneling. The expansive desk was pure oak. A large antique globe rested next to it.

"Someone has serious cash," Kat said.

"My friend who owns the place."

A wistful look crossed her face. The media had had a short period of speculation about the CEO of Lock-Horne Investments and Securities, but like all stories, it died out when nothing new fed it.

"What really happened to him?" Kat asked.

"He just"—she spread her arms and shrugged—"checked out, I guess."

"Nervous breakdown?"

A funny smile came to Stacy's face. "I don't think so."

"Then what?"

"I don't know. His business used to take up six floors. With him gone and all the layoffs, it's down to four."

Kat realized she was asking too many questions, but she pushed past that. "You care about him."

"I do. But it wasn't meant to be."

"Why not?"

"He is handsome, rich, charming, romantic, a great lover."

"I hear a *but*."

"But you can't reach him. No woman can."

"Yet here you are," Kat said.

"After he and I were, uh, together, he put my name on the list."

"The list?"

"It's complicated. Once a woman is on it, they have access to certain spaces, in case they need time alone or whatever."

"You're kidding."

"Nope."

"How many women would you guess are on this list?"

"I don't know," Stacy said. "But I'd guess there are quite a few."

"He sounds like a nutjob."

Stacy shook her head. "There you go again."

"What?"

"Judging people without knowing them."

"I don't do that."

"Yeah, you do," Stacy said. "What was your first impression of me?"

Airheaded bimbo, Kat thought. "Well, what was your first impression of me?"

"I thought you were cool and smart," Stacy replied.

"You were right."

"Kat?"

"Yes?"

"You're asking me all these questions because you're stalling."

"And you're answering them all because you're stalling too."

"Touché," Stacy said.

"So where is Jeff?"

"Near as I can tell, Montauk."

Kat's heart felt as though it'd been kicked. "On Long Island?"

"Do you know another Montauk?" Then in a softer voice: "You could use a drink."

Kat shoved the memory away. "I'm fine."

Stacy moved toward the antique globe and lifted a handle, revealing a crystal decanter and snifters. "Do you drink cognac?"

"Not really."

"He only drinks the best."

"I'm not sure I'm comfortable drinking his expensive cognac."

Another sad smile—Stacy really liked this guy—hit her face. "He would be upset if he knew that we were here and didn't imbibe."

"Pour, then."

Stacy did so. Kat took a sip and managed not to gasp in ecstasy. The cognac was God's nectar.

"Well?" Stacy asked.

"That's the closest thing I've had to an orgasm in liquid form."

Stacy laughed. Kat had never considered herself materialistic or someone who reveled in expensive tastes, but between the Macallan 25 and this cognac, tonight was definitely changing her thinking, at least on the alcohol front.

"You okay?" Stacy asked.

"Fine."

"When I said Montauk—"

"We were there once," Kat said quickly, "in Amagansett, not Montauk. It was wonderful. I'm over it. Move on."

"Good," Stacy said. "So here's the deal. Eighteen years ago, Jeff Raynes leaves New York City and moves to Cincinnati. We know that he got into a brawl at a bar called Longsworth's."

"I remember that place. He took me there once. It used to be a firehouse."

"Wow, great story," Stacy said.

"Was that sarcasm?"

"It was, yes. Mind if I continue?"

"Please."

"Jeff was arrested, but he pleaded down to a misdemeanor and paid a fine. No big deal. But here is where things get a little hairy."

Kat took another sip. The brown liquor warmed her chest.

"There is absolutely no sign of Jeff Raynes after the plea. Whatever made him change his name, it must have had something to do with the fight."

"Who did he fight with?"

"Whom."

"Shut up."

"Sorry. Two other men were arrested that night. They were friends, I guess. Grew up together in Anderson Township. Both also pleaded down to a misdemeanor and paid a fine. According to the arrest report, all three men were inebriated. It started when one of the guys was being rude to his girlfriend. He may have grabbed her arm hard; the testimony is a little fuzzy on that. Anyway, Jeff stepped in and told him to knock it off."

"How chivalrous," Kat said.

"To quote you, 'Was that sarcasm?'"

"I guess so, yeah."

"Because it sounds a little like bitterness."

"What's the difference?" Kat asked.

"Fair point. Anyway, Jeff steps in to protect the girl. The drunk boyfriend, who's been arrested before for these kinds of altercations, snaps back with the classic mind-your-own-business-or-else. Jeff says he'll mind his own business if he leaves the lady alone. You know how it goes."

Kat did. Her earlier comment might have been sarcastic or bitter, but misguided chivalry too often leads to brawls. "So who threw the first punch?"

"Reportedly, the drunk boyfriend. But Jeff supposedly retaliated with a fury. Broke the guy's orbital bone and two ribs. Surprised?"

"Not really," Kat said. "Were there any lawsuits?"

"No. But not long after this, Jeff Raynes quits his job—he was working at *The Cincinnati Post*—and is pretty much never heard from again. Two years later, I have the first sign of Ron Kochman in a byline in something called *Vibe* magazine."

"And now he lives in Montauk?"

"All signs point that way. The thing is, he has a sixteen-year-old daughter."

Kat blinked and took a deeper sip.

"There's no sign of a wife."

"On YouAreJustMyType.com, it says he's a widower."

"That might be true, but I can't say for sure. I only know he has a daughter named Melinda. She attends East Hampton High School, so I was able to access their address via the school records."

Kat and Stacy both stood there, at midnight, alone in some master of the universe's opulent office. Stacy dug into her pocket and took out a slip of paper.

"Do you want me to give you the address, Kat?"

"Why wouldn't I?"

"Because he's done his damnedest not to be found. He changed not only his name, but he's created an entirely new ID. He doesn't use credit cards. He doesn't have bank accounts."

"Yet he went on Facebook and YouAreJustMyType."

"Using aliases, right?"

"No. I mean, he used an alias on YouAreJustMyType. Brandon said his mom called him Jack. But on Facebook, he was Ron Kochman. How do you explain that?"

"I don't know."

Kat nodded. "But either way, your point remains. Jeff doesn't want to be found."

"Right."

"And when I contacted him on YouAreJustMyType, he said that he didn't want to talk to me and that he needed a fresh start."

"Right again."

"So driving up to Montauk out of the blue would be irrational."

"Totally."

Kat stuck out her hand. "So why am I going first thing in the morning?"

Stacy handed her the address. "Because the heart don't know from rational."

30

KAT'S bottle of Jack tasted like fish ass after the cognac and Macallan 25.

She didn't sleep. She barely tried. She just lay in bed and let all the possibilities swirl in her head. She tried to sort through them, tried to figure a way they could make sense, and every time she came up with an answer about what to do next, she'd close her eyes and the swirling would start again and she'd change her mind.

She got out of bed at five in the morning. She could wait and go to Aqua's class—that might help clear her head—but with the way he'd been freaking out lately, it might do more to muddy the waters. Besides, in the end, Kat was again stalling. There really was only one choice here.

She had to drive out to Montauk and figure out what had happened to Jeff.

Yes, she could list a million reasons why that was a

dumb move, but the truth was, until she knew all, Kat could never let Jeff go. She might be able to resist taking the drive for a month, maybe two, but it would be that proverbial itch that would eventually need to be scratched raw. The choice had been made for her. She didn't have the discipline to stay away forever.

There had never been closure with Jeff. There had never been closure with her father. She had let that stand for eighteen years.

No more.

There was no reason to put it off, either. She would drive to Montauk today, right now even. Chaz had already agreed to loan her his car. It was in the garage on 68th Street, waiting for her. She had no idea what she'd find in Montauk. Jeff probably wasn't even there. She could wait to make the trip until . . . until what? He might never return, right? Weren't they moving to Costa Rica?

It might be denial, but she still wasn't buying that. She was missing something here.

Didn't matter. Kat had the time. If Jeff had gone away with Dana Phelps, Kat could find out where and clear up that little mystery too. She grabbed a cup of coffee at the Starbucks on Columbus Avenue and started the drive. She was halfway to Montauk when she realized she had no plan. Would she simply knock on his door? Would she wait till he appeared in his yard or something?

She had no idea.

Kat was driving through East Hampton—she and Jeff had walked these very streets a lifetime ago—when her cell phone trilled. She put it on speaker and said hello.

"I did that image search you wanted," Brandon said. "Wow, do you know this chick personally?"

Men. Or should she yet again say boys? "No."

"She's, uh . . ."

"Yeah, I know what she is, Brandon. What did the image search dig up?"

"Her name is Vanessa Moreau. She's a model. She specializes in bikinis."

Terrific. "Anything else?"

"What else do you want to know? She's five-eight, weight one hundred twelve pounds. Her measurements are thirty-eight, twenty-four, thirty-six; she's a D cup."

Kat kept her hands on the wheel. "Is she married?"

"It doesn't say. I found her modeling portfolio. The picture you sent me is from a website called Mucho Models. They do casting, I guess. It gives her measurements and hair color and says if she'll do nudes or not—she does, by the way. . . ."

"Good to know."

"They also have a part where the model writes a bio."

"What does hers say?"

"Currently looking for paid gigs only. Will travel if expenses paid."

"What else?"

"That's it."

"Home address?"

"Nope, nothing."

So Vanessa was the woman's real name. Kat wasn't sure what to make of that. "Could I ask you another favor?"

"I guess."

"Could you break back into YouAreJustMyType again and access Jeff's communication?"

"That will be harder."

"Why?"

"You can't stay on long. Sites are always changing their passwords and looking for hacking. So I would go in, take a brief look, go out. I never stayed long. The hard part is initially getting in—finding the first portal. Theirs is password protected. It took us a few hours to get past it, but now that I'm out, I'd have to start again."

"Could you do it?" Kat said.

"I can try, I guess, but I don't really think it's a good idea. I mean, maybe you were right. I was invading my mother's privacy. I don't really want to read more of that."

"That's not what I'm asking."

"Then, what?"

"You said that when Jeff was first with your mom, he was still talking with other women."

"Including you," Brandon added.

"Right, including me. What I want to know is if he's still talking to other women."

"You think he's, what, cheating on my mom?"

"You don't have to look at the specific communications. I just need to know if he's communicating with any other women and their names."

Silence.

"Brandon?"

"You still think something is wrong, don't you, Kat?"

"How did your mother sound on the phone?"

"She sounded fine."

"Did she sound happy?"

"I wouldn't go that far. What do you think is going on?"

"I don't know. That's why I'm asking you to check."

Brandon sighed. "On it."

They hung up.

Montauk is located on the far tip of the South Fork of Long Island. It's a hamlet, not a town, and part somehow of East Hampton. Kat made her way to Deforest Road and slowed down. She let the car slide past the address Stacy had given her. The house was what Realtors would probably label a cozy Cape Cod with cedar shingles. Two vehicles were in the driveway, a black Dodge Ram pickup truck loaded up with what appeared to be fishing gear, and a blue Toyota RAV4. Neither was fly yellow. One point for the Kochmans.

Jeff's daughter, Melinda, was sixteen. You don't get your full license in New York State until you are seventeen. So why two vehicles? Both could belong to Jeff, of course. A pickup truck for hobby or work—was he a fisherman now?—and the Toyota for general travel.

So now what?

She parked down at the end of the block and waited. She tried to imagine a car less suited for surveillance work than a fly-yellow Ferrari, but nothing came to mind.

It still wasn't yet eight A.M. Wherever Jeff aka Ron spent his days, there was a decent chance he hadn't gone to it yet. She could wait here a little while and keep watch. But no. There was no reason to waste time. She might as well get out of the Chick Trawler and walk right up to his house.

The front door opened.

Kat wasn't sure what to do. She started to duck down but stopped herself. She was probably a hundred yards away. With the morning glare, no one would be able to see inside the car. She kept her eyes on the door.

A teenage girl appeared.

Could it be . . . ?

The girl turned behind her, waved good-bye to someone in the house, and started down the path. She carried a maroon backpack. Her ponytail sneaked out the back of a baseball cap. Kat wanted to get closer. She wanted to see whether there was any resemblance between the teen with the awkward gait and her old fiancé.

But how?

She didn't know or really care. She didn't think it through. She started up the Ferrari and drove toward her.

It didn't matter. If she blew her cover—though maybe in this car, she could disguise herself as a middle-aged man with erectile dysfunction—so be it.

The girl's steps became more like dance movements. As Kat got closer, she could see that Melinda—why not call her that in her mind?—was wearing white earbuds. The cord dangled past her waist, doing its own little dance.

Melinda turned suddenly and met Kat's eye. Kat looked for a resemblance, an echo of Jeff, but even if she did see one, that could simply have been her imagination.

The girl stopped and stared.

Kat tried to play it cool. "Uh, excuse me," Kat called out. "How do I get to the lighthouse?"

The girl kept a safe distance. "You just get back on Montauk Highway. Keep driving until the end. You can't miss it."

Kat smiled. "Thanks."

"Nice car."

"Yeah, well, it's not mine. It's my boyfriend's."

"He must be rich."

"I guess so."

The girl started walking away. Kat wasn't sure what to do here. She didn't want to lose this lead, but cruising alongside the girl was getting creepy. The girl picked up speed. Up ahead, a school bus made the turn. The girl started to hurry toward it.

Now or never, Kat thought.

"You're Ron Kochman's girl, Melinda, right?"

The girl's face lost color. Something close to panic filled her eyes. She nearly sprinted away now, jumping on the bus without so much as a wave good-bye. The bus door closed and whisked her away.

Well, well, Kat thought.

The bus disappeared down the road. Kat turned the Ferrari around so it faced the Kochman home again. She had clearly spooked the kid. If that meant anything—if she had spooked the girl because she had something to hide or if the girl's reaction had something to do with a weird woman quasi-stalking her—it was hard to say.

Kat waited, wondering if someone else was going to emerge from the house. She took it a step further, moving the car and parking it directly in front of the Kochman home. She waited a few more minutes.

Nothing.

The hell with waiting.

She got out of the car and headed straight up the walk. She hit the doorbell once and knocked firmly for good measure. There was beaded glass on either side of the door. Kat couldn't make anything out through it, but she could see movement.

Someone had passed by the door.

She knocked hard again and, with an internal shoulder shrug of "Why not?", called out, "This is Detective Donovan from the New York Police Department. Could you please open the door?"

Footsteps.

Kat backed off and braced herself. She absentmindedly smoothed out her shirt and even—God help her—patted down her hair. She saw the knob turn and the door opened.

It wasn't Jeff.

A man Kat would estimate to be around seventy years old peered down at her. "Who are you?"

"Detective Donovan, NYPD."

"Let me see some identification."

Kat reached into her pocket and pulled out her badge. She flipped it open. That was usually enough, but the old man reached out and took hold of it. He examined it closely. Kat waited. He squinted and kept examining it. Kat half expected him to break out one of those jeweler's magnifying glasses. Finally, he handed it back to her and gave her the full-on stink-eye.

"What do you want?"

He wore a brown flannel shirt with the sleeves rolled up to the elbow, Wrangler jeans, and brown soft-toe work boots. He was good-looking in a weathered way, the kind of guy you imagined had spent the majority of his life working outdoors and it agreed with him. His hands were gnarly. His forearms were the kind of sinewy you get from life, not a gym.

"May I ask your name, sir?" Kat said.

"You knocked on my door, remember?"

"I do. And I've given you my name. I'd very much appreciate it if you'd extend me the same courtesy."

"Appreciate, my ass," he said.

"I would, really," Kat said, "but those jeans are a little baggy."

His mouth twitched. "You messing with me?"

"Not as much as you're messing with me," Kat said.

"My name ain't important," he snapped. "What do you want?"

There was no reason to play around with this guy. "I'm looking for Ron Kochman," she said.

The question didn't seem to faze him.

"I don't have to answer your questions," he said.

Kat swallowed. Her voice sounded as though it

were coming from someone else. "I don't mean him any harm."

"If that's true," the old man said, "then maybe you should be leaving well enough alone."

"I need to talk to him."

"No, Detective Donovan, I don't think you do."

His eyes pinned her down, and for a moment, it felt as though he knew who she was. "Where is he?"

"He's not here. That's all you need to know."

"Then I'll come back."

"There's nothing left for you here."

She tried to speak, but no words came out. Finally: "Who the hell are you?"

"I'm going to close my door now. If you don't leave, I'm going to call Jim Gamble. He's the chief of police here. I don't think he'll like some NYPD cop hassling one of his residents."

"You don't want that attention."

"No, but I can handle it. Good-bye, Detective."

"What makes you think I'll just go away?"

"Because you should know when you're not wanted. Because you should know that the past is the past. And because I don't think you want to cause any more destruction."

"What destruction? What are you talking about?"

He took hold of the door. "It's time for you to go."

"I just need to talk to him," Kat said. She could hear the pleading in her voice. "I don't want to hurt anybody. Tell him that, okay? Tell him I just need to talk to him."

The old man started to close the door on her. "I'll be sure to pass on that message. Now, get off my property."

31

THE farm, in keeping with the Amish way of life, had no connection to the public electric grid. Titus liked that, of course. No billing, no reading meters, no outside maintenance. Whatever reason the Amish had for not using public energy sources—he had heard everything from a fear of outsiders to blocking access to television and the Internet—it worked well for this operation.

The Amish, however, do not shun electricity altogether. That seemed to be a common myth. This farm had used a windmill to provide enough electricity for their modest needs. But it wouldn't do for Titus. He had installed a DuroMax generator that ran on propane gas. The farm's mailbox was on the edge of the road, far from the house or any clearing. He had put in a gate so no cars could drive through. He never ordered anything, so there were no deliveries. If they needed something, he or one of his people fetched it, usually at a Sam's Club eight miles away.

He tried to give his men time away from the farm. He and Reynaldo enjoyed the solitude. The other men got antsy. There was a strip club twelve miles from there called Starbutts, but to be on the safe side, Titus asked his men to drive the extra six miles to one called the Lumberyard ("Where Real Men Go for Wood"). They were allowed to go once every two weeks, no more. They could do what they pleased, but they could not, under any circumstances, make a scene. They always went alone.

Mobile phones and the like had no reach there, so Dmitry had set up phone and Internet services via a satellite that bounced all web activity via a VPN that originated in Bulgaria. Almost no calls ever came in, so when Titus heard his private account ring at eight in the morning, he knew something was wrong.

"Yes?"

"Wrong number."

The caller hung up.

That was his signal. The government monitored your e-mails. That was no longer a secret. The best way to communicate via e-mail without getting anyone's attention was to *not* send the e-mail. Titus had a Gmail account he kept off-line except when signaled to check it. He loaded the home page and signed in. There were no new e-mails. He had expected that.

He hit DRAFTS and the message popped up. That was how he communicated with a contact. They both had access to the same Gmail account. When you wanted to send a message, you wrote it, but—and this was the important thing—you didn't send it. You just saved it as a draft. Then you signed off, signaled with the call, and your recipient signed on. The recipient, in this case Titus, would then read the message in the draft folder and delete it.

Titus had four such accounts, each communicating with a different person. This one was from his contact in Switzerland:

Stop using 89787198. SAR was filed by a financial firm called Parsons, Chuback, Mitnick and Bushwell and now an NYPD detective named Katarina Donovan has followed up.

Titus deleted the draft and signed out of the account. He wondered about this. Suspicious Activity Reports had been issued on his accounts before. He seldom worried about it. When you moved large sums of money overseas, they were mandatory. But the Department of the Treasury was mostly hung up on possible terrorism financing. Once they checked into the person's background and saw nothing suspicious, they rarely followed up.

But this was the first time he had seen two questions for one account. Moreover, instead of just the Department of the Treasury, Titus had now drawn the attention of a New York City cop. How? Why? None of his recent guests had come from New York City. And what possible connection could there be between a chemist from Massachusetts and a socialite from Connecticut?

He could ask only one of them.

Titus rested his hands on the desk for a moment. Then he leaned forward and brought up a search engine. He typed in the name of the detective and waited for the results.

When he saw the photograph of Detective Donovan, he almost laughed out loud.

Dmitry walked into the room. "Something funny?"

"It's Kat," Titus said. "She's trying to find us."

AFTER the old man slammed the door in her face, Kat wasn't sure what to do.

She stood on the stoop for a moment, half tempted to kick in the door and pistol-whip the old man, but where would that get her? If Jeff wanted to reach out, she had given him all the tools he needed. If he still ignored her, did she really have the right or even desire to force it?

Have some pride, for crying out loud.

She headed back to the car. She began to cry and hated herself for it. Whatever had happened to Jeff in that Cincinnati bar, it had nothing to do with her. Absolutely nothing. Stacy had said last night that she would continue to look into the bar brawl, see if the two drunk guys had additional records, if somehow they were looking for Jeff and that might explain his disappearance, but really, what was the point?

If these two men had been after him, would he still be so afraid to see Kat?

Didn't matter. Jeff had his life. He had a daughter and lived with a grumpy old man. Kat had no idea who the old man was. Jeff's own father had died years ago. Jeff had chosen to go on a dating website. Kat had reached out to him, and he had slapped her hand away. So why was she still pursuing it?

Why, despite all the evidence to the contrary, was she still not buying it?

Kat got back on Montauk Highway and headed west.

But she didn't travel far. A few miles down the road, she turned left onto Napeague Lane. Funny what you remember after nearly twenty years. She made the turn onto Marine Boulevard and parked near Gilbert Path. She took the wooden boardwalk toward the ocean. The waves crashed. The sky darkened, hinting of an upcoming storm. Kat made her way around a pathetic fence with shattered rails. She slipped off her shoes and started on the sand toward the water.

The house hadn't changed. It had been newly built in that sleek modern style that some people found too boxy but that Kat had grown to love. The place would have been way out of their price range, even for a weekend rental, but Jeff had been the owner's TA at Columbia, and loaning him the house had been her way of thanking him.

It had been nearly twenty years, and Kat could still tell you every single moment of that weekend. She could tell you about the visit to the farmers' market, the quiet walks in town, eating three times at the expanded shack restaurant nicknamed Lunch—because they both got addicted to their lobster roll—the way Jeff sneaked up behind her on this very beach and gave her the most tender kiss imaginable.

It had been during that tender kiss that Kat knew she had to spend the rest of her life with him.

Tender kisses don't lie, do they?

She frowned, again hating herself for the sentimentality, but maybe she should cut herself some slack. She tried to find the very spot where she had been standing that day, checking her bearings by using the house, moving a few feet left, then right, until she was certain, yes, this was the spot where that tender kiss took place.

She heard a car engine and turned to see a silver Mercedes idling on the road. She half expected that it would be Jeff. Yes, that would be perfect, wouldn't it? He would follow her here and come up behind her, the same way he had all those years ago. He would take her in his arms, and yeah, it was dumb and corny and hurtful, but that didn't mean the longing wasn't there. You have very few perfect moments in your life, moments you want to put in a box and stick on the top shelf so that when you're alone, you can take the box down and open it up again.

That kiss had been one of the moments.

The silver Mercedes drove away.

Kat turned back to the churning ocean. The clouds were gathering now. It was going to start pouring soon. She was about to head back to the Ferrari, when her phone rang again. It was Brandon.

"Bastard," he said. "That lying, cheating bastard."

"What?"

"Jeff or Ron or Jack or whatever the hell his name is."

Kat stood very still. "What happened?"

"He's still hitting on other women. I couldn't see the communication, but he was in touch with both of them yesterday."

"How many other women?"

"Two."

"Maybe he was saying good-bye. Maybe he's telling them about your mother."

"Yeah, I don't think so."

"Why not?"

"Because that would be one, maybe two, direct messages. These were more like twenty or thirty. That bastard."

"Okay, listen to me, Brandon. Did you get the names of the two women?"

"Yes."

"Could you give them to me?"

"One is named Julie Weitz. She lives in Washington, DC. The other lives in Bryn Mawr, Pennsylvania. Her name is Martha Paquet."

THE first thing Kat did was call Chaz.

He would contact both women and make sure they hadn't gone away with their online paramour. But as Kat made her way toward her car—she was going back to that house in Montauk and she'd kick the old man in the balls if he didn't talk to her—something started bothering her again. It had started to nag her early on, from the beginning of all this, really, but she still couldn't see what it was.

Something was making her hang on to Jeff.

Most would have said that it was the blinding potency of a foolish heart. Kat would have agreed. But now Kat was maybe getting a little clarity on the situation. The thing that had been bothering Kat involved her own messages with Jeff on YouAreJustMyType.com.

She kept going over his words, replaying the ending so many times in her head—all that crap about protecting himself and being cautious and going back to the past would be a mistake and him needing a fresh start— that she hadn't really gone over their earliest communications.

It had all started when she sent him that old music video of John Waite singing "Missing You."

And how had he responded?

He hadn't remembered it.

How could that be? Okay, maybe she had stronger feelings than he did, but he had, after all, proposed. How could he forget something that was so crucial to their relationship?

More than that, Jeff had written that the video was "cute" and that he liked a girl with "a sense of humor" and that he was "drawn" to her photograph. Drawn. Gag. She had been so hurt and surprised, and so she had messaged him and said . . .

It's Kat.

There was a thin man in a dark suit leaning against the yellow Ferrari. He had his arms folded across his chest, his legs crossed near the ankles. Still reeling with the revelations, Kat staggered toward him and said, "May I help you?"

"Nice car."

"Yeah, I get that a lot. You mind getting off it?"

"In a second, sure. If you're ready."

"What?"

The silver Mercedes pulled up next to her.

"Get in the back," the man said.

"What the hell are you talking about?"

"You have a choice. We can shoot you here in the street. Or you can get in and we can have a nice little chat."

32

REYNALDO got the message via the walkie-talkie feature on his smartphone.

"Base to box," Titus said. "Come in."

Reynaldo had been tossing a tennis ball with his Labrador retriever, Bo. Bo lived up to his breed, constantly wanting to play fetch, never ever tiring of the game, no matter how many times or how far Reynaldo threw the tennis ball.

"I'm here," Reynaldo said into the phone, throwing the ball yet again. Bo ran-hobbled after it. Age. Bo was, according to a vet, eleven years old. He was still in good shape, but it made Reynaldo sad to see the sprint slowing to a lumber. Still, Bo wanted to play, always, almost stubbornly insisting on more throws when it was clear that his stamina and arthritis couldn't really handle it. Sometimes Reynaldo tried to stop, for the sake of old Bo, but it was as though Bo could see what his master was trying to do and didn't like it. Bo would whine and bark until Reynaldo picked up the ball and threw it yet again.

Eventually, Reynaldo would send Bo up the path so he could rest on the soft dog bed in the barn. Reynaldo had bought that bed after he found Bo wandering along the East River. The bed had held up well.

Bo looked up at him expectantly. Reynaldo rubbed behind Bo's ear as Titus via the walkie-talkie said, "Escort Number Six up."

"Roger that."

They never used the phones or texts at the farm, just the walkie-talkie app. Untraceable. They never used names for obvious reasons, but Reynaldo didn't know the names anyway. They were all numbers to him, corresponding with their location: Number Six, a blond woman who had arrived in a yellow sundress, was in Box Six.

Even Titus would admit that this sort of security was overkill, but it was always better to err on the side of too much caution. That was his creed.

When Reynaldo rose, Bo stared up at him, disappointed. "We'll play again soon, boy. I promise."

The dog gave a small whimper and nudged Reynaldo's hand. Reynaldo smiled and petted Bo. The dog's tail wagged slowly in appreciation. Reynaldo felt his eyes well up.

"Go get dinner, boy."

Bo looked both disappointed and understanding. He hesitated for another moment and then started trotting up the path. His tail did not wag. Reynaldo waited until Bo was out of sight. For some reason, he didn't want Bo to see inside the boxes. He could smell them, of course, knew what was inside, but when the targets saw Bo, when they sometimes even smiled at the friendly dog, it just . . . it just felt wrong to Reynaldo.

His key chain dangled from his belt. Reynaldo found the proper key, unlocked the padlock, and pulled up the door from the ground. The sudden light always made the targets blink or shield their eyes. Even at night. Even if there was just a sliver of moon. The box was complete and utter darkness. Any illumination, even the slightest from a distant star, hit them like an assault.

"Get out," he said.

The woman groaned. Her lips were cracked. The lines on her face had darkened and deepened, as though the dirt had burrowed into every facial crevice. The stench of her body waste wafted up toward him. Reynaldo was used to that. Some of them tried to hold it in at first, but when you go days in the darkness, lying in what was essentially a coffin, the choice was taken away.

It took Number Six a full minute to sit up. She tried to lick her lips, but her tongue must have been like sandpaper. He tried to remember the last time he had given her a drink. Hours now. He had already dropped the cup of white rice down the mailbox-type slot in the door. That was how he fed them—through the slot in the door. Sometimes, the targets tried to stick their hands through the slot. He gave them one warning not to do that. If they tried it again, Reynaldo crushed their fingers with his boot.

Number Six began to cry.

"Hurry," he said.

The blond woman tried to move faster, but her body was starting to betray her now. He had seen it before. His job was to keep them alive. That was all. Don't let them die until Titus said, "It's time." At that stage, Reynaldo walked them out into the field. Sometimes, he made them dig their own graves. Most times not. He walked them out and then he put the muzzle of the gun against their heads and pulled the trigger. Sometimes, he experimented with the kill shot. He would press the muzzle against the neck and fire up or he'd press it against the crown of the skull and fire down. Sometimes, he put the muzzle against the temple, like you always see suicide victims do in the movies. Sometimes, the kill was quick. Sometimes, they lived until the second bullet. Once, when he had shot too low by the base of the spine, the victim, a man from Wilmington, Delaware, had survived but had been paralyzed.

Reynaldo buried him alive.

Number Six was a mess, defeated, broken. He had seen it often enough.

"Over there," he said to her.

She managed to utter one word: "Water."

"Over there. Change first."

She tried to move fast, but her gait was more like the shuffle Reynaldo had seen on that zombie television show. That, he thought, was appropriate. Number Six was not dead yet, but she wasn't really alive either.

Without prompting, the woman stripped out of her jumpsuit and stood before him naked. A few days ago, when she had first tearfully and reluctantly taken off that yellow sundress, asking him to turn away, trying to duck behind a tree or cover herself with her hands, she had been much more attractive. Today she didn't worry about modesty or vanity. She stood before him like the primitive being she had become, her eyes pleading for water.

Reynaldo picked up the hose with the spray nozzle with the pistol grip. The water pressure was strong. The woman tried to bend down, tried to catch some of the flow in her mouth. He stopped the hose. She stood back up and let him water her down, her skin turning red from the harshness of the jet stream.

When he was finished, he tossed her another jumpsuit. She slipped into it. He gave her water in a plastic cup. She downed it greedily and handed it back to him, indicating that she would do pretty much anything for more. He worried that she would be too weak to make the trip up the path to the farmhouse, so he filled the cup again. She drank this one too fast, almost choking on it. He handed her a breakfast bar he had bought at a Giant food store. She almost ate the wrapper in her haste.

"The path," he said.

The woman started up it, again walking with the shuffle. Reynaldo followed. He wondered how much more money there was to bleed from Number Six. He suspected she was wealthier than most. Surprisingly, Titus preferred male targets to females at a ratio of about three to one. The women were usually higher-profit prey. This one, when she arrived, had expensive jewelry and the certain swagger of the upper class.

Both were gone now.

She walked tentatively, glancing behind her every few steps. She was, he supposed, surprised that Reynaldo was coming with her. Reynaldo was a little surprised too. He was rarely told to escort the targets. Titus somehow liked the idea of making them walk to the farmhouse on their own.

He wondered, since this was her second visit of the day, if this was now her endgame—if Titus would tell him, "It's time."

When they reached the farmhouse, Titus was in his big chair. Dmitry sat by his computer. Reynaldo waited by the door. Number Six—again without prompting—took the hard wooden chair in front of Titus.

"We have a problem, Dana."

Dana, Reynaldo thought. So that was her name.

Dana's eyes fluttered. "Problem?"

"I had hoped to release you today," Titus continued. His voice was always smooth, as if he was always trying to hypnotize you, but today Reynaldo thought he heard a little tension beneath the even tones. "But now it appears that there is a police officer who is investigating your disappearance."

Dana looked dumbfounded.

"A New York City police detective named Katarina Donovan. Do you know her?"

"No."

"She goes by Kat. She works in Manhattan."

Dana stared off, seemingly unable to focus..

"Do you know her?" Titus asked again, a sharp edge in his voice.

"No."

Titus studied her face another moment.

"No," she said again.

Yep, half dead, Reynaldo thought.

Titus glanced at Dmitry. He nodded. Dmitry tugged on his knit cap and then spun the computer monitor so that it faced Dana. There was a picture of a woman on the screen.

"How do you know her, Dana?" Titus asked.

Dana just shook her head.

"How do you know her?"

"I don't."

"Before you left for your trip, did she call you?"

"No."

"You never spoke to her?"

"No, never."

"How do you know her?"

"I don't."

"Have you ever seen this woman before? Think hard."

"I don't know her." Dana broke down and started sobbing. "I've never seen her."

Titus sat back. "I'm going to ask you one more time, Dana. The answer will either get you home with your son or back in the box alone. How do you know Kat Donovan?"

33

KAT had asked the men several times where they were taking her.

The thin man sitting next to her just smiled and pointed the gun at her. The guy driving kept his eyes on the road. From the back, all she could see was a perfectly shaved head and shoulders the size of bowling balls. Kat kept prattling on—where were they going, how long would it take to get there, who were they?

The thin man sitting next to her kept smiling.

The ride ended up being short. They had just gone through the center of Water Mill when the silver Mercedes veered to the left onto Davids Lane, heading toward the ocean. They turned off onto Halsey Lane. Ritzy neighborhood.

Kat now had a pretty good idea where they were heading.

The car slowed past an enormous estate blocked off by a solid wall of high shrubs. The hedge wall stretched for several hundred yards before being interrupted by a drive protected by a completely opaque gate. A man in a dark suit and sunglasses, with an earpiece, talked into a sleeve microphone.

The gate opened, and the silver Mercedes pulled up the drive toward a sprawling Gatsby-esque stone mansion with a red tile roof. White Greco-Roman statues and cypress trees lined the drive. The courtyard featured a round pool with a high-spouting fountain.

The smiling thin man said, "If you please."

Kat got out on one side of the car, Smiley on the other. She stared up at this mansion from another era. She had seen old photographs of it. A wealthy industrialist named Richard Heffernan had it built in the 1930s. His family had held on to it until about ten years ago, when the current owner purchased it, gutted it, and, if rumors were true, spent ten million dollars on the renovation.

"Lift your arms, please."

She complied while yet another dark-suited man in sunglasses frisked her with so much enthusiasm Kat almost asked for a penicillin shot. Smiley had already taken her gun and her phone, so there was nothing to find. Back in the day, her father had always carried a spare gun in his boot—Kat had often debated doing the same—but this guy would have found it for sure. When he was finished (and was practically smoking a cigarette, for crying out loud), he nodded toward Smiley.

Smiley said, "This way, please."

They headed past a lush garden that seemed to be straight out of some glossy high-end magazine, which, Kat supposed, it probably was. The ocean was spread out in front of them now, almost as though it had gathered on command for a postcard shot. Kat could smell the salt air.

"Hello, Kat."

He was waiting for her on a porch with cushioned teak furniture. He wore all-white, too-fitted clothing. This was maybe a passable look on a young, well-built man. On a squat, flabby man in his seventies, it was nearly obscene. The buttons of his shirt strained against his gut—that is, the buttons that weren't already undone, revealing a line of chest hair long enough for a curling iron. He wore gold rings on pudgy fingers. He had either a full head of sandy hair or a great toupee; it was hard to tell which.

"So we finally meet," he said.

Kat wasn't sure how to react. After all these years, after all the reading and obsessing and hating and deserved demonizing, Willy Cozone finally stood in front of her.

"I bet you've pictured this day for a long time," Cozone said to her.

"I have."

Cozone spread his arms toward the ocean. "Was it anything like this?"

"No," Kat said. "You were in handcuffs."

He laughed at that as though he had never heard anything so funny in his life. Smiley, the thin man, stood next to her, hands folded. He didn't laugh. He just smiled. One-trick pony.

"You can leave us, Leslie."

Smiley Leslie did a half bow and walked away.

"Would you care to sit?" Cozone asked.

"No."

"How about some iced tea or lemonade?" He held up

his own glass. "I'm having an Arnold Palmer. Do you know what that is?"

"I do, yes."

"Would you like one?"

"No," Kat said. "Not to put too fine a point on this, but it is against the law to kidnap a person at gunpoint, especially a police officer."

"Please," Cozone said. "Let's not waste time with minutiae. We have matters to discuss."

"I'm listening."

"Are you sure you won't sit?"

"What do you want, Mr. Cozone?"

He took a sip of his drink, watching her the whole time. "Perhaps this was a mistake."

Kat said nothing.

He started walking away. "I will have Leslie drop you back at your car. My apologies."

"I could charge you."

Cozone waved a hand in her direction. "Oh, please, Kat. May I call you Kat? I've beaten far more solid charges. I can produce a dozen witnesses who will verify my whereabouts. I can produce a surveillance video showing you were never here. Let's not waste our time playing games."

"That goes two ways," Kat said.

"Meaning?"

"Meaning, don't give me the 'I'll have Leslie drop you back' crap. You brought me here for a reason. I would like to know what it is."

Cozone liked that. He took a step toward her. His eyes were a light blue that somehow on him still looked black. "You are stirring up trouble with your current investigation."

"My investigation isn't current."

"Good point. Your father has been dead a long time."

"Did you have him killed?"

"If I did, what makes you think I'd ever let you leave here alive?"

Kat knew everything about Cozone—his birth date, his family history, his arrest record, his residences (like this one)—from studying his file. But it was always different when you saw someone in person for the first time. She stared at his light blue eyes. She thought about the horror that those eyes had seen over their seventy-plus years. And how, in a sense, that horror never reached them.

"Theoretically," he continued, in a tone that bordered on bored, "I could put a bullet in your brain right here. I have several boats. We could dump you at sea. Yes, your fellow officers would search hard, but we both know that they would find nothing."

Kat tried not to swallow. "You didn't bring me here to kill me."

"How can you be so sure?"

"Because I'm still breathing."

Cozone smiled at that. He had small peg teeth that looked like decaying Chiclets. His face was the kind of smooth that suggests a chemical peel or Botox. "Let's see how our conversation goes first, shall we?"

He collapsed into the cushioned teak and patted the seat next to him.

"Please sit."

As she did, a shiver passed through her. She could smell his cologne—something cloying and overly potent. The two chairs faced the ocean rather than each other. For a moment, neither of them said anything, both staring out at the churning surf.

"A storm is coming," he said.

"Ominous," Kat said, aiming for sarcasm and falling a little short.

"Ask the question, Kat."

She said nothing.

"You've waited nearly twenty years. So here's your chance. Ask me."

She turned and watched his face. "Did you have my father killed?"

"No." He kept his gaze on the water.

"Am I just supposed to believe you?"

"Do you know I'm from the old neighborhood?"

"Yep. Farrington Street near the car wash. You killed a kid when you were in fifth grade."

He shook his head. "May I share a secret with you?"

"Sure, go ahead."

"That story about me and the hammer is an urban myth."

"I talked to someone whose brother went to school with you."

"It's not true," he said. "Why would I lie to you about that? I like the myths. I've even had a hand in cultivating them. They've eased my way, to some degree. Not that it was easy. Not that my hands are clean. But fear is a wonderful motivating tool."

"Is that a confession?"

Cozone put his wrists together as though waiting for the cuffs. She knew that nothing he said here would be admissible or even helpful, but that didn't mean she wanted him to stop talking.

"I knew your father," he said. "We had an understanding."

"Are you saying he was crooked?"

"I'm not saying anything. I'm explaining to you that

I had nothing to do with your father's death—that we were from the same world, he and I."

"So you never killed anyone from Flushing?"

"Oh, I wouldn't say that."

"So what exactly are you saying?"

"Over the years, you have caused several of my enterprises to, let us say, interrupt services."

She had busted the heads of any "enterprise" even rumored to be connected to Cozone. She had, no doubt, cost Cozone money.

"Are you trying to make a point?" Kat asked.

"I don't want those days brought back again."

"So you thought by telling me that you didn't kill my father, it would all end?"

"Something like that. I thought—or rather I hoped—that we could come to an understanding."

"An understanding."

"Yes."

"Like the one you claimed to have with my father."

His eyes stayed on the surf, but a smile played at the corner of his mouth. "Something like that."

Kat wasn't sure how to react to that. "Why now?" she asked.

He lifted his drink and brought it to his lips.

"You could have told me this years ago, if you thought it would lead to"—air quotes—"'an understanding.' So why now?"

"Things have changed."

"In what way?"

"A dear friend has passed away."

"Monte Leburne?"

Cozone took another sip of his drink. "You're tough, Kat. I'll give you that."

She didn't bother responding.

"You loved your father dearly, didn't you?"

"I'm not here to talk about me or my feelings."

"Fair enough. You asked why I told you this now. It is because Monte Leburne is now dead."

"But he confessed to the killing."

"Indeed. He also said that I had nothing to do with it."

"Right, but he also said you had nothing to do with the other two hits. Are you going to deny those too?"

He turned his head toward her just a little bit. His face hardened. "I'm not here to talk about the other two. Not in any way. Do you understand my meaning?"

She did. He wasn't confessing, but then again, as opposed to with her father, he wasn't denying it either. The message was clear: Yeah, I did those two, but not your dad.

But that didn't mean she had to believe him.

Cozone wanted her off his back. That was the point of all this. He would spin any tale to get his way.

"What I'm going to tell you now is confidential," Cozone said. "Are we clear on that?"

Kat nodded because, again, it didn't matter. If he gave her information and she needed to use it, her quasi promise to a prominent killer wouldn't stop her. He probably knew that too.

"Let's travel back in time, shall we? To the day Monte Leburne was arrested. You see, when the feds nabbed Monte, I was somewhat worried. No reason to talk about why. Monte had always been one of my most loyal employees. I reached out to him immediately."

"How? He was in isolation."

He frowned. "Please."

He was right. Cozone would have his connections. It was also irrelevant.

"Anyway, I promised Monte that if he continued to be the loyal employee I knew that he was, his family would receive a generous compensation package."

A bribe. "And if he didn't stay loyal?"

"We don't need to go into hypotheticals, Kat, do we?" He looked at her.

"I guess not."

"Besides, even with strong threats, many employees have sold out their bosses to better their own lot. I hoped to discourage Monte Leburne from doing that with a carrot rather than a stick."

"Seems you were successful."

"Yes, I was. But it didn't work out exactly as I had planned."

"How so?"

Cozone started to twist a ring around his finger. "As you probably know, Monte Leburne was originally arrested on charges involving two homicides."

"Right."

"He asked me for permission to confess to a third."

Kat just sat there for a moment. She waited for him to say more, but he suddenly seemed exhausted. "Why would he do that?"

"Because it didn't matter. He had a life sentence."

"Still. He didn't confess for the fun of it."

"No, he didn't."

"So why?"

"Let me explain why we haven't talked before. Part of my arrangement with Monte Leburne was that it would remain between the two of us. I won't hand you a line about honor among thieves, but I want you to understand. I couldn't say anything because I was sworn to secrecy. If I did, I would be betraying a loyal employee."

"Who might in return change his mind about not implicating you."

"The pragmatic is always a consideration," Cozone agreed. "But mostly, I wanted to demonstrate to Monte and to my other employees that I am a man of my word."

"And now?"

Cozone shrugged. "He's dead. The agreement is therefore null and void."

"So you're free to talk."

"If I wish. Naturally, I would prefer that you kept this between us. You've always believed that I killed your father. I am here to tell you that I didn't."

She asked the obvious: "Who did?"

"I don't know."

"Did Leburne have anything to do with it?"

"No."

"Do you know why he confessed?"

He spread his arms. "Why would anyone?"

"Money?"

"For one thing."

"What else?"

"This is where it gets trickier, Kat."

"What do you mean?"

"He was promised favors."

"What kind of favors?"

"Better treatment in prison. A better cell. Extra rations. Employment help for his nephew."

Kat frowned. "Who provided him with that?"

"He never told me."

"But you have your suspicions."

"It does me no good to talk about hypotheticals."

"So you've said. What kind of job did the nephew get?"

"It wasn't a job. It was more getting into a school."

"What kind of school?"

"The police academy."

The skies opened up as though on cue. The rain began over the ocean, swirling the current. It slowly moved over the yard and toward them. Cozone rose and stood back a little, so as to stay fully under the roof. Kat did the same.

"Leslie will give you a ride back to your car," Cozone said.

"I have more questions."

"I've said too much as it is."

"And if I don't believe you?"

Cozone shrugged. "Then we continue as we have."

"With no understanding?"

"So be it," he said.

She thought about all he had said, about honor among thieves, about understandings and agreements. "Understandings don't matter after someone dies, right?"

He said nothing.

"I mean, that's what you said. Whatever deal you and Leburne worked out, it's over now."

"Correct."

Smiley Leslie appeared. But Kat didn't move.

"You also had an understanding with my father," Kat said. Her voice sounded funny in her own ears. "That's what you said."

The rain pounded down on the roof. She had to speak louder to be heard.

"Do you know who Sugar is?" she asked him.

Cozone looked off. "You know about Sugar?"

"To some degree."

"So why are you asking me?"

"Because I want to talk to her."

His face tilted in a question.

"If you don't know anything about who killed my father," Kat said, "maybe Sugar does."

Cozone might have nodded. "Maybe."

"So I want to meet her," Kat said. "Does that make sense?"

"In some ways," he said almost too carefully.

"Could you help me find her?"

Cozone looked toward Leslie. Leslie didn't move. Still Cozone said, "We could try, yes."

"Thank you."

"Under one condition."

"That being?"

"You promise to leave my operation alone."

"If you're telling the truth about no involvement—"

"I am."

"Then no problem," she said.

He stuck out his hand. She reluctantly shook it, imagining all the blood that had once been on it, imagining it all flooding back and then splashing onto her. Cozone held on.

"Are you sure that's what you want, Kat?"

"What?"

"Are you sure you want to meet Sugar?"

She pulled her hand away. "Yes, I'm sure."

He looked back toward the churning waves. "I guess maybe that's okay. I guess that maybe it's time to let all the secrets out, no matter how destructive."

"What's that supposed to mean?" Kat asked.

But Cozone turned then and started to head inside. "Leslie will drive you back to your car. He will call you when he's found an address for Sugar."

34

TITUS asked Dana the same question a dozen more times. As he'd more or less expected, she stuck to her story. She didn't know Kat. She had never seen her. She had no idea why she would be investigating anything involved with Dana's disappearance.

Titus believed her.

He leaned back and rubbed his chin. Dana stared back at him. The slim flicker of hope remained in her eyes. Behind her, Reynaldo was leaning against the doorjamb. Titus wondered whether he could use Dana to get another payout, but no, he had always lived by the rule of patience. Don't get greedy. It was time to cut the line. He would bet that Detective Kat Donovan hadn't told anybody about her investigation yet. She had too little evidence, for one thing. For another, she wouldn't want to admit how she had stumbled across this particular crime.

By stalking a former boyfriend.

He debated the pros and cons. On the one hand, once he removed Dana Phelps, it would be over. She would be dead and buried. There would be no clues. On the other hand, Kat Donovan had gotten further than anyone else. She had put together Gerard Remington's disappearance with Dana Phelps's. She had a personal stake in this now.

She might not give up all that easily.

Eliminating a cop was extremely risky. But so, in this case, was letting her live.

He needed to run a full cost-benefit analysis—kill her or not—but in the meantime, there was another matter that needed attending.

Titus smiled at Dana. "Would you like some tea?"

She nodded with everything she had, which wasn't much. "Yes, please."

Titus looked toward Dmitry. "Would you make Ms. Phelps some tea?"

Dmitry got up from the computer and headed into the kitchen.

Titus rose. "I'll be back in a moment," he told her.

"I'm telling the truth, Mr. Titus."

"I know that, Dana. Please don't worry."

Titus moved toward where Reynaldo was standing by the door. The two men stepped outside.

"It's time," Titus said.

Reynaldo nodded. "Okay."

Titus looked over his shoulder. "Do you believe her?"

"Yes."

"So do I," Titus said, "but we need to be absolutely certain."

Reynaldo's eyes narrowed. "So you don't want me to kill her?"

"Oh. I do," Titus said, looking toward the barn. "But take your time about it."

CHAZ called Julie Weitz. A woman answered the phone and said, "Hello?"

"Is this Julie Weitz?"

"It is."

"I'm Detective Faircloth from the New York Police Department."

Chaz asked her a few questions. Yes, she was talking to a man online, more than one actually, but that wasn't anyone's concern but her own. No, she had no plans to go away with him. How on earth was that police business anyway? Chaz thanked her and hung up.

Strike one. Or maybe the more apropos baseball term would be *safe*.

Then Chaz called Martha Paquet's house. A woman answered the phone and said, "Hello?"

"Is this Martha Paquet?"

"No," the woman said. "This is her sister, Sandi."

SMILEY Leslie and the silver Mercedes dropped Kat back at Chaz's yellow Ferrari. Before she got out, Leslie said, "I'll call you when I have an address."

Kat almost thanked him, but that seemed woefully inappropriate. The driver handed her back her gun. She could tell from the weight that he had removed the bullets. Then he handed her back her cell phone.

Kat got out. They drove away.

Her head was still spinning. She didn't know what to make of what Cozone had said. Actually, even worse, she knew exactly what to make of it. Wasn't it obvious now? Stagger had gone to visit Monte Leburne immediately after his arrest. He hadn't told Suggs or Rinsky or anybody else. He had made a deal with Leburne, so that Leburne would take the fall for Dad's murder.

But why?

Or was that getting obvious too?

The real question was, what could she do about it? It wouldn't pay to confront Stagger anymore. He would just continue to lie. Or worse. No, she would have to prove him a liar. How?

The fingerprints found at the murder scene.

Stagger had covered them up, hadn't he? But if they belonged to Stagger, they would have shown up in the first fingerprint search Suggs and Rinsky ran. All cops' prints are on file. So they couldn't belong to Stagger.

Still, when they did get a hit, Stagger had inserted himself in the investigation, pretending (or probably pretending) that the prints belonged to a random homeless guy.

The fingerprints were the key.

She called Suggs on his cell phone.

"Hey, Kat, how's it going?"

"Good. Have you had a chance to look at those old fingerprints?"

"Not yet."

"I hate to be a pest, but they are really important."

"After all these years? I can't see how. But either way, I put the request in. All the evidence is boxed up at the warehouse. They tell me it'll take a few more days."

"Can you push it?"

"I guess, but they're working active cases, Kat. This isn't a priority."

"It is," she said. "Believe me, okay? For my father."

There was silence on the other end of the line. Then Suggs said, "For your father," and hung up.

Kat looked back toward that damn stretch of beach, and now she remembered what she'd been thinking about before Leslie had shown up, leaning against Chaz's car.

It's Kat.

She had been the one to type that in an instant message to Jeff/Ron. First, she had sent him a link to the "Missing You" video. Then he had responded as though he didn't know who she was. Then she wrote . . .

It's Kat.

Her body felt cold. She, Kat, had told him her name. He hadn't said it first. He started referring to her as Kat, as though he knew her, *after* she had already told him her name.

Something was wrong.

Something was very, very wrong with Dana Phelps and Gerard Remington and Jeff Raynes aka Ron Kochman. She couldn't prove it yet, but three people had disappeared.

Or two anyway. Gerard and Dana. As for Jeff . . .

One way to find out. She slid into the Ferrari and started it up. She wasn't going back to New York City. Not yet. She was going back to Ron Kochman's house. She would knock down his goddamn door if she had to, but she was going to learn the truth one way or the other.

When Kat turned back onto Deforest Street, the same

two vehicles were in the driveway. She pulled her car right behind them and slammed the stick into park. As she reached for the door handle, her cell phone rang.

It was Chaz.

"Hello?"

"Martha Paquet went away last night for a weekend getaway. No one has seen her since."

TITUS thanked Dana for her cooperation.

"When can I go home?" she asked.

"Tomorrow, if all goes well. In the meantime, Reynaldo here is going to let you sleep in the guest quarters in the barn. There's a shower and a bed. I think you'll find it more comfortable."

Dana had the shakes, but she still managed to say, "Thank you."

"You're welcome. You can go now."

"I won't say a word," she said. "You can trust me."

"I know. I do."

Dana trudged toward the door as though walking through deep mud. Reynaldo waited for her. The moment the door closed behind them, Dmitry coughed into his fist and said, "Uh, we got a problem."

Titus's gaze snapped toward him. They had never had a problem. Not ever.

"What's wrong?"

"We're getting e-mails."

Once they got the passwords, Dmitry set it up so all the e-mail accounts for all their guests would be forwarded to him. This way they could monitor and even answer e-mails from concerned family or friends.

"From?"

"Martha Paquet's sister. I guess she's been calling the cell phone too."

"What do the e-mails say?"

Dmitry looked up. He pushed his glasses up his nose with his pointer finger. "It says that a New York City police detective called and asked where Martha was. The cop seemed worried when she said she'd gone away with her boyfriend."

A blinding bolt of anger crashed through Titus.

Kat.

The balance of his internal cost-benefit analysis—kill or not kill—had now tilted to one side.

Titus grabbed his keys and hurried for the door. "E-mail back to the sister that you're fine and having a great time and will be home tomorrow. If any other communications come in, call me on my cell phone."

"Where are you going?"

"To New York City."

KAT pounded on the front door. She looked through the pebbled glass for movement again. She saw none. The old man had to be home. She had been here, what, an hour ago? Both cars were there. She knocked some more.

No answer.

The old man had told her to get off *his* property. His. So Ron or Jeff might not be the owner. The old man was. Maybe Jeff and his daughter, Melinda, rented space. She could easily find the old man's name in the records, but really, what would that do?

Chaz was supposed to notify the FBI about this case now, though again, they still didn't have much. Adults are allowed to be out of touch for a day or two. She hoped the circumstantial consistencies would give the case some urgency, but she wasn't sure. Dana Phelps had actually spoken to both her son and her financial adviser. Martha Paquet could just be holed up in bed with her new lover.

Except for one thing: Both women were supposedly away with the same man.

She circled the house, trying to peer into the windows, but the shades were drawn. She found the old man in the backyard on a chaise longue. He was reading a paperback by Parnell Hall, gripping the book as though it were trying to run away.

Kat said, "Hello?"

The old man sat up, startled. "What the hell are you doing here?"

"I knocked on the door."

"What do you want?"

"Where is Jeff?"

He sat up. "I don't know anybody by that name."

She didn't believe him. "Where is Ron Kochman?"

"I told you. He's not here."

Kat moved to the chaise, looming above him. "Two women are missing."

"What?"

"Two women met him online. Both of them are now missing."

"I don't know what you're talking about."

"I'm not leaving until you tell me where he is."

He said nothing.

"I will call the cops. I will call the FBI. I will call the media."

The old man's eyes widened. "You wouldn't."

Kat bent so that her face was inches from his. "Try me. I will tell everyone I know that Ron Kochman used to be a guy named Jeff Raynes."

The old man just sat there.

"Where is he?"

The old man said nothing.

She almost reached for her gun but stopped herself. This time she shouted, "Where is he?"

"Leave him alone."

Kat gasped at the sound of the voice. Her head turned toward the house. The screen door opened. Kat felt her knees buckle. She opened her mouth, but no sound came out.

Jeff stepped out of the house and spread his arms. "I'm right here, Kat."

35

WHEN Reynaldo and Dana arrived at the barn, Bo was by the door, tail wagging. He leapt toward his master, who got down on one knee and scratched behind the ears.

"Good boy."

Bo barked his approval.

Behind him, Reynaldo heard the farmhouse's screen door slam. Titus jumped the porch steps and hurried toward the black SUV. Clem Sison, who worked as the driver now that Claude was gone, got behind the wheel. Titus jumped in on the passenger side.

The SUV sped off, kicking up dirt in its wake.

Reynaldo wondered what had happened. Bo barked and Reynaldo realized that in his distraction, he had stopped scratching. He smiled and got back to it. Bo made his happy face. It was a wonderful thing about dogs. You always knew exactly what they were feeling.

Dana stood perfectly still. There was a small smile on her lips as she watched him with Bo. Reynaldo didn't like that. He stood and ordered Bo to go back toward the underground boxes. The dog whined in protest.

"Go," Reynaldo said again.

Reluctantly, the dog left the barn and started toward the path.

Dana watched the old dog go, her smile fading away to nothing. "I have a Lab too," she said. "Her name is Chloe. She's black, though, not chocolate. How old is your dog?"

Reynaldo didn't reply. From where he now stood at the barn entrance, Reynaldo could see the old Amish pruning saw on the wall. Reynaldo had once wondered whether the blade could cut through finger bones. It had taken a while. It had been messy, more of a ripping and tearing of bone than anything resembling a clean cut, but Reynaldo had made it all the way through one finger at a time. That man—he had been in Box Three—had screamed. The noise bothered Titus, so Reynaldo jammed a cloth in Number Three's mouth and then sealed it with duct tape. That muffled the shrieks of agony. Number Three started passing out when the blade got caught up in the cartilage. The first two times, Reynaldo had stopped what he was doing, gotten a pail of water, and thrown it on the man. That had woken him back up. After he passed out for the third time, Reynaldo had kept pails of water by his side.

"Would you like some water?" he asked Dana now.

"Yes, please."

He filled two buckets with water and placed them at the ready on the tool table. Dana lifted one to her lips and drank straight from it. Reynaldo found a hand towel that would make a good gag, but he couldn't find duct tape. He could threaten her, of course, tell her that if the towel came out of her mouth, he would make it much worse, but on the other hand, Titus had just driven off, so he wouldn't be bothered by the noise.

Maybe Reynaldo would just let her scream.

"Where's the bed?" Dana asked. "And the shower?"

"Sit," he said, pointing to the chair.

He had tied Number Three down with rope and trapped whatever hand he was cutting in the large vise on the tool table. Number Three had started to resist when he first saw the ropes, but Reynaldo had silenced him with the gun. He could do that again here, he supposed, but Dana seemed more pliant. Still, once the cutting began, he would need restraints.

"Sit," he said again.

Dana immediately sat in the chair.

Reynaldo opened the bottom tool drawer and pulled out the tying rope. He wasn't good at knots, but if you stayed near your victim and if you wrapped it enough times around, you didn't have to be.

"What's that for?" Dana asked.

"I need to make up your bed. I can't risk you running off while I do that."

"I won't. I promise."

"Sit still."

When he wrapped the rope around her chest, Dana started to cry. But she didn't resist. He wasn't sure if that pleased or disappointed him. Reynaldo was about to do a second go-around, when he heard the familiar whimper.

Bo.

Reynaldo looked up. Bo was standing right outside the barn door, looking at his master with sad eyes.

"Go," Reynaldo said.

Bo didn't move. He whimpered some more.

"Go. I'll be down in a few minutes."

The dog started pawing the ground and looked toward his bed. Reynaldo should have anticipated this. Bo liked his bed. He liked the barn, especially when Reynaldo was here. The only time Reynaldo had locked Bo out was when he was working on Number Three. Bo hadn't liked that—not the part about sawing the man's fingers off; Bo cared only about Reynaldo—but he was upset at being locked away from both his bed and his master.

For days afterward, Bo would sniff where the blood had spilled.

Reynaldo rose and moved toward the barn door. He gave the dog a quick scratch behind the ears and said, "Sorry, boy. I need you to stay outside." He backed the dog away from the doorway and got ready to close it. Bo started toward him.

"Sit," Reynaldo said sternly.

The dog obeyed.

Reynaldo's hand had just taken hold of the handle on the barn door when he felt something crash into the back of his head. The blow knocked Reynaldo to his knees. His head vibrated like a tuning fork. He looked up and saw Dana holding the metal chair. She reared back and with a guttural scream swung it at his face.

Reynaldo ducked just in time, the chair flying over him. He could hear Bo starting to bark out of concern. Reynaldo reached up, grabbed the chair, and pulled it away from her.

Dana ran.

Reynaldo was still on his knees. He tried to get up,

but his head reeled in protest. He dropped back down. Bo was there now, licking his face. It gave him strength. He made his way to his feet, pulled out his gun, and ran outside. He looked to the right. No sign of her. He looked to the left. Again nothing.

He spun to the back just as Dana disappeared into the woods. Reynaldo raised his gun, fired, and ran after her.

TITUS had been so careful.

The setup for what he considered to be the perfect crime didn't come just with a cry of "Eureka!" It had been the result of evolution, survival of the fittest—an idea that had evolved from all the other career dealings in his lifetime. It combined love and sex and romance and longing. It was primitive in its instinct and modern in its execution.

It was perfect.

Or at least, it had been.

Titus had seen small-time hustlers think small-time. They'd put ads up for sex on websites, make a date with a guy, and then roll him for chump change.

No, that wouldn't do.

Titus had gathered all of his past operations—prostitution, extortion, scams, identity theft—and taken them to the next level. First, he created the perfect fake online profiles. How? There were several ways. Dmitry helped him find "dead," "deleted," or inactive social media accounts on sites like Facebook or even MySpace—people who had created a page, thrown up a few photographs, and then never used it. Most of the ones he ended up using were from canceled accounts.

Take Ron Kochman, for example. According to the

cache, his account had been set up and then deleted two weeks later. That was ideal. Take Vanessa Moreau. They had found her bikini portfolio on a casting site called Mucho Models. Not only had Vanessa not updated her account in three years, but when a fictional magazine tried to "book" her for a job, Titus got no reply.

In short, both were dead accounts.

That was step one.

Once Titus had located potential IDs he could exploit, he ran a more thorough online search because any potential suitor would do that. It was the norm nowadays. If you met someone online—or even in person—you Googled them, especially if they were potential suitors. That was why a completely fake identity wouldn't really work. You'd be able to sniff it out in a Google search. But if the person was real and just unreachable . . .

Bingo.

There was virtually nothing on Ron Kochman online, though in that case, Titus had still had "Ron" be "cautious" and call himself Jack. It worked well. The same was true of Vanessa Moreau. After a ton of extra research—which the average person would never be able to muster without hiring a private eye—Titus had found out that Vanessa Moreau was just a professional name, that she was really Nancy Josephson and was now married with two kids and lived in Bristol, England.

The next important criterion was looks.

Vanessa, he had figured, would be a problem. She was simply too attractive in a pinup-model-type way. Men would be suspicious. But, as Titus would have learned during his days in prostitution, men are also dumb when it comes to the female sex. They all have this misguided belief that they are somehow God's gift to women. Gerard Remington had even waxed on to Vanessa about how superior specimens—him in terms of brains, her in terms of looks—should naturally gravitate toward each other.

"Special people find one another," Gerard had argued. "They procreate and thus enhance the species."

Yes, he had said that. For real.

Ron Kochman had been a perfect and rare find. Normally, to be on the absolute safest side, Titus used each profile to nab only one target. After that, he deleted the ID and started using another. But locating ideal identities—people who had some online presence but couldn't be found—was difficult. Kochman had also had the look and age he wanted. Wealthy women would be suspicious of someone too young and figure that they were perversely into cougars or after their money. They would have less interest in being romantic with someone too old.

Kochman was both a widower (women loved those) and "real world" handsome. Even in photographs, he looked like a nice guy—relaxed, confident, comfortable in his own skin, nice eyes, an endearing smile that drew you in.

Women fell for him hard.

From there, the planning was pretty simple. Titus took the photographs he'd harvested from their old Facebook or Mucho Model or whatever accounts and put them on various online dating services. He kept the profiles simple and clean. When you do this often enough, you learn all the tricks. He was never lecherous toward the women or overly sexual to the men. Titus thought that the communications—the seduction—was his forte. He listened to his suitors, truly listened, and responded to their needs. This was his strength, going back to the days of reading the young girls at the Port Authority. He never oversold himself. He kept far away from "personal ad" speak. He showed his personality (his comments, for example, were lightly self-deprecating) rather than telling it ("I'm really funny and caring").

Titus never asked for personal information, though once the communications began, the target always gave him enough. Once he knew the name or address or other key information he would have Dmitry run a full check on them and try to figure out a net worth. If they didn't reach high six figures, there was no reason to continue the flirtation. If they had a ton of family ties and would be missed, that was also reason to bail.

At any one time, Titus could have ten identities flirting with hundreds of potential marks. The large majority fell by the wayside for one reason or another. Some were just too much work. Some would not go away without first meeting for a coffee. Some did the research and, with IDs not quite as off the grid as Ron Kochman or Vanessa Moreau, saw that they were being tricked.

Still, there was a never-ending stream of potential targets.

Currently, Titus was holding seven people at the farm. Five men, two women. He preferred men. Yes, that might sound strange, but a single man going missing drew almost no attention. Men disappear all the time. They run away. They hook up with some woman and move. No one questioned when a man wanted to move his money to another account. People do wonder—and yes, this was pure old-fashioned sexism—when a woman starts going "crazy" with her finances.

Think about it. How often did you hear on the news

that a forty-seven-year-old single man had vanished and the police were searching for him?

Almost never.

The answer becomes "completely never" when the man is still sending e-mails or text messages and even, when needed, making phone calls. Titus's operation was simple and precise. You keep the targets alive for as long as you need them. You bleed them in a way that might cause a raised eyebrow but rarely more. You bleed them for as long as it is profitable. Then you kill them and make them disappear.

That was the key. Once their usefulness is over, you don't let them live.

Titus had been running his operation at the farm for eight months now. In terms of geography, he cast his net within a ten-hour ride to the farm. That gave him a great deal of the East Coast—from Maine to South Carolina, and even the Midwest. Cleveland was only five hours away, Indianapolis about nine; Chicago was right about at the ten-hour mark. He tried to make sure that no two victims lived too close to each other or had any connection. Gerard Remington had been from Hadley, Massachusetts, for example, while Dana Phelps lived in Greenwich, Connecticut.

The rest was simple.

Eventually, most online relationships had to progress to the point where you had in-person contact. Titus had been surprised, though, at how intimate you could become without ever meeting face-to-face. He'd had some form of online sex or sexting episode with more than half his victims. He'd had phone sex, always using a disposable mobile device, sometimes hiring a woman who didn't really know what was going on, but most of the time, he used a simple voice changer and did it himself. In every case, words of love were exchanged before a face-to-face meet was even set up.

Odd.

The getaway—be it a weekend or a week—evolved into a given. Gerard Remington, who clearly had some social issues (he almost ruined the plan by insisting on taking his own car—they ended up improvising, conking him over the head in the airport parking lot), had bought a ring and prepared his proposal—this despite never laying eyes on Vanessa in the flesh. He wasn't the first. Titus had read about relationships like this, people who talked online for months or even years. That star linebacker from Notre Dame had fallen in love without ever seeing the "girl" who was conning him, even believing that she had died from a bizarre mix of leukemia and a car accident.

Love blinds, yes, but not nearly as much as wanting to be loved.

That was what Titus had learned. People weren't so much gullible as desperate. Or maybe, Titus concluded, those were two sides of the same coin.

Now his perfect operation seemed to have hit a major snag. Looking back on it, Titus could blame only himself. He had grown lazy. It had all gone so smoothly for so long that he let down his guard. Immediately after "Kat"—he recognized her as the woman who had reached out to Ron Kochman at YouAreJustMyType.com—had contacted Ron Kochman, Titus should have closed down the profile and cut the line. He hadn't for several reasons.

The first was, he was close to nailing two other victims using that profile. It had taken a lot of work to get there. He didn't want to lose them over what at first blush seemed to be nothing but contact with an ex. Second, he had no idea that Kat was an NYPD officer. He hadn't bothered to check her out. He had simply assumed she was a lonely ex-girlfriend and that his "let's not go back to the past" spiel would be the end of it. That had been incorrect. Third, Kat hadn't called him Ron. She called him Jeff, making Titus wonder whether she had mistaken him for another guy who looked like Ron, or whether Ron had once been known as Jeff, therefore making it even harder to find him and an even better fake profile.

That too had been a mistake.

Still, even if hindsight is twenty-twenty, how had Kat put it together? How, from a small communication on YouAreJustMyType, had Detective Kat Donovan found Dana Phelps and Gerard Remington and Martha Paquet?

He needed to know.

So now Titus couldn't just kill her and be done with it. He had to grab her and make her talk to see the level of threat. He now wondered whether his perfect operation had run its course. That could be. If he learned that Kat was closing in on him or had shared the information with anyone, he would hit the DELETE button on the whole enterprise—that is, kill the rest of the targets, bury them, burn down the farmhouse, move on with the money they'd made.

But a man had to find balance too. A man could panic under these circumstances and make the mistake of being overcautious. He didn't want to make a final decision until he knew more facts. He needed to get ahold of Kat Donovan and find out what she knew. He would have to make her disappear too. For some reason, there seemed to be this myth that if you killed someone, the law would come down on you harder. The truth was, dead people tell no tales. Missing bodies give no clues. The risk was greater, far greater, when you let your target or enemies work with impunity.

Remove them entirely and you're always better off.

Titus closed his eyes and leaned his head back. The ride to New York City would take about three hours. He might as well take a nap so he could be well rested for what might come.

36

KAT stood frozen in the backyard of this ordinary house in Montauk and felt the earth open up and swallow her whole. Eighteen years after saying that he no longer wanted to marry her, Jeff was a scant ten feet away. For a few moments, neither one of them spoke. She saw the look of loss and hurt and confusion on his face and wondered whether he was seeing the same on hers.

When Jeff finally spoke, it was to the old man, not Kat. "We could use a little privacy, Sam."

"Yeah, sure thing."

In her peripheral vision, Kat saw the old man close the book and go in the house. She and Jeff didn't take their eyes off each other. They had either become two wary gunfighters waiting for someone to draw or, more likely, two disbelieving souls who feared that if one of them turned away, if one of them so much as blinked, the other would vanish into the eighteen-year-old dust.

Jeff had tears in his eyes. "God, it's so good to see you."

"You too," she said.

Silence.

Then Kat said, "Did I really just say 'you too'?"

"You used to be better with the comebacks."

"I used to be better with a lot of things."

He shook his head. "You look fantastic."

She smiled at him. "You too." Then: "Hey, that's becoming my new go-to line."

Jeff started toward her, arms spread. She wanted to collapse into them. She wanted him to take her in his arms and press her against his chest and maybe pull back and kiss her tenderly and then just wait for the eighteen years to melt away like the morning frost. But—and maybe this was more a protective maneuver—Kat took a step back and held up her palm to him. He pulled up, surprised, but only for a moment, and then he nodded.

"Why are you here, Kat?"

"I'm looking for two missing women."

She felt on firmer ground when she said this. She hadn't gone through all this to rekindle a flame her old fiancé had long ago extinguished. She was here to solve a case.

"I don't understand," he said.

"Their names are Dana Phelps and Martha Paquet."

"I've never heard of them."

She had expected this answer. Once Kat put together that she was the one who said, "It's Kat," first, the rest had fallen into place.

"Do you have a laptop?" she asked.

"Uh, sure, why?"

"Could you get it, please?"

"I still don't—"

"Just get it, Jeff. Okay?"

He nodded. When he went inside, Kat actually dropped to her knees and felt her entire body give out. She wanted to sink to the ground and forget about these women, just lie on the earth and let go and cry and wonder about all the what-ifs that this stupid life brings us.

She managed to get back up a few seconds before he returned. He turned on the laptop and handed it to her. She sat at a picnic table. Jeff sat across from her.

"Kat?"

She could hear the pain in his voice too. "Not now. Please. Let me just get through this, okay?"

She got to the YouAreJustMyType page and brought up his profile.

It was gone.

Someone was closing ranks. She quickly opened up her old e-mail and found the link Brandon had sent her with Jeff's inactive Facebook page. She brought it up and spun the laptop toward him.

"You were on Facebook?"

Jeff squinted at the page. "That's how you found me?"

"It helped."

"I deleted the account as soon as I found out about it."

"Nothing online is ever deleted."

"You saw my daughter this morning. When she was going to school."

Kat nodded. So the daughter had called him after she made contact. Kat had figured as much.

"A few years ago, Melinda—that's her name—she thought I was lonely. Her mother died years ago. I don't date or anything, so she figured that the least I could do was have a Facebook page. To find old friends or meet someone. You know how it is."

"So your daughter set up the page?"

"Yes. As a surprise for me."

"Did she know you used to be Jeff Raynes?"

"She didn't then, no. As soon as I saw it, I deleted it. That's when I explained to her that I used to be someone else."

Kat met his gaze. His eyes still pierced. "Why did you change your name?"

He shook his head. "You said something about missing women."

"Yes."

"And that's why you're here."

"Right. Someone used you in a catfish scheme."

"Catfish?"

"Yeah. I mean, that's what they call it. Have you seen the movie or TV show?"

"No."

"A catfish is a person who pretends to be someone they're not online, especially in romantic relationships." Her voice was flat, matter-of-fact. She needed that now. She needed to just spout facts and figures and definitions and not feel a damn thing. "Someone took your pictures and created an online profile for you and put it on a singles' site. Two women who fell for the catfish-you are missing."

"I had nothing to do with it," Jeff said.

"Yeah, I know that now."

"How did you get involved in all this?"

"I'm a cop."

"So was this your case?" he asked. "Did someone else recognize me?"

"No. I joined YouAreJustMyType. Or a friend did for me. It doesn't matter. I saw your profile and I contacted you." She almost smiled. "I sent you that 'Missing You' video."

He smiled. "John Waite."

"Yeah."

"I loved that video." Something like hope lit up his eyes. "So you're, uh, you're single?"

"Yeah."

"You never got—"

"No."

Jeff's eyes started to well up again. "I got Melinda's mother pregnant in a drunken haze during a really self-destructive period for both of us. I managed to get out of the self-destruction. She didn't. That's my former father-in-law inside. The three of us have lived together since she died, when Melinda was eighteen months old."

"I'm sorry."

"It's fine. I just wanted you to know."

Kat tried to swallow. "It isn't my business."

"I guess not," Jeff said. He looked to the left and blinked. "I wish I could help you with your missing women, but I don't know anything."

"I know that."

"And yet you still came all this way to find me," he said.

"It wasn't all that far. And I had to make sure."

Jeff turned back so that he was facing her. God, he was still so damn handsome. "Did you?" he asked.

The world was crashing around her. She felt dizzy. Seeing his face again, hearing his voice—Kat hadn't really believed it would happen. The pain was more acute than she could have imagined. The rawness of how it all ended, the suddenness, was made all the worse by seeing his beautiful, troubled, haunting face.

She still loved him.

Goddamn it to hell. Goddamn it all and she hated herself for it and she felt weak and stupid and like a sucker.

She still loved him.

"Jeff?"

"Yes?"

"Why did you leave me?"

THE first bullet hit the tree six inches from Dana's head.

Bits of bark hit her left eye. Dana ducked and scampered away on all fours. The second and third bullets hit somewhere above her. She had no idea where.

"Dana?"

She had only one conscious thought: Keep as much distance between her and the juicehead as possible. He had been the one who locked her in that damn box. He had been the one who made her take off her clothes. And he had been the one to make her wear the jumpsuit with only socks.

No shoes or sneakers.

So here she was, running through these woods to escape from this psycho—in her stocking feet.

Dana didn't care.

Even before the big juicehead had locked her underground, Dana Phelps had realized that she had been had. At first, the worst part of it wasn't the pain or the fear but the humiliation and self-loathing for falling for a few photographs and well-turned phrases.

God, how pathetic was she?

But as the conditions worsened, that stuff flew out the window. Her only goal became survival. She knew that there was no point in fighting with the man who called himself Titus. He would do what he had to in order to get the information. She might not have been as broken as she pretended—she'd hoped it would make them let their guard down—but the sad truth was, she had been pretty badly cracked.

Dana had no idea how many days she had spent in the box. There was no sunrise or sunset, no clocks, no light, no dark even.

Just stone-cold blackness.

"Come out, Dana. There's no need for this. We're going to let you go, remember?"

Yeah, right.

She knew they were going to kill her and maybe, from the looks of what Juicehead had been up to, even worse. Titus had made a good sales pitch when he first met with her. He had tried to give her hope, which in the end was probably crueler than anything in that box. But she knew. He had shown his face. So had the computer geek and Juicehead and the two guards she had spotted.

She had wondered, lying in the dark all those hours and days, how they intended to kill her. She had heard the sound of a gun once. Would that be how they'd do it? Or would they just decide to leave her in that box and stop throwing down the handfuls of rice?

Did it even matter?

Now that Dana was aboveground, now that she was finally in the great, beautiful, spectacular outdoors, she felt free. If she died, she would at least die on her own terms.

Dana kept running. Yes, she had cooperated with Titus. What good would it have done not to? When she was forced to call to confirm the bank transfers, she hoped that Martin Bork would hear something in her voice or that she could try to slip him some kind of subtle message. But Titus kept one finger on the hang-up button, the other on the trigger of a gun.

And then of course, there was Titus's big threat. . . .

Juicehead shouted, "You don't want to do this, Dana."

He was in the woods now. She ran faster, knowing she could battle through the exhaustion. She was gaining ground on him, moving deftly through the foliage, ducking branches and trees, when she stepped on something and heard a sharp crack.

Dana managed not to scream out loud.

Her body tumbled to the side, a tree preventing her fall. She stayed up on one leg, cupping her left foot in her hand. The stick had broken into two sharp pieces, one of them slicing through and then embedding itself in the bottom of her foot. She tried to ease it out, but the stick wouldn't budge.

Juicehead was running toward her.

In a blind panic, Dana broke off what she could and left the splinter sticking out of the sole of her foot.

"There are three of us coming after you," Juicehead shouted. "We will find you. But if we don't, I still have your cell phone. I can text Brandon. I can tell him it's from you and that the stretch limousine will take him to his mommy."

She ducked down, closed her eyes, and tried not to listen.

This had been Titus's big threat—that if she didn't cooperate, they would go after Brandon.

"Your son will die in your box," Juicehead shouted. "If he's lucky."

Dana shook her head, tears of fear and fury running down her cheeks. Part of her wanted to surrender. But no, don't listen. Screw him and his threats. Her going back didn't guarantee her son's safety.

It only guaranteed that he'd be an orphan.

"Dana?"

He was gaining on her.

She hobbled back to standing. She winced when her foot hit the ground, but that couldn't be helped. Dana had always been a runner, the kind who jogged every day without fail. She had run cross-country at University of Wisconsin, where she'd met Jason Phelps, the love of her life. He had teased her about her addiction to the runner's high. "I'm addicted to *not* running," Jason had told her on too many occasions. But that hadn't stopped Jason from being proud of her. He traveled with her to every marathon. He waited by the finish line, his face lighting up as she crossed. Even when he was sick, even when he could barely get out of bed, Jason would insist that she still run, sitting at the finish line with a blanket on his thinning legs, waiting expectantly with his dying eyes for her to make the final turn.

She hadn't run a marathon since Jason died. She knew that she never would again.

Dana had heard all the great lines about death, but here was the universal truth: Death sucks. Death sucks, mostly because it forces those who stay behind to survive. Death isn't merciful enough to take you too. Instead, death constantly jams down your throat the awful lesson that life does indeed go on, no matter what.

She tried to run a little faster. Her muscles and lungs may have been willing, but her foot would not cooperate. She tried to put weight on it, tried to fight past the shooting pain, but every time her left foot hit the ground, it felt as though a dagger was being jammed through the sole of it.

He was getting closer.

The woods were spread out in front of her as far as the eye could see. She could keep running—would keep running—but suppose she didn't find her way out? How long could she keep going with this splinter in her foot and a maniac chasing her down?

Not very.

Dana jumped to the side and rolled behind a rock. He wasn't far away now. She could hear him pushing through the brush. She had no choice now. She couldn't keep running.

She would have to stand her ground and fight.

37

"WHY did you leave me?"

Jeff winced as though the five words had formed a cocked fist. For some reason, Kat reached across the table and took his hand in hers. He welcomed it. There was no jolt when they touched, no huge spark or grandiose physical current. There was comfort. There was, oddly enough, familiarity. There was the feeling that despite everything, despite the years and heartache and lives lived, that this was somehow right.

"I'm sorry," he said.

"I don't want an apology."

"I know."

He threaded his fingers in hers. They sat there, holding hands. Kat didn't press it. She let it happen. She didn't fight it. She embraced the connection with this man who had shattered her heart, when she knew she should have pushed it away.

"It was a long time ago," Jeff said.

"Eighteen years."

"Right."

Kat tilted her head. "It seem that long ago to you?"

"No," he said.

They sat there some more. The skies had cleared. The sun shone down upon them. Kat almost asked if he remembered their weekend in Amagansett, but what was the point? This was dumb, sitting with this man who gave her a ring and then a pink slip, and yet for the first time in a long time, she didn't feel the fool about him. She could be projecting. She could be deluding herself. She knew the dangers of trusting instinct over evidence.

But she felt loved.

"You're in hiding," she said.

He didn't reply.

"Are you in the Witness Protection Program or something?"

"No."

"So what, then?"

"I needed a change, Kat."

"You got into a bar fight in Cincinnati," she said.

A small smile came to his face. "You know about that, huh?"

"I do. It happened not long after we broke up."

"The beginning of my self-destructive period."

"And sometime after the fight, you changed your name."

Jeff stared down, as though noticing for the first time that they were holding hands. "Why does this feel so natural?" he asked.

"What happened, Jeff?"

"Like I said, I needed a change."

"You're not going to tell me?" She felt herself start welling up. "So I, what, just get up and leave now? I drive back to New York City and we forget all this and never see each other again?"

He kept his eyes on her hands. "I love you, Kat."

"I love you too."

Foolish. Dumb. Crazy. Honest.

When he looked up at her, when their eyes met, Kat felt her world crash down on her once again.

"But we don't get to go back," he said. "It doesn't work that way."

Her cell phone buzzed yet again. Kat had been ignoring it, but now Jeff gently pulled his hand away from hers. The spell, if that was what you'd call it, broke. Coldness spread up her abandoned hand and up her arm.

She checked the caller ID. It was Chaz. She stepped away from the picnic table and brought the phone to her ear. She cleared her throat and said, "Hello?"

"Martha Paquet just sent her sister an e-mail."

"What?"

"She said all is okay. She and her boyfriend ended up at another inn and they're having a great time."

"I'm with her supposed boyfriend right now. It's all a catfish."

"What?"

She explained about the use of the faux Ron Kochman. She left out the part about Ron being Jeff and her connection to him. It wasn't so much embarrassment anymore as much as not wanting to muddy the water.

"So what the hell is going on, Kat?" Chaz asked.

"Something really, really bad. Have you spoken to the feds yet?"

"I did, but I mean, they just sort of go silent on me. Maybe this catfish thing will help move things along, but right now, there is almost no proof of a crime. People do this all the time."

"Do what all the time?"

"Have you watched the *Catfish* TV show? People set up fake accounts on these websites all the time. They use photos from someone who is hotter-looking. To break the ice. Pisses me off, you know? Chicks are always talking about how all they care about is personality, but then, bam, they fall for the cutie too. That might be all this is, Kat."

Kat frowned. "And what, Chaz—this ugly guy or girl ends up getting them to transfer hundreds of thousands of dollars to Swiss bank accounts?"

"Martha's money hasn't been touched."

"Not yet anyway. Chaz, listen to me. I need you to look for any missing adults over the last few months. Maybe they were reported. Maybe they just claimed to run off with a lover. There wouldn't be major attention because there would be texts or e-mails or whatever, just like with these three. But cross-reference any kind of concern with singles' websites."

"You think there are more victims?"

"I do."

"Okay, I get it," he said. "But I don't know if the feds will."

Chaz had a point. "Maybe you can set up a meet," Kat said. "Call Mike Keiser. He's the ADIC in New York. We may be able to do better face-to-face."

"So you're coming back to the city now?"

Kat looked behind her. Jeff was standing. He wore denim jeans and a fitted black T-shirt. All of this—sights, sound, emotions, whatever—was almost too much to take in at once. The rush was overwhelming to the point of threatening.

"Yeah," she said. "I'll leave now."

THEY didn't bother with good-byes or promises or hugs. They had said what they wanted to say, Kat guessed. It felt like enough and yet more incomplete than ever. She had come here hoping for answers, and as is the way of the world, she was leaving with even more questions.

Jeff walked her to the car. He made a face when he saw the fly yellow Ferrari, and despite everything, Kat actually laughed.

"This yours?" Jeff asked.

"What if I said yes?"

"I would wonder if you grew a very small penis since we were last together."

She couldn't help herself. She threw her arms around him hard. He stumbled back for a second, got his footing, and hugged her back. She put her face against his chest and sobbed. His big hand cupped the back of her head and pulled her closer. He squeezed his eyes shut. They both just held on, changing their grips, pulling each other closer and with more desperation, until finally Kat pushed away all at once and, without another word, got into the car and drove away. She didn't look back. She didn't check the rearview mirror.

Kat drove the next thirty miles in a fog, obeying the GPS as though she were the machine, not it. When she had her bearings, she made herself concentrate on the case, only the case. She thought about all she had learned—about the catfishing and the money transfers and the e-mails and the stolen license plate and the phone calls.

Panic began to harden in her chest.

This couldn't wait for a face-to-face.

She started making pleading phone calls, working connections, until she reached Mike Keiser, the Assistant Director in Charge of the FBI. "What can I do for you, Detective? We're working an incident that took place at LaGuardia Airport this morning. I also have two drug busts going down. It's a busy day."

"I appreciate that, sir, but I have a case involving at least three missing people across at least three states. One is from Massachusetts, one from Connecticut, one from Pennsylvania. I think there may be many more victims that we don't know about yet. Have you been briefed on any of this?"

"I have. In fact, I know your partner, Detective Faircloth, has been trying to set up a meeting with us, but we're really crazed with this LaGuardia situation. It may involve national security."

"If these people are being held against their will—"

"Which you have no proof of. In fact, hasn't each of your supposed victims been in touch with family or friends?"

"None is currently answering their phones. I suspect that the e-mails and calls are being coerced."

"Based on?"

"Look at the whole picture," Kat said.

"Make it fast, Detective."

"Start with the two women. They both have an online relationship with the same guy—"

"Who isn't really the guy."

"Right."

"Someone else was just using his pictures."

"Right."

"Which I gather is not uncommon."

"It's not. But the rest is. Both of these women go away with this same guy about a week apart."

"You don't know it's the same guy."

"Pardon?"

"Several guys could be using the same fake profile."

Kat hadn't thought of that. "Even if that were the case, neither woman is back from her trip."

"Which also isn't surprising. One had extended her trip. The other just left, what, yesterday?"

"Sir, one of the women transferred a ton of cash and is supposedly moving to Costa Rica or something. I don't know."

"But she called her son?"

"Yes, but—"

"You think the call was coerced."

"I do. We also have to look at the case of Gerard Remington. He started an online relationship and now he's gone too. He also transferred money to that Swiss account."

"So what exactly do you think is going on here, Detective?"

"I think someone is preying on people, maybe a lot of people. We've stumbled across three possible victims. I think there are more. I think someone lures them away with promises of a vacation with a potential life partner. He grabs them and gets them somehow to cooperate. So far, none of them have come back. Gerard Remington has been off the grid for weeks."

"And you think—"

"I hope he's alive, but I'm not optimistic."

"You really believe that these people have all been, what, kidnapped?"

"I do. Whoever is behind this has been smart and careful. He's stolen license plates. With one exception, none of these three has used their credit cards or ATM charges or anything else we can trace. They just vanish."

She waited.

"Look, I have to go into a meeting on this LaGuardia mess, but okay, yeah, this doesn't pass the smell test. Right now, I don't have a ton of manpower, but we'll get on it. You gave us the three names. We will put a watch on their accounts, run their credit cards, check phone records. I'll get a subpoena for this singles' website and see what they can tell us about who put up the profile pages. I don't know if that will give us anything or not. Criminals use anonymous VPNs all the time. I'll also see if we can get that singles' site to put up some kind of warning on their home page, but since it will hurt their bottom line, I doubt they will want to cooperate. We can also see if Treasury can go after the money trail. Two SARs were issued, right? That should be enough to get the ball rolling on that end too."

Kat listened to ADIC Keiser continue to go down his checklist and came to a horrible, awful conclusion:

It wouldn't do any good.

Whoever was behind this had been efficient. He had even gone so far as to steal a license plate from another Lincoln Town Car. So yes, the feds would work the case, even though it couldn't yet be a priority. Maybe, if they got lucky, they'd find something.

Eventually.

But what else could she do?

When ADIC Keiser finished, he said, "Detective? I need to go now."

"I appreciate your believing me," Kat said.

"Sadly, I think I do believe you," he said, "but I hope to hell you're wrong about all this."

"Me too."

They hung up. Kat had one more card to play. She called Brandon.

"Where are you?" she asked him.

"I'm still in Manhattan."

"I found the guy your mother supposedly went away with."

"What?"

"I think you were right from the start. I think something bad has happened to your mother."

"But I spoke to her," Brandon said. "She would have told me if something was wrong."

"Not if she felt it would put her—or you—in danger."

"You think that's what happened?"

There was no reason to sugarcoat it anymore. "Yeah, Brandon, I do."

"Oh God."

"The FBI is looking into it now. They will go through every *legal* channel they can to find out what happened." She repeated the word that she had emphasized. "*Legal.*"

"Kat?"

"Yes?"

"Is that your way of asking me to break in to the website again?"

Screw the fancy talk. "Yes."

"Okay, I'm at a coffee shop not far from your house. I'm going to need more privacy and stronger Wi-Fi."

"Do you want to use my apartment?"

"Yeah, that'll work."

"I'll call and tell the doorman to let you in. I'm on my way too. Call me if you find anything—who put up the profiles, if they put up any other profiles, who else they've contacted, anything. Get your friends to help, whatever. We need to know everything."

"On it."

She hung up, called her doorman, hit the accelerator, though she felt as if she were rushing to nowhere. Panic was beginning to creep in and take hold. The more she learned, the more helpless she felt. Professionally and personally.

When the phone sounded again, the caller ID read BLOCKED.

Kat picked it up. "Hello?"

"This is Leslie."

Cozone's thin man. Even his phone voice had a creepy smile. "What is it?" she asked.

"I found Sugar."

38

JUICEHEAD was getting closer.

From her spot behind the boulder, Dana Phelps searched for some kind of weapon. A rock maybe. A fallen branch. Something. She started digging her hands around the dirt near her, finding nothing more lethal than pebbles, and twigs too flimsy for a bird's nest.

"Dana?"

The timbre of his shout told her that he was closing the gap in a hurry. Weapon, weapon. Still nothing. She wondered about the pebbles. Maybe she could mix them with the dirt and then fling it in his face, hitting his eyes, blinding him for a second or two and then . . .

Then what?

The whole plan was moronic. Dana may have been able to temporarily escape using the element of surprise. She might have been able to put some distance between

them because of some fortuitous blend of lifelong training and adrenaline. But when she stopped and looked at
it now, he had a gun and size and strength. He was well
fed and healthy while she had been locked underground
for she had no idea how long.

She had no chance.

What did Dana have on her side in this David and
Goliath battle? Not even a slingshot. The only thing she
maybe had was, again, the element of surprise. She was
ducking behind this boulder. He would be passing by it
any minute now. She could leap out, catching him off
guard. She would go for the eyes and the balls and attack
with the ferocity only someone fighting for her life could
muster.

But did that even sound feasible anymore?

No, not really.

She could hear that he had slowed his pace. His steps
were more deliberate now. Terrific. Even the element of
surprise was gone.

So what did she have left?

Nothing.

Exhaustion emanated from every part of her body.
Part of her wanted to just stay here, on the ground, and
get it over with. Let him do what he wanted. He could
kill her right away. Probably would. Or he could bring
her back to that barn and do whatever monstrous thing
he had been planning in hopes of extracting information
relating to that police detective Titus had asked about.

Dana hadn't been lying. She had no idea who Kat
Donovan was, but that didn't really seem to matter to
Titus and Juicehead. Pathos never entered the equation
with these two. She was less than an animal (witness
Juicehead's dog) to them. She was something inanimate,

something lifeless, like this boulder, an object to be removed or bulldozed or broken into bits, depending on their want or convenience. It would have been one thing if they were simply cruel or sadistic. What they were, though, was something worse.

They were completely pragmatic.

Juicehead's steps closed in on her. Dana tried to adjust her body, tried to find a way to pounce when he passed, but her muscles wouldn't obey. She tried to find hope in the fact that this Kat woman had spooked Titus.

Titus was worried about her.

Dana could hear it in his voice, in his questions, in his leaving her in the hands of Juicehead. Dana remembered seeing him rush out the door and drive away.

How worried was he?

Was Detective Kat Donovan, with the sweet, open face Dana had seen on that computer screen, onto him? Was she right now on her way to rescue Dana?

Juicehead was fewer than ten steps away.

Didn't matter. Dana had nothing left. Her foot ached. Her head thrummed. She had no weapon, no strength, no experience.

Five steps away.

It was now or never.

Mere seconds until he reached her . . .

Dana closed her eyes and chose . . . never.

She ducked low and covered her head and said a silent prayer. Juicehead stopped at the boulder. Dana's head was down, her face almost buried in the dirt. She braced for the blow.

But it never came.

Juicehead started up again, pushing his way through the branches. He hadn't seen her. Dana didn't move. She lay still as that boulder. She couldn't say how long. Five minutes. Maybe ten. When she risked a look, Juicehead was nowhere in sight.

Change of plans.

Dana started heading back toward the farmhouse.

COZONE'S man Leslie had given Kat the address of a town house on the corner of Lorimer and Noble streets in Greenpoint, Brooklyn, near the Union Baptist Church. The neighborhood had redbrick and concrete stoops. She drove past a broken-down building with a temporary sign reading HAWAIIAN TANNING SALON and couldn't imagine any odder juxtaposition than a Hawaiian tan and Greenpoint, Brooklyn.

There were no free parking spaces, so she stuck the fly yellow Ferrari in front of a fire hydrant. She climbed the stoop. A plastic name tape reading A. PARKER was peeling off by the second-floor buzzer. Kat pushed it, heard the sound, and waited.

A black man with a shaved head trudged down the stairs and opened the door. He wore work gloves and blue coveralls with a cable company logo. A yellow hard hat was tucked under his left arm. He stood in the doorway and said, "Can I help you?"

"I'm looking for Sugar," she said.

The man's eyes narrowed. "And you are?"

"My name is Kat Donovan."

The man stood there and studied her.

"What do you want with Sugar?" he asked.

"It's about my father."

"What about him?"

"Sugar used to know him. I just need to ask her a few questions."

He looked over her head and then down the block. He spotted the yellow Ferrari. She wondered whether he too would make a comment. He didn't. He looked the other way.

"Pardon me, Mr. . . . ?"

"Parker," the man said. "Anthony Parker."

He glanced to his left again, but didn't really seem to be checking the street so much as buying time. He seemed uncertain what to do.

"I'm here alone," Kat said, trying to reassure him.

"I can see that."

"And I don't want to cause any trouble. I just need to ask Sugar some questions."

His eyes rested on hers. He managed a smile. "Come on inside."

Parker opened the door all the way and held it for her. She stepped into the front foyer and pointed up the stairs.

"Second floor?" she asked.

"Yes."

"Is Sugar up there?"

"She will be."

"When?"

"Right behind you," Anthony Parker said. "I'm Sugar."

DANA had to move slowly.

Two other men had joined the search. One had a rifle. One had a handgun. They were communicating with

Reynaldo via some kind of hands-free mobile phone or walkie-talkie. They swept back and forth, preventing her from making a straight line back to the farmhouse. Often, she had to stay perfectly still for minutes at a time.

In a very odd way, it was almost as though being buried underground had helped train her for this. Every part of her body ached, but she ignored it. She was too tired to cry. She thought about hiding out here, finding a covered spot and just staying put in the hopes that someone would come and rescue her.

But that wouldn't work.

For one thing, she needed sustenance. She had been dehydrated before all this started. Now it was getting worse. For another, the three men after her kept crisscrossing the woods, keeping her on the move. One of the men had been so close to her at one point that she could overhear Juicehead say, "If she's out that far, she'll die before she ever gets back."

It was a clue. Don't keep running in that direction away from the farm. There was nothing for her out that way. So what to do?

She had no choice. She had to get back to the farmhouse.

So for the last . . . she had no idea how long; time had become irrelevant—Dana kept on the move, moving a yard or two at a time. She stayed low. She didn't have a compass, but she thought she still knew the general direction. She had run out here in pretty much a straight line. The return was more a zigzag.

The woods were thick, making her rely more on sound sometimes than sight, but finally, up ahead, she thought that she saw a clearing.

Or maybe that was just wishful thinking.

Dana commando-crawled toward it, moving with everything she had, which wasn't all that much. It wouldn't do—commando-crawling was simply too exhausting. She risked getting to her feet, her head reeling from the blood rush, but every time her foot touched down on the dirt, a fresh jolt of agony rushed up her leg. She got back down and tried all fours.

It was slower going.

Five, maybe ten minutes later, she broke through the last line of trees and reached the farmhouse clearing.

So now what?

She had somehow managed to come back to exactly the place she had entered the woods. Up ahead of her was the back of that barn. To the right stood the farmhouse. She had to move. Staying where she was left her too exposed.

She made a dash for the barn.

With death so close behind her, Dana figured that she'd be able to push past the pain in her foot. But that wasn't working. The daggers turned her sprint into a spastic one-legged hop. Her joints ached. Her muscles tightened.

Still, if she stopped, she would die. A simple equation when she thought of it that way.

She half fell against the side of the barn, pressing her body tight against the wall as though that might make her invisible.

So far, she was in the clear.

Okay, good. No one had spotted her yet. That was the key. Next step?

Get help.

How?

She thought about running down the drive. That had

to lead to an exit, right? But she had no idea how far it was, and worse, it was wide-open. She would be spotted and picked off easily.

Still, it was an option.

Dana craned her neck, trying to see to the end of the road. It was too far away.

So now what?

She had two choices. One, run down the road. Take her chances that way. Two, hide someplace. Hope someone comes to rescue her or maybe she could sneak out under nightfall.

She couldn't think straight. Hiding till nightfall seemed somewhat feasible, but she couldn't count on anything approaching an immediate rescue. Her tired, confused brain added up the pros and cons and reached a conclusion: Making a run for it was the best of a lot of bad options. No, she had no idea how far it was to the road. No, she didn't know how close any other people or traffic were.

But she couldn't just stay here and wait for Juicehead to come back.

She had gone only about ten yards toward the road when the front door of the farmhouse opened. The computer guy with the knit cap, tinted glasses, and wild shirt stepped onto the porch. Dana hopped to the left and dove headfirst into the barn. She scrambled on all fours toward the metal tool table. The rope—the one Juicehead had planned to tie her with—was still on the floor.

She waited to see if the computer guy came into the barn. He didn't. Time passed. She had to risk it. This "hiding" spot was too exposed. She slowly crawled out from under the table. Tools were hung on the wall in front of her. There were several saws, a wooden mallet, a sander.

And an ax.

Dana tried to stand up. Whoa, the head rush again. She started to black out, forcing her to take a knee.

Slow down. Steady.

Running down that road wasn't feeling like much of an option anymore.

Deep breaths.

She had to move. Juicehead and his friends would be coming back soon. Dana struggled to her feet and reached for the ax. She pulled it off the wall. It was heavier than she'd thought, almost knocking her back to the floor. She regained her balance and gripped the ax with two hands.

It felt good.

So now what?

She took a peek out the barn door. The computer guy was smoking a cigarette near the drive.

Running was definitely out.

So what was option two again? Hiding, right?

She took a look behind her. There was no decent place in the barn to hide. Her best bet, she realized, was to get to the farmhouse. She looked toward the back. The kitchen, she knew, was there.

Kitchen. Food.

Just the thought of that—of getting food in her belly—made her dizzy.

But more than that, there was a computer in the farmhouse. A phone too.

A way to get help.

The guy with the knit hat still had his back to her. There wouldn't be a better chance. Keeping one eye on him, Dana crept toward the kitchen door of the farmhouse. She was completely exposed now, tiptoeing at a spot about halfway between the barn and the back of the house, when the guy with the knit hat dropped the butt of his cigarette onto the ground, stomped on it, and turned toward her.

Dana lowered her head and sprinted with all she had to the back of the house.

TITUS waited in the car near the corner of Columbus Avenue. He didn't like being back in the city, even though the ritzy Upper West Side had about as much to do with his old life as a vagrant has to do with a hedge fund manager. It was almost as if something were drawing Titus back to the life he had neatly put behind him.

He didn't want to be here.

Clem Sison crossed the street and slid back into the driver's seat. "Donovan's not home."

Clem had gone into Kat Donovan's building with a "package" that needed her signature. The doorman had informed him that she wasn't home right now. Clem thanked him and said that he'd return.

Titus didn't like staying away from the farm any longer than necessary. He considered heading back and leaving Clem behind to make the grab, but Clem wouldn't be able to handle this alone. He was muscle, good with a gun and taking orders and not much else.

So what now?

Titus plucked at his lip and considered his options. His eyes were still locked on the front of Kat Donovan's building, when he saw something that stunned him.

Brandon Phelps was walking through the door.

What the . . . ?

But hold on. Maybe this explained everything. Had Brandon Phelps initiated all this? Was the problem here Kat Donovan or Brandon Phelps—or both? Brandon Phelps, Titus knew, had been something of an issue from the start. The mama's boy had sent dozens of homesick e-mails and texts. Now all of a sudden, here he is with Kat Donovan, an NYPD cop. Titus ran the scenarios through his head.

Had Kat Donovan been onto Titus earlier than he'd suspected?

Could that be? Could Kat have been pretending to be Ron Kochman's ex to draw him out in some way? Had Brandon gone to Kat—or had Kat gone to Brandon?

Did it even matter?

Titus's mobile phone buzzed in his pocket. He pulled it out and saw that it was Reynaldo.

"Hello?"

"We have a problem," Reynaldo said.

Titus's jaw clenched. "What is it?"

"Number Six is on the run."

39

TWO crocheted afghan blankets covered the couch. Kat sat on the small space between them. Anthony Parker tossed his yellow hard hat onto a spare chair. He took off one work glove, then the other. He carefully put them on the coffee table, as though this was a task of great importance. Kat let her eyes wander around the apartment. The lighting was poor, but maybe that had something to do with the fact that Anthony Parker had switched on only one dim lamp. The furniture was old and made of wood. There was a console TV on top of a bureau. The wallpaper was busy blue chinoiserie with egrets and trees and water scenes.

"This was my mother's place," he said by way of explanation.

Kat nodded.

"She died last year."

"I'm sorry," Kat said, because that was what you said under such circumstances and she couldn't think of anything else right now.

Her entire body felt numb.

Anthony "Sugar" Parker sat across from her. He was, she guessed, in his late fifties or early sixties. When he met her eyes, it was almost too much. Kat had to angle her body away, just a little, just enough so that they weren't so face-to-face. Anthony Parker—Sugar?—looked so damned normal. His height and build would have been listed on a police blotter as average. He had a nice face, but nothing special or even feminine.

"You can imagine my shock at seeing you," Parker said.

"Yeah, well, I think I may have you beat in that area."

"Fair enough. So you didn't know I was a man?"

Kat shook her head. "I'd guess you'd call this my personal *Crying Game* moment."

He smiled. "You look like your father."

"Yeah, I get that a lot."

"You also sound like him. He always used humor to deflect." Parker smiled. "He made me laugh."

"My father did?"

"Yes."

"You and my father," she said, with a shake of her head.

"Yes."

"I'm having trouble believing it."

"I understand."

"So are you telling me my father was gay?"

"I'm not defining him."

"But you two were . . . ?" Kat made her hands go back and forth in a near clap.

"We were together, yes."

Kat closed her eyes and tried not to make a face.

"It's been nearly twenty years," Parker said. "Why are you here now?"

"I just found out about you two."

"How?"

She shook it off. "It's not important."

"Don't be angry with him. He loved you. He loved all of you."

"Including you," Kat half snapped. "The man was just so full of love."

"I know that you're in shock. Would it be better if I were a woman?"

Kat said nothing.

"You have to understand what it was like for him," Parker said.

"Could you just answer my question?" Kat said. "Was he gay or not?"

"Does it matter?" Parker shifted in his seat. "Would you think less of him if he was?"

She wasn't sure what to say. She had so many questions, and yet maybe all of this was indeed beside the point. "He lived a lie," she said.

"Yes." Parker tilted his head to the side. "Think about how horrible that is, Kat. He loved you. He loved your brothers. He even loved your mother. But you know the world he grew up in. He fought what he knew for a long, long time until it consumed him. It doesn't change who he was. It doesn't make him any less manly or any less a cop or any less of the things you think he is. What else could he do?"

"He could have divorced my mother, for one thing."

"He suggested it."

That surprised her. "What?"

"For her sake, really. But your mother didn't want it."

"Wait. Are you saying my mother knew about you?"

Parker looked down at the floor. "I don't know. What happens with something like this, with a huge secret you can't let anyone know, everyone starts living the lie. He deceived you, sure, but you also didn't want to see. It corrupts everyone."

"Yet he asked her for a divorce?"

"No. Like I said, he suggested it. For her sake. But you know your neighborhood. Where would your mother go from there? And where would he go? It wasn't as though he could leave her and let the world know about us. Today, it's better than it was twenty years ago, but even now, could you imagine it?"

She couldn't.

"How long were you two"—she still couldn't believe it—"together?"

"Fourteen years."

Another jolt. She had been a child when it started. "Fourteen years?"

"Yes."

"And you two were able to keep it secret all that time?"

Something dark crossed his face. "We tried. Your father had a place on Central Park West. We would meet up there."

Kat's head started to swim. "On Sixty-Seventh Street?"

"Yes."

Her eyes closed. Her apartment now. The betrayal just grew and grew, and yet should it be worse because it was a man? No. Kat had prided herself on being more open-minded, right? When she assumed her father had had a mistress, she had been upset but understanding.

Why should it be worse now?

"Then I got a place in Red Hook," Parker said. "We'd

go there. We traveled together a lot. You probably re-member. He'd pretend to be away with friends or on some kind of bender."

"And you cross-dressed?"

"Yes. I think it was easier for him. Being with, in some ways, a woman. Freaky in his world was still better than being a faggot—you know what I'm saying?"

Kat didn't respond.

"And I was in drag when we first met. He busted a club I was working in. Beat me up. Such rage. Called me an abomination. I remember there were tears in his eyes even as he was hitting me with his fists. When you see a man with such rage, it is almost like he's beating himself up—do you know what I mean?"

Again Kat didn't respond.

"Anyway, he visited me in the hospital. At first, he said it was just to make sure I didn't talk, you know, like he was still threatening me. But we both knew. It didn't happen fast. But he lived in such pain. I mean, it came off him in waves. I know you probably want to hate him right now."

"I don't hate him," Kat said in a voice that she barely recognized as her own. "I feel sorry for him."

"People are always talking about fighting for gay rights and acceptance. But that isn't really what a lot of us are after. It's the freedom to be authentic. It's living honestly. It is so hard to live a life where you can't be what you are. Your father lived under that horrible cloud for his entire life. He feared being exposed more than anything, and yet he couldn't let me go. He lived a lie and he lived in terror that someone would find out about that lie."

Kat saw it now. "But someone did find out, didn't they?"

Sugar—suddenly, Kat was seeing him as Sugar, not Anthony Parker—nodded.

It was obvious now, wasn't it? Tessie knew about it. People had seen them together. To the neighbors, it meant her father had a thing for black prostitutes. But to someone savvier, someone who could use the information for his own good, it would mean something different.

It would mean an "understanding."

"A lowlife thug named Cozone gave me your address," Kat said. "He found out about the two of you, didn't he?"

"Yes."

"When?"

"A month or two before your father's murder."

Kat sat up, pushing aside the fact that she was the daughter, taking on the cop role. "So my father was onto Cozone. He was getting close. Cozone probably sent men to follow him. Dig up dirt, if they could. Something he could leverage to stop the investigation."

Sugar didn't nod. He didn't have to. Kat looked at him. "Sugar?"

Sugar's eyes slowly came up and met Kat's.

"Who killed my father?"

"NUMBER Six is on the run," Reynaldo said.

Titus squeezed the phone. Something inside of him exploded. "How the hell . . . ?" He stopped himself and closed his eyes.

Composure. Patience. When Titus lost those, he lost everything. He fought back the anger, and in as calm a voice as he could muster, he asked, "Where is she now?"

"She ran north behind the barn. The three of us are trying to find her."

North, Titus thought. Okay, good. North was straight

into miles and miles of forest. In her current condition, she couldn't last out there. They had never had anyone successfully run from them for more than a minute or two, but one of the beauties of the farm was the remoteness and security. To the north, it was all forest. Go south from the farmhouse and you still had almost a mile before you reached the main road. The entrance was fenced, as was the land east and west.

"Let her run," Titus said. "Start back to the farm. Post Rick and Julio in position in case she circles back."

"Okay."

"How long has she been gone?"

"She ran a few minutes after you left."

Three hours ago.

"Okay, keep me in the loop."

Titus hung up. He sat back and tried to analyze this situation rationally. To date, the operation had grossed more money than he had ever imagined. The current count was $6.2 million. How much, he asked himself, would be enough?

Greed brought men down more than anything else.

In short, was this the endgame? Had this profitable operation, like all others before it, run its course?

Titus had planned for this day. He knew that no business venture could last forever. Eventually, too many people would be found missing. The authorities would have to take a good, hard look, and while Titus had tried to think of every eventuality, it would be hubris to think that if he continued, he would never get caught.

He called back to the farmhouse. It took four rings for Dmitry to answer. "Hello?"

"Are you aware of our problem?" Titus asked.

"Reynaldo said Dana is on the run."

"Yes," Titus said. "I need you to bring up her phone information."

Mobile phones are traceable if left on, so when a new "guest" arrived, Dmitry transferred all the phone information onto his computer, basically duplicating the contents onto the hard drive. Once that was done, the batteries were pulled out of the phones and dumped in a drawer.

"Dana Phelps," Dmitry said. "I got it up. What do you need?"

"Bring up her contacts. I need her son's phone number."

Titus could hear the typing.

"Here it is, Titus. Brandon Phelps. Do you want his mobile or his number at school?"

"Mobile."

Dmitry gave him the phone number. Then he asked, "Do you need me to do anything else?"

"It may be time to abort," Titus said.

"Really?"

"Yeah. Set up the self-destruct on the computers, but don't enact yet. I'm going to grab the kid and bring him back."

"Why?"

"If Dana Phelps is still hiding somewhere, we need to flush her out. She'll come out when she hears his screams."

"I don't understand," Sugar said. "I thought they caught the man who killed your father."

"No. He just took the fall."

Sugar stood up and stared, pacing. Kat watched him.

"Cozone found out about you two a few months before he died, right?" Kat asked.

"Right." There were tears in Sugar's eyes now. "Once Cozone started to blackmail your father, everything changed."

"Changed how?"

"Your father broke it off with me. Said we were through. That I disgusted him. That rage, like when we first met—it came back. He hit me. You have to understand. He directed the rage at me, but it was mostly toward himself. When you live a lie—"

"Yeah, I get it," Kat said, cutting him off. "I really don't need the pop psychology lesson right now. He was a self-hating gay man trapped in a straight, macho world."

"You say it with such coldness."

"No, not really," Kat said. She felt the lump in her throat and tried to make it go away. "Later, when I have the time to think about all this, it will break my heart. And when that happens—when I let it in—it will crush me that my father was in such pain and I couldn't see it. I will crawl into bed with a bottle and vanish for as long as it takes. But not right now. Right now I need to do what I can to help him."

"By finding out who killed him?"

"Yes, by being the cop he raised. So who killed him, Sugar?"

He shook his head. "If it wasn't Cozone, then I really don't know."

"So when was the last time you saw him?"

"The night he died."

Kat made a face. "I thought you said you broke up."

"We did." Sugar stopped pacing and smiled through the tears on his face. "But he couldn't stay away. That was the truth. He couldn't be with me, but he couldn't let me go, either. He waited for me behind the nightclub where I was working." Sugar looked up, lost in the memory. "He had a dozen white roses in his hands. My favorite. He wore sunglasses. I thought they were to disguise himself. But when he took them off, I could see his eyes were red from crying." The tears were flowing freely down Sugar's cheeks now. "It was so wonderful. That was the last time I saw him. And then later that night . . ."

"He was murdered," Kat finished for him.

Silence.

"Kat?"

"Yes?"

"I never got over losing him," Sugar said. "He was the only man I ever really loved. Part of me will always hate him too. We could have run away. We could have found a way to be together. You and your brothers, you'd have understood eventually. We'd have been happy. I stayed with it all those years because that chance existed. You know what I mean? As long as we were alive, I think we both stupidly believed we would find a way."

Sugar knelt down and took both of Kat's hands in his. "I'm telling you so you understand. I still miss him so damn much. Every day. I would give anything, forgive anything, just to be with him for even a few seconds."

Block, Kat thought. Keep the blocks up for now. Get through this.

"Who killed him, Sugar?"

"I don't know."

But Kat thought that maybe now she knew who could give her the answer. She just had to make him finally tell her the truth.

40

STANDING outside the precinct, Kat called Stagger's cell phone.

"I don't think we have anything more to say to each other," Stagger said.

"Wrong. I just talked to Sugar. I'm thinking there's still a lot to say."

Silence.

"Hello?" Kat said.

"Where are you?"

"I'm coming down to your office right now, unless this is yet again a bad time."

"No, Kat." She had never heard Stagger sound so weary. "I think it's a good time."

When she arrived, Stagger was sitting at his desk. The photographs of his wife and kids were in front of him now, as though that could somehow shield him. Kat started in on him pretty hard, accusing him of lying and worse. Stagger came right back at her. There were shouts and tears, but finally Stagger made several admissions.

Yes, Stagger knew about Sugar.

Yes, Stagger had promised Monte Leburne favors for a simple confession.

Yes, Stagger had done that because he feared the affair would become public.

"I didn't want that for your father," Stagger said. "I didn't want his name dragged through the mud. For his sake. For yours and your family's too."

"And what about yours?" Kat countered.

Stagger made a maybe-yes/maybe-no gesture.

"You should have told me," Kat said.

"I didn't know how."

"So who killed him?"

"What?"

"Who killed my father?"

Stagger shook his head. "You really don't see?"

"No."

"Monte Leburne killed him. Cozone ordered him to."

Kat frowned. "You're still trying to peddle that story?"

"Because it's true, Kat."

"Cozone had no motive. He had my father right where he wanted him."

"No," Stagger said in that same tired tone. "He didn't."

"But he knew about—"

"Yeah, he knew about it. And for a little while, Cozone had your old man under his thumb. I sat back and watched your father back off. I even let him, so maybe I had something to lose here too. Once Cozone learned about Sugar, your father changed. He was trapped. He saw no way out until he just . . ." Stagger's voice faded away.

"He just what?"

Stagger looked up at her. "Had enough, I guess. Henry had lived with all those years of deception, but it hadn't affected his job. Now all of a sudden, in order to protect his lies, he had to compromise his police work. All men have their breaking point. That was your father's. So he told Cozone to go to hell. He didn't care anymore."

"How did Cozone react to that?" Kat asked.

"How do you think?"

They stood there in silence.

"So that's it?" she asked.

"That's it. It's over, Kat."

She didn't know what to say.

"Take a few more days. Then come back to work."

"I'm not being transferred?"

"No. I'd like you to stay. Do you still want a new partner?"

She shook her head. "No, I was wrong about that."

"About what?"

"About Chaz Faircloth."

Stagger picked up his pen. "Kat Donovan just admitted she was wrong. Will wonders never cease?"

THE kitchen door of the farmhouse was unlocked.

With the ax in one hand, Dana Phelps eased the screen door open, entered, and guided it to a close with a barely audible click. She stopped for a second and tried to gather herself.

But only for a second.

Food.

There, on the table in front of her, was a giant box of granola bars, the kind you buy at one of the price club stores. She had never experienced the horror of hunger before. She knew it would probably be smarter to search for a phone—and she would—but when she saw the food right there, so close by, it became beyond irresistible.

Stop, she told herself. Take care of the task at hand.

She checked for a phone in the kitchen. There were none. Now that she thought about it, there were no wires anywhere. She had heard the roar of a generator outside. Was that how they got electricity? Was there no phone hooked up?

Didn't matter.

There was, she knew, a computer with Internet in the other room. She could get help that way. If she could get to it. She wondered how much longer the computer guy would be outside on his smoke break. She had seen him throw down his cigarette and start turning toward her. Would he be lighting up another one or . . . ?

She heard the front door open.

Damn.

Dana looked for a hiding spot. The kitchen was small and sparse. There were cupboards and a table. Ducking beneath the table would do no good. There was no table-cloth. She would be completely exposed. The refrigerator was small and brown, the same kind she'd had in college in Wisconsin when she first met Jason. There was no room to hide there. There was a door, probably leading to a cellar. She could maybe go down there, if there was time.

Footsteps.

Then another thought came to Dana: the hell with hiding.

A swinging door separated the kitchen from the living room where Titus had grilled her. If the computer guy came in here, if he decided to make his way into the kitchen, Dana would hear and see him coming. It wasn't like before in the woods. Yes, she was exhausted. Yes, she needed one of those damn granola bars. But right now, if the computer guy entered this kitchen, she had the element of surprise in a big bad way.

And she had an ax.

The footsteps were coming toward her.

She slid off to the side behind the door. She wanted to make sure she had room to wield the ax—yet she needed to leave herself enough of an angle so that he wouldn't be able to see her until it was too late. The ax was so damned heavy. She debated how to swing it exactly. An overhead chop would be a tough angle. If she aimed for his neck, if she tried to slice his goddamn head off, the target area would be pretty small. Her aim would have to be precise.

The footsteps were right on the other side of the door now.

Dana gripped the handle with both hands. She lifted the ax up and held it like a batter waiting for the pitch. That would be the best angle. Swing like a baseball bat. Aim for the center of the chest and hope to bury the blade deep in his heart. If she missed a little right or left or up or down, it would still cause massive damage.

The footsteps stopped. The door began to creak open.

Dana's body shook from the strain, but she was ready.

Then a phone rang.

For a moment, the door stayed still. Then a hand released it and the door swung back. Dana let the ax collapse back to her side. For a moment, her eyes fell back on the granola bar.

The guy in the house would be busy, at least for the next few seconds. She grabbed a bar and tried her best to quietly unwrap it.

From the other room, she heard the computer guy say, "Hello?"

New plan, she thought. Grab a few granola bars. Go down into the cellar. Hide there with the ax and granola bars. Rest. Draw strength. Find a place where she could see someone coming and maybe take him down with the ax.

Her jumpsuit had pockets. A break, for once. Still chewing, she jammed granola bars into the pockets. They might notice if the entire box was missing from the table, but five or ten bars gone from a box that had originally held sixty wouldn't draw anyone's suspicion.

Dana reached for the cellar door when she heard the computer guy tell whoever was on the other end of the line: "Reynaldo said Dana is on the run."

She froze and listened. She heard typing and then the computer guy spoke again.

"Dana Phelps. I got it up. What do you need?"

She kept her hand on the cellar door. Again she could hear the clacking of his fingers on the keyboard.

"Here it is, Titus. Brandon Phelps. Do you want his mobile or his number at school?"

Dana jammed her hand in her mouth so she wouldn't scream out loud.

Her hand dropped back to the ax handle. She heard the computer guy give Titus her son's cell phone.

No, oh God, no, not Brandon . . .

She moved closer to the kitchen door and tried to hear what was being said, tried to figure out what Titus wanted with her son's phone number.

But wasn't it obvious?

They were going after her son.

Conscious thought no longer entered the equation. It was now very simple. No hiding. No staying in the cellar. No worrying about her own safety. Only one thing consumed this mother's thoughts: Save Brandon.

When the computer guy hung up the phone, Dana ran out of the kitchen and straight toward him.

"Where's Titus?"

The computer guy jumped back. When he saw Dana coming toward him, he opened his mouth to scream for help. That would be it. If he screamed, if he got the attention of the other guys . . .

Dana moved with a speed and ferocity she didn't know she possessed. The ax was already in position, swinging toward the seated man at the computer with full force.

She didn't aim for the chest. He was too low for that.

The blades of the ax slammed straight into the mouth, smashing his teeth, ripping right through the lips and mouth. The spray of blood nearly blinded her. He fell back off the chair, his back slamming hard on the ground. Dana pulled back hard as he did, trying to free the blade. It came out of his face with a wet sucking pop.

Dana didn't know if he was dead yet or not. But there was no hesitation, no squeamishness. The blood had already reached her face. The rust taste was already on her tongue.

She lifted the blade again, this time straight up in the air. He didn't move or resist. She brought the ax down hard, cleaving his face in two. The blade sliced through the back of the skull with surprising ease, as though it were a watermelon rind. His tinted glasses split in two, dropping to either side of what had once been his face.

Dana wasted no time. She dropped the ax and started to fumble for the phone.

It was then that she saw the front door was open.

The old dog stood there, watching her, his tail wagging.

Dana put her finger to her lips, tried to smile, tried to convince the old dog that all was okay.

Bo's tail stopped wagging. And then he began to bark.

REYNALDO was carefully going through the woods when he heard the bark.

"Bo!"

He knew all of Bo's barks. This one was not for greeting a friendly face. This was a bark of fear and panic.

With the other two men following him, Reynaldo took out his gun and sprinted back toward the farmhouse.

41

BRANDON was just settling onto a barstool in Kat's apartment when a blocked call came into his mobile phone.

He had already contacted as many of his friends as he could to start hacking into YouAreJustMyType.com. Six of them were with him right now, on Skype, all their faces on the computer screen. Back on campus, his friends had the powerful mainframe and so would be able to handle the hack better. Brandon would work it remotely in conjunction with those on campus.

He picked up the phone. "Hello?"

A voice he didn't recognize said, "Brandon?"

"Yes. Who is this?"

"Just listen. You have two minutes. Go downstairs and out the door. Turn right. On the corner of Columbus Avenue, you'll see a black SUV. Get in it. Your mother is in the backseat."

"What—?"

"If you're not here in exactly two minutes, she dies."

"Wait. Who is this—?"

"One minute fifty-five seconds."

Click.

Brandon jumped off this stool and sprinted to the door. He threw it open and pressed the button for the elevator. It was on the ground floor. He was six floors up.

Better to take the stairs.

He did, more tumbling down them than running. His phone was still in his hand. He crossed the lobby and burst through the door. He leapt down the stoop to street level and veered right on 67th Street, nearly knocking over a man in a business suit.

He didn't let up. He dashed down the street, looking at the cars ahead of him. There, at the corner per the phone call, was the black SUV.

He was getting closer, when his cell phone rang again. Still in stride, he checked the caller ID.

A blocked number again.

He was near the SUV now. The back door opened. He put the phone to his ear and heard a barking dog. "Hello?"

"Brandon, listen to me."

His heart stopped. "Mom? I'm almost at the car."

"No!"

Brandon heard a man shouting in the background. "What was that? Mom?"

"Don't get in the car!"

"I don't un—"

"Run, Brandon! Just run!"

Brandon stopped, tried to back up, but two hands reached out of the back of the car and grabbed his shirt.

His cell phone dropped as a man tried to drag him into the SUV.

KAT welcomed the walk across the park, a chance to clear her head and think, but the familiar sites didn't offer any of their usual solace. She thought about the Ramble a few blocks north, how her father had worked the area, what must have been going through his mind.

When she looked back on it, when she looked back at her father's behavior, his drinking, his rage, his disappearances, it all made sad, pathetic sense. You hide so much. You hide your heart. You hide your true self. The facade becomes not just the cruel reality.

It becomes your prison.

Her poor father.

But none of this mattered anymore. Not really. It was in the past. Her father's pain was over. To be the best daughter she could be, to honor his memory or offer whatever comfort you could offer to the dead, she had to be the best cop she could be.

That meant figuring a way to nail Cozone.

Her cell phone buzzed as she exited the park on the west side. It was Chaz.

"Were you just here?"

"Sorry, yeah. I was with the captain."

"He told me you're coming back."

"Maybe," she said.

"I'd like that."

"Me too."

"But that isn't why I called," Chaz said. "I'm working the missing-people angle like you asked. What I have is only preliminary."

"But?"

"I have eleven missing adults, including Dana Phelps, Gerard Remington, and Martha Paquet, across four states. All had recently met someone online."

The hairs on her neck stood up. "My God."

"I know, right?"

"Did you contact ADIC Keiser?" she asked.

"I sent it to his point man. They're going to dive into it further. But eleven missing, Kat. I mean . . ."

Chaz just left it at that.

There was nothing more that needed to be said. The feds would know what to do now. They had done more than their part here. Kat hung up the phone as she crossed onto 67th Street. That was when she saw the ruckus down at the Columbus Avenue corner.

What the . . . ?

She broke into a sprint. As she got closer, she could see Brandon Phelps struggling. Someone was trying to pull him into the back of an SUV.

THE old dog ran a few steps into the house, almost sliding on the mix of hardwood floors and blood, and kept barking at Dana.

She knew, of course, what that meant. Juicehead—the computer guy she had just killed had called him Reynaldo on the phone—would hear the distress in his beloved dog's bark. He would hurry back here.

Her first thought was to hide.

But that was not going to happen.

A strange calmness spread across her. She still knew what she had to do.

She had to save her son.

There was no mobile phone in sight. The only phone she could see, the only one on the desk, was a regular gray house phone connected into the back of the computer. It wasn't portable. If she wanted to use it, she would have to stay where she was. In plain view.

So be it.

She lifted the phone, put it to her ear, and dialed her son's phone number. Her hand shook so badly that she almost misdialed.

A voice shouted, "Bo!"

It was Reynaldo. He wasn't far away. It would be only a matter of time. Still, she had no choice. From what she had overheard, Titus was planning on grabbing her son. She had to stop him. Nothing else mattered. There was no question, no regret, no hesitation.

The phone began to ring. Dana braced herself, but when she heard her son say, "Hello?" she almost lost it.

Footsteps pounded heavily on the porch now. Bo stopped barking and trotted toward his master.

No time left.

"Brandon, listen to me."

She heard him gasp. "Mom? I'm almost at the car."

"No!"

Reynaldo shouted, "Bo!" again.

"What was that?" Brandon asked. "Mom?"

Her hand tightened on the receiver. "Don't get in the car!"

"I don't un—"

Reynaldo would be at the door any second now.

"Run, Brandon! Just run!"

*   *   *

KAT pulled out her gun and sprinted down the block.

In the distance, she could see Brandon was putting up a good struggle, almost breaking free. Someone on the street came over to help him, but then the driver of the SUV got out.

He had a gun.

Pedestrians began to scream. Kat yelled, "Freeze!" but the distance and the screams drowned her out. The Good Samaritans backed away. The driver hurried around toward Brandon.

Kat saw him lift the gun and bring it down hard on Brandon's head.

The struggle ended.

Brandon fell inside. The back door slammed shut.

The driver hurried back toward his door. Kat was getting closer now. She was about to take a shot at him, but something akin to instinct made her pull up. There were too many civilians on the street to risk a gun battle, and even if she got lucky and hit him, whoever was in the backseat—whoever had grabbed Brandon—could be armed too.

So what to do?

The black SUV quickly shot out and made the left onto Columbus Avenue.

Kat spotted a man getting out of a gray Ford Fusion. She flashed her badge and said, "I'm commandeering this car."

The man made a face. "You're kidding me, right? You're not taking my car—"

Without breaking stride, Kat showed him the gun. He raised his hands. She grabbed the keys from his right hand and hopped into the car.

A minute later, she was heading down 67th Street behind the SUV.

She grabbed the cell phone and called Chaz. "I'm following a black SUV, turning right on Broadway at 67th Street."

She gave him the license plate and quickly filled him in on what had happened.

"Someone on the street is probably already calling nine-one-one," Chaz said.

"Right, look, make sure they keep all marked squad cars away. I don't want them spooked."

"You have a plan?"

"I do," Kat said. "Call the FBI. Tell them what's up. Let them get a chopper in the air. I'll keep tailing them."

SITTING in the back of the SUV, Brandon was still dazed from the blow to his head. Titus pointed his gun at him.

"Brandon?"

"Where's my mother?"

"You'll see her soon enough. For now, I want you to stay still. If you do something I don't like, your mother will be killed immediately. Do you understand?"

Brandon nodded and stayed still.

Titus was nervous as they crossed the George Washington Bridge. He feared that the police might be on them, that someone who had witnessed Clem's exuberance on 67th Street might have notified the authorities. But the traffic had been slim on the West Side Highway. The ride took less than fifteen minutes, not enough time, Titus surmised, to start mounting a full-fledged APB on their SUV. Still, Titus had Clem pull over at the Teaneck Marriott right off Route 95. He debated stealing another car, but it would be better to just change license plates. They found another black SUV parked in the back and using a battery-operated screwdriver, Clem switched plates in a matter of seconds.

They drove back onto the New Jersey Turnpike and headed south toward the farm.

"DO they have the chopper up?" Kat asked.

"They said it'll take another five minutes."

"Okay, good," she said. Then: "Wait. Hold up."

"What?"

"They just pulled into the Marriott."

"Maybe that's where they're staying."

"Let the feds know."

She took the ramp, staying two cars behind them. She saw them pull into the lot and circle toward the back. She stopped on the side, inching her way so that she had an angle but could stay out of sight.

The driver got out. She considered making a move, right here and now, but as long as she couldn't see what was going on with Brandon in the back, it would be too risky. She waited and watched.

A minute later, she was on the line again with Chaz.

"They just switched license plates and headed back onto the road."

"Which way?"

"South. Looks like they're getting on the New Jersey Turnpike."

REYNALDO ran with everything he had toward Bo's bark.

If that woman has done something to Bo, if she has so much as touched a hair on his head . . .

Reynaldo now wanted her to die slowly.

Bo was still barking when Reynaldo reached the clearing. His legs pumped hard as he ran with everything he had toward the house. He leapt the steps, landing hard on the wraparound porch.

Bo had stopped barking.

Oh God, oh God, please don't let anything happen to . . .

He started running toward the front door when Bo appeared. He dropped to his knees in relief.

"Bo!" he shouted.

The dog ran toward him. Reynaldo spread his arms and hugged his dog. Bo licked his face.

From inside the house, he heard Dana scream, "Run, Brandon! Just run!"

Reynaldo took out his gun. He was only a few steps away from the doorway now. He rose, ready to end this problem once and for all, when something made him pull up in panic.

Bo's paws were covered in blood.

If she hurt my dog, if she hurt this sweet, innocent dog who never did anyone any harm . . .

He checked the front paws for wounds. Nothing. He checked the back paws. Nothing. Reynaldo looked into Bo's eyes.

The dog wagged his tail as though to tell Reynaldo he was fine.

Relief flooded his veins, but then another thought hit him.

If the blood didn't belong to Bo, whose was it?

He had his gun at the ready. He put his back against

the door. When he turned and entered the house, he ducked low just in case she was waiting for him.

No movement.

Then Reynaldo saw the mess on the floor that had once been Dmitry.

Had Dana done that to him?

Rage consumed him. That bitch. Oh man, she was going to pay.

But how? How had she done that to Dmitry? Answer: She must now be armed. She must have grabbed something from the barn. There was no other explanation for so much blood.

Next question: Where was she now?

Reynaldo spotted the bloody footprints on the floor. His eyes followed them to where they stopped—at the kitchen door. He grabbed his walkie-talkie and called Julio. "Are you at the back of the house?"

"Just arrived."

"Do you see any blood by the kitchen door?"

"No, nothing. It's clear back here."

"Good." He smiled now. "Have your guns ready and pointed that way. She may be armed."

42

BEHIND the copper-roofed Kerbs Boathouse in Central Park, Aqua sat cross-legged. His eyes were closed. His tongue was pressing against the roof of his mouth. His thumbs and middle fingers formed circles. His hands rested near his knees.

Jeff Raynes sat next to him.

"She found me," Jeff said.

Aqua nodded. He had loaded up on his meds today. He hated them. They made him miserable and depressed, like he was underwater and couldn't move. They made him feel lifeless. Aqua often compared himself to a broken vending machine. When it was on, you never knew what you got. You might get scalding-hot coffee when you asked for cool water. But at least the machine was on. When he was on his drugs, it was as though the machine was unplugged.

Still, Aqua needed the clarity. Not for long. But for a few minutes anyway.

"Do you still love her?" Aqua asked him.

"Yes. You know that."

"You've always loved her."

"Always."

Aqua kept his eyes closed. "Do you believe that she still loves you?"

Jeff grunted. "If only it were that simple."

"It's been eighteen years," Aqua said.

"You're not going to tell me time heals all wounds, are you?"

"No. But why are you here, Jeff?"

He didn't respond.

"Isn't your talking to me a futile exercise anyway?"

"What do you mean?"

"You saw her today."

"Yes," Jeff said.

"You let her go once. Do you really think you have the strength to do that again?"

Silence.

Aqua finally opened his eyes. The pain etched on his friend's face made him wince. He reached out a hand and put it on Jeff's forearm.

"I made my choice," Jeff said.

"And how did that work out for you?"

"I can't regret it. I wouldn't have my daughter if I hadn't left."

Aqua nodded. "But it's been a long time."

"Yes."

"Maybe everything happened for a reason. Maybe this was how your love story was supposed to go."

"She'll never forgive me."

"You'd be surprised what love can overcome."

Jeff made a face. "Time heals all wounds, everything happens for a reason, *and* love conquers all? You're loading up on your clichés today."

"Jeff?"

"What?"

"My meds aren't going to hold me together much longer. In a few minutes, I will crash and start panicking again. I will think about you and Kat and I will want to kill myself."

"Don't say that."

"Then listen to me. Einstein described insanity as doing the same thing over and over again and expecting different results. So what are you going to do, Jeff? Are you going to run away and crush both your hearts again? Or are you going to try something different?"

REYNALDO knew he had Dana trapped.

Still staring at the bloody footprints, he worked the mental layout of the kitchen. The table, the chairs, the cupboard—there was no place for her to hide. Her only hope was to attack him when he entered. Or . . .

Without warning, he shoved the door hard with both hands.

He didn't follow the door into the kitchen. She might be expecting that. If she were waiting near the door, if she were hoping for him to enter blindly so she could surprise him, Reynaldo would see it.

She would make a move, cry out, flinch, something.

Just to be on the safe side, he took a step backward as he shoved the door.

It flew open, banged against the wall, and then swung

closed again. The wood vacillated a few times before coming to rest.

There had been no movement on the other side.

He had, however, seen more bloody footprints.

With the gun drawn now, he entered the kitchen. He aimed the gun right, then swung it left.

It was empty.

Then he looked down at the floor and saw the bloody footprints again.

They led to the cellar door.

Of course. Reynaldo almost slapped himself in the head. But no matter. He knew there was only one other exit from the cellar—an outdoor storm door with a padlock on it.

Number Six was truly trapped now.

His cell phone buzzed. It was Titus. Reynaldo brought the phone to his ear.

"Have you found her yet?" Titus asked.

"I think so."

"You think so?"

He quickly explained about the cellar door.

"We are on our way back," Titus said. "Tell Dmitry to start destroying the computer files."

"Dmitry is dead."

"What?"

"Dana killed him."

"How?"

"From the looks of it, I think she has the ax."

Silence.

"You still there, Titus?"

"There's gasoline in the barn," Titus said. "A lot of it."

"I know," Reynaldo said. "Why?"

But Reynaldo knew the answer, didn't he? He didn't

like it. He knew this day was coming. But this farm had been his home. He and Bo liked it here.

It made him angrier than ever at that bitch who was ruining everything.

"Start spreading it throughout the house," Titus said. "We're going to burn down the entire operation."

KAT had no idea where they were headed.

For over two hours, she had followed the SUV down the New Jersey Turnpike, getting off on the Pennsylvania Turnpike, traveling north of Philadelphia. The FBI had sent out a chopper. It was following from a safe distance, but that didn't mean Kat was ready to relax.

The Ford Fusion had enough gas. She wasn't worried about that. Kat was in constant contact with the FBI agents. They had no new information to give her. The black SUV's original plates had been stolen too. YouAreJustMyType.com was dragging its heels and demanding a subpoena. Chaz had located what he thought might be two more victims, but he couldn't be sure. It would take time. She got that. On cop shows, it all got wrapped up in an hour. In reality, it always took much longer.

She tried not to let her mind wander to either her father or Jeff, but as time passed, she couldn't help it. Sugar's words kept reverberating in her ears, about what he'd sacrifice, what he'd forgive, if he could have just a few more seconds with Kat's father. She could see that Sugar's love was real. It wasn't an act. It made her wonder. Had her father been happy with Sugar? Had he known passion and love? Kat hoped he had. When she stripped it down, when she dismissed her not so subconscious prejudice—she was, after all, from the neighborhood too—maybe Kat could be grateful for that.

She started playing what-if, wondering what would happen if her father suddenly materialized in the seat next to her, if she told him that she knew everything and that he had been given a second chance. What would her father do? Death was probably a great educator. If he could do it over again, would her father come clean to Mom? Would he live his life with Sugar?

That would be what Kat would want for him. That would be what Kat would want for her mother too.

Honesty. Or how had Sugar put it? The freedom to be authentic.

Had her father been close to coming to that realization? Had he grown tired of the lies and deceptions? When he arrived at that club with flowers for Sugar, had he finally found the strength to be authentic?

Kat would probably never know.

But the larger question, when she let herself go there, when she let her mind wander away from the far more important task of saving Brandon and his mother from whatever evil this was, ended up being more present-day. Suppose her dad did indeed materialize in the seat next to her. Suppose she told him she had seen Jeff again, that she was convinced they had a chance, that when she saw Jeff, she understood what Sugar had meant about giving up anything for just a few more seconds with him.

What would her father tell her to do?

The answer was so obvious now.

It didn't matter why Jeff ran off, why he changed his name, none of that. Sugar wouldn't care. Dad wouldn't care. Death teaches you that. You would give anything, forgive anything, for just one more second. . . .

When this was over, Kat would drive back up to Montauk and tell him how she felt.

The sun was setting, coloring the sky a deep purple.

Up ahead, the black SUV finally exited the turnpike onto Route 222.

Kat followed. It couldn't be too far now.

BRANDON asked, "What do you want with my mother?" one time too many.

Titus clocked him in the mouth with the butt of his gun. Brandon's teeth broke. Blood flowed from his mouth. Brandon ripped off his T-shirt and pressed it against the wound. He stopped talking then.

When they hit Route 222, Titus checked his watch. They were less than forty minutes away. He did a few calculations in his head—the size of the fire, the visibility, how long it would take local firefighters to arrive, especially if he called them and told them he had it under control.

An hour, at least.

That was all the time he would need.

He called Reynaldo. "Have you finished spreading the gasoline?"

"Yes."

"Is she still trapped in the basement?"

"Yes."

"Where are Rick and Julio?"

"They're in the yard. One in the front, one in the back."

"You know what has to be done."

"I do."

"Take care of it. Then set the fire. Make sure it burns

all the way to the ground. Then get to the boxes and finish cleaning up."

REYNALDO hung up the phone. Bo stood by the barn. He'd be safe. That was the important thing now. Rick was in the front of the house. Reynaldo walked toward him.

"Did you speak to Titus?" Rick asked.

"Yes."

"Are we going to set the fire?"

Reynaldo had the knife hidden in his hand. He stabbed him fast and deep in the heart. Rick was dead before he slid to the ground. Reynaldo took out a book of matches. He headed back to the house, lit one, and dropped it on the front steps.

The flames leapt to life, traveling in a fast blue line.

Reynaldo kept walking. He reached the back door. His gun was by his side. He aimed and shot Julio in the head. Reynaldo lit another match and threw it by the back door. Again, flames exploded in a glorious blue wave. He took a few steps back so he could see both exits.

There was no other way out. He saw that right away. Dana would burn to a crisp in the fire.

He watched the flames climb higher and higher. He wasn't a pyromaniac or anything like that, but he couldn't help but be enthralled by the sheer power of the blaze. It quickly ran through the house, eating everything in sight. Reynaldo listened for her screams. He had hoped to hear them. But there were none. He kept his eyes on the doors, especially the kitchen one, hoping that the fire would drive her out, that a flaming figure would whirl into sight, driven by agonizing pain, pirouetting in a final death dance.

But that didn't happen either.

Reynaldo lifted Julio's body and tossed it into the flames. He and Rick would end up charred but perhaps identifiable. That might help. If anyone would take the fall, it would be the dead.

The blaze was at full power now.

Still no screams, no sightings.

He wondered whether the fire or the smoke had killed Dana. He might never know, of course. He was sure, however, that she was dead. He could see no way she could have escaped.

And yet, as he turned away from the wreckage, he felt a funny sense of unease.

43

WHEN Dana Phelps saw the flames, she hurried down the awful path she had taken too many times before.

Where, she wondered, would be the last place he would look for her?

Back with the boxes.

It was odd about what we consider luck, fate, timing. Her husband, Jason, had grown up in Pittsburgh and was an avid Steelers, Pirates, and Penguins fan. He loved cheering his teams, but he understood better than most how random the whole world was. If there had been full-replay rules with HD cameras back in the seventies, many believed that we would see the ball hit the ground before Franco Harris made the catch on the Immaculate Reception. Did it? If so, would the Steelers have then lost that game and not won four Super Bowl titles in six years?

Jason loved asking questions like this. He didn't care

about the big stuff—the work ethic, the schooling, the training. Life, he suspected, hinges too often on chance. We all want to convince ourselves that it is about hard work and education and perseverance, but the truth is, life is much more about the fickle and the random. We don't want to admit it, but we are controlled by luck, by timing, by fate.

In her case, the luck, the timing, the fate had been blood on Bo's paws.

Checking the dog for injuries had slowed Reynaldo down just a few seconds, but it was long enough. It was long enough for her to drop the phone and run into the kitchen and realize that he would quickly find her because of her bloody footprints.

So what did she do?

There was no time to consider a bunch of cute plans or alternatives. The idea was there and, if she did say so herself, near genius. She walked straight to the cellar door, opened it and tossed her socks down the stairs.

Then, fully barefoot, she managed to hop-sprint outside. She made it to the woods and ducked down to hide. A few seconds later, Julio appeared.

As soon as the fire started, as soon as the flames began to crawl up the sides of the wooden frame, Dana realized that they were covering their tracks. It was all coming to an end. So she ran down the path, remembering that when she had first arrived, when she was first forced to take off her yellow sundress, she had seen something that troubled her.

Other clothing.

The sun was setting fast. Darkness had already started to settle in when she reached the clearing. There was a small tent where Reynaldo hung out. She quickly looked inside. There was a sleeping bag and a flashlight. No phone. Nothing she could use as a weapon.

Of course, she still had the ax.

She took the flashlight although she didn't dare turn it on yet. The clearing in front of her was flat. The box where she had been forced to live for—again, she had no idea how long—was camouflaged. Even she couldn't remember exactly where it was. She walked over, bent down, and finally found the open padlock. Amazing. Without the padlock, she would have passed right over the door.

A crazy idea darted through her head—get into the box and hide there. Who in their right mind would look for her there? But then again, who in their right mind would ever, even if it meant helping themselves, voluntarily go underground again?

Not her.

This was all beside the point anyway. The house was burning.

Darkness had fallen now. She could barely see. She started to crawl across the grass, still not sure what she should do here. She had gone about ten yards when her hand hit something metallic.

Another padlock.

This one was locked.

It took Dana two blows with the ax to break the lock open. The door was heavier than she would have imagined. She needed all her strength to pull it up off the dirt.

She peered down into the dark hole. There was no sound, no movement.

Behind her the blaze was still burning. No choice now. She had to risk it.

Dana turned on the flashlight. She pointed it down to the box and gasped out loud.

The sobbing woman looked up at her. "Please don't kill me."

Dana nearly started to cry. "I'm here to save you, not hurt you. Can you get yourself out?"

"Yes."

"Good."

Dana crawled another ten yards and found yet another padlock. She broke that one open on the first try. The man inside was also weeping and too weak to climb out. She didn't wait. She moved toward a third box and found the padlock. She broke it, opened the door and didn't even bother checking inside. She moved to a fourth box.

She had just cracked that lock with her ax when she saw headlights by the farmhouse.

Someone had come up the drive.

CLEM opened the gates. Then he got back behind the wheel.

It wasn't until they were halfway up the drive that Titus saw the flames.

He smiled. This was a good thing. If he couldn't see the fire from the road, there was an excellent chance that nobody would notify the fire station. It gave him plenty of time to finish up and clear out.

Reynaldo was up ahead, dragging a body toward the flames.

"What the hell?" Clem said. "Isn't that Rick?"

Titus calmly put the muzzle of the gun against the back of Clem's head and fired one shot. Clem slumped forward on the wheel.

This had all begun with Titus and Reynaldo. That was how it would end too.

Brandon cried out in shock. Titus swung the gun back toward the kid's chest. "Get out of the car."

Brandon stumbled out. Reynaldo was there to greet him. Titus followed. For a few seconds, the three of them stood there together and watched the flames.

"Is his mother dead?" Titus asked.

"I think so."

Brandon let out an agonizing, primitive cry. He lunged toward Reynaldo, hands raised. Reynaldo stopped him with a deep punch in the gut. Brandon fell to the ground, gasping for air.

Titus pointed the gun at the boy's head. To Reynaldo he asked, "Why did you say 'I think so'?"

"Because I think she was in the basement. Like I said."

"But?"

Bo's bark shattered the night air.

Titus grabbed a flashlight and moved it around until he located Bo standing on the right. The old dog was looking down the path to the boxes and barking like mad.

"Maybe," Titus said, "you were wrong about her being in the basement."

Reynaldo nodded.

Titus handed him the flashlight. "Start down the path. Have the gun ready. Shoot her as soon as she reveals herself."

"She could be hiding," Reynaldo said.

"Not for long she won't be."

Brandon yelled, "Mom! Don't come this way! Run!"

Titus pushed the gun into Brandon's mouth, silencing him. With as loud a voice as he could muster, he shouted, "Dana? I have your son." He hesitated before adding, "Come out or he will suffer."

There was silence.

He called out again. "Okay, Dana. Listen to this."

Titus pulled the gun out of Brandon's mouth. He aimed for the boy's knee and pulled the trigger.

Brandon's scream shattered the night.

KAT stayed on the road, making sure not to slow down and give the SUV a bead on her. She was in constant phone contact with the FBI now. She gave them the locale and pulled off the road about a hundred yards up.

"Good work, Detective," ADIC Keiser told her. "Our people should be there in fifteen or twenty minutes. I want to make sure we have enough men to take them all down."

"They have Brandon, sir."

"I know that."

"I don't think we should wait."

"You can't just barge in. They have hostages. You have to wait for our team, let them get a dialogue going. You know the drill."

Kat didn't like it. "With all due respect, sir, I'm not sure there's time. I would like permission to go in on my own. I won't engage unless absolutely necessary."

"I don't think that's a good idea, Detective."

That wasn't a no.

She hung up the phone before he could say more and put it on silent. Her gun was in its holster. She left the car where it was and started back. She would have to be careful. There could be security cameras at the gate, so she entered from the side and hopped the fence. It was dark now. The woods were thick. She used her iPhone—thank goodness the guy with the Ford Fusion had a built-in charger—as a dim flashlight.

Kat was walking slowly through the trees, when up ahead, she saw the flames.

DANA managed to get another box open when she heard Brandon shout:

"Mom! Don't come this way! Run!"

She froze at the sound of her son's voice.

Then she heard Titus: "Dana? I have your son."

Her whole body began to shake.

"Come out or he will suffer."

Dana almost dropped the heavy door, but the first woman she'd helped was suddenly beside her. The woman took the door from Dana and let it drop to the ground. Someone inside the box groaned.

Dana started toward the path.

"Don't," the woman whispered to her.

Confused, dazed, Dana turned toward the voice. "What?"

"You can't listen to him. He's just playing games with you. You need to stay here."

"I can't."

The woman put her hands on Dana's cheeks and made her look her straight in the eye. "I'm Martha. What's your name?"

"Dana."

"Dana, listen to me. We need to get the rest of these boxes open."

"Are you out of your mind? He has my son."

"I know that. And once you show yourself, he'll kill you both."

Dana shook her head. "No, I can save him. I can make a trade—"

Titus's voice cut through the night like a reaper's scythe. "Okay, Dana, listen to this."

The two women turned as the gunshot blasted through the still night air.

Dana's son's scream got lost in her own.

Before she could react more, before she could surrender and save her son, this woman—this Martha—tackled her to the ground.

"Get off me!"

Martha stayed on top of her. Her voice was remarkably calm. "No."

Dana bucked and fought, but Martha held on with everything she had.

"He'll kill you both," Martha whispered in her ear. "You know that. For your boy's sake, you can't run out there."

Dana started twisting and turning in panic. "Let me go!"

And then Titus's voice again: "Okay, Dana. Now I'm going to shoot his other knee."

KAT was moving forward a few trees at a time, making sure per protocol that she stayed out of sight, when she heard the man threaten Brandon.

She needed to move faster.

A few seconds later, when Kat heard the gunshot and Brandon's scream, she tossed all protocol to the wind. She veered from the woods onto the main drive where she could run at full speed. She would, of course, be easy pickings if anyone saw her, but that didn't seem like such a big deal right now.

She had to save Brandon.

Her gun was in her right hand. Her breath echoed in her ears as though someone had pressed seashells against them.

Up ahead, she saw the SUV. A man holding a gun stood next to it. Brandon was on the ground, writhing in pain.

"Okay, Dana," the man shouted. "Now I'm going to shoot his other knee."

Kat was still too far away for a shot. She yelled, "Freeze!" without slowing down her sprint.

The man turned toward her. For a half second, no more, he looked perplexed. Kat kept running. The man swung the gun toward her. Kat dove to the side. But the guy still had her in his sights. He was about to pull the trigger when something made him stop.

Brandon had grabbed his leg.

Annoyed, the man pointed the gun toward Brandon.

Kat was ready now. She didn't bother shouting out another warning.

She pulled the trigger and saw the man's body fly backward.

FROM a spot midway through the path, Reynaldo was able to hear the screams in stereo. From behind him, the sound came from the boy who'd just been shot. In front of him, he heard the more anguished cry of a mother who was paying the price for trying to escape.

Now he knew for certain where she was.

The boxes.

He wouldn't let her escape again.

Reynaldo rushed down into the clearing that he had called home for these many months. It was dark, but he had the flashlight. He cast the beam to his right, then his left.

Dana Phelps was lying on the ground about twenty yards away. There was another woman—it looked like Number Eight—on top of her.

He didn't ask why Number Eight was out of the box or how. He didn't call out or give them any kind of warning. He simply raised his gun and took aim. He was about to squeeze the trigger, when he heard a guttural, primitive shout.

Someone jumped on his back.

Reynaldo stumbled, dropping the flashlight but holding on to the gun for dear life. He reached behind him, clawing for whoever was on his back. Someone else picked up the flashlight and struck him in the nose. Reynaldo howled in pain and fear. His eyes watered.

"Get off me!"

He reared back, trying desperately to buck the person off his back. It didn't work. An arm snaked around his enormous neck and started to squeeze.

They were everywhere, swarming all over him.

One bit his leg. Reynaldo could feel the teeth digging into his flesh. He tried to shake his leg loose, but that just made him lose balance. He teetered before falling hard to the ground.

Someone jumped on his chest. Someone else grabbed his arm. It was as if they were demons coming out of the dark.

Or out of the box.

Panic engulfed him.

The gun. He still had the gun.

Reynaldo tried to raise his gun, tried to blast all these demons straight back to hell, but someone was still holding his arm down.

They wouldn't stop attacking him.

There were four of them. Or five. He didn't know. They were relentless, like zombies.

"No!"

He could make out their faces now. There was the bald man in Number Two. The fat guy in Number Seven. That man from Number Four had joined in too. Someone smashed him in the nose with the flashlight again. The blood started flowing down into his mouth. His eyes started rolling back.

With a desperate roar, Reynaldo started pulling the trigger on the gun. The bullets dug harmlessly into the ground, but the shock and suddenness made whoever was holding his arm loosen their grip.

One last chance.

Reynaldo used all his strength to pull free.

He swung his gun up in the air.

In the light of the moon, Reynaldo could see the silhouette of Dana Phelps rising above him. He started to take aim, but it was too late.

The ax was already on its way toward him.

Time slowed.

Somewhere in the distance, Reynaldo heard Bo bark.

And then there was no sound at all.

44

THE full accounting would take weeks, but here was what they learned in the first three days:

Thirty-one bodies had so far been dug up at the farm.

Twenty-two were men, nine were women.

The oldest was a seventy-six-year-old man. The youngest was a forty-three-year-old woman.

Most had died of gunshot wounds to the head. Many were malnourished. A few had severe injuries beyond the head wounds, including severed body parts.

The media came up with all kinds of terrible headlines. CLUB DEAD. THE DATE FROM HELL. DOA CUPID. WORST DATE EVER. None was funny. None reflected the pure, undiluted horror of that farm.

The case was no longer Kat's. The FBI took it over. That was fine with her.

Seven people, including Dana Phelps, had been rescued. They were all treated at a local hospital and released within two days. The exception was Brandon Phelps. The bullet wound had shattered his kneecap. He would need surgery.

All of the perpetrators of this horror were dead, with one notable exception: The leader, Titus Monroe, had survived Kat's bullet.

He was, however, in critical condition—in a medically induced coma and on a respirator. But he was still alive. Kat didn't know how she felt about that. Maybe if Titus Monroe woke up, she would have a better idea.

A few weeks later, Kat visited Dana and Brandon at their home in Greenwich, Connecticut.

As she pulled into the driveway, Brandon hobbled out on crutches to greet her. She got out of the car and hugged him, and for a moment or two, they just held on to each other. Dana Phelps smiled and waved from the front lawn. Yep, Kat thought, still stunning. A little thinner perhaps, her blond hair pulled back into a ponytail, but now her beauty seemed to emanate more from resiliency and strength than privilege or good fortune.

Dana lifted a tennis ball into the air. She was playing fetch with her two dogs. One was a black Lab named Chloe.

The other was an old chocolate Lab named Bo.

Kat walked toward her. She remembered what Stacy had said about Kat being quick to judge. Stacy had been right. Intuition was one thing. Preconceived notions—about Dana, about Chaz, about Sugar, about anyone—were another.

"I'm surprised," Kat said to her.

"Why's that?"

"I would think the dog would bring bad memories."

"Bo's only mistake was loving the wrong person," Dana said, tossing the ball across the green grass. There was a hint of a smile on her face. "Who can't relate to that?"

Kat smiled too. "Good point."

Bo sprinted toward the ball with all he had. He picked it up in his mouth and jogged toward Brandon. Leaning on one crutch, Brandon lowered himself and patted Bo's head. Bo dropped the ball, wagged his tail, and barked for him to throw it again.

Dana shaded her eyes. "I'm glad you could come out, Kat."

"Me too."

The two women watched Brandon with the dogs.

"He'll always have a limp," Dana said. "That's what the doctors told me."

"I'm sorry."

Dana shrugged. "He seems okay with it. Proud even."

"He's a hero," Kat said. "If he hadn't broken into that website, if he hadn't somehow known you were in trouble . . ."

She didn't finish the thought. She didn't have to.

"Kat?"

"Yes?"

"What about you?"

"What about me?"

Dana turned to her. "I want to hear everything. The whole story."

"Okay," Kat said, "but I'm not sure it's over yet."

*　　*　　*

WHEN Kat arrived back home on 67th Street the day after they brought down the farm, Jeff was sitting on the stoop.

"How long have you been waiting here?" she asked him.

"Eighteen years," he said.

Then Jeff begged her for forgiveness.

"Don't," she said.

"What?"

But how could she explain? As Sugar had said, she would have given or forgiven anything. She had him back. That was all that mattered.

"Just don't, okay?"

"Yeah," he said. "Okay."

It was as though some invisible giant had grabbed ahold of eighteen years ago in one hand, grabbed ahold of today in the other, pulled them together and then sutured them up. Sure, Kat still had questions. She wanted to know more, but at the same time, it no longer seemed to matter. Jeff began to fill her in bit by bit. Eighteen years ago, there was an issue at home, he explained, forcing him to go back to Cincinnati. He foolishly believed that Kat wouldn't wait for him or it wouldn't be fair to ask her to wait, some chivalrous nonsense. Still, he had hoped to come back to her and, yep, beg her forgiveness, but then he got into that fight at the bar. The drunk boyfriend whose nose he had broken was Mobbed up. They wanted revenge, so he ran and got a new ID. Then he got Melinda's mother pregnant and . . .

"Life got away from me, I guess."

Kat could see that he wasn't telling all, that he was shading the story for reasons still unknown. But she didn't rush it. Oddly enough, the reality was better than she could have imagined. They had both learned much over the painful years, but perhaps the greatest lesson was also the simplest: Cherish and take care of what you value. Happiness is fragile. Appreciate every moment and do everything you can to protect it.

The rest of life, in a sense, is background noise.

They had both been hurt and heartbroken, but now it felt as though it had been meant to be, that you can't reach this high without at one point being that low, that she and Jeff had to go their separate ways so that, surreal as it sounded, they could end up together in this better place.

"And here we are," she said, kissing him tenderly.

Every kiss was like that now. Every kiss was like that tender one on the beach.

The rest of the world could wait. Kat would get her revenge on Cozone. She didn't know how or when. But one day, she would knock on Cozone's door and finish this for her father.

Just not right now.

Kat asked for a leave from the force. Stagger gave it to her. She needed to get out of the city. She rented a place in Montauk, near Jeff's house. Jeff insisted that Kat stay with them, but that felt like too much too soon. Still, they spent every second together.

Jeff's daughter, Melinda, had been wary at first, but once she saw Kat and Jeff together, all doubts fled. "You make him happy," Melinda told Kat with tears in her eyes. "He deserves that."

Even the old man, Jeff's former father-in-law, welcomed her into the fold.

It felt right. It felt wonderful.

Stacy visited for a weekend. One night, when Jeff was

barbecuing for them in the yard, both women holding wineglasses and watching the sun set, Stacy smiled and said, "I was right."

"About?"

"The fairy tale."

Kat nodded, remembering what her friend had said so long ago. "But even better."

A month later, Kat was lying on his bed, her body still humming from the pleasure, when the fairy tale came to an end.

She hugged the pillow postcoital and smiled. She could hear Jeff singing in the shower. The song had become the ultimate delight and the ultimate dreaded earworm, never leaving them: *"I ain't missing you at all."*

Jeff couldn't carry a tune if you tattooed it on him. God, Kat thought with a shake of her head. Such a beautiful man with such a horrible voice.

She was still feeling deliciously lazy when she heard her cell phone ring. She reached over and hit the green answer button and said, "Hello?"

"Kat, it's Bobby Suggs."

Suggs. The old family friend. The detective who had worked her father's homicide.

"Hey," she said.

"Hey. You got a minute?"

"Sure."

"You remember you asked me to look into those old fingerprints? The ones we found at the murder scene."

Kat sat up. "Yes."

"I gotta tell you. It was a pain in the ass. That's why it took so long. The warehouse couldn't find them. No one had the results anymore. I guess Stagger must have thrown them away. I had to run them again."

"Did you find the fingerprints?" she asked.

"I got a name, yeah. I don't know what it means, though."

The shower had stopped running.

"What's the name?" she asked.

And then he said it.

The phone slipped from Kat's hand. It dropped onto the bed. She stared at it. Suggs kept talking. Kat could still hear him, but the words no longer reached her.

Still lost, she slowly turned toward the bathroom door. Jeff stood in the doorway. A towel was wrapped around his waist. Even now, even after this ultimate betrayal, she still couldn't help but think he was beautiful.

Kat hung up the phone. "You heard?" she asked.

"Enough, yeah."

She waited. Then she said, "Jeff?"

"I didn't mean to kill him."

Her eyes closed. The words landed like the most crushing blow. He just stood there and let her take the eight count.

"The club," Kat said. "The night he died, he went to a club."

"Right."

"You were there?"

"No."

She nodded, seeing it now. A club for cross-dressers. "Aqua?"

"Right."

"Aqua saw him."

"Yes."

"So what happened, Jeff?"

"Your father went into that club with Sugar, I guess. They were— I don't know. Aqua never told me any details. That's the thing. He would have never said a word. But Aqua saw him."

"And Dad saw Aqua too?"

Jeff nodded.

Dad knew Aqua from O'Malley's. She could hear the disapproval in her father's voice whenever he saw her with him.

"What happened, Jeff?"

"Your father lost it. He called Stagger. Told him that they had to find this guy."

"Aqua?"

"Yes. Your father didn't know we were roommates, did he?"

Kat had seen no reason to tell him.

"It was late. I don't know. Two, three in the morning. I was downstairs in the laundry room. Your father broke in. I came back up. . . ."

"And what happened, Jeff?"

"Your father was just beating on him. Aqua's face . . . he was a mess. His eyes were closed. Your dad was straddling his chest, just whaling on him. I shouted for him to stop. But he wouldn't listen. He just kept . . ." Jeff shook his head. "I thought maybe Aqua was already dead."

Kat remembered now that Aqua had been hospitalized after her father's death. She'd figured he had been admitted for psychiatric help, but now she realized that he had been dealing with other problems as well. He would eventually recover from the physical injuries, but the truth was, Aqua's mental health had never recovered.

There had been psychotic episodes before. But after that night, after her father had beaten him . . .

It was why Aqua kept saying it was his fault. It was why he blamed himself for the breakup, why he wanted to return the debt and protect Jeff, even going so far as to attack Brandon.

"I jumped on top of him," Jeff said. "We fought. He knocked me over. I was on the floor. He stood up and kicked me in the stomach. I grabbed his boot. He started to reach into his holster. Aqua regained consciousness and tackled him. I still had him by the boot." Jeff looked off now, his eyes twisted in pain. "And then I remembered you telling me that he always kept a weapon there, a throw-down gun."

Kat started shaking her head no.

"He was reaching into his holster again. I told him to stop. But he just wouldn't listen. So I reached into his boot and grabbed his spare gun. . . ."

Kat just sat there.

"Stagger heard the shot. Your dad had told him to be a lookout or something. He rushed in. He was panicked. His career, at the very least, was on the line. We would all go to jail, he said. No one would believe us."

She found her voice. "So you covered it up."

"Yes."

"And then you just pretended that nothing happened."

"I tried to."

Despite it all, a smile came to her lips. "You're not like my dad, are you, Jeff?"

"What do you mean?"

"He could live with the lies." One tear slid down her face. "You couldn't."

Jeff said nothing.

"That was why you left me. You couldn't tell me the truth. And you couldn't face me with that lie for the rest of your life."

He didn't respond. She knew the rest now. Jeff had run away and started what he had called his self-destructive stage. He got into the fight at that bar. Once he was booked, once his fingerprints had finally gotten a hit, they showed up in the homicide file. Stagger had covered it up, but that might not last forever. Stagger had probably gone to Cincinnati then, explained to Jeff that he had to hide, that if anyone ever looked for him, he couldn't be around.

"Did Stagger help you get the Ron Kochman identity?"

"Yes."

"So you ended up living a lie anyway."

"No, Kat," he said. "It was just a different name."

"But now you are, right?"

Jeff said nothing.

"These past weeks with me, you've been living with the lie. So what were you going to do, Jeff? Now that we're back together, what was your plan?"

"I didn't have one," he said. "At first, I just wanted to be with you. I didn't care about anything else. You know?"

She did know, but she didn't want to hear it.

"But after a while," he said, "I started to wonder."

"Wonder what?"

"Would it be better to live a lie with you or a truth without you?"

She swallowed. "Did you ever come up with an answer?"

"No," Jeff said. "But now I'll never have to. The truth is out. The lies are gone."

"Just like that?"

"No, Kat. Nothing with us is ever 'just like that.'"

He moved toward the bed and sat next to her. He didn't try to embrace her. He didn't try to get too close. She didn't move toward him either. They just sat there, staring at the wall, letting it all rush over them—the lies and secrets, the death and murder and blood, the years of heartbreak and loneliness. Finally, his hand moved toward hers. Her hand closed the gap, covered his. For a very long time, they both stayed like that, frozen, touching, almost afraid to breathe. And somewhere, maybe on a car radio driving by, maybe just in her head, Kat could hear someone singing, "I ain't missing you at all."

ACKNOWLEDGMENTS

The author wishes to acknowledge the following in no particular order because he can't remember exactly who helped with what: Ray Clarke, Jay Louis, Ben Sevier, Brian Tart, Christine Ball, Jamie McDonald, Laura Bradford, Michael Smith (yes, "Demon Lover" is a real song), Diane Discepolo, Linda Fairstein, and Lisa Erbach Vance. Any mistakes are theirs. Hey, they're the experts. Why should I take all the heat?

If I accidentally left your name off this list, just let me know and I'll throw you in the next book's acknowledgments. You know how forgetful I am.

I'd also like to give a quick shout-out to:

Asghar Chuback
Michael Craig
John Glass
Parnell Hall
Chris Harrop
Keith Inchierca
Ron Kochman
Steve Schrader
Joe Schwartz
Stephen Singer
Clemente "Clem" Sison
Sylvia Steiner

These people (or their loved ones) made generous contributions to charities of my choosing in return for having their names appear in this novel. If you'd like to participate in the future, visit harlancoben.com or e-mail giving@harlancoben.com for details.

New York Times bestselling author
Harlan Coben is back with another thriller.
Read on for a preview of

DON'T LET GO

Available from Dutton.

1

DAISY wore a clingy black dress with a neckline so deep it could tutor philosophy.

She spotted the mark sitting at the end of the bar, wearing a gray pinstripe suit. Hmm. The guy was old enough to be her dad. That might make it more difficult to make her play, but then again, it might not. You never knew with the old guys. Some of them, especially the recent divorcés, are all too ready to preen and prove they still got it, even if they never had it in the first place.

Especially if they never had it in the first place.

As Daisy sauntered across the room, she could feel the eyes of the male patrons crawling down her bare legs like earthworms. When she reached the end of the bar, she made a mild production of lowering herself onto the stool next to him.

The mark peered into the glass of whiskey in front of

him as though he were a gypsy with a crystal ball. She waited for him to turn toward her. He didn't. Daisy studied his profile for a moment. His beard was heavy and gray. His nose was bulbous and putty-like, almost as though it were a Hollywood silicon special effect. His hair was long, straggly.

Second marriage, Daisy thought. Second divorce in all likelihood.

Dale Miller—that was the mark's name—picked up his whiskey gently and cradled it in both hands like it was an injured bird.

"Hi," Daisy said with a much-practiced hair toss.

Miller's eyes slid toward her. He looked her straight in the eyes. She waited for his gaze to dip down to the neckline—heck, even women did it with this dress—but they stayed on hers.

"Hello," he replied. Then he turned back to his whiskey.

Daisy usually let the mark hit on her. That was her go-to technique. She said hi like this, she smiled, the guy asked whether he could buy her a drink. You know the deal. But Miller didn't look in the mood to flirt. He took a deep swallow from his whiskey glass, then another.

That was good. That was helpful.

"Is there something I can do for you?" he asked her.

Burly, Daisy thought. That was the word to describe him. Even in that pinstripe suit, Miller had that burly-biker-Vietnam-vet thing going on, his voice a low rasp. He was the kind of older guy Daisy found sexy, though that was probably her now legendary daddy issues rearing their insecure head. Daisy liked men who made her feel safe.

It had been too long since she'd known one.

Time to try another angle, Daisy thought.

"Do you mind if I just sit here with you?" Daisy leaned a little closer, working the cleavage a bit, and whispered, "There's this guy. . . ."

"Is he bothering you?"

Sweet. He didn't say it all macho poseur like so many d-bags she had met along the way. Dale Miller said it calmly, matter-of-factly, chivalrously, even—like a man who wanted to protect her.

"No, no . . . not really."

He started looking around the bar. "Which one is he?"

Daisy put a hand on his arm.

"It's not a big deal. Really. I just . . . I feel safe here with you, okay?"

Miller met her eyes again. The bulbous nose didn't go with the face, but you almost didn't notice it with those piercing blue eyes. "Of course," he said, but in a cautious voice. "Can I buy you a drink?"

That was pretty much all the opening Daisy needed. She was good with conversation, and men—married, single, getting divorced, whatever—never minded opening up to her. It took Dale Miller a little more time than usual—Drink Four, if her count was correct—but eventually he got to the impending divorce to Clara, his, yup, second wife who was eighteen years his junior. ("Should've know, right? I'm such a fool.") A drink later, he told her about the two kids—Ryan and Simone—the custody battle, his job in finance.

She had to open up, too. That was how this work. Prime the pump. She had a story at the ready for just such occasions—a completely fictional one, of course—but something about the way Miller carried himself made her add shades of candor. She would never tell him the truth. No one knew that in this town, except Rex. And even Rex didn't know it all.

He drank whiskey. She drank vodka. She tried to move at a slower pace. She took her full glass twice to the bathroom, dumped it into the sink, filled it with water. Still, Daisy was feeling a little buzzed when the text came in from Rex.

R?

R for *Ready*.

"Everything okay?" Miller asked her.

"Sure. Just a friend."

She texted back a Y for *Yes* and turned back to him. This was the part where she would normally suggest that they go someplace quieter. Most men jumped at the chance—men were nothing if not predicable—but she wasn't sure that direct route would work with Dale Miller. It wasn't that he didn't seem interested. He just seemed to be somehow—she wasn't sure how to put it— somehow above it.

"Could I ask you something?" she began.

Miller smiled. "You been asking me things all night."

There was a slight slur in his voice. Good.

"Do you have a car?" she asked.

"I do. Why?"

She glanced about the bar. "Could I, uh, ask you for a ride home? I don't live far."

"Sure, no problem." Then: "I may need a little time to sober up—"

Daisy hopped off the stool. "Oh that's okay. I'll walk then."

Miller sat upright. "Wait, what?"

"I kinda need to get home now, but if you can't drive—"

"No, no," he said, managing to stand. "I'll take you now."

"If it's trouble . . ."

He hopped off the stool. "No trouble, Daisy."

Bingo. As they started for the door, Daisy quickly texted Rex:

OOW

Code for *On Our Way*.

Some might call it a con or swindle, but Rex insisted that it was "righteous" money. Daisy wasn't sure about *righteous*, but she didn't feel a lot of guilt about it either. The plan was simple in execution, if not motive. A man and a woman are getting divorced. The custody battles turn nasty. Both sides get desperate. The woman—technically speaking, the man could use their services, too, though so far it had always been the woman   hired Rex to help them win this bloodiest of battles. How did he do it?

Nail the husband on a DUI.

What better way to show the man is an unfit parent?

So that was how it worked. Daisy's job was twofold: Make sure the mark was legally drunk and then get him behind the wheel. Rex, who was a cop, pulled the guy over, arrested him for driving under the influence, and boom, their client gets a big boost in the court proceedings. Right now, Rex was waiting in a squad car two blocks away. He always found an abandoned spot very close to whatever bar the mark would be at the evening.

The fewer witnesses, the better. They didn't want questions.

Pull the guy over, arrest him, move on.

They both stumbled into the lot.

"This way," Miller said. "I parked over here."

The lot was made up of loose pebbles. Miller kicked them up as he led her to a gray Toyota Corolla. He hit the key fob. The car gave a muted double honk. When Miller headed toward the passenger door, Daisy was confused. Did he want her to drive? God, she hoped not. Was he more wasted than she thought? That seemed more likely. But she quickly realized it was neither of those things.

Dale Miller was opening the door for her. Like a real gentleman. That was how long it had been since Daisy had known a real gentleman. She hadn't even realized what he was doing.

He held the door and waited. Daisy slid into the car. Dale Miller waited while she was all the way in and properly situated before he carefully closed the door behind her.

She felt a pang of guilt.

Rex had pointed out many times that they weren't doing anything illegal or even ethically dubious. For one thing, the plan didn't always work. Some guys don't hang out in bars. "If that's the case," Rex had told her, "then he's in the clear. Our guy is already out drinking, right? You're just giving him a little push, that's all. But he doesn't have to drink and drive. That's his choice in the end. You're not putting a gun to his head."

All of which was true.

Daisy put on her seat belt. Dale Miller did the same. He started the car and put it in reverse. The tires crunched the pebbles. When he was clear of the spot,

Miller stopped the car and looked at her a long moment. She tried to smile, but it wouldn't hold.

"What are you hiding, Daisy?" he asked.

She felt a chill but didn't reply.

"Something happened to you. I can see it in your face."

Not sure what else to do, Daisy tried to laugh it off. "I told you my life story in that bar, Dale."

Miller waited another second, maybe two, though it felt to her like an hour. Finally, he looked forward and put the car in drive. He didn't say another word as they made their way out of the parking lot.

"Take a left," Daisy said, hearing the tenseness in her own voice. "And then it's the second right."

Dale Miller was silent now, making the turns deliberately, the way you do when you've had too much to drink but don't want to get pulled over. The Toyota Corolla was clean and impersonal and smelled a little too strongly of deodorizer. When Miller took the second right, Daisy held her breath and waited for Rex's blue lights and siren to come on.

This was always the scary part for Daisy, because you never knew how someone was going to react. One guy tried to make a run for it, though he realized the futility before he reached the next corner. Some guys started cursing. Some guys—too many of them—started sobbing. That was the worst. Grown men, coolly hitting on her moments earlier, some still with their hand sliding up past her bare knee, suddenly starting blubbering like preschoolers.

They realized the severity in an instant. That realization crushed them.

Daisy didn't know what to expect with Dale Miller.

Rex had the timing down to a science, and as though on cue, the spinning blue light came to life, followed immediately by the squad-car siren. Daisy pivoted and studied Dale Miller's face to gauge his reaction. If Miller seemed distraught or surprised, neither emotion was showing on his face. He was composed, determined, even. He used his blinker to signal before carefully veering to a proper stop by the curb as Rex pulled up behind him.

The siren was off now, the blue light still circling.

Dale Miller put the car in park and turned to her. She wasn't sure what expression to go with here. Surprise? Sympathy? A what-can-you-do sigh?

"Well, well," Miller said. "It looks like the past has caught up with us, eh?"

His words, his tone, his expression, unnerved her. She wanted to yell for Rex to hurry, but he was taking his time the way a cop does. Dale Miller kept his eyes on her, even after Rex did a knuckle knock on his window. Miller slowly turned away and slid open the window.

"Is there a problem, Officer?"

"License and registration, please. Have you been drinking tonight?"

"Maybe one," he said.

With that answer, at least, he was the same as every other mark. They always lied.

"Do you mind stepping out of the car for a moment?"

Miller turned back toward Daisy. Daisy tried not to cringe under his gaze. She stared straight ahead, avoiding eye contact.

Rex said, "Sir? I asked you—"

"Of course, Officer."

Dale Miller pulled the handle. When the interior car light came, Daisy closed her eyes for a moment. Miller rolled out with a grunt. He left the door open, but Rex reached past him and slammed it closed. The window was still open, so Daisy could hear.

"Sir, I would like to run a series of field sobriety tests on you."

"We could skip that," Dale Miller said.

"Pardon me?"

"Why don't we go right to the Breathalyzer, if that would be easier?"

That offer surprised Rex. He glanced past Miller for a moment and caught her eye. Daisy gave a small shrug.

"I assume you have a field Breathalyzer in your squad car?" Miller asked.

"I do, yes."

"So let's not waste your time or mine or the lovely lady's."

Rex hesitated. Then he said, "Okay, please wait here."

"Sure."

When Rex turned to go back to his squad car, Dale Miller pulled out a gun and shot Rex twice in the back of the head. Rex crumbled to the ground.

Then Dale Miller turned the gun toward Daisy.

They're back, she thought.

After all these years, they found me.

HARLAN
COBEN

"Coben is simply one of the all-time greats."

—Gillian Flynn, bestselling author of *Gone Girl*

For a complete list of titles,
please visit prh.com/HarlanCoben